LIKE LESSER GODS

MARI TOMASI

AFTERWORD BY ALFRED ROSA

D1230683

THE NEW ENGLAND PRESS
SHELBURNE, VERMONT

Second printing, January 1999

For additional copies of this book or for a copy
of our catalog, please write:

The New England Press
P.O. Box 575
Shelburne, Vermont 05482

or e-mail: nep@together.net

Visit us on the Web at www.nepress.com

The little city of Granitetown, the story, and the characters
between the covers of this book are wholly fictitious.

Tomasi, Mari, 1907-1965.
    Like lesser gods / Mari Tomasi ; afterword by Alfred Rosa.
— 1st New England Press ed.
        p.   cm.
    Reprint. Originally published: Milwaukee : Bruce Pub. Co., c1949
    ISBN 0933050-62-3
    I. Title.
PS3539.0344L5 1988
813'.54—dc19   88-29117
                                                                          CIP

For Marguerite,
who kept the study quiet;
and for
Andy, Bert, and Dr. Ernie

And he cried out from the steeple,
"Where art thou, Lord?"
And the Lord replied,
"Down here among my people."

Author Unknown

```
┌─────────────────────┐
│                     │
│      BOOK I         │
│                     │
│      1924           │
│                     │
└─────────────────────┘
```

CHAPTER I

A deep-throated whistle announced the arrival of the train as it labored up an incline past the giant, spruce-flanked sign which read:

WELCOME TO GRANITETOWN, VERMONT,
THE LARGEST GRANITE CENTER
IN THE WORLD

Most of the twenty passengers in the Granitetown coach were men. They peered intently from the windows at the greening countryside which rolled gently upward to the darker sky line of the Green Mountains, and which was thinly spangled now by the April sunshine of late afternoon. On the sign someone had recently scrawled, in red stonecutter's chalk, the addenda — *Strikebreakers! Go on back to your own jobs!* The men in the train could not distinguish these words. Nevertheless, an atmosphere of reluctance permeated the homely confusion of assembling their scant luggage and of straightening ties and socks.

Only the frail-looking little man, crumpled in sleep against a

1

red plush seat, remained oblivious to the tension. He slept deeply.
With each breath his silky white mustache quivered, and his
lower lip flapped noisily forward. His white head was cushioned
against the shabby luxury of an ancient pigskin bag, and his
slender legs, sheathed in rich but worn suiting of decided foreign
cut, were stretched out onto the seat facing him.

The conductor halted impatiently beside him. "Granitetown,"
he announced. His eyes swept over the makeshift pillow and
then held to the upper left corner of the bag where faint delineations of a coat of arms were visible. The conductor's curiosity
mounted. Yes, those were the traces of a shield, all right. Even
the four quarters were well defined. The coat of arms had either
worn off or someone had tried to rub it off. A down-at-the-heel
foreigner, that's what he was. One who had seen better days. But
surely a fellow of fifty-five or so — and one who carried a cane —
hadn't come here to quarry stone like some of these other passengers, had he? The conductor shrugged and reached over to shake
the man. "Your stop, Mister! Granitetown."

The man's pale blue eyes blinked open. His right hand had
lain at his breast, concealed under the jacket; now it darted out,
and the conductor saw clenched there a miniature silver figure
of a young man thrusting a spear through the head of a serpent.
The conductor's mind made an agile about-face. One of those
traveling magicians, that's what he was. He'd come to Granitetown
to put on his act between shows at one of the movie houses. He'd
probably picked up the bag in a secondhand shop. Secondhand
shops were a happy hunting ground to third-rate actors. His interest soured. "Guess this is where your ride ends." He passed
on, calling, "Granitetown!"

Excitement glowed in the little man's slender face. He held the
figurine in the open palm of his hand. "Eh, so we are here at last!"
he whispered in his native Italian. "Let this be a good life, yes,
San' Michele? And please, please, spare me Mafalda's 'I-told-
you-so.'" He placed the tiny statue in his pocket, but not before

it had stirred in him, as always it did, a poignant memory of the milestones that had punctuated his life.

One of his sister Mafalda's early "I-told-you-so's" dated back to his youth when, newly orphaned, he had spoken of his intention of entering a seminary in Turin.

"Pah," she sniffed. "*You* made of the same stuff that makes good priests! Nonsense!"

And not two years later, kindly, wise old Don Benedetto, prefect of juniors at the seminary, said to him: "Michele Tiffone, you are a good young man. Of that I am certain. Your intentions are always good. But, my boy! The means you sometimes take to achieve these ends! To be sure, they may not be exactly sinful, but —" He raised a white hand in desperation. "Last week we were all delighted to hear the report that the children at the neighboring school were saying the rosary each day. But now we find those children — one hundred and two of them! — clamoring for one hundred and two tickets for the Pinocchio show! Tickets that *you* promised them!"

A deep flush spread to the very rims of the young man's blue eyes. "Please, Father — it was not bribery. Believe me. I simply wanted to show my appreciation —"

"How were you planning to pay for those tickets? Your inheritance is spent. When did you expect to buy show tickets for those children? In a few years when their hearts are yearning not for Pinocchio but for wives and families?"

Don Benedetto sat with his fingers laced across his shrunken abdomen. He did not admit aloud that, had he not been called to God's work, he would have liked to father a son exactly like this now wretchedly unhappy, long-nosed young seminarian standing before him. Instead, with head lowered to conceal the twinkle he could not keep from his old eyes, he sternly reviewed in painful detail the many instances of Michele's zealous activities. And with each he found some question. "My dear Michele," he added, and in his voice was genuine sadness, "I have no alternative but to advise you not to continue your studies for the priesthood."

The silver figure of San' Michele had been Don Benedetto's parting gift, but even that did not help dull Mafalda's sharp, "You see, brother? What did I tell you?"

The ex-seminarian then chose a career of teaching. He did not listen to Mafalda's plea that he take a position at one of the Turin academies. He became a general instructor in an obscure Piedmont village school where he could spend many an evening chatting with his friend the young, land-loving Count Mattzo, who had lost an arm and a leg in an African expedition. Mafalda predicted dryly, "You will not save a single *lira* in this village. You will dole out your teacher's salary to the needy, and when you are hungry you'll be bowed into the Count's dining room — just because you were once his corporal. But me — I will sit at home and eat crusts."

In the years to come whenever — and it was not often — the Tiffone table failed to measure up to Mafalda's truly epicurean standards, she lamented, "Didn't I tell you so! You give the villagers everything and what do you get from them except that ridiculous land-worker's habit of wearing a kerchief at your neck." Michele invariably replied in variable degrees of patience, "The villagers give me much more than what little I can give them. And I wear the kerchief because I *am* a villager."

One evening this past winter, when his sandy hair and mustache had already turned white, he sat reading and musing in front of Count Mattzo's fireplace. He found himself blinking into the glowing heart of the logs and rubbing meditatively at the mole on his beak of a nose. "Strange, isn't it, friend Mattzo," he murmured, "I can tell you what the queen of Ethiopia prefers for breakfast; I have learned to keep score in that game of baseball which exercises the lungs of American sports fans; I know that in the little American state named Vermont the cows exceed the humans in population; I can name the colors of the flowers that grow in the fields of Bethlehem and — I have never set foot beyond our *Italy*." There was gentle resolution in the closing of the book on his lap. "I have done enough traveling by print. I think I shall take a trip by rail and by boat. I think I shall go to America, to Rich Haven, Vermont, where my bachelor nephew has just bought himself a store."

In vain Mafalda daily protested, "Fifty-five is too ripe an age for you to go courting adventure across the water. You will return with your rheumatic leg and your purse more weakened than they already are."

At Count Mattzo's offer of money and a new wardrobe, he shook his head. But reluctantly. Instead he accepted one of his friend's old suits and a discarded pigskin bag. He scraped long and conscientiously trying to remove the impressive Mattzo coat of arms from the bag. And he blushed in happy resignation when he finally had to admit that he could not possibly remove the insignia of aristocracy without sinfully ruining the bag.

Afterward, events moved swiftly: he turned over his home and possessions to Mafalda . . . the Ibena villagers bade him farewell at the largest party ever recorded in the history of the village . . . he arrived in Rich Haven, Vermont, to find his nephew on his deathbed and the unpaid-for store already returned to its former owners . . . the nephew died . . . the former *maestro* of Ibena, alone and rheumatic in a new world, found himself the possessor of two twenty-dollar bills plus the nephew's wardrobe. He discovered with a pang of guilt that his heart-spoken *Pater Nosters* were being directed less for the repose of his nephew's soul than for a merciful act of God which would keep him in this America and which would prevent another justifiable "I-told-you-so" from Mafalda. It was Pietro Dalli, a former student in Ibena and now a granite cutter in Granitetown, who learned of his plight and sent word that his home was open to him.

The train lurched to a final stop. Two scrawny children, a boy and a girl who had been sitting in front of the *maestro* with their father and grandfather, pointed eagerly to the depot square where a small group of men was gathered. The two men in the train looked for a moment upon the scene, then their unsmiling eyes locked in wordless conversation. The *maestro*, his nose pressed to the window, knew a mellow surge of happiness: hah, Pietro Dalli must have come to welcome him.

He rose unsteadily, tucked the pigskin bag under his left arm, and tried his cramped legs in an experimental step. But it was strange, no, that his fellow passengers were revealing none of his eagerness to leave the train? Along the aisle the men, standing now, were drawing aside to let him pass. *Dio mio,* was it Count Mattzo's half-deleted coat of arms that was reaping this respect? He bowed his thanks right and left, his cheeks humbly scarlet, and as he reached the top step of the train and looked down upon the little knot of men it came to him with a great pounding of heart and with a rush of moisture to his eyes that perhaps Pietro had arranged this welcome for him.

"*Amici!*" he called impulsively.

An object hit at the pigskin bag, and he saw that someone had thrown a withered head of cabbage. In that second of horror he could notice that a boy of fifteen was trying to climb the train steps and that a blue-suited man, with the authoritative air of a *carabiniere,* ordered briefly, "Scram!" He could even note that the unfamiliar word possessed magical properties, for the boy suddenly halted and then drew back. And in that same second, from the dozen or so men gathered on the square, one low jeer fractured the air. "Strikebreakers!" An arm reached from behind the *maestro* and drew him back into the coach.

"But, what is it? What is wrong?" he gasped in his native tongue when the conductor led him, startled and trembling, to a seat.

The conductor pushed his cap to the back of his head. "You asked for it, didn't you, sticking your neck out by starting to make a speech —"

Pale blue eyes stared back, blank with incomprehension, into his. "What is wrong?" the *maestro* repeated dully.

The conductor's voice grew louder, as if volume could force understanding where mere English proved sterile. "The granite workers in this town are striking, and some of these fellows," his thumb indicated the *maestro's* fellow passengers, "are going to fill in on their quarrying jobs. Well, they don't like it — the granite workers, I mean."

It was Vitleau, the father of the two scrawny children, who translated the conductor's words into a barely intelligible jargon of English, French, and Italian. And the *maestro's* first horror lessened. At least it was not really he, the *maestro*, for whom the cabbage was intended. His head spun with the complexity of the situation: the granite workers were striking, they were out of jobs; his own fellow passengers had come to Granitetown to earn their bread and butter; and if one must win, the other must lose, no? And there would still be mouths left to be fed. And, he thought bleakly, Pietro Dalli with whom he was to make his home, he must be striking, too.

Police and deputies now formed a thin cordon from the steps of the train, and a few of the *maestro's* fellow passengers had already left the train and filed their way to Main Street where cars awaited them. He stepped breathlessly from the train. In a less confused state of mind he might not have taken this first step onto the earth of his new home without a Columbian prayer in his heart. He was reflecting, with a rueful glance at the cabbage spots on his bag, that the things for which one waited so impatiently, the big moments of life — they were seldom what one dreamed they would be. Hah, well, it was one of the *Dio's* many ways of pointing out the finiteness of mortal minds.

The *maestro* looked in vain for the face of Pietro. Beside him a robust young man with a boldly handsome face lunged forward against the pale newcomer, Vitleau.

"So you've come to grab our jobs," Tip Gioffi sneered at the straight, unretreating form. "You've come to kill our chances for better pay!" His fist swung upward.

A pair of blue-clad arms grasped Tip firmly. "Enough of that, Tip!" Officer Riley ordered curtly. "Get going before you get yourself into trouble — scram!"

The *maestro's* ears cocked at this second meeting with the fascinating word, and he would have been disappointed had not the young man, with a conciliatory "O.K., O.K.," rejoined his silent companions.

Vitleau spoke harshly, angrily to Officer Riley, "By God, I came here to earn my living — I got a right to that. If anything happens to my kids and my old man —"

"Nothing'll happen. It's been a peaceful strike, and it's going to stay so."

He stopped abruptly and listened. The *maestro* listened, too. From near by a child's voice whispered blissfully in singsong chant — "Strikebreaker's little girl, strikebreaker's little girl."

They saw Vitleau's daughter, Jean, frozen into a rigid figure. A long stick was lightly basting the child's thin legs, and her eyes were held terror bound to where the stick disappeared behind a stout man's leg. Another child crouched there, an elfin-faced girl with light brown braids dangling to her shoulders. She was wielding the stick, her wide mouth rapturously forming the chant — "Strikebreaker's little girl."

Officer Riley lifted her to her feet. "I'll give you ten minutes to get home!" Suspicion grew in the policeman's eyes: for where Petra Dalli was, his own daughter was likely to be. "Where's Peggy?"

"Gone home." She flashed him an understanding smile. "I guess she got scared."

The *maestro* cleared his throat. Here was opportunity to test the word he had already heard twice this afternoon. He said pleasantly, "Sc-ram."

Petra's tranquil gray-green eyes widened. They traveled over his own mild eyes, the silky wisp of a mustache, the blue kerchief at his neck, and dwelt with lively interest on the tight black shoes with their built-up heels.

"Sc-ram," he repeated expectantly and knew a tinge of pleasure when she walked streetward tossing him a final, puzzled look.

Behind him two men were speaking in his native tongue. He asked them where he might find the home of one Pietro Dalli, stone-cutter. Four blocks along Main Street, and then the first street to the right, he was told. There would be a sign on the corner announcing Pastinetti Place. And the third house on the right — that would be Pietro Dalli's house.

He walked slowly along Main Street. Except for counting the street blocks carefully he paid little attention to his new surroundings or to the groups of men loitering at the store fronts in animated conversation. He was thinking of the letters he had received in Italy from his nephew, from Pietro, and from other friends. They had painted a rich canvas of life in this Vermont. They had written of *hills that are more gently rounded than those in Italia, hills that are near and friendly and that boast an evergreen coat all winter long . . . the wages are good . . . there is work for everyone . . . in Granitetown the Italian, Spanish, Scotch, Irish, French — all live together in harmony. . . .* Why, then, this situation which was influencing even a pig-tailed, elfin child to torment another in the unconsciously cruel mimicry of youth?

The street sign "Pastinetti Place" reminded him to turn right. His heels crunched into a path of granite chips. So, this was the stone that Pietro cut? One house, two — hah, this third, this humble frame house painted a fresh huntsman's green, this was Pietro's. The tiny lawn was enclosed within a fence heavy with vines. The *maestro* touched eager fingers to a hard, rosy bud bursting from its covering of brown bark and rejoiced that here was an old friend from Ibena — a grapevine. And bordering the piazza were surely the first green shoots of the familiar chicory. A large wooden ball, the *bocce*, lay half hidden in the grass where it had spun from some adult's hand. Pietro has not changed, he reassured himself.

He stared before him, unseeing, his mind drawing a picture of the Pietro and Maria he once knew. He failed to hear the Dalli door close and failed to see the girl and boy who stood there hand in hand watching him.

The girl's whisper was tense. "Vetch, he's that little man I told you about, the one at the station —"

The boy's close-cropped head rose but an inch above his sister's. Arms and legs protruded, brown and wiry, from last year's suit. His usually restless eyes were fixed suspiciously on the strange, slender man whose shoes had absurd heels like his mother's Sunday shoes. The man's feet were planted on either side of a bulging pigskin bag. A cane was crooked over an elbow, and his right hand gently stroked a great mole that spread from a thin nostril and lost itself in a wisp of a mustache. He was staring into the very midst of the lilac tree on the neighboring lawn.

The girl knew with swift ecstasy that the stranger was looking *at* the tree but that he was not *seeing* it. She knew! For didn't his face wear the still, rapt look that was her own when she was playing her "guessing" game? His eyes were wide open; yet she felt he was purposely blinding them so that his mind could take a picture of its own choice.

"Hi!" she greeted.

The *maestro* was startled to quick attention.

Vetch scowled. "You want my father?"

Petra flew down the steps her eyes bright with sudden enlightenment. "I know — you're my father's teacher —"

Then Pietro's plump figure was at the door, his brown eyes warmly luminous, his hand extended in greeting. The *maestro's* lips smacked Pietro's cheeks, and he smiled when the younger man tweaked the blue kerchief at his throat and chuckled, "The same *maestro,* even to the kerchief."

Pietro Dalli took his guest's arm. "You must forgive me for not meeting the train, *si?* It was tonight, late, I thought you were coming." To his wide-eyed children, he said, "This is a day of days for us! Here is the teacher who pounded my young mind into shape."

Vetch felt the pressure of his father's hand and heard him say proudly, "This one is Elvecchio, my first-born."

"Vetch," the girl corrected quickly. This stranger must not hurt Vetch's feelings by laughing, "Elvecchio, that means old man, eh?" as did so many of Papa's friends. The man flashed a look at Petra's earnest eyes and at the sullen hardness in those of the boy, and his hand went out to the boy. "Vetch, eh?"

She said, "You don't look like a teacher. You don't look like a Miss Gossard or a Mr. Abbot."

"Speak Italian to the maestro," her father reminded.

It was Pietro's wife, Maria, again swollen with new life and sitting in the kitchen with the baby Gabriella on her lap, who showered questions upon the newcomer. How was every one of the friends in Ibena? Her mother? Her brother? Pietro's family? Was the old church of Santa Margherita at last boasting a new roof? Indeed, the steady flow of questions, pouring out after each answer was barely given, so completely flooded any other attempted channel of conversation that the maestro suspected Maria of secret purposes. Even Petra's proud "Mama, I saw the maestro at the station" was ignored in favor of another question.

Three children and a fourth on its way had instilled a softness to the almost severe classic beauty that was Maria's, the maestro decided. She wore the remembered night-black hair rolled in a loose knot at the nape of her white neck. As in childhood her eyes were still her soul: alert, constant, and, he thought uneasily, possessing a gleam of determination that was twin to the firmness of her full, red lips. Was it the details of the strike she wished to keep from him? And why?

They ate supper at the kitchen table under a low-swinging naked electric light bulb. He was stabbing contentedly at the last delicate stem of spaghetti coiled in its pool of spicy red sauce when Pietro pushed back his chair and urged, "Hurry, Maestro, I promised

Ronato I would match him at *bocce* tonight before it darkens. You must come along, *si?* Ronato is eager to see you again."

"Tired as he is after today's trip?" Maria demanded. "No, no, *Maestro,* you must rest! That is it. You must sit here, and while I do the dishes you will tell me about the rest of our Ibena friends. Tell me, how can I expect to sleep tonight if I do not know what has become of Iolanda and Giuseppe and Tilda?"

She laughingly pushed Pietro toward the door. The husband turned for a moment, hesitant, his hand at his mustache.

The *maestro* could not mistake the plea in his eyes. But, *per Baccho,* could a guest refuse a simple request from the woman whose tastily cooked dishes had just comforted a stomach abused by rude food these two weeks?

The door closed behind Pietro. Petra was immediately assigned to upstairs duty with the baby. Vetch was sent into the small living room to do his studying.

The *maestro* sat stiffly erect in his chair, waiting, feeling more a pupil than a teacher. Could it be that in this humble home where another life was soon to be born there would not be room for him? Is that what she wanted to say? Could it be that in this cozy kitchen he would be told of Dalli financial straits and thus be doomed to another I-told-you-so from Mafalda? But no. Maria, bent over the sink, was truly pelting him with questions about the distant Iolanda and Tilda, and he was making response in a voice pitched high against the rattle of the dishes. She at last flipped the dish towel to a peg above the sink and came to sit beside him, a rounded elbow poised resolutely on the kitchen table.

He breathed tremulously. Whatever it was, it was coming now.

"You know, *Maestro,* that Pietro has a deep affection for you —"

A prelude, he suspected. That is merely a prelude. "Hah, Maria, good. But, as you say, it is hardly news — I knew it."

"I can honestly say that you come next to his family in affection," she added. "And in his respect for wisdom — there, I think, you come first —"

He shook his head. "You refer to the Pietro of childhood who looked up in awe at a more mature mind. But now his mind is as adult as mine, and more youthfully alert."

She was not listening to him. He knew that. She was silently forming thoughts behind that Mona Lisan mask, and now she put them into speech. "You would advise Pietro for his own good, wouldn't you? He might listen to the advice of his teacher. . . . Advise him, *Maestro*, to forget going back to the sheds, advise him to find other work. There could be no better time to try another job — and to keep it!"

"But he likes his work!" he blurted. How well he recalled those letters from Pietro — *It is beautiful, this Vermont granite we work, and its lifetime is that of the pyramids. . . . You ask me if here I am content? I am happy at my work, and happy with my family. Therefore, according to your own teaching that two united affirmatives can but result in a more positive affirmative — I am a happy man, Maestro!*

"Likes it!" She laughed bitterly. "A baby, too, may like a piece of poisoned candy, but the mother keeps him away from that candy, no?"

"Poisoned? You don't mean the stone?" Alarmed, he began riffling the pages of his limited mental encyclopedia.

"It might as well be! A few years of work in those houses of dust and their lungs are thick with powder."

"The silica." He was on firm ground now. "But it hardly kills like poison, Maria —"

"It is the beginning!" she exclaimed. "Their dusty lungs are no longer able to resist any infection they may get. I know. I have seen them. Jo and Luigi, the Scotsman Andy, the Spanish Carlos, the Irishman Ike, and now Italo — the Italo you taught." She was not aware of his sharp intake of breath. "And his Lucia will be left with three growing boys. The sheds you knew in the old country were more open to air — here they must be closed against the cold winters; there the stone was softer, here it is hard and heavy with silica. And the floors — they are kept wet to hold down the dust, but don't you think it will also hold their legs to rheumatism!"

He smiled gently. "I have the rheumatism, too, yet I have never worked on a shed floor. I do not say you are not justified, my Maria, but each industry has its own hazards. Pietro has worked here for more than ten years, no? And others of his age have died from other causes in that time, no? The industry here is young — they will find a way to fight the dust —"

"Pietro's words!" she scoffed. "And in the meantime, Italo, Pietro, and how many others must pay the price?"

He could not help asking, "Pietro — what does he say? Have you asked him to find other work?"

"Asked him! *Dio mio*, hear him! I have pleaded, prayed, threatened. And what does he do but look at me with the innocent, hurt eyes of a child and mutter, 'But I like to work the stone, *cara*. It is a part of me.' He is for all the world as foolishly stubborn about stone as that friend of yours, Count Mattzo, who prefers his Ibena chestnut trees to a palace in Turin. When I was carrying Vetch, he promised, 'We will think about it.' When I was carrying Petra, he offered, 'But there will be additional expense now, and other jobs might not pay as well.' When Gabriella was nearing birth, he changed his tune to, 'But next to Ronato and the other really excellent carvers I am among the highest paid at the shed. It would be foolish to seek a lower salary when there will be five mouths to feed.' And now that I am with the latest Dalli and there is every reason to find a job, he says, 'But, *cara*, I must not let my fellow workers down, and besides I like my work.' And to think that I was almost happy over this strike, hoping that newcomers would take his job and keep it! How many times I have told him: 'Let us do as the Ciarlotti's down the street. Let us put shelves in our little living room. Let us have a store, with a bell on the front door to tell us when customers arrive. We can dress always in Sunday best, and you can sell bread to the living instead of cutting stones for the dead.'"

He was strangely quiet.

"You do not agree with me?" she demanded hotly.

"*Si*, I believe, Maria." His hand sought his pocket, fingered the two twenty-dollar bills and the little statue of San' Michele. There was frustration in the droop of his shoulders. "I think you will not want me to stay here tonight. I think I shall find a room somewhere. You see, Maria, I will gladly tell Pietro all of these things you have pointed out to me. But to ask him to quit?" He shook his head sadly. "Sometimes for a man there is only one job at which he can be truly happy, and unless he is happy how can he give the best of service to his fellow man and to God?"

"What about service to his wife and children?" she cried. "What service can he give anyone when he is under the ground?"

He said quietly, "I promise. I will point out the truths you have said." He rose; picked up his bag, hat, and cane; and put his hand to the door. His smile was feeble. "I am sorry, Maria. You will tell Pietro, please, that with an old man's sudden whim for adventure, I decided to get a room downtown."

Maria pulled the bag from his hands, her eyes blazing. Her voice flung quick irritation at him. "What kind of a woman do you think I am? Do I love Pietro the less because in this matter he has a mind of his own? Strong willed, my father and mother called me! Yet the moment Pietro touches me, I am no longer Maria — I am Pietro, thinking and feeling as Pietro, as rapturously as would a new bride! And me wearing a wedding ring these eleven years!" He lowered his head so that she would not see the red of embarrassment that crowded into his pale face. "And you," she continued, "do I like you any the less because you have a ridiculous code of living which you think must follow?" Her breasts rose and fell fiercely. She stared at him, pressed hard against the wall. And suddenly she saw him as he was, utterly weary, puzzled, defeated, and alone. And in that moment her dark eyes softened. She took him by the hand. "Your place is here with us, *Maestro*, until you find a good job. Remember that. Now, come up to your bedroom, which you must share with Vetch."

A few minutes later he was sitting on one of the bedroom's two cots removing his shoes and pressing his lips tightly to imprison a groan. Petra's pig-tailed head appeared at the door.

She said breathlessly, "You got to tell me, Mister *Maestro!* This afternoon, when you were looking at the lilac tree next door — did you really *see* it? Did you?"

"Hah, am I blind, my Petra, that I should look and see nothing?"

His were the mildest blue eyes she had ever seen. The fragile blue of the Dresden shepherdess doll Miss Gossard had given her at Christmas. The faint blue of robin eggs found in the sugar bush on the hill. The delicate blue of the feathery, wild chicory blossoms she loved. "Oh, no," she added, with a shyness new to her, "sometimes on washdays when the window is all steamed up, I wipe a clear spot and close my eyes, and I guess how things will look when I open them."

"So my eyes were closed then?"

He had rolled his pants' legs up to his knees and was tenderly massaging his legs. His thin legs in the long, clay-colored underwear reminded her of cleanly picked drumsticks. "No," she said. "But —"

"Hah, a 'but' we have! But — what?"

He detected a churning gray-green confusion in her eyes, and he admitted, "I think you have guessed it! I looked at the tree, indeed, but I did not see it. My memory was sketching a picture of your father, the Pietro I used to know in Italy. And my common sense was erasing lines where here he may have added a few pounds to his body, and where there he may have lost a few. And, yes, I was picturing his children: would they be like Pietro, or like Maria?"

She breathed from a tense throat, "Gee!"

"It amazes you?"

"I didn't know anyone else did my guessing game. Anyone besides Denny Douglas." She sank cross-legged to the floor. "Did you guess me right?"

"Hah, no." The blue eyes twinkled. "I foolishly and completely forgot your grandfather. And in so doing I failed to consider the wisdom of a man named Mendel. I thought only: the children will be Pietro's — square of body, hard workers, with a simple pattern of life. Or, they will be Maria's — handsome, practical. . . ." He cleared his throat. "A bit inflexible. And now this disregard for Mendel shames me. It points its finger at me. For I see in your face the white, slender face of your grandfather. The same wistful gray eyes. And I see his dreamer's soul —"

"Father Carty says we can't see souls."

"Hah, yes and no. You do not see the wind, but you feel it. And feeling it, you know it is there. And so knowing, in this instance, is almost equal to seeing, no?"

He was unpacking his bag as he spoke. He drew out an English-Italian grammar which he had studied aboard ship, and a scroll which, unfurled, proved to be a calendar of the saints, each page bearing the picture of a saint in rich Moorish colors. He placed it on the dresser top beside the figurine of San' Michele.

"We have a St. Michael in our church — St. Michael's church. And we have a calendar like that in Mama's room," she informed him. She was disappointed. She had expected something unusual among this little man's possessions.

"Then I need not look for today's saint on the calendar. You can tell me. I was in such a hurry to leave this morning that I had no time to consult the calendar."

He was waiting, she saw. She drew back a little under the amazing blue of his eyes.

"Well," he asked, "what saint has blessed this day?"

"I don't know."

"Yet you have a calendar —"

"I never look, Mister *Maestro*. I can't read Italian."

"A pity." He stroked his slender beak of a nose, and it came to him with a jolt of pleasant surprise that much of the weariness he had felt in the kitchen had now vanished. "Think of it, a saint for each day in the year. Hah, you have missed something! A saint is enough to keep the mind in virtuous and exciting occupation for a full twenty-four hours."

"Look," she bargained. "I'll teach you English after I do my lessons every night, if you teach me to read Italian. I'll — gee, I don't even know your name —"

"I have a name, and to spare," he assured her gravely. "*Maestro* Michele Pio Vittorio Giuseppe Tiffone."

"Gee —"

He counted them off on his fingers. "Michele for the great Archangel — this one." He indicated the silver San' Michele figurine on the dresser. "Pio for the pope who reigned when I was born and whom you may some day call *Santo Pio;* Vittorio, who is king and whose birthday is November 11 — the same as mine; and Giuseppe for my father, who humbled his name into obscurity by tacking it at the end."

Tiffone. She frowned. *Maestro* Michele Pio. . . . A happy thought smoothed the wrinkles from her brow. "I'll call you Mister Tiff. I'm glad, glad I saw you first — I mean at the station."

"You weren't being very kind to another girl when I saw you."

"She's a strikebreaker's kid, isn't she? The strikebreakers take bread from poor children's mouths, don't they?"

She stirred uncomfortably under his silence.

She had overheard those words from a stonecutter as he stood talking on a street corner. But no one had actually taken bread from her mouth. It was true that she and Vetch no longer had their candy at recess, and that Mama had forbidden her to jump rope lest she scuff her shoes to shreds. But wasn't there always Papa's 'trust slip' at Pepino Stoffi's store, and didn't they always have enough to eat? Her braids swung defiantly over her shoulders. "Anyhow, I'm glad, glad there's a strike! Once, just once, a smarty-pants boy called me 'wop,' but now everyone's too busy calling the others 'bozos' to bother with me."

He winced, not at the alien word spoken with such hearty contempt that it could hardly be complimentary, but because here among the Dallis there were already two who welcomed the strike, and for vastly different reasons.

Vetch had been standing these last minutes in sullen silence by the door, his eyes on the man's shoes that stood neatly upright under the cot, side by side. He said gruffly in his poor Italian, "The kids'll laugh at those shoes. Those heels — they're just like women's heels."

"Laugh? But I was in Rich Haven two weeks and no one laughed —"

"That's a hick town. This is, well, it's Granitetown."

The *maestro* heard him go down the stairs. He returned carrying a saw.

"*Dio mio,*" the man chuckled. "Is it suicide you wish me to consider this first night in your father's home."

But, together, they sawed at the heels until even the boy admitted that the shoes looked as if they might have come from the shelves of any Granitetown shoe store.

He had barely propped himself to a half-sitting position in his cot, his lips telling each brown, wooden bead and his ears conscious of the regular breathing of Vetch sleeping in the cot beside him, when he heard heavy footsteps on the porch. He prophesied with a wry smile, "*Et tu,* Pietro," and resigned himself to a postponement of sleep until another session with a member of the Dalli family was ended.

Later Pietro sat beside him in the dark, and the *maestro* assured him that the cot was most comfortable; *si,* he had had sufficient to eat; *si,* he had already become well acquainted with Maria, Vetch, and Petra; and, *si,* he was sure to have a good night's sleep.

Pietro lingered, tugging at his brown mustache. He shifted his weight awkwardly, crossing a leg, uncrossing it. "Maria spoke to you tonight — about my work, no?" It was more apology than question.

"*Si,*" agreed the older man.

A long sigh quivered from the very depths of Pietro. "I guessed. And when supper was finished I was sure of it. Maria's tongue prefers to lie still; when it is active there is always good reason. She tried to avoid talk of stonecutting tonight until she could speak to you alone — that was it?"

"And she thwarted your own attempt to do the same?" came the gentle suggestion. The *maestro* slipped his rosary under the pillow. Prayers would have to wait. In Ibena it had been customary for the villagers to discuss their little problems with the village teacher. But he had not expected the custom to flower in a distant soil and after an uprootal of eleven years. In promise to Maria he began: "Listen, my Pietro, perhaps she is justified in wanting you to find other work." And here he dutifully pointed out all the reasons Maria had listed.

Pietro heard him through without comment. He murmured with shamed cheeks, "What a poor welcome we Dallis have given you, overwhelming you with our little burdens on your first night." He groped for words, continued haltingly, "I have a confession to make, *Maestro*. I, too, like Maria, was going to 'talk' to you tonight. But now I see it is not fair to you, nor to Maria and me. Think of it, I was going to enlist your aid in making Maria understand that for me there is no work but stonecutting!"

"If you have not tried other work, how can you be so sure?" The words rose halfheartedly from the darkness of the cot, and the *maestro* felt that his was the joyless but necessary role of devil's advocate.

"What else can I do here? Street cleaning? Pour heart and soul into the dung I sweep? Run a store? Hand over the counter the products that other hands have made? No, no. For me there can never be anything like cutting a beautiful stone and knowing it will last, as I have fashioned it, long after all of us have gone."

"Once in a great while the second best can make one moderately happy — if one will but let it." The *maestro* spoke with calm conviction, seeing again the seminary in Turin and feeling again the pain it had cost to take Don Benedetto's advice. For a long time there had been that loneness of heart, almost as if God had withdrawn His hand, but in extending his own hand to the villagers he had somehow reached again into God's.

After Pietro said his good nights, the older man tossed in his bed, his mind twisting through a miasma of confused thoughts. First his mind was on Maria. On Pietro. On himself. He had come to Pietro's home at a poor time indeed. When there was no wage earner in the house, when his own rheumatic leg would balk at regular work hours. And there were six mouths to feed. . . . Had he done wrong this time in not listening to Mafalda? His eyes sought San' Michele dimly outlined on the dresser. Please, he prayed, do not let this one trip of my life prove a mistake for myself and a tribulation to my friends. . . .

He was dropping off to sleep when there loomed before him the two mind-teasing question marks that had lost themselves tonight under the avalanche of Dalli conversation. He drew aside the bedclothes, put his feet to the bare planks of the floor, and bent over the sleeping boy.

"Vetch!" he whispered. "Vetch!"

The boy muttered drowsily in the darkness.

"Vetch, the strikers — why are they striking? Do they want more pay?"

The boy was too drenched in sleep to answer other than an affirming, "Uh-huh."

"And that word *sc-ram* — what might that mean?"

But the boy's cheek had already turned again to the pillow in sleep.

CHAPTER II

A 7 o'clock stone-shed whistle shattered the morning quiet. It was making its first rasping efforts to achieve a single, steady note. From the Dalli bathroom echoed a loud clearing of throat followed by a vibrating screech. Mister Tiff lifted bewildered ears from the pillow and listened to the alien sounds. He saw the girl Petra by his cot, her brown braids shining from recent brushing. She was quietly surveying him, her slender body straight and still under a freshly ironed red gingham dress. She had been considering, briefly, the practical nature of the blue kerchief which yesterday Mister Tiff had worn as a neck decoration and which this morning was a nightcap drawn to skull smoothness over his head.

She said to the perplexity in his eyes, "It's the stone-shed whistle, the bathroom pipes, and Papa. I think Papa has worked in the sheds so long he sounds just like the whistle." She giggled. "They're both clearing their throats."

His blue eyes blinked. With the startling quickness of a jack-in-the-box her words had catapulted before him a vision of a gigantic whistle, its long stem of a throat throbbing noisily as it cleared itself of phlegm.

He shook his head to clearer wakefulness. "So."

"Let's get started, Mister Tiff," she urged, and drew herself to a comfortable sitting position on Vetch's empty cot. "Vetch is up already," she observed unnecessarily. "Let's get started. Pretty soon I got to dress baby Gabriella."

"Started for what?"

"The saints. You said we'd start this morning."

Together they studied the saints' calendar. She listened with sober politeness when he read the short biography — "St. Mark, the Evangelist, born of Jewish parents, died about 68, founder of the church at Alexandria, Egypt. Patron saint of Venice and of notaries." But when he laid aside the calendar, leaned his kerchiefed head to the wall and described to her Mark's labors with Peter and Paul in a Rome running Christian blood under Nero, and when he pictured from memory the magnificent basilica in Venice where the martyred saint's body was now at rest, the child's eyes glowed and she hugged herself in rapt silence.

"There," he concluded. "Wasn't I right? Won't Mark provide enough food for thought for the rest of the day?"

"It's almost better than my 'guessing game,'" she admitted. "Want me to show you?" She took slow steps to the window, her hand making a blindfold over her eyes. "When I open my eyes I bet I won't be able to see the top of Camel's Hump on account of it's gray weather outdoors. That really isn't fair," she added parenthetically, "because I looked at it already from my own window. But I bet the pasture trees don't show their green yet. I bet the branches are all black and stiff, stiff like hypnotized circus snakes. And I bet Ellie Marclay'll be coming down the street, because she always takes the trolley car to Montpelier, where she works in an insurance office. And Robbie — Ellie's his aunt, and he lives with her, you know — he'll be out sweeping the porch because it's Saturday and no school. And Aggie — she works for them — she'll be shaking rugs." She drew her hands from her eyes. After a moment she chanted, "I was right! I was right! There's Ellie and — gee." She stopped. Her fingers pressed taut and white against the pane. Her elfin face, the man thought uneasily from the cot, was transfigured with the same glee it had shown yesterday at the station when she was slapping at the legs of the Vitleau child.

He pushed aside the bedclothes, shook down his twisted nightshirt to its modest length and limped beside her. The window scene appeared innocent enough. The young woman with the milk-white face and curly, red hair, walking sedately down the street, must be Ellie. But there was no boy sweeping the porch as Petra had expected. Perhaps he was the lad up there on the hilly pasture with Vetch. The two boys were prodding three cows through a gateway into an adjacent lot.

"Gee! Conway's going to be ripping mad!" she exulted. "And it's good enough for him —"

Under the man's probing the little story was unfolded: the land adjacent to the pasture had belonged to St. Michael's parish and had been used by the neighborhood boys for a baseball field. Three weeks ago a fire had destroyed several pews in the church, and in order to replace them old Father Down had sold the lot to Asa Conway who ran a general store on Main Street. Asa had immediately posted a *No Trespassing* sign on the lot.

"The cows'll tear it up worse than baseball ever would," she predicted hopefully. Absorbed in this blissful contemplation she automatically obeyed the man's request that she wait in the hall outside his door until he dressed.

Maria was measuring out the morning coffee when they appeared hand in hand in the kitchen. "Five minutes, *Maestro,* and you will have your first Dalli breakfast. You slept well, *sir?*"

Her smile embraced them both, and the man sought in vain for a single trace of the grimly and passionately pleading Maria of last night. Under the first tantalizing aroma of fresh coffee, yesterday's embarrassing scene at the station, Maria's fears, Pietro's hesitant conversation at his bedside — all seemed part of a fanciful dream which only a travel-wearied mind could have fashioned. Only the coffee, the smiling Maria, the pressure of Petra's fingers twined about his own were reality, as was the knowledge that up there in that pasture two boys at this moment were acting with the but human weakness of boys in any country under the sun. And those two boys must be stopped now. . . .

Maria agreed that, *si,* a short walk to the top of the first hill would whet his appetite. Her eyes followed his halting steps across the porch, and she resolved that even though Pietro was temporarily without work they must not hurry their guest into finding work and other lodging. Indeed, what kind of work could a teacher do if, like the *maestro,* he were possessed of aching legs and a foreign tongue?

The pasture land rose in a crude terrace just above the vacant house next to Ellie Marclay's house. Mister Tiff's slow steps brought them to the pasture gate in five minutes. Vetch and the freckled Robbie sat on a stone watching the cows browsing contentedly in their newly acquired lot.

The man asked without preamble, "You own that land, Vetch?"

"You know I don't," the boy mumbled in Italian. He was aware of Robbie's staring eyes, and realized, uncomfortably, that this was the first time the other boy had heard him speak Italian. He finished sullenly, "It's Skinflint Conway's land." He glared resentfully at his sister, suspecting her to be the root of this intrusion.

"If it belongs to Conway," the man continued mildly, "then surely he has the right to say who or what goes on it, no?"

"We weren't hurting his old field playing ball on it, were we? Now we have to go clear to the other end of town to play."

"Hah! And suppose your shirt is hanging on your mother's line, and suppose your friend Robbie's only shirt is somewhere at the other end of town. Does that give him the right to make use of your shirt, especially if you have refused it to him?"

Vetch forbore to argue. He turned helplessly to Robbie. "Guess we might as well put the cows back. He will, anyway — if we don't." He paused. "He was my father's teacher in Italy," he concluded, explaining the stranger and presenting, he thought, adequate reason for obeying the little man.

Back in Maria's fragrant kitchen the lean, sad-faced Ronato was waiting to greet his former teacher.

"Our Ronato is the most skilled carver in Granitetown," Pietro boasted over his coffee to Mister Tiff. He bit into his slice of bread which, these days, was folded over a single slice of salami. Despite Pietro's passion for working stone it did not occur to him to be envious of Ronato's greater talent for carving. Nor was he envious of Ronato's studies at the *Reale Academia of Belle Arti di Brera* in Milan. Ronato was born in Ibena, but he had early left for the stone-working district of Lake Como, a district which had provided many fine workers for Granitetown.

Maria, ladling hot corn porridge into Ronato's bowl, murmured, "Italo was a fine carver, too. What good is that to him or Lucia now?"

She regretted the words the moment she spoke them. For a silence strained across the table, engulfing its occupants. She saw Pietro's head dip in embarrassment, and it seemed that the very silence was shouting, "How this Maria nags her husband!" Maria could not bear to see him pitied by his friends, and her fingers scurried to play a contrite caress in the short hair that curled on the back of his neck. She said lightly over his head to the *maestro*, "Lucia can hardly wait to see you. She promises to stop by today."

Now it was Ronato who lowered his head. Each time he heard Lucia's name, a swift flow of color dyed his thin face. In Italy all of his friends had witnessed his fruitless courtship of Lucia, and had seen her choose the handsome Italo for a husband. But, he was thinking wretchedly, could they know that at this moment he felt himself a Judas, that he was sorrowing deeply over the approaching death of his friend, Italo, and that at the same time he was nourishing a budding hope that Lucia, in widowhood, might some day open her heart to him?

When the house was empty of the children, Pietro and Maria disappeared behind their bedroom door. Ronato whispered to Mister Tiff, "Pietro and I have been told we are welcome to work in the Quincy, Massachusetts, sheds until this strike is settled. But with Maria having her baby soon —" He left the sentence unfinished, and shrugged his doubts.

Behind the closed door Maria was saying in brittle tension,

"Always there is an excuse, Pietro, always!" Her laugh was dry. "This time, to be sure, you can honestly say you have double reason for not missing any more wages — there's the baby on his way, and there's the *maestro*, who surely is unfit for work and who must eat."

"*Si*," he admitted miserably. "Those are exactly the words I might have spoken."

Her voice snapped, "Then, you know you will have your way again! Why bother to talk, talk, talk —"

He interrupted hesitantly, "But there is more I want to say." He laid a hand gently to her swollen front. "Always I have been with you when a new life comes to us, Maria. You know that. And I want to be here this time."

Theirs was an old-fashioned, towering bed of brass, made higher by two mattresses, a custom rooted from Ibena days. Pietro had cut and polished a round block of granite and placed it by the bed to serve as a step for Maria when her body, as now, reached unwieldy proportions. Now he took her by the hand, and together they sat on the edge of the bed, his brown mustache brushing her cheek. As always, a part of her wondered if twenty years from now his touch would still grow these cool little hills of delight along her arms and breasts.

"I have figured it carefully." He tried to speak confidently, but uncertainty lurked in his brown eyes. "The strike cannot last much longer. If I don't go to Quincy it will mean we must spend our savings to eat. But if you tell me to stay, I shall. Truly, up here," he tapped his brow with a plump finger, "it tells me, 'Go to work in Quincy, earn the money you need.' But here," he tapped at his heart, "it tells me, 'Stay with Maria.' So, what shall I do?"

She bit her lips to choke down the emotion that was half anger, half joy. Was ever woman so torn between despair and bliss! How could she be angry when his simple honesty was trying to reconcile action to both conscience and heart? Her eyes fell to the gleaming surface of the granite step. The dark mica flecks glinted up at her maliciously, mockingly, she thought. She sometimes asked herself if she could be foolish enough to be jealous of his love for stone and if, subconsciously, this constituted a good share of what she believed was her fear of stone. But even though he loved to work granite and even though it might treacherously bring him to his sickbed, she knew that stone would always remain cold, insensate matter. While here within her, patterned body and soul to the Creator of all love, was living proof of their love for each other. Ah, a few weeks in Quincy would not harm him; besides, in another month or so he would be back in the Granitetown sheds. . . . Pietro's lips grazed her cheek, settled on hers. Her own full lips instantly kindled under the fire in his. "Go to Quincy, it will be for only a short time." She whispered the words quickly, knowing that in a half hour he and Ronato would be happily anticipating again the feeling of chisel on stone, and that she would be angry with herself for neglecting this opportunity of keeping Pietro from the sheds.

Pietro and Ronato left for Quincy late the following afternoon. And in that last minute before train time Pietro said to his former teacher, "Remember, *Maestro,* I am turning over to you my place as head of the family. Do not think, for even a second, of looking for work until I come back, eh, please?"

The little man gratefully agreed. His tired legs were as yet revealing no inclination to tire themselves further on job-hunting trips. He saw the two men to the station, and before returning to Pastinetti Place he made a visit to St. Michael's church. His eyes clung to the life-size, familiar statue of his patron saint, Michael. The archangel stood, with militant arm upraised, in a sanctuary niche. Meeting St. Michael in the Granitetown church bathed the man in warm security; it was reunion with a dear and a powerful friend.

During the next week as he limped about the kitchen helping Maria with the dishes and the laundry, he chuckled, "Head of the family, indeed!" He wrote Mafalda: "Three months ago I was standing on twitching legs stuffing knowledge into the unwilling heads of Ibena youths, and today with twitching nostrils I am removing diapers from the chafed underside of Maria's beautiful baby." But the possibility of even a written "I-told-you-so" from Mafalda sent his pen scratching out the lines, and he tore up the letter.

He knew a nostalgia these days for the balmy spring of his Italian Piedmont, and he learned to be tolerant of the whims of a Vermont spring. He told Maria that the maples behind the Marclay house were beginning their first symphony in green with a maddening adagio; yet he held his breath in sheer ecstasy as the fragrant white-pink of chokecherry blossoms foamed gloriously among them in brief crescendo before falling in silent requiem to the earth.

He worked the Dalli back-yard vegetable patch where onion sprouts had already broken earth. The sprouts were tender, more delicately flavored than their rooted bulbs. The Dallis never dug up the onions. They were allowed to relive each spring, tirelessly sending up new shoots. Mister Tiff broke off the tops. Maria chopped them fine. With these she flavored soups, meats, and the salads which invariably constituted the summer's evening meals. The lightly serrate leaves of new chicory were picked for salads. Maria yearly allowed some of these plants to live their full, productive span of life. The fibrous stalks grew high and banked the house in a profusion of feathery blue flowers.

He sweated through his *English conversation-Grammar* for the second time, and nodded doubtfully when Petra exclaimed, "You're learning English awfully fast, Mister Tiff." To Count Mattzo he wrote rambling letters: "In Italy one speaks Italian. In France, French. Here in America we speak not American but England's English spiced with a pungent slang. Indeed, one hardly has to employ dictionary words to make one's self understood. On the other hand, the genuine dictionary words conspire diabolically to frighten away new students. A *pear* is fruit; *pair* means two of a kind; *pare* may mean to peel — and all pronounced the same! A *soul* is that God-given, invisible immortality; yet *sole* (pronounced the same) is the flat bottom of one's shoe! And as if that were not enough, words identical in spelling may differ vastly in pronunciation and meaning. *Tear* might be a drop of body water glistening in the eye; or it might well be the rip in the seat of one's trousers. A language of whimsies, no?" And, ". . . at last I am unburdened of my weighty name. To all but my few old friends I am now Mister Tiff. Pronounce it, dear Count, and roll it on your tongue like Mattzo wine if you would savor the piquant dryness of the name I now enjoy."

After school hours he met Petra and they walked the broad Main Street of the business section, beside the granite-paved road. When they reached the brick public library facing the park he avidly searched out any and all literature pertaining to his newly adopted home and to the granite which his friends worked. Before long he was making bedtime a magic hour for Petra and Vetch and he was practicing his English by relating the information he had gleaned. And when Vetch would boast, as often he did, that some day he would be a quarrier and would scale the great gray ledges of The Hill's greatest quarry, come sleet or rain, Mister Tiff might paint for them stories of the ancient pyramid builders, their bronzed, sweating bodies straining at blocks of stone, stone which in Granitetown would be cut and carried by tireless machinery. The listening Vetch, long enthralled with the romance of quarrying, felt a warm understanding for those men of antiquity, and the past became for him not dead but living. His eyes were sparked with adventure at the man's stories of the great Carrara quarries. Mister Tiff found for the children pictures of the *Mona Lisa* and *The Madonna of the Rocks,* and he chuckled, "None other than the painter of these masterpieces, the painter-sculptor-scientist-inventor da Vinci, opened at Carrara the most celebrated and the most continuously used quarry for any stone!"

The first Granitetown quarry, he told them, was opened by a war veteran after the War of 1812. At first only simple necessities like door sills and window sills were made; but soon cutters were making memorials and stone blocks for building. And by the end of the nineteenth century a rising tide of Scotch cutters with Italian cutters and carvers from the Como area, Carrara, and other stone-working districts of Italy flowed into Granitetown to contribute talent and brawn to the work. And if Petra wondered aloud where all the granite came from, the man let them sip generously from his cup of newly acquired knowledge. Here in the granite area, he told them, millions of years ago the hot, molten center of the earth was forced to the top. Intruded into this were masses of molten, glass-like matter containing highly heated water. The enormous weight of the rock above caused this granite to crystallize very slowly into its most beautiful and lasting form. It cooled, he told them, into the fine, tiny crystals which were the delight of true artists like Ronato.

Nor did it occur to the children to question Mister Tiff's words, nor to wonder why these things had not been told them by their father and mother who had lived in Granitetown much longer than this little man. Mister Tiff, they told themselves, was a teacher, wasn't he? He was expected to know such things, wasn't he?

It was Italo from his sickbed on Willow Hollow Road who gave Mister Tiff the details of the granite workers' strike. And the little man rubbed his nose meditatively and began to understand why Ronato and the honest Pietro had been reluctant to discuss it with him. The producers and the granite cutters, said Italo from his pillows, were bound to an agreement calling for $6.40 a day for a year's time, and then for $6.80 for the following year. But in March of this year the Granitetown branch of the workers' association requested an $8 day to take effect the following month, instead of the $6.40 agreed upon. The request failed, and the workers struck April 1. "It is the first breaking of a granite workers' agreement in Granitetown." Italo's smile was wan. "Some call it the 'illegal strike.'"

"So," murmured Mister Tiff.

Seeing Italo in his bed, his cheeks aglow not with health but with the fever of his illness, it was easy to believe that the workers were justified in demanding more pay. But the kindly, haunting face of old Don Benedetto quickly made discipline of his mind, and he was forced to admit that whether or not they deserved more pay they should have abided by their agreement, or should not have made it in the first place. For, he was thinking, if man's word is abused, then agreements — whether they be between individuals, labor unions, or nations — become so much worthless scraps of paper, and no one has faith in them. The first Word had been duly fulfilled, and faith and hope had been instilled in millions. And surely society must follow this example if it wished to live in a world of order.

Tonight Italo Tosti was dying.

He lay asleep in his bed, hearing neither Josie Blaine's gay victrola music in the tenement beyond the partition nor the drizzle as it tapped the moaning river willows across the road. In his dream he was in a familiar field in northern Italy. He was twelve years younger. His chest was carved bronze and strong over lungs as clean as newly fashioned bellows. He and a lustrous-eyed Lucia sat beneath a chestnut tree whose breeze-tossed foliage made a fickle awning against the sun. Italo's rich voice soared high in *Santa Lucia,* expanding under the admiration in her eyes, and breaking rudely for the sudden tumble of words — "Marry me, Lucia! Yesterday I received a letter from America, from our friend Pietro. He says over there I can earn a fine living from granite." And because her glance quickly sought the green of the familiar foothills, he added, "Pietro says this Vermont has the beauty of our own hills —"

Lucia's young lips met his. Her brown fingers touched his cheek.

Italo Tosti awoke. And the little ecstasy was not of Lucia's making, but the warm red life of him oozing upward in his throat and trickling out. He was conscious of an ethereal quality of person so strange that he knew he must be hovering on the brink of eternity.

He pulled feebly at the cord dangling on his pillow. He heard the tinkle in Lucia's room, and then saw a plump, black braid swinging against the red-stained pillow.

In a moment Lucia's bare feet were flying up to the attic room where Gino, Ito, and the baby Bert slept. In another five minutes the two brothers, hand in hand, hurried into the wet night for the doctor and the priest. The stiff willows near the river creaked under the cool drizzle. In all Willow Hollow Road only Josie Blaine's windows were lighted. Her victrola played loud and gay. Across the road the river was a quiet, dark strangeness to the boys. Gino knew that in the daytime its edges were filmed with twigs, oil, and stone dust. The machine sheds upstream dripped oil into these waters. Daytimes he liked to watch the yellow spheres winking in the sun. Across the river the weathered buildings of Shed Row loomed black and cheerless.

Ito panted to keep up with his brother. "What's *die*, Gino?"

"It's — well, you're dead."

"Like Josie's cat that got run over last week?"

"Uh-huh."

"All still?"

"You're dead — you can't move or talk any more."

The spring rain had softened the earth. Their feet sloshed into the muddy ruts. Gino was grateful for the sidewalk and brighter lights of Main Street. Below the park he shook off his brother's hand. "I'm going up there for the doctor, Ito. You got to go alone now. It's the white house next to the church — tell the priest to hurry."

His own legs ached from running. The quiet, inactive city seemed strange to him. He was accustomed to the Main Street of noontime and four o'clock when yellow trolley cars drummed a rhythm along the rails, when the air was alive with blaring auto horns and when hearty-voiced stonecutters poured out of Shed Row to merge with pedestrians and school children. Main Street tonight was as unnatural to him as the yellow-white face of his father. Tears smarted under his lids. His lips were blue with cold when he reached Dr. Renaud's house and rang the bell.

Amy Hickox, the buxom, middle-aged housekeeper, opened the door. The released hall light sprang a bright path across the porch.

"Goodness, you're dripping like a beaver," she began, eyeing the soaked jacket and rain-thinned hair.

The boy's voice strained to a frightened, high pitch. "It's my father — we want the doctor quick —" He let himself be drawn into the living room.

Gino's eyes traveled the cozy room and came to rest on a square granite door stop. It was the gray of Granitetown's best granite, highly polished, and it bore the sunken letters R E N A U D . He remembered that Pietro Dalli had worked that stone last year and had given it to the doctor, not as pay, but as an extra thank you. And there on the seat of an armchair was a patchwork pillow of bright silks which Josie Blaine had made and had given to the doctor after he treated her for the red, itchy spots she had on her arm. Josie had made a similar pillow for Gino's mother. Amy Hickox bustled back into the room and insisted upon laying a shawl to Gino's shoulders before he climbed into the doctor's car.

As they turned into Willow Hollow Road Gino saw that young Father Carty had already arrived for there beside the Dalli porch stood the priest's black, shiny coupe. Father Carty was the recently assigned assistant to old Father Down.

The lights of Dr. Renaud's car picked out another car parked a discreet distance from Josie Blaine's side of the house. It was half hidden between a clump of young willows and a heap of discolored waste granite. The doctor's lips twitched wryly. Josie Blaine was entertaining a guest tonight. A discreet guest.

Gino raced ahead of the doctor into the house. Halfway up the bare stairway they could hear Father Carty's low voice — "*De profundis clamavi ad te, Domine: Domine, exaudi vocem meam* — Out of the depths I have called to thee, O Lord: Lord, hear my voice —" Mingling faintly with the invocation were occasional notes from Josie's victrola. The doctor hesitated for a moment, frowning, then quickly ascended the stairs.

Lucia was holding her husband's limp hand deep between her breasts, her lips following the priest's prayers. Each of her words came on a deep breath which slanted the flame of the blessed candle in its crucifix holder on the bedside table. Surprisingly Mister Tiff was there, the wailing Tosti baby in his arms. Ito had been afraid to ring the bell of the priest's darkened house, and had run instead to the Dalli's where he could see a light burning.

Dr. Renaud's eyes dwelled briefly on Italo's shrunken face, the half-closed eyes. His fingers reached over a wrist. He turned aside silently. It always gave him a feeling of guilt to say, "He is dead." It was ridiculous, he knew, for how could his spoken judgment take away life where life no longer was?

Gino pressed hard to his mother's side. Her grief distressed him more than the still face on the pillow. "Don't, Mama!" he begged. If death did this to Mama then it must never again come to the Tosti house. Once he had heard Dr. Renaud tell Mama that many sicknesses could be prevented. He thought simply: if I were a doctor I wouldn't let my family get sick, Mama wouldn't have to see any of us die. He said with young assurance, "It'll be all right, Mama. Some day I'll be a doctor."

Afterward Father Carty and Mister Tiff approached Josie Blaine's door. Inside, the victrola was announcing cheerfully — *You're Nobody's Sweetheart Now.* The priest removed the black hat from his red head. Mister Tiff's knuckles rapped lightly at the door. "Josie has the visitor, *si?*"

Father Carty's freckled cheeks flushed a deep red at the hint of a chuckle in the other man's voice.

Josie's door opened. "Oh." Her startled eyes rested on the clerical collar, and traveled with some relief to Mister Tiff. "You're Gino's Tiff, aren't you? I've seen you around the past few weeks." Her eyes swung with reluctance back to the priest. "You must be the new priest —" Her hands flew to her crisp, short hair. It was late. It was a miserable night, too. What in the world did they want?

Mister Tiff gently prodded the priest into the room. Father Carty wasn't certain he had seen a shadow slip behind the spangled portieres, even though the colored glass strings of the portieres were still swaying and tinkling. Mister Tiff did not entertain the priest's doubts: he had seen the flash of a trouser leg. It was the garish green of Asa Conway's everyday suit. Once a week Mister Tiff and Petra stopped in Asa's store for a bag of Canadian peppermints, and always Asa wore that torturing shade of green.

Granitetown said that Josie's husband, Johnnie Blaine, was in northeastern Vermont, working in a lumber camp. In two years he had made one or two brief visits with Josie and the two children. And now Mister Tiff's eyes rested with alarm on Josie's plump, filling figure. Lost in his own unhappy conjectures he had paid no attention to the priest's monologue.

Father Carty was finishing in competition with the victrola. "— and Mrs. Tosti will be alone except for the baby. Gino and Ito are going to the Dalli home with Mr. Tiffone."

"Tiff," corrected his companion irritably, and had the grace to blush. It gave him unique pleasure to hear the name Petra had fashioned for him.

The priest cleared his throat. "— with Mr. Tiff. If you would be kind enough to go in with her until Mr. Tiff returns —"

Josie's red mouth had fallen open, and her chin quivered. "Dead!" In a subconscious gesture of modesty, extended not to her callers but to the dead Italo who could not see her, she drew higher the already high neckline of her dress. "Poor Lucy." She had never had the patience to pronounce the Italian name correctly — *Loo-chee-a*. "Say, you don't have to *ask* me to go in. I'll be glad to. They've been nice neighbors, and he was a swell fellow."

"— *and you're nobody's sweetheart now*," ended the victrola record. The needle scratched noisily. Josie clicked it quiet. Her pert, pretty face revealed sincere dismay. "I wouldn't have played it if I knew he was dying —"

CHAPTER III

"— twenty-two cars, twenty-three, twenty-four —" Joey Mull, Granitetown's occasional man-of-odd-jobs, counted through the rain-sheeted windows of Asa Conway's store.

Asa's wide nostrils flared angrily. He was a wiry man, of slight frame. The high cheekbones and finely chiseled features might have high-lighted a handsome face were it not for the almost perpendicular droop of his mouth, which rendered his expression perpetually sour. "Dammit, how many times I got to tell you to keep your elbows out of them oranges! You spoiled three last week."

Joey's ferret eyes broke reluctantly from the funeral cars moving slowly up granite-paved Main Street. "Hell, you made me lose count." His grimy monkey face grinned good-naturedly. Asa's growls lost strength through frequency. Each morning and each night when Joey swept the Conway floor for his two packages of cigarettes, one ear received the growls, the other promptly dismissed them. He slouched to the door, wiping orange juice from the frayed elbow of his sweater. "Made me miss three, maybe four cars. I think Tosti had a few more'n old MacMurphy had a few weeks ago. Leave it to them Eyetalians to show up for a funeral."

Asa picked out the damaged oranges, gouged out the squashed sections with a banana knife and offered one to Tip Gioffi who had dashed in from the rain for his daily bag of licorice drops. Tip shook his head. "Give it to Joey." He flipped a drop high in the air and caught it in his mouth. He stood by the door waiting for the spring rain to spend itself. "My old man died in the spring, too. That's when they go — spring and fall."

37

Joey rolled the orange between his palms to ease the flow of juice. He sucked noisily. "Damn near every Eyetalian in Granite-town was at Tosti's wake last night. Even some of the cutters who went to Quincy showed up."

Asa's question was world-old. "How'd he look?"

"His mustache was gone." Joey smacked juice-wet lips. "Wouldn't have known him."

Tip laughed. "My mother used to get after my old man to shave his off. Then someone told her a mustache caught up lot of stone dust and kept it from his nose. So she quit asking him."

Joey licked orange juice from his fingers. "Funny the Tostis don't live up this end with most of the Eyetalians —"

"Rent's cheaper in Willow Hollow Road," Tip volunteered with an impatient eye on the downpouring rain. He was scheduled to go on a bootlegging trip to the line tonight. If the rain continued, his favorite back road, a short cut which twisted between the Canadian-Vermont border, would be a river of mud too treacherous for a speeding, heavily laden car.

Joey darted cunning eyes at Asa. "Didn't I see you comin' from that way the night Tosti died? Sunday night?"

The storekeeper shot him a venomous glance. He was spared an answer, for at that moment his twin daughters, Ester and Hester, came stamping down the stairs from the Conway living quarters above. At the same time four of the Pastinetti Place children — Vetch, Petra, Robbie, and Peggy Riley, the policeman's daughter — tramped in from the rain. Asa's sister, Louella, who had kept house for Asa since his wife's death three years ago, called down to the twins from the head of the stairs admonishing them not to dawdle on their way to school.

Peggy Riley, more affluent during the strike period than the Dalli children, carefully laid a nickel on the glass counter. It was typical of Peggy's quiet nature that the deposited coin made no clatter as it touched the glass. "Five popcorn balls, Mr. Conway." She tucked two into her schoolbag and gave one each to Petra,

Vetch, and Robbie. Asa drew out two more balls and handed them
to his daughters.

Tip Gioffi shrugged at the tireless rainfall. He turned up the
collar of his well-tailored coat, and said, "Come on, kids, I'll give
you a ride to school."

He held the door open for Aggie Rugg, who was doing the morning shopping for the Marclay house. She eyed Tip with disfavor.
She had made up her mind that bootleggers were as bad as people
who drank the stuff. Years ago, if old Grandpa Eb Rugg had been
less thirsty, he might not have sold his pasture land to Enoch
Douglas for a song. Old Eb sang his song to a last hilarious note in
six weeks of drinking, then he hired out to Enoch to clear the
pasture of trees. Afterward Enoch opened the earth, found good
granite, and made money. Today his grandson Alvah Douglas was
enjoying that money in his yellow brick house on Douglas Hill. In
Aggie's simple mind the Douglas family should be blamed for her
financial straits, for the unhappy lines in her plain face. She
shrugged bony shoulders at Ellie's frequent, "They're nice folks,
Aggie. Old Enoch drove a keen bargain, but he was honest." Ellie's
grandfather had been one of the half-dozen quarriers who helped
Enoch open the quarry.

Aggie was in her middle twenties, and of a shapeless thinness.
Her face, sprinkled with sprawling brown freckles, started with a
very narrow chin but blossomed into an unexpectedly wide forehead crowned with thick, dun-colored hair. Mister Tiff, when he
had gazed upon her for the first time, murmured to himself, "Like
a mottled mushroom, and she doesn't look bright." Yet his heart
bowed to the soft, bovine eyes that were beautiful with childish
innocence. Ellie Marclay had not regretted having employed Aggie
two years ago. At first she was reluctant to entrust Robbie to her
care from seven o'clock in the morning until five in the afternoon.
But the Pastinetti Place neighbors assured her that for all Aggie's
strange looks and slow ways, she loved children and she lived an
innocent, hard-working life.

This morning Aggie smiled slowly at Joey, who was slouched against the counter. Perhaps, if he could keep a job for more than a week or two, she'd accept him as a real boy friend. He was nice to her, and he didn't make her feel that he knew more than she did.

She gave Asa the grocery slip Ellie had written.

"Want I should carry it up for you, Aggie?" Joey suggested. He'd get wet but, hell, there wasn't much else to do.

"If you want. My umbrella's big."

Later they started down Main Street, he with a bag under each arm, Aggie holding the umbrella.

"Maybe I'll come to see you again tonight." It was more question than statement.

Aggie looked at him silently. It would have been fun to have Joey to talk to after Robbie went to bed. But tonight Ellie was going out with Pete Rocco and she'd asked Aggie, please, not to have callers when she was alone. Ellie'd said, "I like you, Aggie. It's for your own good." And Aggie believed her.

"Make it tomorrow night, Joey," she said.

CHAPTER IV

On Douglas Hill the sun made splendor of new elm leaves and wove brilliance into the carpets of gently sloping lawns. Beyond Douglas Hill, and rising above it, towered The Hill, its huge bulk pitted with quarries. At a distance the deep, open wounds lost their dimensions: they appeared to be gigantic scars.

Mister Tiff, a limp burlap bag slung over his shoulder, was accompanying the Dalli children on the last dandelion pick of the season. Pietro had made a hurried trip from Quincy to attend Italo's funeral this past week, and he had lamented to Maria that no restaurant in Quincy served dandelion greens in as savory a dish as she when she piled their boiled tenderness high over spicy *salsigi*. And so today, if he filled the burlap bag, Maria would can a few jars of dandelions for Pietro. As he walked Mister Tiff's mild blue eyes held thoughtfully to The Hill in the distance. Like in Petra's game, he was not seeing it, but seeing beyond it to a glorious tapestry of other hills of the ages: Christ crucified on Calvary; Moses receiving the tablets of stone on Mt. Sinai; Noah's ark salvaged on the double peaks of Ararat; Rome built on its seven hills. And here was Granitetown. To be sure, it was not built on a hill, but it was dominated by a hill. The Hill was Granitetown's very lifeblood. It was not as beautiful as its storied sister hills of Vermont. It reared gaunt and despoiled, its rock-ribbed sides shattered and lacerated.

The Hill dominated Granitetown, yet it stood there defenseless against the many and deeper wounds man would inflict in years to come. For, as long as this beautiful stone was available, there

41

would be men to work it, reflected the little man. To hew it. To carve it. To ship it to the four corners of the country, and beyond, where it would pile into lasting buildings, or stand as memorials to fellow men who had paid their visit to the world and departed. He thought of the dead Italo. Hah, The Hill was not without its own brand of revenge, and its avenging weapon was the very stone the men worked. Dust slowly took its toll of men. He pictured the quarriers' steel drilling into the granite womb, and The Hill retaliating with a gush of gray dust. And he pictured its continued vindication when, after the stone was dislodged and freighted down the tracks to the finishing sheds, the men further cut it or carved it to finished perfection. But man's inventive mind, he told himself, would some day control dust, just as it had eased stone production with its pneumatic and electrical tools, its derricks and its transportation devices. . . .

The dandelion pickers climbed the elm-shaded walk of Douglas Hill. Petra, her hand tucked into the man's, squinted against the slant of sun. "It's funny, this is steeper than our street, but it doesn't *feel* steeper."

Robbie was lightly slapping at a greening box hedge with a sumach wand. "That's because this is a smooth cement walk. All Pastinetti Place's got is a granite-chip walk — that's why."

"Well, why don't we have one like it?"

Vetch grumbled, "Denny Douglas' feet aren't any better than mine just because his family owns a quarry."

A smile tugged at Mister Tiff's heart for, despite the boy's plaint, Vetch was this minute returning a joyous wave of the hand to Denny Douglas, who was running down the flagstone walk which bisected the Douglas lawn. He must remember to write to Count Mattzo that in this little city of imported bloods, even though there might be strikes, stone, which was the city's very blood, made itself felt as a common denominator. . . . Count Mattzo, he suspected, would tap the letter on his desk, and he would wish to heaven that he had these Granitetown people as tenants instead of the wealthy tenants who leased his farms and who subleased them to less wealthy tenants — and between whom flared perpetual bickering and snobbery.

As Denny reached the group, there was a sudden decision to race to the spruces atop the hill and thence to the green field beyond. Petra fled with the boys, calling over her shoulder, "We'll wait for you there, Mister Tiff."

Alone, and welcoming a rest, the man set down bag and cane, and sank gratefully to the narrow lip of green that curved beneath the Douglas hedge. Dandelions were growing tantalizingly within his reach. He drew out his jackknife, unfolded the blade, and bent sideways to cut the greens.

An icy voice trickled down at him from above the hedge. "Look here, I won't have my lawn dug up!"

Even as she spoke the words Minna Douglas realized that ordinarily she would not have interrupted anyone picking dandelions here. It was only the hedge-enclosed lawn which she insisted be kept smooth as the nap of a Persian rug. But today a headache frayed her nerves.

She looked down at the man. She had not expected a pair of mild eyes that were a faded blue against the bright blue of his kerchief, nor did she expect an English that halted broken at his lips.

"Me, I don't dig — I cut at the top. See?"

"I don't care how you pick them, I just don't want them picked. There are any number of dandelions over the hill, in the field below."

He wiped his hands on the grass. "Your hair — it is the same color as the boy Denny's."

She heard the slight rise in his voice which signaled a question and which, if answered, would direct conversation into other channels. She had the uncomfortable feeling that he was laughing at her; moreover, that she was deserving of it. It came to her that he must be the teacher from Italy about whom Denny often spoke after he had spent an hour or two with the Dalli children.

She was silent. He ventured guilelessly, his eyes on the fine greens growing on either side of him, "*Dio mio,* you planted these dandelions?"

"Of course not. How foolish! People don't plant dandelions in their lawns. It spoils them."

"Hah, really then you don't *want* them here, no?"

His manner waxed humble, yet again she sensed a suppressed chuckle in his voice. Minna Douglas, like her son, Denny, was slender and white; a sallowness was beginning to shade the appealing curve of her cheeks. She said coldly, "It's our gardener's business to take care of that!"

"I go, I go," Tiff agreed softly. He wiped the blade of his knife on the burlap bag, and rose painfully to his feet. He began conversationally, "The gardener — he eats the dandelions?"

"How do I know!" She was angry with him and with herself.

"At our house, we eat them. You know, in soup and in *insalata* —"

"*Insal* —" In spite of herself she queried, "You mean salads? You eat raw dandelions?"

"You eat the lettuce raw, no? And the endive?" he countered.

That evening she laughingly told her husband that she could not remember exactly what had transpired except that Denny's Mister Tiff waved aside her protests, and she found herself crossing the lawn with him, entering the kitchen, and helping him clean a half-dozen dandelions while the maid, at his bidding, boiled three eggs. When he asked for garlic and was told they had none, he surprisingly produced a clove of garlic from his shirt pocket. He explained shyly that the child Petra often carried ham sandwiches on these excursions for dandelions. And since the flat taste of ham pleased him not at all, he had fallen into the habit of carrying a clove of garlic. With this, he added, he seasoned the sandwiches to his liking.

Mister Tiff sliced a garlic kernel in two, and rubbed the moist sides to Minna's salad bowl. He diced a small onion and the hard-boiled eggs. These he put into the bowl with the greens. And over the whole he let trickle a thin flow of olive oil. A heavier stream of vinegar broke up the golden globules of oil and sent them shimmering between the greens. He added salt and pepper, and tossed the salad lightly until each dandelion leaf was coated with yellowed vinegar. He urged Minna to try it.

She put the fork to her mouth. She chewed warily, at first. The faint bitterness of the cut greens and the tang of the seasoned vinegar teased her tongue pleasantly. "Why, it *is* good!" And she was thinking, as he abruptly said his good-bys and murmured that he must catch up with the Dalli children, that Alvah would like this salad, and that she might mix some for the bridge club tomorrow.

Mister Tiff joined his young friends at the brow of the spruce wood topping Douglas Hill. The little party dipped out of sight onto a sharp drop of stubble field. Here a wanton grass grew and lived its life unmolested by Douglas Hill gardeners. Even in adolescence it was a tough, dry grass that lisped rebellion to the slightest stir of breeze. A decrepit stone fence lurched diagonally down the incline, and ended by tumbling into the shallow water of a wooded gorge. Scaly lichens grew in the interstices of the stones. Sections of the fence were of old wood. They were the stumps of trees Aggie's grandfather had cleared off this land for Enoch Douglas years ago. They were great, black, interlaced roots. Jagged and grotesque. They were rotting now, but in their day the stiff upthrusts had warded off man and beast.

Denny crooked his slim arm through the brown, sturdier one of Vetch. He looked accusingly at the paper bag rustling in the pit of his friend's arm. "Are you really going to pick dandelions with the rest? You promised we'd go to our quarry today." Under the warming sun fine beads of perspiration gleamed over his delicately molded lips, and his bronze hair was sculptured to a moist, white brow.

Vetch's gaze swept Denny's shoes, the unblemished brown and

white of which proclaimed their newness. His glance lowered to his own scuffed shoes. He suggested roughly, "Let's go barefoot." And when Denny's bare feet sank beside his into the prickly green stubble, he could forget the small resentment and could enjoy an equality with this schoolmate whom he liked. He assured Denny: "O.K., we'll go to our quarry. Let's lag behind the others — you, Gino and me."

The trio fell behind Petra, Robbie and the man; the boys pressed steadily downward toward the ravine. When a satisfactory distance separated the two groups, Vetch horned his hands and shouted to Petra that they were going to the opposite slope. She looked back at him silently, a slim hand making a visor against the sun. Noting her indecision, Vetch thought: she knows I'm going to the quarry. She knows Mama doesn't want me to go, yet she doesn't want to remind me in front of my friends. . . . He was filled with an awkward tenderness. Petra was all right — Petra wouldn't squeal. His open palm swept upward in a gesture that assured her, "Everything's O.K. You won't have to lie for me when we get home."

The boys bore downward, now, at a fast clip. They scrambled down sun-warmed stones of the gorge, waded the brook, scaled the opposite rocky wall. In a brief woodland they walked the shadows of thin spruces and scraggy pines, their naked feet sinking into last year's needles, their toes digging into the slippery, spongy surface. The sudden coolness sent a ripple to Denny's sensitive skin. The beads of perspiration became a cool, short-lived dew. He spied the fuzzy curls of new fern against exposed spruce roots, and he could not help drawing one from the ground and holding its woody fragrance to his cheek, adding coolness to coolness.

The woodland opened abruptly to vast sunlight, to early crickets chanting underfoot, and to an immediate flight of knolls treading one above the other to meet with a mountainous bulk. Its side was gashed with long-abandoned quarries. Gray pyramids of grout stood like battered fortresses beside the yawning cavities. The waste granite had lain there many years. Leaves, dirt and dust had gathered in its crevices to become a poor soil; and now a scrawny tree or two jutted out from the piles, as if poised for flight, as if at any moment they might lose their precious roothold. Beyond this hill, and below, lay the broad flat of Peter's Gate, a community picnic ground. And above this plain towered The Hill with its active quarries.

On the shelf of the first knoll the boys put on their shoes. They walked the rusted rails of an old freight track half hidden under weeds. Their destination was a slight, circular depression on the second knoll. It was scoured of earth, and barren with flat, gray rock. Vetch went at once to a clump of chokecherry bushes; he pushed aside the branches and drew out two rusty picks, a shovel, and crowbar. He and Denny wasted no time. They swung their picks into a jagged indentation which had taken them two weeks to dig. Gino sprawled lazily on a hummock at a safe distance from flying splinters.

He could see no fun in their useless labor. It was too much like the wood chopping he did daily at home. At least the wood gave warmth, but this stone gave only blistered hands and an aching back. He watched the picks rise and fall; he saw the boys' faces gradually grow a mottled red-white and then settle to a hot, wet scarlet. He wondered idly if Denny's father ever sweated like that in his Main Street bank or in his quarry office. He said flatly, "That stone's no good."

"So what?" Vetch ground out. He struck his pick into the stone with all his might.

"So you're working for nothing. Even if it *was* good, what would you get out of it? It's old man Salvatore's land. Denny's father sold it to old man Salvatore; didn't he, Denny?"

Denny nodded. Vetch straightened his throbbing body and turned a grimy face full to Gino. It was hostile, sullen. "Maybe we like to dig for nothing, see?"

Gino's little flow of conversation was dammed by his friend's fury. He reached beside him for the paper bag Vetch had carried.

Crystals of sugar rustled in its bottom. He shook them out. A few ants fell out with them. He might as well pick dandelions, Mama would be pleased with them.

With Gino gone, Vetch's brown square face turned upward to The Hill. For the hundredth time he said to Denny, "That big quarry up there — where you see the top of the derrick, that's where I'm going to work some day."

Denny drew a quivering breath of relief. He knew from past experience that when Vetch began talking about quarries, it was a prologue to the stoppage of work. He thrust the steel deep into the earth, and leaned upon the handle. His back ached. His arms ached. If he rubbed his arms to comfort them, Vetch would scoff at him. He walked from the rock bed and sank to the ground. "Wouldn't you like to work with your father?"

"In the sheds?" Vetch shrugged off the question as undeserving of a reply. He flung himself prone beside Denny, his forehead on a curved arm. "What about yourself? Do you want to work with your father?"

"No —"

"Well, then, why should I?"

"It's all granite — you like granite —"

"So do you."

Denny admitted, "Yes."

"Well, do you want to quarry stone like me?"

"You know I don't." Denny's smile was tolerant. He had answered this same question a dozen times. "I don't care where I work as long as I can carve it."

It was all so strange, he thought. Father and Mother spoke proudly of Great-grandfather Douglas who had carved beautiful monuments in Aberdeen, Scotland, years ago. But when they came upon Denny last winter carving a small dog from a piece of soft grout, she ordered him to throw it away. At first, Father had exclaimed with something of pleased surprise, "Maybe he takes after Gramp, Minna." But afterward the colored clays, molding

knives, and chisels disappeared from his playroom. They were replaced with other gifts.

Denny's thumping heart was quieting now. He collected his and
Vetch's quarry tools and concealed them once more behind the
bushes. From a shoe box, also hidden there, he took a tiny earthen
church he had molded from the reddish clay of the brook, and a
small steepled square of granite which was already showing a
resemblance to its clay model. With a small chisel and hammer
he hewed away at the diminutive steps. It was for this moment
that Denny accompanied Vetch and worked with him at their
little quarry. Denny did not like to dig, but the few moments of
rest Vetch afterward claimed afforded him this opportunity to work
at his carving. He wondered how long he would have to wait before
the little finger of his left hand became chisel distorted and swollen
— like Ronato's and Pietro Dalli's, and those of hundreds of granite
carvers.

Vetch, his eyes entrenched in the cleft their picks had dug, said
dreamily, "It's one of the oldest jobs in the world — "

"What is?"

"Quarrying — "

"Who said so?"

"Mister Tiff."

"Oh." He added in quiet satisfaction, "Then carving must be
the second oldest." For surely those thousands of years ago when
stone was first taken from the earth there must have been someone
like himself who had to put his hands to it, to give it shape and
meaning.

"It's in the Bible," Vetch added.

"That it's the oldest job?"

"Well — that they dug stone, and made buildings. Mister Tiff
said so." Vetch lay there, his cheek to the ground, envisioning
Mister Tiff's picture of the ragged bondmen in Egypt. Straining
under their leashes. Sweat pouring from their backs. Flayed, driven
on at whips' end to draw huge blocks of stone for some mighty

pharaoh. And all that work done by hand, Mister Tiff had said. Nowadays, quarriers had derricks, trucks, flatcars, to haul away the stone, they had drills that ate into stone at the press of a button, they had powder to break it from its rock bed. But he and Denny — his heart swelled proudly — he and Denny did it all by hand. Like the stoneworkers of long ago.

"Denny, what're bondmen?"

"I don't know."

"I think rich guys must've owned them."

"Maybe they were slaves, then, like the Negroes used to be," Denny ventured. He suddenly remembered a bit of information a dinner guest had given last night, information Vetch would like to hear. "You know that memorial they're putting up in the park, the one to the soldiers and sailors? Well, before the sculptors started to work on it the piece of granite weighed 36 tons."

"Gee!" But for Vetch the glory of idle moments had paled. He was eager, now, to climb the topmost knoll and to look down on Granitetown. Denny reluctantly replaced the granite church and its clay model beneath the chokecherry bushes. Then he panted up the hill beside Vetch and Gino. He could not understand this craving that Vetch had to stand on some high hill, his sturdy legs wide apart, his brown arms folded to his chest, like the man in *Gulliver's Travels*. Vetch's eyes would light up as he looked down upon the countryside, and Denny felt that he could almost see power, pride, and strength flowing into him, and out.

Denny was ever content in looking up to the hills. And above, to the skies. So many beautiful things pointed upward. The cone-shaped hills. The trees. All the church steeples of the world pointed upward. There was a strange, sweet mystery to the heavens, he thought, something that made throat and heart swell with some soundless harmony. Once he had tried to discuss with Vetch this which he himself did not understand, and Vetch had cut him short with, "Nuts!" Denny, at times, was envious of his friend's rough voice, his brown, husky body, his spirit of independence. Vetch seemed to him a small edition of those hearty, boisterous men who came daily down The Hill, dinner pails in hand, tongues quick to lash out in irritation and just as quick to shake the world with laughter.

When fingers of shadow crept longer and wider over the sun-drenched hills, the boys remembered they must go home. It would never do, the trio decided, to trace their steps back to Douglas Hill. They cut into a steep field and soon they were on a hard surface road, the main artery leading to Granitetown. They sat to catch their breath on the wooden blocks supporting the enormous roadside sign which announced:

GRANITETOWN, THE WORLD'S
GREATEST GRANITE CENTER

Vetch rolled blades of dusty grass into pellets and aimed them at the letters in Granitetown. He reminded, "One of us got to hitch a ride."

In pity for Denny's drooping shoulders and weary face, Gino said to Vetch, "Let's you and me play a game of *mora*. The loser — two out of three — does the bumming. O.K.?" And so they played the game their fathers played, the game the Italian stonecutters played at Mama Gioffi's house to see who would pay for the wine. Simultaneously each boy flung down his right hand with any number of fingers outstretched, and each called aloud the number which he guessed to be the total of outstretched fingers.

"Six!" Vetch cried.

"Eight!" Gino guessed.

"It's seven. Neither of us won." It was Gino who finally won the game. Vetch pocketed his hands and took a stand on the gravel shoulder. He kicked desultorily at pebbles. An elderly woman in a black coupe sounded her horn in annoyance and passed them by. It was Tip Gioffi and Pete Rocco, in Tip's sleek black touring car, who picked them up.

Gino settled himself in the back seat and whispered to Denny that Tip was a bootlegger.

Denny's eyes widened; his fingers gingerly explored the seat.

Vetch laughed his scorn. "There's nothing here now — they go after their loads at night."

CHAPTER V

At noon, on June twelfth, Pietro burst radiantly into Maria's kitchen where she was bathing the two weeks' old Americo. "No more Quincy," he announced. "I am home for good!"

So much of happiness radiated from his round face that she did not dare entertain the hope that he had come home to employment other than the cutting of stone. As if in communion of thought he explained, "I start work again for Gerbatti day after tomorrow."

The old vexation pulsed wearily at her temples. She had heard no word of a settlement between the Granitetown manufacturers and the strikers. "Gerbatti's?"

"I know, I know. It is not yet common knowledge in Granitetown. Gerbatti wrote to us in Quincy. The papers of settlement will probably be signed tomorrow. Some of the other sheds will open this week, too."

"And those who have been taking your places, and the quarriers — what will happen to them?"

"Ah, to be sure, some will keep their jobs — "

Petra interrupted, "There's a bozo family living right up the street, Papa! In the house next to Robbie Marclay's — "

Maria ordered, "They have a name, call them by their right name." And to Pietro's questioning glance, "Yes, a young quarrier named Vitleau has bought the house and pasture land. There are himself, his father, and a little boy and girl. He is the one, they say, with whom Tip Gioffi had words at the station."

"Words!" Pietro fingered his silky mustache. "You know, Maria, I cannot bear a grudge against them. They were made offers that would tempt any man who carries a hungry belly. For them it was a job. And all are entitled to that. Some of them had never worked granite before. They didn't know that our strikes are justifiable." He remembered the conditions of the present strike, and he added, "Well, most of them."

Maria's laugh was hollow. "They'll learn. A few years in those houses of dust — " She stopped abruptly. Vetch and Petra, caught by a grim quality in her voice, were listening with avid attention. And she was determined that whatever differences of opinion she and Pietro might have concerning his work would not be poured into the ears of the children.

Mister Tiff's search for a job was proving fruitless. As a last resort he appeared at the stonesheds, where a glance at his gray hair (he was too old, the glance said, to come in as an apprentice) and his rheumatic legs (how could those legs, the glance asked, support him in the tiring job of even a handy man?) brought him a kindly shake of the head. Hah, he thought, if only his English were better, and if only the *paesani* were wealthy enough to hire him to teach their children Italian! The idea was so golden that he tucked it away for use when the opportune time might present itself.

For days since Pietro's return Mister Tiff had been on the verge of raising the delicate question of whether, with the recent addition of the baby Americo, he was not crowding the little Dalli home. But each time he found himself strangling the words in his throat. For, if Pietro said, "*Sì*, we are crowded," where would he go? How would he support himself? And the mere thought of writing to his sister in Ibena for his fare back to his homeland grew a cold sweat on his brow.

It was Maria who set his mind at temporary ease. One warm evening they had been sitting on the porch listening to Petra and Vetch read Italian from the saints' calendar, while from the Rossi's back-yard *bocce* course sounded the bop of wooden balls being rolled by Pietro and his friends. Maria said, "It is truly our good fortune that you came to us, *Maestro*. I would never have had the time or patience to teach the children to read Italian." And in the next breath she added the housewifely detail, "I changed your room around today. The window is now between your bed and Vetch's. With the hot weather coming you will both need that window."

Few words, and simple, yet for the man they were enough to assure him that his welcome had not worn thin. Heartened, he decided that if he could not find a job, he must create one.

So it was that on a warm afternoon of blue sky and persistent sun, Mister Tiff crossed the bridge to Shed Row. He paused under a willow at the river bank and let the wheelbarrow rest on its own supports. The metal rests dug into the pulverized earth, much of which was stone dust. The barrow was heavy. It carried a metal pail of ice and two dozen bottles of soda in assorted flavors. Too, it carried two shoe boxes filled with oranges, bananas, and chocolate bars. The man untied the blue kerchief at his neck and applied it to his forehead where it soaked up the perspiration. He hoped Pepino Stoffi and Asa Conway had not been looking from their store windows as he passed with this little store on wheels. He had bought the stock at a chain store. It cost less. True, Pepino might have sold him the stock at cost — but how, then, would Pepino make a profit for himself?

The sun was beating destruction on the ice; he gathered fresh willow leaves and strewed them over the ice and fruit. Then, he sat on the edge of the barrow and rubbed his legs. This idea of peddling drinks to the stonecutters had come to him in the fanciful hours of night. With his legs at ease between crisp sheets, it had seemed a silvery avenue of grace. . . . Mafalda, if she knew it, would throw up her hands in horror; but Mafalda, fortunately, was across the ocean. He would not have to remind her, futilely, that Christ had carried lumber in His father's humble woodshop, and that the Paduan Anthony had exercised his scholar's hands in scullery work. With dogged perseverance he lifted the barrow and started across the hot steel of the tracks to the sheds.

At the bend of the road, just before the string of weather-beaten sheds became visible, he heard the tireless hiss of air compressors punctuated by violent, explosive blasts. Threading the din was the nearer staccato *clat-aclat-clat* of drills on stone. This would be the MacDougal shed. And here was big Tony Bottelli, dark of face and massive of shoulder, bent over a drill in the roofed yard. Mister Tiff chuckled. This giant Bottelli might well have been a model for Michelangelo's great Jeremiah. The cutter's long, muscular legs were set, firm and widespread, on a huge granite block, and the thick flesh quivered to the vibrations of the drill. Dust fanned upward to his narrowed eyes. The sight of this chalky spray dried the juices of Mister Tiff's nose and throat. Tony shifted the quid in his mouth and squirted a brown stream which seeped into the dusty earth.

The cutter and his fellow workers drank gratefully from the cold stock, and the vendor left the MacDougal shed with the barrow lighter by six bottles, two oranges, and three chocolate bars. He limped into the dusty coolness of the Gerbatti shed and shouted through the clamor of drills and saws, "Hah, Pietro, a businessman I am these days!"

He was unprepared for the sudden start and slump that sent the pneumatic hose sliding from Pietro's shoulder, and for the quick flash of pity in the brown eyes facing him. Mother of God, was there a trace of Mafalda in this Pietro!

But although Pietro could not disguise the feeling mirrored in his eyes, yet his tongue could choose words carefully. And he insisted, "Two bottles I can drink, right away!"

Ronato, the bachelor carver, bought. And Gerbatti. And others. And afterward Pietro, in clumsy effort to nip this peddling business in the bud for today at least, said in his native tongue. "A thought comes to me, *Maestro*. Since well before Americo was born I have not surprised the children with a gift. Today I will buy all of your stock, yes?"

"The barrow, too?" the other man asked dryly. But understanding suddenly flowed easily between them.

"To be sure! I can use it in the vegetable garden."

Mister Tiff shook his head. "I have already promised soda to the men in the yard."

Gerbatti, the boss, jowls blue from a three days' beard and red faced from standing over the forge, interrupted to call Pietro and Ronato to him. He was holding a print Jeff Doyle had just brought him from the drafting room. "You two, you like this design for Tosti's stone?"

Ronato looked. "For Tosti? But it is the design you asked me to make for the Chicago customer. You said, 'Make it beautiful, he is a special customer.' "

Gerbatti grinned. "I fooled you, eh? Good. Well, do we make it for Tosti? Yes? No?"

Pietro and Ronato exchanged a look which said plainly: how can Lucia Tosti ever pay for so fine a stone?

Gerbatti said, as he lighted a black stogie, "Me and MacDougal, we give the stone. You two, you do the work — O.K.?"

It was a small memorial standing no higher than four feet. An ancient Greek stele. The motif — delicately wrought passion flowers — was concentrated at the top. Below was the lettering; and beneath this a plain polished field. Ronato was eyeing his own work approvingly. He had liked this design so much that he had made an oil painting of it — the raw umber and white blending subtly to create the lustrous dark gray of the granite — and had hung it on the wall of his room. Pietro, studying the design Gerbatti held in his hand, wished wordlessly that it might have included a cross smothered in a shaft of lilies or a tangle of grapevine. But Ronato's eye, he acknowledged in silent tribute, was far the more artistic. Strange, he thought, I am a simple man, my pleasures are simple, yet for me beauty in art is an intricacy of design. Whereas this

Ronato, whose hands can draw and carve all but life — he seeks the simple.

Gerbatti was thrusting the print into Ronato's hands. "See if Lucia Tosti likes the design, eh, Ronato?"

Ronato's melancholy face flushed. He massaged his cramped right hand and turned to the stone he was carving. The design would be a good reason for appearing at Lucia's door again tonight. Last night when the three Tosti boys were abed he had intended to say — with no mention of love, for Italo was buried but a few weeks — "Lucia, we should marry, yes? We can make a nice home for the boys." But she cleverly veered him from the subject of matrimony, and spoke chiefly of the *maestro* who, she said, would certainly lose his self-respect if he did not find work. She suggested that Pietro might take up a collection, and that he might then travel back in comfort to Italy where he would again be the respected village teacher. Ronato sighed. He was about to relate Lucia's suggestion to Pietro, but he noticed that Tiff, soda bottle in hand, was beside him watching him at his work. The carver's hand closed snugly around the chisel. He worked.

Mister Tiff marveled at the rapt expression that transfigured Ronato's face. He was carving a nude cherub which had the plump, swelling curves of a Raphael angel. Later this summer it would stand on a cemetery lot where the little daughter of a wealthy Granitetown merchant was laid. The stone cherub must possess all but breathing life; its eyes must hold delight and love, as if it were quite by choice that its naked feet had paused there in the grass to keep company with the other child. Ronato said, half to himself, "So fine is this stone that I swear I could cut lashes to the little one's eyes."

The little man nodded in humble silence. He moved across to Pietro's corner. The din of the shed was deafening. Traveling cranes careened thunderously overhead. At Gerbatti's forge, steel tempered steel in sharp clangs. From the four corners of the room came the vicious chatter of pneumatic drills. In the next room giant circular saws sliced ravenously into stone; near by, chisels bit more fastidiously into it. Everywhere, thought Mister Tiff, steel on stone. Steel cut the stone and shredded the air into a million splinters of sound, and the wooden shed shuddered with vibrations. Pietro was standing on the newly wet floor. He slid the steel over the calloused little finger of his left hand and guided it carefully into the outlined letters, carving the name *Jerrod Aldrich Eckles* into a small marker. *Gurra-urra-urra* rang the steel as it cut into the stone, and Pietro's thoughts rang with it: *So, Jerrod Aldrich Eckles, you are a stranger to me. Nor are you a* paesano, *not with that name! Is your skin of my whiteness, or are you black or yellow? I don't know you. Nor do you know me. I am but one poor Pietro Dalli, yet my hands are making a memory of you in stone. The* Dio *created you, He let you live and die, and now I am creating a memory of you in stone. Perhaps to the end of the world there will be an occasional one who will pass your way and who will look at this stone and say — "A certain Jerrod Aldrich Eckles once lived, may he rest in peace —"*

A quiet smile played at Pietro's full lips. Mister Tiff recognized that smile. It was the smile that flowered from a heart at peace — whether the heart belonged to the teacher in the classroom, the priest making his evening recollection, a mother tucking her children abed at the end of the day, the student closing the volume from which he has gleaned knowledge, the smithy contentedly surveying his handwork. It was the smile of simple satisfaction, contentment. Mister Tiff understood that smile. He sighed for all those who could never fashion such a smile, and he lifted the handles of his barrow and slowly went out to the shed yard.

Joey Mull lay on his side, sunning himself on a roughly cut block of granite. A soiled cap tipped over his left eye; the other eye watched a cutter chalking stone. A rope was tied around Joey's wrist; at the end frisked a shaggy black puppy. The pup scrambled to the wheelbarrow and thrust an exploring paw into

the pail of ice water. He withdrew it quickly, and tried to rub
it dry against his other front paw.

"*Io mi lavo gli mani*," Mister Tiff chuckled.

Joey sat up. "Huh?"

"I wash my hands," the man translated. "Remember — Pontio
Pilato did that."

"Who's he?"

The Irishman Sweeney wiped his red-chalked hands along his
thighs. "Pontius Pilate. The Bible guy who got cold feet."

Joey shrugged disinterest. That funny Tiff fellow was playing
with the mutt as if he liked him. "Want to buy the dog?"

The man hesitated. Certainly, Petra, Vetch, and Gabriella would
love this dog. But in his pocket there was but ninety-five cents. . . .
And for Pietro only a rabbit dog like Rossi's flap-eared hound
would be truly appreciated.

Joey broke the sulphurous cap from a match with his fingernail.
"Want to buy him?"

"Us, we use mostly hunting dogs."

"Hell, you can borrow a huntin' dog any time you get the urge.
This one's good — Spitz and Scottie. Chopped wood all mornin' for
old lady Martin to get him."

The dog sat up to sniff the chocolate bars. Sweeney's fingers
combed through the matted silky hair. "Give you a dollar, Joey."

Joey shook his head.

Mister Tiff made a hurried survey of his stock. One dollar and
fifty-cents worth, retail. Should he trade? So much humiliation —
and pity — had shone from Pietro's eyes that never would he have
the heart to take his barrow on another peddling tour. It was
one thing to feel that he should accept any job, but quite another
to humiliate the man who was giving him a home. He drew a
speckled banana from the willow leaves, peeled it leisurely, and
ate with loud relish.

Sweeney made his second offer. "I'll give you a dollar and
this jackknife."

Joey's eyes fastened to the pulpy white fruit at Mister Tiff's mouth. He'd planned to present the pup to Aggie. She hadn't looked at him this week, ever since he borrowed the dollar from her. But, hell, the pup was lousy with fleas. Old Mrs. Martin had told him to drown the pup. Sure, he'd chopped wood for her, but she paid him a dollar for that, and gave him an extra quarter to drown the pup.

Joey fingered the dice in his pocket. "Tell you what, let's make a jackpot of the dog, your stock, and Sweeney's knife and dollar. High score out of five rolls takes all. O.K.?"

And so they rolled. Joey chalked the totals of their four rolls on the granite block, and handed the dice to Mister Tiff. The little man's every pore prickled with excitement. The score read: Sweeney 22, Joey 24, Tiff 20. *Dio mio,* he thought, I must roll high, high. . . . He wondered, with something of guilt, if there were a patron saint for gamblers. Thieves irreverently claimed St. Nicholas — but, he was hardly a thief playing at this game about which he knew so little. On a breath of desperation and self-reproach he whispered a prayer to his St. Michael. He rolled, and stared. Each die showed double rows of three's. "One whole dozen!" he cried. His index finger caressed his nose in great hope.

"Twelve," Joey mumbled after him. He chalked "Tiff — 32."

Sweeney's roll sent one of the dice over the granite edge, onto the ground.

"It counts," Joey warned. He scrambled in search of it.

Mister Tiff took advantage of their turned backs, and swiftly stuffed a handful of chocolate bars into his shirt. If he were to lose, why lose all?

Joey said, "Eight. That gives you thirty, Sweeney. Two less than Tiff." He blew in his hands, mumbled an abracadabra, and made the final roll. He spat. "Hell, seven — "

Mister Tiff's pale eyes shone. He was possessor of stock, dollar, knife, and dog.

Joey muttered, "He's full of fleas anyway."

Mister Tiff set the pup in the barrow and wheeled it down the road to the Tosti's Willow Hollow Road home. Lucia sat on the porch, her listless attention on her playing children. Over the plain black dress she wore the heavy blue-and-white-striped stone-cutter's apron which Italo had worn in the sheds. The man un-buttoned his shirt and distributed the sweets and half of the barrow's stock to the Tosti boys and Josie Blaine's children. The remainder he would present to the Dalli children; and Pietro would have his barrow, after all. From Lucia be begged a pail of warm, soapy water, and into this he crumbled two black stogies. He soaked the squirming pup in this brew. "No more fleas for you, my Pilato."

The four o'clock shed whistle had blown, and he was saying his farewells to Lucia on the little square of lawn when big Tony Bottelli and two fellow stonecutters appeared around the bend. They greeted the man and woman briefly, slapped stone dust from pants and caps, and strode, without more ado, into Lucia's kitchen. Mister Tiff turned puzzled eyes after them. Lucia quickly excused herself. It was not until Tony's hearty — "*Maestro*, come join us in a glass of wine," boomed from the doorway that the man realized that Lucia had decided to earn money for her family by selling liquor in her home.

"Another time," he called back. He sat there on the edge of the barrow waiting until the three men had quenched their thirst and departed.

Lucia, edged with a defiance that was alien to her soft, dark prettiness, came out to stand before him. "Say it, say whatever you will! If you think I like to turn my kitchen into a taproom for thirsty men — you are mistaken — "

"How long have you been 'selling'?"

"A week."

"But, Lucia, it is against the law."

"Others in Granitetown do it."

"It is still against the law."

"Is it against the law to feed my boys? Back in the Ibena schoolroom you always said, 'Be prudent, be prudent.' Well, I am being prudent. The very little money Italo left I am going to keep — every cent — for an emergency, and to help later on with the boys' education. But — " a white hand waved expressively toward the kitchen " — in the meantime we have to eat. How can I get an outside job when there is a baby to look after? Selling wine is better than charity."

He winced at the word, remembering himself under Pietro's roof. But he persisted, "Would you have your children pointed at? They have but one parent now, Lucia. And for you they must have all the love and respect other children give to two parents. How will they feel later if some schoolmate taunts, 'Your mother breaks the law — she makes her living by breaking the law'?"

"Others do it," she repeated.

"Your children are yours, they don't belong to these 'others.'"

Josie Blaine's pert face was smiling at them from her screen door. She shooed her two children out into the sunshine. "Hello —" she called before closing the door.

Lucia spoke soberly. "I break a law of the land. Josie breaks a law, too. I sell only wine. . . ."

The man's slight figure squirmed uncomfortably. True, just before reaching the Tosti house, he had seen Asa Conway's car making a wide arc around Willow Hollow Road. "Hah, quiet," he urged, hoping to interrupt both his own and Lucia's worthless thoughts, "we must not set ourselves as judges." And now he was wearily comparing his own problem of earning a living with that of Lucia. She could not take an outside job because of her children; he could not take on a real job because of his legs. His eyes fell to the strings of the stonecutter's apron; she was languidly twining the coarse ribbons around her little finger.

"Hah!" He sprang to his feet heedless of the twinge of pain shooting through his knee. "I have it, Lucia! And, *per Baccho,* it is the solution for both of us." He rubbed hard at the mole on his nostril. "That apron you are wearing — you made it, no?"

"Yes." She could not share the excitement that quivered in the usually serene features and calm eyes. "I have a fine machine." It was the last expensive gift Italo had given her, just before he stopped work.

"Then, see, the *Dio* takes care of us both in one stroke, and with no evasion of the law. Look, you are the production line; I am the salesman. You make the greater profit because you do the greater amount of work — I get the commission." He wondered uneasily if self-promotion from peddler to salesman in one afternoon would be social advancement enough in Pietro's eyes, and profit enough for himself. At least, it would be helping Lucia plant her feet on the right side of the law. . . .

In the face of his eagerness Lucia's reserve broke. She smiled tolerantly. "What *are* you talking about?"

"The aprons, of course!" His job, he told her, would consist of going to the sheds and taking orders for aprons which she would make at home. "Your sewing may grow into a business. If the aprons are not enough, you can take orders among your acquaintances for children's clothes. You shall have a sign in the window — *Lucia Tosti, Seamstress.* And you will not be living furtively, breaking the law —"

Under the magic of his words she could almost hear the busy whirring of the sewing machine and picture herself sewing dresses, aprons, curtains, while her three boys sat safely in the same room playing or studying.

He took her hands in his thin ones, swinging them in playful fashion. "You promise, eh? No more of this 'selling' business?"

Beneath the bantering tone she read earnest appeal, and she felt herself back in an Ibena schoolroom facing a kindly but determined teacher. "I promise."

Jubilantly he swung the barrow with the now sleeping pup down the road, almost colliding with Asa Conway, who was getting into his car at the river bend. "Excuse me, excuse me," Mister Tiff sang. And because in his hour of happiness for Lucia's future he could find benediction for all human beings, he added blithely, "Your Josie looks very pretty today, yes?"

"Mind your own damn business!"

The words stopped Mister Tiff with the efficiency of a well-aimed shot. The metal wheelbarrow stands thudded to the ground. He was still for a moment, making up his mind. He turned and limped to the car. "Wait, it is two weeks now that something is bothering me. That field on Pastinetti Place, the one you own — it is a pity the children cannot play ball there."

"That's none of your business, too —"

Asa's fingers, the man saw, were blundering with the ignition switch. In a moment he would be gone. Hah, he would have to talk fast and to the point. "It would be a pity if your two little girls had to come way down here to play — " He halted, then added, " — by the river." But the eloquent gesture of his hand indicated plainly not the river, but Josie's home.

"They play at home," Asa snapped. He had not missed the other man's meaning which hinted — "You wouldn't want them to see you visiting Josie, would you?" He stared at him balefully and met only the guileless look of innocent eyes.

"The boys and Petra," Mister Tiff continued, "have to come 'way down this end to find a good baseball field. You can never tell, can you, when your girls may take it into their little heads to come along with them? It is safer to have them home, no? If you take down that sign —"

Asa's bony hand tightened over the wheel. His face was tinged a choleric purple. There was a chance that this interfering foreigner was bluffing, but he dared not take that chance. He forced himself to say, "Maybe you're right."

"Hah, then you will take it down?"

"Take it down yourself!" Asa growled over the roar of the motor. "And hereafter keep your blackmailing nose out of my business!"

He met the Pastinetti Place children in front of St. Michael's church. They were homeward bound after the walk to the ball field at the other end of the town. Mister Tiff greeted them with: "Meet Pilato, whose fur is as silky as in the inside of milkweed." He could not tell which pleased them most — the dog, the stock in the wheelbarrow, or the assurance that they had permission from Asa Conway to march to the Pastinetti Place field and remove the *No Trespassing* sign. He shook his head in disapproval of their grimy, heat-wet faces, and he bade them pluck a few cool leaves from underneath the roadside shrubs and wipe their faces. "Then St. Michael will finish the job of cooling us," he promised.

As usual they trooped into church, a bedraggled and tired group. The man limped ahead of them, his cane tapping the wooden floor, its echo knocking hollowly somewhere above the choir gallery. Last week on one of Denny Douglas' visits to Pastinetti Place and on his first visit to the church, he asked curiously why they dipped their hands in the holy water font and why they made the sign of the cross. The man explained that the water was blessed and that when one made the sign of the cross it expressed his belief in the Trinity of the Father, Son, and Holy Ghost. And he told them that in years long past men cleansed their hands at the font in preparation for placing Christ — the Host — on their tongues with their own hands.

Petra marveled at the information which came from the slender, frail body. She bet herself that Papa and Mama didn't know that. Nor even Father Carty. For surely no one had ever told her that priests had not always themselves laid the Host on the tongues of communicants.

If Petra happened to be alone with him, the man would lead her to the statue of St. Peter. There, beneath the austere and bearded face, he would whisper, "Your patron saint, my Petra. And your father's. Peter means 'rock' — think of it, your name has lived from the very beginning of the Church."

The girl would quickly hide her cheeks that stung with guilty red, for she could find no joy in the knowledge that Petra meant "rock." Why couldn't it mean something pretty? Her mind droned dismally — *"rock, gravel, stones, granite chips —"* And she tried hard to picture the chubby cherub Papa said Ronato was carving, for that must be truly lovely if Papa said so, and it was made of stone.

Best she liked Mister Tiff's patron saint, St. Michael. It was an old-fashioned wooden statue carved by a man who lived across Lake Champlain. She liked the rich, Moorish colors, and the handsome, young face of the warrior-saint. Michael was clad in mail of resplendent crimson and silver. His sandaled feet pressed the scaly neck of a writhing serpent-devil. His uy right arm bore a spear and was ready to transfix the devil's fangs. Petra liked the great white wings — so disproportionate to the slender body — spreading at least six feet from tip to tip.

Always when the little knot of grimy pilgrims huddled their sweaty bodies under those wings, the man would say a prayer in Italian and follow it with the English invocation Father Carty made after Mass. "Saint Michael, the archangel, defend us in battle, be our protection against the wickedness and snares of the devil." If the church happened to be empty of other visitors, he would kneel on the worn baize of the prie-dieu and he would recount legends and Bible stories of the saint: how Michael had thrust the proud Lucifer from heaven; how he had stayed the hand of Abraham in the sacrifice of his son; how he had safely led the Israelites in their desert journey.

The children listened under those wings. Their sticky bodies dried; their hot cheeks cooled. They did not reason that the statue of St. Michael stood near the east wall of the church which was built against a hill of spruces, and that wings or no wings that corner of the church would always be cool.

Redheaded Father Carty often entered the church through the sacristy. The first time he came upon the strange little tableau he stood for a time in the doorway, unseen, and then withdrew with warming heart.

CHAPTER VI

Maria Dalli lay beside her husband, in the borderland of sleep; she was free of thoughts, yet conscious of Pietro's warm arms. The metallic screech of the alarm clock shattered her little moment of luxury. She felt the quick start of Pietro's body, then his hands slipping gently from her to quiet the clock. And she would have stretched an arm to draw him back to her, but she remembered that it was Sunday — picnic day, that food must be packed, and that first the children must be dressed for Mass. Pietro began to clear his throat. He stopped abruptly, guiltily. And she knew he would stifle the needs of his throat until he reached the bathroom.

But a frown lined his brow. He yawned, tugged his brown mustache and yawned again before he said, "You know, Maria, now that the big day is here I am worried. The *maestro* may feel that we have collected the purse to get rid of him, that we consider him a nuisance."

"Ridiculous. No one could love him more than Petra and Vetch. And he knows it." She sat up beside him, swinging her dark braids over her shoulders. "Actually, I myself hate to see him go." It was more than simply because he had a way with the children; it was something she could not, at the moment, put into words.

"Suppose he is embarrassed by an outright gift of money, that he looks upon it as charity?"

Her kindly laugh tinkled close to his ears. "All these excuses! The trouble is, Pietro, that you, too, would rather have him stay here."

" 'Too!' " he repeated. "But I thought having him here meant too much work for you." His face brightened and he threw his arms around her. Arms entwined they sat there on the bed laughing at each other's attempt to keep his feeling secret, and warming to a new closeness of heart because those secrets had in reality been but one.

"But he must go back to Italy." Maria disengaged herself. She must be firm. "It would be cruel of us not to remember that it is for his own good. He makes hardly enough from his commissions on Lucia's aprons to keep him in cigars. In a few years he will be an old man, and the old like to be beside their kin. His only close relative is his sister in Ibena. They should be together. We must remember that he came to America to make his home with his nephew, not with us. Now that the nephew is gone it is natural that he should want to return to his homeland, his sister, and a good job."

"Yes," Pietro sighed. "Yes."

In the next room Petra awoke to the sound of air whistling in the bathroom, and of her father clearing his throat. A pink gingham dress — sewn by Lucia the day after the neat seamstress' sign was hung in her window — lay over the back of a chair. The new dress reminded her that it was Sunday, the day for the Italian picnic. She jumped from the bed thrilling to the threads of gold sunlight that pierced the pinpricks in the olive-green window shade. In her impatience to call Vetch and Mister Tiff she might have neglected the picture of the Infant Jesus, but Mister Tiff would surely question her sometime during the day. . . . She knelt on the wide planks of the floor, padding her knees with a double fold of nightgown:

> "Baby Jesus, I offer Thee this day
> All I think and do and say.
> Ever this day be at my side
> To rule and guide —"

She faltered, wriggling her toes fretfully. "To rule and guide — to rule and guide — well, anyway, to rule and guide me, Amen."

Vetch's door was ajar. He and Mister Tiff were already dressed. She went in to consult the man's wall calendar. It was fun every morning at recess to tell Peggy Riley and her friends that this was Blessed Theresa's day, the Little Flower who died only a few years ago in a convent in France — or St. Jean, the brave Joan of Arc. This morning she struggled over the Italian words. "What saint for today?" she finally asked. "It ought to be a good one; today's Sunday, and picnic day."

The man smiled. "In heaven every day is picnic day. Everyone must be good to be in heaven, so every saint is good, my Petra."

She scratched at her thigh, nodding absently. Some of the saints were more exciting than others. She could lie abed at night, for a whole hour after Gabriella slept, picturing Joan of Arc. Always, Joan of Arc was a slender, fair-haired, wide-eyed Petra. But the hair was not braided; it fell long and loose down her back. Sometimes it flew high in the wind as her great steed leaped forward to meet the enemy. She never came into actual conflict with the enemy. That wasn't fun. Better to feel the wind tugging at her hair. Whistling "Onward! Onward!" in her ears, as the horse strained beneath her. Always, the steed was the dappled gray of Veet Palingetti's plodding creature that trudged up Pastinetti Place each morning with the meat van. But it was a more slender and a swifter steed with a long arched neck, alert eyes, and dainty hooves. And always those that Joan of Arc led were an army of Vetches, Dennys, Leos, Robbies, and Ginos.

Later in the morning Petra squeezed through the congregation pouring from St. Michael's church. She pulled the whimpering Gabriella behind her. They hurried up Church Street, across backyards that were still morning wet, and up Pastinetti Place. Veet's meat van stood before her house. The Dallis and Rossis were piling the shelves high with boxes of food. Papa and Mama were Sunday dressed, ready for the next Mass. One of Papa's striped shed aprons covered Mama's green silk dress. She was loading Pete Rocco's Ford car with boxes and saucepans. Pontius Pilate yapped joyfully at the excitement. Last night Petra had seen her mother knead flour into raw egg yolks and mashed potato, cutting the rolled dough into little diamond shapes that would be flapped over into triangles to seal a meat filling. Hundreds of these *ravioli* her mother had made. And the house, from bedrooms to cellar, smelled deliciously of the rich red sauce made of olive oil, butter, garlic, onion, sage, rosemary, tomato paste, and tomatoes.

Petra spied a carton containing a jar of pickled mushrooms, a long arm of *salami*, and hundreds of thin slices of *prosciutto*. "Gee whiz, we going to eat all that?"

"Pete Rocco is eating with us," her mother reminded, "and Ellie and Robbie. And you invited Peggy —"

From the Vitleau porch steps a boy and a girl looked down upon the neighborhood activities. Their faces were envious, Petra thought. She said impulsively, "And Leo and Jean, too, Mama?"

Today Granitetown's Italian picnic was held at Peter's Gate, the plateau linking The Hill with its twin hill of abandoned quarries. Granitetown's first Catholic priest had purchased the stretch of land for a parish cemetery, but traded it later for a plot nearer the church. Strolling the plateau for the first time he had christened it Peter's Gate. For, though sentineled as it was by two scarred and mutilated hills, it offered westward a vista of rolling valley land. It was drowned that morning in a pearly mist and underneath the mist, the priest was sure, lay green pastures veined with brooks and dotted with browsing cows and houses.

Petra preferred for picnics the little pond areas fringing the outskirts of town. The ponds were cupped, cool, and half hidden in circles of spruce and tasseled pine. Or they lay in the open, wearing the sky on their clear breasts. But in these delightful spots the grownups must keep so constant an eye on the children, Papa said, that their own good time would be lessened.

By noontime the flat of Peter's Gate was alive with picnickers. The men were building makeshift fireplaces of stones gathered by the children. Pastinetti Place neighbors spread their tablecloths edge on edge so that they might eat and make merry together. Tip's mother, Mama Gioffi, kept constant vigil at a great iron *polenta* pot; its black bottom reached into the crackling wood fire. Each picnicker would have a slab or two of this *polenta*. A checkered bandanna bound Mama Gioffi's head. Her ample bosom swelled and fell under the heat of the sun and the open fire. The salted water in the pot must be boiling rapidly before she allowed each house-wife to sift into it her portion of cornmeal. And as each poured her pint of meal, Mama Gioffi tested and stirred the gruel with a broom handle scraped clean of paint. It required a practiced eye and touch to anticipate correctly the final thickness. The meal ab-sorbed the water quickly; yet the batter must remain thin enough to allow a long period of cooking. Then the finished *polenta* could be turned out, a firm yellow mound, ready to be sliced. Mama Gioffi turned up her nose at those who sliced *polenta* with knives. She stretched a fine, yet strong cord between her hands. This she slipped under the *polenta* and drew upward, cutting neatly through the mound lengthwise and then crosswise to form long, thin slabs. As she bent to feed the fire, she saw a slowly approaching car driven by Ronato.

"Look at Ronato," she whispered to Tip. "How lovesick he looks."

Tip could well picture the carver's mournful eyes. He said with-out as much as a glance at Ronato, "Don't know that I blame him. Lucia's got looks."

Mama Gioffi puffed, "A widow, and with three children!"

"She's still got looks —"

His mother bit her thick lips uneasily. Ever since he had started bootlegging his attitude about girls had changed. There was always one girl after another, and he didn't seem to care deeply for any one of them. She said tartly, "She's twelve, thirteen years older than you!"

Ronato had rented a car to carry his Lucia and her three sons to Peter's Gate. He wore somber black, and he sat straight, his long face void of animation. The youngest Tosti was burrowed in Lucia's lap, slapping contentedly at Ronato's accordion which made a thick wall between the man and the woman. In the back seat slumped Gino and Ito, their legs resting on boxes of food piled seat-high on the floor. The car rolled past the picnic throng and stopped beside a tar-papered structure. It was a wooden pavilion, boasting a small stage for musicians and entertainers, and a rough floor that tried the patience of dancing feet. Benches lined the four sides of the pavilion. Here the older picnickers would later rest and pamper the inertia resulting from rich food eaten under a hot sun.

Gino murmured, "Call me, Mama, when it's time to eat," and disappeared behind the pavilion where Vetch and Robbie were swinging in high arcs. They stood face to face on a broad swing seat, their bodies bending, taking turns pumping themselves through the air. Peggy Riley and Petra seesawed spasmodically on a teeter-board. If he were Vetch, Gino reflected, he'd tell his sister to pull her dress down. The skirt was pulled up to her waist; her pink-sheathed buttocks bobbed up and down, up and down. Her feet scuffed up bubbles of dust.

In front of the pavilion the men had slanted a plank from Veet Palingetti's van to a deeply notched tree trunk. They slowly rolled a barrel in place. The picnickers knew Gerbatti's wine to be Granitetown's best — ruby red, clear, and extra dry. Each year the shed owner made it; and he was careful to use only the best grapes. Mama Gioffi bought of him for her customers; and Lucia had bought, too, during her short-lived experience of selling wine to thirsty stonecutters.

Gerbatti drew a brimming glass from under the spigot and handed it to Mister Tiff. "Here, *Maestro,* the first glass for you!" Perhaps he shared Pietro's uneasiness about presenting the man with money for a return trip to Italy, for now the shed owner was thinking: the *maestro* may be proud, but wine has been known to soften backbone into putty. The more he drinks, the less unwilling he will be to accept the collection of money. . . . Gerbatti made a trumpet of his hands and shouted, "Everybody, come on! The wine is ready — ten cents a glass!"

They came, men and women, even though a jug of wine already graced each family tablecloth. They came and bought, aware of what the *maestro* was ignorant: that the proceeds from this barrel would be Gerbatti's contribution toward the little man's ocean trip. The men drank and drifted off into little groups.

The younger men wandered off to a field for a game of baseball. The women were left bustling about their duties, half an eye on the younger babies who lay in the shade of the spruces. The women's hands were grimy from the blackened cooking pans; their crisp aprons were streaked with the same blackness. For a time a refreshing scent of spruce, mingled with the acrid smell of burning wood, clung in the air. Then it was lost in the melee of cooking odors. Peter's Gate, on picnic day, was a great earthen dish of spicy, spiraling vapors.

Mama Gioffi's slicing of the *polenta* signaled the beginning of the luncheon. It signaled, too, the collection for Mister Tiff. And the little man, bent on amusing the baby Americo, failed to observe that each man of the family, as he approached Mama Gioffi for his share of *polenta*, handed her a coin. Some, a bill.

After they had eaten and wined, they gathered for the dance in the pavilion. Mister Tiff was curling himself to comfort on a corner bench when Ronato stepped to the stage. A cascade of accordion notes immediately claimed the attention of the crowd. Ronato spoke a few words.

Mister Tiff cocked bewildered ears. Unless his ears, after his wining, played tricks upon him, this Ronato was calling him forward to the platform. Truly, his name *had* been spoken! The glances of the *paesani* all shifted to Mister Tiff. And the face of each was smiling, eager, expectant. It is pleasantry, the little man thought.

They know I have no voice and they want me to stand up there for their amusement, to bray an accompaniment to Ronato's accordion music. Well, he determined, they shall have it. . . . He limped across the floor and up the steps. Pietro was suddenly beside him. A mysterious Pietro who was a little excited and who wore an uncomfortable look of importance on his plump face.

Pietro had prepared a fine speech for this occasion. Now the sea of faces before him seemed to surge into his very brain and drown the words. In a panic he wordlessly extended to Mister Tiff a small canvas bag bulging with money. It was boldly lettered — *Granitetown Bank.*

Mister Tiff stared.

And Pietro could stammer only, "For you, *Maestro,* with the compliments of all of us — so that you may return to your beloved Ibena." Even as he spoke the words Pietro was struck again with the chilling thought: *Dio mio,* has my tongue blundered? And my actions as well? Will he be embarrassed? Or can it be that in so short a time he has found happiness in my home and has no wish to recross the ocean?

But, no, the *maestro* was accepting the gift, and his quiet voice was saying, "My thanks to all of you — you are friends to be proud of."

The picnickers murmured happily among themselves. They wore the complacent smiles of those who know they have done a good deed, and who know the deed is appreciated. They would have turned now to dancing but a shrill scream from the doorway held them rooted to their places.

"No, no, Mister Tiff!"

Petra jostled her way through the crowd. Her hands clutched the man's in a frenzied grasp. Her voice rose high and frantic, "No, don't go away!"

A hush fell upon the picnickers.

Under the barrage of curious eyes Pietro reproved faintly, "Quiet, Petra."

Mister Tiff cupped the girl's hands in his own. He tried to still the pounding of his heart. "Hah, my Petra, you would ask me not to return to my homeland?"

"Don't go!"

"You don't want me to return to my friends?" Friends? Mother of God, were not these his friends who had given him a roof over his head? And all of these today who had dug into their moneybags for him? And had they not tried sincerely to please him?

The girl's wide gray eyes shone with a dry reproach. "I'm your friend. You said so yourself. You —"

"Hah, but I mean my *old* friends —"

She wrenched her hands free. Perhaps, across that ocean, there were other Petras who would dream at night of his stories of the saints. Other Petras who would tramp the fields with him, play their guessing games. . . . And she would be without him. Lonesome. A liquid self-pity flooded her eyes. Through the blur she saw Leo Vitleau staring curiously at her. Her cheeks flamed high with shame and anger. Leo's face looked pinched, sad. She wanted no sympathy; she wanted to slap that pitying face and yell, "Don't look at me! Go away!" Instead, she turned upon Mister Tiff and gave vent to her fury, screaming in wild crescendo, "Go on, then! Cross the old ocean — stay there!" Her fists rained blows upon his midriff. "I don't care!" She jumped from the platform, and pushed her way to the door.

Maria whispered through firm lips, "Tonight, Pietro, you will really punish her. Many a time before she has deserved it."

"Ah, Maria, it is affection she feels for him." And he was glad that Mama Gioffi chose this time to beckon him to her side. They rolled a victrola to the stage. Soon it ground out the gay *Chiribiribin.* The music was swelled by Ronato's accordion, and tempered with the melody of two violins. Pietro's heart ticked happily to the music; his arm encircled Maria. "We'll dance, eh?"

Mister Tiff limped quietly from them into the sunlight. Earlier in the afternoon the sun had laid a pleasant warmth to his bared head. It had soothed his rheumatic legs. Now it was a wearying hotness. He sank to the narrow green between the pavilion steps and the almost emptied wine keg where the merging shadows gave promise of coolness and seclusion. His chin drooped to his chest, and his index finger slumped to the arch of his nose. He would have to return, a failure, to Ibena. He tried to blind out the recurring picture of himself in Count Mattzo's library, eagerly planning this trip to America. "Well, San' Michele," he sighed wryly, "for once you and I are not of the same opinion. I want to stay here. You want me back in Ibena. You even wish to submit me to another I-told-you-so from Mafalda. But, well — so be it. . . ." He argued sensibly: I know I should be pleased to return to Ibena. There is so much to discuss with Count Mattzo. And by fall, when these legs of mine are less determined to torture me, I will sit again at my desk in front of the class; I will be earning a good living again. . . . But through these forced thoughts danced an uninvited procession of friends crowding from him everything but the desire to remain here in Granitetown: wide-eyed Petra, Vetch, Denny, the good Pietro, the mourning Lucia, Ronato, the boyish Father Carty, even the monkey-faced Joey Mull, Asa Conway, and Aggie Rugg. . . .

In the parking lot Vetch's brown face scowled down from the back of Veet Palingetti's horse. He said to the panting newcomer, "It's about time you came. The picnic's almost over."

Denny struggled to breathe normally. He had run almost all the distance from Douglas Hill. Yet he did not care to have the boys know it. "We had guests for lunch. It kept us at the table longer. Shall we go?" It was a whole week since he and Vetch had been to their miniature quarry, and his hands fairly ached to do more carving on his little granite church.

Vetch slid from the horse; his eyes swept the half-dozen boys around him. He said to Denny, "There's too many of us to go up there. Besides, how can you dig in those clothes?" Vetch's dark eyes scorned the crisp white of Denny's starched blouse and the black velvet knee pants, and they held no compassion for Denny's humiliated cheeks. And when Gino suggested, "Let's go swimming — it's so hot," Vetch agreed, "All right. Up to the old quarry." And Denny swallowed his disappointment, wordlessly, and followed them.

Mister Tiff, from his secluded spot, saw the boys plunge into a spruce thicket that seemed to hinge Peter's Gate to The Hill. He saw them emerge to the scrubby incline, their bodies straining upward. He noted, too, a rainbow of bright colors flowing more slowly and cautiously over their footsteps, and he knew it was Petra and her companions bent on following the boys.

Someone opened the pavilion door. For a moment the music grew louder; he heard the scraping of dancing feet. Voices sounded from the steps:

"You've got a good job in the shed office, why play around with this?"

The mumbled reply could not be clearly heard. The first voice came again, loud and clear, and it surely was the voice of Tip Gioffi. He was saying impatiently, "O.K., then. Tonight, at ten-thirty. And no bellyaching about it afterward, see? You take your own chances."

"Sure, sure."

Mister Tiff decided that those last two words might be Pete Rocco's. When he turned to look, there was no one on the steps and the door was opening to Lucia and Ronato. The man and woman walked down the steps and settled themselves beneath a spruce. Lucia held her head high, her earrings glittering in the sun. She did not look into Ronato's face; it was as if she feared those passionately melancholy eyes might wrench from her an answer her heart was reluctant to give.

Now a giggle floated down the steps. Mister Tiff twisted his slight body. It was a too-much-wine giggle, he decided, even before he saw the high flush of Ellie Marclay's usually milk-white cheeks, and the smile her round mouth was making for Pete Rocco. She clung to the swaggering youth's arm, yet her slender blue-clad body kept a good distance from him. Mister Tiff chuckled and corrected himself: no, it was a just-enough-wine giggle . . . Pete's wavy brown hair mingled for a moment with the red of Ellie's. He bent to kiss her, but she drew back swiftly. The little man sighed. Hah, Lucia and Ronato, Ellie and Pete. Here was another pair he would sometimes think about when he was far from Granitetown. Scotch, Italian. They were good bloods to fuse. But Ellie, he wagered, would never get Pete with that prudish regard for her lips. If she were wise she might give him a taste.

The couple strolled the breadth of Peter's Gate and disappeared over the ferny lip of a knoll. The little man in the shadow of the wine barrel was still considering the desirability of a Scotch-Italian union when from a corner of an amazed eye he detected the blue of Ellie's skirt close beside him. She carried an empty glass.

"Hah, you want wine?"

The voice from the shadows startled her.

"Oh, it's you. Yes, Pete wants wine." She turned the spigot. Dregs of the nearly empty barrel dripped into the glass.

The man fingered his nose thoughtfully. With a shrug that meant, "I am going away from here — what difference if she resents me if, in so doing, she has won a husband." He said timidly, "Maybe you love this Pete, yes?"

No man had ever mentioned the word *love* to Ellie. The pale, blue-veined lids fluttered. Why, the busybody! Or could he have had too much wine? She curbed the desire to snub him and said, stiffly noncommittal, "I *like* Pete."

The mild blue eyes twinkled. He spoke his English with great care and accompanied by many gestures. "That wine, Ellie — throw it away! Listen to me. And believe me. Never in my life have I seen the man who would rather taste the dregs from a barrel's bottom than the sweetness of his girl's lips. And a woman's lips, my Ellie, are more potent than any wine. *Dio*, more powerful than the best in King Vittorio's cellar. . . . Ah-h," he murmured sadly, "now you go away mad." For Ellie's suddenly rosy face had lowered, and she was running across the flat. She hesitated among the ferns. He saw a determined hand fling the glass and its cloudy contents high in the air. Her fingers fussed for a moment with her hair. Mister Tiff settled back contentedly.

Pete Rocco sprawled on the grass, his eyes closed to the sun. His heart was tripping in excited anticipation of the ride he would take to the Canadian line with Tip tonight. He could picture Ellie's eyes widening into fear and almost hear her gasp, "Oh, no, Pete — not bootlegging! It's dangerous!" Well, he wouldn't tell her. He grinned. The movement of his lips shook the hot ash from the cigarette at his mouth. He raised his head, spat out the cigarette. Ellie was standing studying him with a curious expression on her face.

"Where's the wine?"

"It's all gone —"

"The barreled wine — sure, it must be all gone. Why didn't you ask Rossi, Dalli, or anyone — they all brought gallons with them." He expected her to say, "I'll go back and see, Pete." But she shrugged her slim shoulders and sat down beside him.

He sprang to his feet. "I'll go myself." His smoldering eyes hinted: I'll take a damn long time about it, too. . . .

She said with an indifference that fired him with resentment, "I'll nap while you're gone."

She relaxed against the tree; the sun touched a gold sheen to her red hair. Her head lowered a bit to avoid the sun glare, and brilliant strands of hair held to the rough bark. Pete hesitated. With the absence of that timid look Ellie was really pretty, as pretty as she was nice. There had been one night in her kitchen when she was, as now, so appealing. He had made something of a fool of himself. Since then she kept a cool distance from him. As if she were afraid of him. Or, of herself.

"It's too hot for wine." He barely recognized his own voice.

He dropped down beside her; and Ellie's lips, that moment, rounded into a smile, and his mouth quickly sought hers, crushed it. Ellie's white finger tips were caressing his cheeks. He had never looked into her eyes as they now were, opened full into his, shot with a sweet brilliance. His rigid hands loosed her. They stroked her gently.

Ellie, basking in the tenderness she craved, was kindled to warm pliancy. She drew closer to him.

"Ellie," he breathed. He felt strangely mellow, protective. A feeling he would never describe to Tip. He whispered into her shoulder. "Look, Ellie, shall we get married?"

An apologetic cough from near by sent Ellie back against the tree, her cheeks flaming red.

"Excuse me. Excuse," Mister Tiff offered with a mildness he did not feel. He busied himself untying his blue kerchief and mopping a pink brow. *Dio mio*, for all this Scotch lass's reserve, she had certainly taken his advice, and to spare! Botticelli's Venus, bursting shyly from her shell into blushing, radiant life, had nothing on this Ellie. . . . May God forgive him this role of zealous counselor, he prayed, though a part of him could not help rejoicing over the transformed Ellie. The reproachful eyes of old Don Benedetto gave him the trembling courage to ignore Pete's darkening brow. He held his ground. He knelt awkwardly to the ferns, and he exclaimed in joyful surprise at fronds that were no different from a hundred other fronds he had seen. And when his glad cries attracted a bevy of children, and he heard Pete's resigned, "Let's go back to the dance hall, Ellie," he finally enjoyed a lightness of heart. He rose painfully on stiff legs and wandered slowly across Peter's Gate toward the spruce thicket.

Petra, with Peggy Riley and Jean Vitleau, had left the picnic grounds intent on following Vetch and his friends, but now they loitered at the iris marsh below the abandoned quarry. Petra, loving the blue-purple of the flowers, said, "It's the only pretty color on the whole hill." She pointed to where a breeze bent the darkness of marsh grass to a creamy green. "And that's the next best." Her hands pulled at the flat iris blades until the whitish, water-weakened bases came free of mud with a soft *plop*. It was more difficult to break the fibrous green spikes that bore the flowers. She bent the spikes, twisting and fraying them until they tore raggedly loose in her smeared fingers. In the bouquet of irises she inserted the dainty white of Queen Anne's lace which grew in the drier stretches of the hill.

Jean Vitleau remembered that tomorrow was the last day of school. "I'm going to give my flowers to Miss Gossard."

"I'll give mine to St. Margaret." Petra smiled archly. "Today's St. Margaret's day. Margaret means *pearl*."

Peggy's voice was shaded with envy. "Does the calendar say so?"

Petra nodded. "She was queen of Scotland, and her name means *pearl*." (Oh, why couldn't Petra mean *pearl* instead of *stone*. . . .) She studied one of the flat, lacy clusters of Queen Anne's lace. "You think these look like pearls?"

Jean shook her head. "They look more like the lace Denny Douglas had under the ice-cream plates at his birthday party."

"Anyway, I'm going to bring them to church for St. Margaret."

Peggy countered in some satisfaction, "There's no St. Margaret statue in our church —"

"Then I'll give them to God — right up on the altar. I'll ask Father Carty to put them there." Yes, that was better, she'd pray direct to God. Mister Tiff said it was nice to pray to the saints; they were so good, and such close friends of God that He wouldn't refuse what they asked for. It was like begging Papa to ask Veet Palingetti to give her a ride in his meat van. Papa was such a good friend that Veet wouldn't refuse him. But Petra's request today was most urgent. She would not waste time in roundabout praying to the saints. She'd take a short cut to God Himself, and beg Him not to let Mister Tiff go away. Mister Tiff always assured her that if you prayed for something hard, hard, you would get it. Oh, Infant Jesus, little *Bambino* — don't take Mister Tiff from Granitetown. . . . The picture of Pastinetti Place without her friend was a sad one. She was swept in a floodtide of emotion. Tears spilled from her eyes; she darted from the curious stares of her friends, running further uphill. A light breeze molded the pink dress to her body; it dried the tears on her cheeks. Pontius Pilate galloped after her. A rusting elbow of pipe, jutting from the grass, warned the girl that she was nearing a quarry hole and must slacken her pace.

The Hill had a spinal column of solid granite. Alvah Douglas had hollowed this quarry from a thin rib, and had then abandoned it for one of The Hill's richer vertebrae. It was a small quarry, no more than seventy-five feet deep. This was part of the rocky pasture old Enoch Douglas had bought of Aggie Rugg's grandfather. Splintered masts of long dismantled derricks now protruded from the quarry's shoulders. They were black, rotting. A cable or two dangled to the ground. In the tough grass lay discarded tools, broken, rusted, half buried.

Pontius Pilate frightened a bird from the quarryside weeds. Its black wings bore it forward where it circled uncertainly over the pit, calling an eerie cry of confusion, then it launched itself surely in a swift, clean arc to the derrick mast. The girl's eyes followed its flight to where a breeze was moving a loose cable end. The metal coil whined as it swung back and forth. It glanced a heap of waste granite blocks piled on the ground, and scraped out a mournful note. From the iris marsh a frog sang its throaty, lonely song. The girl hugged the flowers to her breast and stood very still, alert to the melancholy around her and in communion with it.

Pontius Pilate, poised rigidly at the rim of the great hole, rumbled softly in his throat. A faint splash sounded from the quarry's depth. Petra advanced slowly. She lay flat on her stomach, peering over the edge.

Robbie and Leo were sunning themselves on a broad granite shelf halfway down the wall. Below, in the cool green water that was nearly always in shadow, Vetch and Denny swam. Petra held her breath. She loosened a pebble from the soil and let it fall close to the wall. In its downward journey it clattered a few times against jagged granite and then met the water with a *plop*. She held the dog to her, waited for the boys' reaction. She laughed in high glee, for they paused but a second in their fun, convinced that it was only the wind that had dislodged the pebble. She loosed another stone. Robbie and Leo, at last suspecting intruders, rolled over prone, and in that position pulled on their trousers.

Peggy's voice drew itself out behind her, small and shocked. "They're naked — "

Petra laughed. "Sure, they're swimming, aren't they?"

"Well, maybe we shouldn't stay — "

The dog, his head over the quarry lip, barked loud and long. The swimmers cast a hasty upward glance and fled for shelter behind a gray ledge. In a few minutes they appeared, fully dressed.

Vetch's voice was as sharp as the cracking of an icicle. "Go on home, you!"

Petra shivered at his anger. But she laughed at the echo of his voice, and watched him climb a rickety ladder to the sun-splashed shelf of stone. Over this terrace, extending from one side of the quarry to the other and running parallel to the terrace, ran a cable. It had been side guyed at a point directly over the terrace, perhaps to facilitate the moving of equipment from the rock floor when the quarry was abandoned. The smaller wire held the cable taut over the boys' heads. Vetch and Robbie stood on tip-toe, grasped the cable, and began chinning themselves. The girls entrenched their flowers in the marsh to keep them fresh, skirted the quarry hole, and descended an old, shaky ladder to the terrace.

It was not the first time Petra had stepped into a quarry. As always she sat down breathlessly, staring up at the blue circle of sky and the weeds fringing the quarry's lip, and then downward to the green water. It was thrilling to be inside the earth, not on top. . . . Yet she knew that this was a very small quarry and that it would fit more than a dozen times into the great, gaping chasm where Lancelotto Rossi and the other quarriers worked.

Vetch ground his teeth at Petra. "You wait — you'll get it when Papa hears you were snooping around here."

She was tranquil. "You won't tell."

"Oh, no?"

"No." Her gray eyes were serene.

"Wait and see — "

"You won't." She was confident. "You aren't supposed to be here, either."

He flung back at her, "Anyway, I'm ashamed you're my sister, see?"

Vetch turned back to the cable where Leo Vitleau was waiting to match him in a chinning contest. The boys stretched their arms over their heads, grasped the cables in their hands and making themselves rigid began to pull themselves up until their under-chins rested on the cable. Then they lowered themselves. Robbie was counting for Leo; and Denny, for Vetch.

"One, two, three — "

Their mouths suddenly froze into silence. A small area of the granite wall, where the temporary guy wire had been pinned, was shattering into splinters. Fragments of granite clattered to the rock floor. For a fleet second the children saw the pin slipping, slipping. Then it broke loose from the stone, and their horrified eyes followed the released cable as it swung down and out from the terrace, carrying Vetch and Leo with it. The boys clung to the slowly swinging cable, their bodies suspended over the cragged, watery pit.

After the first paralyzing moment, Leo Vitleau began to cry in terror, his eyes shut tight to the water and the sharp boulders beneath him. Vetch strained a white face upward toward the terrace. It was hopelessly out of reach. He heard Petra's frantic scream, "Don't let go, Vetch! Don't let go!" And then her plea to Denny, "Do something, Denny, quick, quick — "

Robbie's voice was a thin wraith. "They're out too far, Denny. We can't reach them — "

Denny echoed Petra's first cry. "Hold on!" he cried. "I'll get someone to help."

His trembling body sped up the ladder and over the quarry's brim. He stumbled blindly down the hill, and he thought miserably: any other time I could run much faster. There was a loud, fast throbbing at his temples. He tried to make his strides longer, swifter.

Mister Tiff, emerging from the spruce thicket, stared at the boy running drunkenly toward him. *Dio mio,* had the little Denny drunk of the picnic wine, too? He grasped the boy's arm, for Denny was passing the man without seeing him.

"Don't you see me, boy?" the man demanded. He felt the trembling of Denny's arm and saw the pallor of his face, and he listened to the broken sentences. And when Denny continued to the picnic ground for Pietro Dalli, Mister Tiff limped up the hill, cursing his weak legs and the pain in them that prevented speed. When his foot at last touched the top rung of the quarry ladder, he closed his eyes against dizziness and crept down, step by step.

Petra's fingers, for the second time that day, dug hysterically into his arms. "Quick, Mister Tiff, quick! Do something — "

He called out to the boys to hold their grip. He tried to hide the fear in him. Holy Mother of God, what could he do? How could he reach that cable without help? The green fright in Leo Vitleau's face tore at his heart. Leo's stiff finger grip on the cable could surely not last much longer; the hands seemed drained of blood. Vetch, he thought, had a firmer grip.

Vetch heard Mister Tiff, and because the pain in his arms was unbearable, he cried weakly, "Shall we try to jump — in the water?"

"No, no!" the man implored. "Try to hold on!" He lay flat on the terrace stretching his right arm to the limit, and reached out between the boys with his cane. Ah, good *Dio,* it reached! He crooked the handle over the cable. "You, Petra," he panted in

Italian, for in this moment his tongue could form no English, "and all of you, hold fast to me!" And when he felt their hands upon him he drew at the cane with all his strength, yet slowly, smoothly, fearful lest a jerk might loosen their already wearied fingers.

Petra's eyes were glued to the cable. It was coming closer, closer. She prayed: "Look, Infant Jesus, don't let him fall. Please don't! If I'm asking you for too many favors I'll take one back — You can let Mister Tiff go away, I won't mind, only please don't let Vetch fall, and don't let Leo fall — "

"Hah," the man breathed. He had done it! The cable was as close as he could draw it. Close enough, if the boys had the strength and the nerve to reach out an arm. . . .

Overhead came the voices of the men Denny had brought from the picnic ground, and the stifled high-pitched cry of a woman.

From the cable Vetch was trying to follow Mister Tiff's advice. He timidly stretched an arm to the terrace, his trembling finger tips just brushing its stone wall. And Pietro and Pete Rocco were there now to clutch the arm, and to pull the exhausted boy to safety. The boy crumpled on the terrace. Now that danger was past, he put his face to his father's breast, and his body shook with sobs.

Leo Vitleau dared not follow the example of Vetch; he would not reach an arm into space toward the two men who were pleading with him. He hung rigid, unwilling to release the life grasp of one hand. He was deaf to their pleas, and to the men's promises that their hands, grasping his, would save him. His blue blouse clung wet to his sweating back. He wept quietly, his teeth biting into his lips. Blood oozed from them and trickled to his chin.

One of the men was throwing a rope to him when Leo's fingers at last slipped from the cable. The boy's lips opened in a cry of despair. "Papa!"

Mister Tiff was glad that Leo Vitleau's father was not there to hear, to see. There was no outcry from the helpless group standing at the rim of the quarry. In the dead hush came the soft thud of Leo's body against a boulder. Then a splash.

CHAPTER VII

Mister Tiff could not sleep.

The Dalli house at ten o'clock lay dark and quiet. True, it was early yet for sleep; but the man, anticipating wakeful hours, had hastily swallowed one of the white capsules Dr. Renaud left for the distraught Vetch.

The boy lay in the near-by cot in half-drugged sleep. Once he chilled the man's veins with his cry — "Leo, Leo, hold on!" The man deafened his ears between pillow and quilt. He struggled to blot out the picture of Tip Gioffi and Pete Rocco carrying the crushed, lifeless Leo from the quarry hole. Even in the limbo darkness of Mister Tiff's tightly closed eyes, the deep gash across Leo's forehead persisted in flaming before him, red and livid. When finally he was able to blind his mind's eye to the picture, another sorrow beset him: he felt the hard lump of the moneybag through his pillow, and he remembered that soon he would be returning to Ibena.

Perhaps, all these years, he had been belittling Mafalda's judgment. For when he had yearned for the priesthood she had surely scoffed, "You, made of the same stuff that makes good priests! Ridiculous!" And certainly Don Benedetto had implied the same thing, though in more kindly rhetoric. He had not been a financial success in Granitetown, nevertheless he felt that he belonged here. And now Granitetown, like the priesthood, was being snatched from his reluctant heart.

Restlessness grew into feverish tossing. He tried in vain to relive the more pleasant scenes of the day — Mama Gioffi at the *polenta* pot, the dancing, Ellie's radiant cheeks, the lusty voices of the men accompanying the victrola music. And he remembered himself in the shadow of the wine barrel, and remembered the voices that might be Tip's and Pete's agreeing to meet at ten-thirty tonight. Now, *Dio mio*, what was going to happen at ten-thirty that in its planning required secrecy and whispers? He suffered the disquieting conviction that any plan of Tip's foreboded little good, especially since Tip had added, "You take your own chances." The thought of Ellie's glowing face, close to Pete's and flushed of its rabbitlike timidity, spurred Mister Tiff from his bed.

He tucked his nightshirt flaps into his pants, drew on his shoes, his jacket, tied the blue kerchief around his neck, and stole silently from the house.

Pete's bedroom, over the poolroom around the corner from Pastinetti Place, was in darkness; Tip's long, black touring car was parked in front. It was empty. Perhaps they were in the lunch cart next door where laughter was rolling from the upraised windows. Hah, well, it was not yet ten-thirty. He would wait. He climbed into the back of Tip's car. The seat was gone; yards of canvas were piled on the floor. He spread them and made himself comfortable. And now when wakefulness was welcome, sleep came unbidden.

He dreamed he was aboard the *Stella D'Italia* en route to Italy. So rough were the waters, so deep the lunges of the ship that he must hold hard to the posts of the berth to stay himself. His steerage companions suffered audibly in seasickness and fear. They held to their beds and muttered prayers against the wrath of the waters. Now, in spite of himself Mister Tiff was torn from his hold, and he pitched sharply to the rolling floor. Icy ocean spray slapped at him; before he could wonder where it was coming from pain plunged him into darkness. At last he saw that the ceiling was a star-splashed sky, the ocean spray was a cool night breeze, and the *Stella D'Italia* had transformed itself into a speeding touring car. The moans of his companions became a lusty duet of male voices singing *Oh Susannah.*

He scrambled, swaying, to his feet. "Holy Mother of God, what happens?"

The wheel jerked under Tip Gioffi's hand. "What the hell!" He pulled the car off the road, and stopped in a potato field.

Pete Rocco twisted in his seat. "Tiff!"

"Who else, then?" the softly spoken man remarked crossly. The air was chill. The sudden lunge to his feet had sent a knifelike pain into his cramped legs. A tender spot on his head throbbed persistently.

Tip's two follow-up cars drew up beside him. A figure vaulted from one of them and ran to Tip. "What's up?"

Tip shrugged. He held a flaring cigarette lighter before Mister Tiff's blinking eyes. Above the glare Tip's nose twisted grotesquely. His eyes bored the man's, cold and unfriendly. "Where in hell'd you come from?"

Mister Tiff, buffeted from discomfort to curiosity and thence to an ardent desire to present a diplomatic account for his presence, struggled for a time and could only murmur indignantly in Italian, "Hell? Young man you insult my mother's womb — "

"Quit it!" Tip ordered. And at Pete Rocco he whipped suspiciously, "Was this your bright idea?"

"No, Tip. I swear it — "

"O.K. Forget it." Tip groped on the seat for the ever-present bag of licorice drops. This was one hell of a laugh. Old Tiff going up the line for a load! His voice was hard, cold. "Look, Tiff, spill it. How'd you get in this car, and why?"

The man sighed. "I couldn't sleep — I was thinking of the Vitleau boy, and other things. I went for a walk. Just when my legs decided to feel tired, I saw your car. I fell asleep — and here I am." His roving eyes searched the landscape. Even in the dark it appeared flat, flat. "Holy Mother of God, this isn't Granitetown — "

Neither Tip nor Pete offered an explanation.

He cried in agitation, "Where are we, eh? Where are we?"

"You're three miles from Canada."

"The French country that is English?"

Teen McLeary, driver of one of the follow-up cars, laughed.

Tip lashed at him, "Quit it, will you?"

Mister Tiff knew a little thrill. "Think of it — in a short time I will return to Italy, and I can say to my sister, 'I have visited the two big countries of America — the United States and Canada.'"

"Listen, this isn't a joy ride. Get that in your head." Tip's hands played sharp slaps on the wheel. "You sit tight and mind your business and you'll be all right. If there's excitement on the road, sit tight, see? We're getting a load tonight — "

"Load?"

"Load."

Pete explained patiently, "Liquor, Mister Tiff."

The little man thought sadly: why didn't I guess it? He protested, as he had protested to Lucia, a few weeks ago, "But it is against the law, no?"

Teen McLeary laughed.

Tip repeated harshly, "I said quit it, McLeary. Come on, get going — same as before. And wrap yourself in that canvas," he advised Mister Tiff, "before you get pneumonia."

The man draped himself well and sank to the floor. His heart was bumping at his ribs, but not unpleasantly. Granitetown told stories of wild chases between bootleggers and revenue officers in their high-powered cars. Mister Tiff guiltily thrilled to tonight's trip, even as he deplored it. For the second time tonight the wrinkled face of old Don Benedetto haunted him and he could almost hear his — "See, my son, where your untempered zeal has led you. If you had exercised prudence — " And even Lucia's face bobbed before him, her lips saying ironically — "So, *Maestro,* you are one of those do-as-I-say-and-not-as-I-do unfortunates."

The twisted, rutted country road bounced the slight figure from side to side. And now he wished wholeheartedly for the comfort of his bed. At road bends the lights of the car revealed smooth plains, traversed intermittently by wild, wooded country and fields of discolored rock protrusions that lacked the beauty of the familiar Granitetown stone.

Tip swung the car into a narrow, elm-bordered wagon road. At a distance the soft, wavering glow of kerosene lamps shone from two farmhouses. The dwellings were not much more than a hundred yards apart. The first house stood on Vermont soil. It had proved a reliable hideout for Tip these many months. Only one light glimmered.

Tip broke into a happy whistle. If old Joe had spotted revenue men around, he would have had another light in the second story. A warning light. He drove up to a sagging doorway. He said abruptly to Mister Tiff, "Here's where you park yourself for an hour."

"This is Canada?"

This time it was Tip who laughed. He said shortly, "Up there, on the other side of that elm — that's Canada."

"And I must stay here? No Canada?" The man suddenly pictured aged Moses wistfully looking upon the Promised Land, yet powerless to tread upon it.

Tip impatiently urged him up the lilac-flanked walk. Mister Tiff reflected that Petra would like a lilac or two on her lawn. Tip pushed open the door to an untidy kitchen and to its occupant, a man clad in baggy khaki trousers and plaid shirt. "Hi, Joe. Everything O.K.?"

Joe nodded. He was bent over the stove where a saucepan of potatoes was boiling.

The man owned a face that was a match for Aggie Rugg's, decided Mister Tiff. He had, besides, an ugly back, for the plaid shirt bulged over a double hunch. And he had never seen so wispy a mustache on anyone but himself; and hardly aware of the action he touched his fingers to his own,

Tip fed himself another licorice drop. "This fellow's staying here while we load up, Joe."

"How many of you this time?"

"Five." The door closed behind Tip.

Mister Tiff waited in vain for an invitation to sit. "You live alone?" he inquired.

"Yeah." Joe melted butter in a heavy skillet and laid in it five rounds of steak.

Mister Tiff loosened his blue kerchief. "Your own beef?"

"Yeah."

Mister Tiff leaned to the stove; his long nose quivered. *Dio*, that fine steak was beginning to sizzle, yet it gave off none of the tantalizing bouquet of well-seasoned meat. He slapped at his pockets in eager search.

Joe lifted his eyes. "Lose something?"

"Hah!" The pale blue eyes livened with success. He drew a plump clove of garlic from his pocket. "That meat is intended for us?" he inquired.

"Yeah."

"Then you feel no offense if I cook it the way I like it?" At the man's shrug, Mister Tiff opened his jackknife and sliced the clove into thin disks, sprinkling them over the meat.

Joe was not unfriendly, for when Mister Tiff suggested sitting on the steps to await Tip, the man again shrugged indifferent shoulders. The older man did not linger on the steps. He crossed the unkempt lawn and limped up the dark road, feeling the ruts with his cane; and when he reached the elm he made sure to take a few more steps beyond. There — now it would indeed be no mental fabrication when back home he told his sister and Count Mattzo that he had visited Canada. . . .

The farmhouse on the Canadian side was in darkness now. But cracks in the old barn behind it had become splinters of light. Tip must be there loading his car. He shook his head. So many illegal proceedings. The Vermont farmer and the Canadian farmer aiding the bootleggers; Tip buying and selling illegally; and in Granitetown Mama Gioffi and others buying illegally; to say nothing of the Granitetown men and women who would quench their thirst over illegal glasses. He walked slowly back to the farmhouse and to Joe.

With Petra in mind, he asked Joe's permission to dig a few lilac sprouts.

The man drawled, "Dig all you want." And he accommodatingly dragged an iron shovel from beneath the kitchen stove.

Later Tip's nostrils flared to the odor of seasoned steak. He was gay. "You're learning to cook, Joe."

The man's stub of a chin indicated Mister Tiff. "*He* fooled with it."

While they were eating Joe volunteered, "Revenuers was sniffin' these parts yesterday an' the day before. Been quiet today. But you never can tell."

On the return trip to Granitetown Mister Tiff was told to ride with McLeary. He viewed the empty tonneau with conflicting emotions. "We carry no liquor?"

"No liquor." Tip repeated the words automatically. He was busy directing the pilot drivers, McLeary and Marc Lantalvi. It was the usual plan: McLeary was to take the lead. A light signal given by Tip at the Canadian farmhouse would tell them when to start. "If you meet anything, don't stop. Let them chase you. Let them tail you over to Pell's Road — that'll clear the road for us. And, Lantalvi, you follow." Tip gave no further instructions to Lantalvi. Lantalvi knew his business.

Joe and Mister Tiff were alone in the kitchen for a few minutes, and the latter suddenly remembered the two pints Tip had given Joe. He tried to strike a bargain. Joe looked up morosely from the dishes he was washing. "I ain't givin' away the only pints I got."

"See," Mister Tiff encouraged, "One dollar and this knife." It was the jackknife he won at dice with Joey Mull and Sweeney. "See, pictures of pretty women with veils."

Joe wiped a palm on his plaid shirt and picked up the knife. His dull eyes scrutinized it. "Huh!"

The little man pressed temptingly, "One woman on each side. And the blade is sharp."

Joe finally succumbed to the charms of the knife, and the other man tucked the bottles into his nightshirt and tightened his belt. He chose a time — when Tip and Pete left for the Canadian farmhouse and McLeary and Lantalvi were gulping a last whiskey and coffee — to lay the pints carefully under the rug in the back of McLeary's car, and to pile over them the lilac sprouts he had uprooted. McLeary, he feared, would give little co-operation in his plan to bootleg two pints, and perhaps less to transport lilac sprouts for Petra. He caressed the curve of his nose, anticipating Count Mattzo's surprise when, if ever conversation should lag before his Ibena fireplace, he would murmur, "Once I helped smuggle liquor from Canada — "

As he rode on the return trip with McLeary, awareness of those two bottles in the back of the car became an exhilaration. More exhilarating than the night air that slapped briskly, and with a hint of damp coolness, at his face.

The night was clear, though moonless. McLeary knew the roads. On straight stretches the car tore along without lights, at such speed that, in spite of the ecstatic tingle in his breast Mister Tiff knew a little fear. He shrank down into his seat, but not before offering McLeary the favorite advice of old Don Benedetto. "Prudence," he begged. "Drive with prudence, eh, please."

McLeary laughed. "Sit tight, fella." He misjudged a right turn. Brakes screeched. The car traced the bend on two wheels. Mister Tiff waited until he felt capable of infusing a calmness into his voice. He said, as if he were continuing a dinner-table conversation, "In school we learn that faith, hope, and charity are the cardinal virtues. Hah, they forgot prudence — "

"Who's *they?*"

"Great men."

"Well, if they were great and could forget it, why don't you?"

The older man shifted in his seat. If only he could keep this towheaded idiot talking, perhaps he would drive more slowly, more carefully. After a moment he asked, "You truly like this — business?"

"Why not?"

"You're young and strong — you ought to do other work."

McLeary tossed a shoulder. "You get out of high school — then what? I tried the sheds a year — "

His companion was silent.

"The old man cut stone twenty years," McLeary said. He laughed again. "I'll take mine this way — it's easier."

Suddenly he was tense. Was that a flash of light down there among the trees? He switched on his lights; twin beams played over the dark road. If it happened to be coppers, they'd suspect blind driving. He strained forward, eyes alert. He distinguished the vague outline of two men in the road. Now he saw the blue of their uniforms. He spoke rapidly to his companion. "We're going by those guys, see? Whether they try to stop us or not. When we do stop on Pell Road, you keep your mouth shut — hell, we're safe anyway — "

Safe anyway? Mister Tiff sat up uneasily, and his hand sought the comforting crook of his nose. Should he tell McLeary of the two concealed bottles? And what did the law do to a man who smuggled two pints?

McLeary's lips were grim; his hands tightened on the wheel. He saw that one of the revenue men handled a revolver, and the other's raised hand was ordering the approaching car to stop. McLeary stepped hard. The touring car leaped forward. The men retreated from the center road, and the touring car roared between them. McLeary's lips relaxed. "We'll give them a chase!"

Mister Tiff gasped, "You give them one already!" For the officers had wasted no time. Their sedan was roaring along the road behind them. The older man craned his neck backward; the wind tore open the knotted kerchief, slapped it flat to his face for a second, and then carried it off.

"Hah, it's gone," he mourned against the wind.

"What's gone?"

"The kerchief — the blue one from Torino — "

McLeary swore.

Mister Tiff, his eyes still fastened on the pursuing car, reported on a high note of ecstatic dread, "They come closer and closer — "

"Good!" In full speed the touring car seemed to rise from the ground. It twisted in and out of ruts. Bouncing. Careening. And at the Pell's Road bend it hurled the older man against McLeary and then sent him sprawling to the floor.

After a mile of Pell's Road, McLeary gradually cut the speed. The sedan passed them and held them to the middle of the road. McLeary stopped. "I'll do the talking," he warned.

A lean, sharp featured officer advanced. For the first time Mister Tiff saw the black automatic in his hand. He was startled. "Will he use it?"

McLeary hissed, "Shut up!"

The second officer was but a youth, the ex-teacher decided. A snub-nosed, black-haired lad whose face under that tangle of black curls should be merry and not — as now — white and bleak. And what a nice blue was the blue of their pants! A blue-gray. Truly, the American government had good taste. . . .

The sharp-faced officer put a foot to McLeary's running board. "What's the idea?"

"Oh, you're the police!" Mister Tiff murmured in wide-eyed approval of their uniforms. And his mild voice informed McLeary, "They are police."

The officer ignored him. "Why don't you stop when you're ordered to?" he demanded of McLeary.

"Thinking it might be a holdup? Hell, I wasn't taking any chances."

"You were driving without lights."

"We were having ignition trouble." McLeary laughed. "Good thing the ruts were deep enough to keep the car on the road."

"Let's see your license." The officer shot a beam of light on McLeary's open billfold. "Well, McLeary, what're you doing in these parts?" Granitetown had its share of bootleggers, he knew from experience.

Mister Tiff cleared his throat. He said eagerly, "We picked sprouts, lilac sprouts —" He felt the kick of McLeary's foot against his leg, but he continued, "for the girl, Petra." He thrust out his grimy, slender hands, and he was glad that he had not washed them at Joe's iron sink. "See, my hands are still dirty from digging."

"Where are they?"

"The lilacs? In back, of course." He held his breath as the flashlight sent its beam over the green sprouts. "Fine ones, no?" he asked with great enthusiasm, and trembled lest they search beneath and find the two pints.

McLeary darted a bewildered look at the lilacs and stifled an exclamation. The older officer touched the fresh soil that clung to the lilac roots. From the corner of his eye Mister Tiff detected, in the distant darkness, a darker object, moving swiftly along the road they had just left. His heart beat faster. Tip and Pete Rocco! Now, for sure, he must keep these uniformed ones talking, talking. . . . And McLeary must have seen, too, for he felt the steel tensing of the body beside him. Mister Tiff continued in friendly discourse with the officers, "You would like some lilacs, maybe?"

The snub-nosed officer grinned. "No, thanks —"

"They're easy to grow. Me, I just soak them two days, three days, in a pail of water —"

The other officer cut short his words. "What's your name?"

"Michele Pio Vittorio Giuseppe Tiffone." Hah, here opened quite miraculously a long avenue of grace for Tip. He beamed, "*Michele* for the archangel Michael, *Pio* for the pope, and —"

But the officer abruptly walled this channel. "Never mind the trimmings."

McLeary put in, "He hasn't been in this country long. We call him Mister Tiff."

"Where do you live?"

"Ibena, Italy — that's in the north," he explained. "Nice hill country, like Vermont. I was born there. But I live in Granitetown, too."

"Make up your mind —"

"But it is true. Until a few months ago I lived in Italy. Next month I will be living there again. But right now I live in Granitetown —"

"Vermont?"

Mister Tiff stroked his nose. "Where else is there a Granitetown? Italy, to be different, has her Venice; Vermont has her Granitetown. Me, I say Granitetown is no more typical —"

The lights of a speeding car swiftly swept them, left them again in darkness. As the officers swung around, a shot shattered the quiet of the night. It sounded as if it had glanced a rock and gone screeching into the dark void. A dense smoke wave hovered over the distant road, so dense that the powerful lights of the car behind could not pierce it. The older officer snapped, "Let's get going, Neilson! Johnson's after somebody."

Their car sped off Pell's Road.

McLeary said nervously, more to himself than to the little man beside him, "It's the works, all right. But Gioffi'll make it. He always does. He'll give them a chase — and he'll make it."

Mister Tiff stared at the smoke. "Tip's car is afire?"

McLeary shook his head. "Smoke screen from Lantalvi's car — so they can't see to pass — or fire." He started the car. "Nothing we can do — we'll meet them at the halfway house." They rode on at a leisurely pace. In silence. Only once McLeary spoke, complimenting grudgingly, "You sure got the gift of gab, fella. You sure stalled those guys."

Landow's Place, a neat, rambling, white farm some twenty miles from the Canadian line, advertised from planks nailed to its front-yard elms:

Fresh Buttermilk
Strawberries & Asparagus (In season)
Pure Vermont Maple Syrup

Henry Landow kept stocked with his advertised products, but pleasure cars seldom left the cement highway to patronize this country-road farm; and, of late, Henry could appreciate the money paid him from bootleggers seeking brief hideout.

McLeary drove into the dark driveway and beyond to an isolated barn. Tip's car stood, a vague bulk, close to the barn. In the night it appeared to be a low extension of the building.

Henry Landow was nervous. "You sure you lost them?" he was saying to Tip. "I don't want you leading them here. I got enough troubles, without that."

"I tell you it's O.K. Soon as Lantalvi finds the other fellow we'll clear out." Suddenly Tip was gruff. "What the hell, we pay you enough; don't we? You expect to take chances; don't you?"

A coldness trembled at Mister Tiff's spine. *Find the other fellow!* Pete Rocco was "the other fellow." Pete was missing!

Beside him McLeary was asking, "What's the matter, Tip? Where's Pete?"

For once, Mister Tiff reflected, this Tip Gioffi's voice told a strain. "Everything was all right," Tip was explaining, "till we got to those straight flats. Then a revenue car tailed in on Lantalvi. He gave us the light sign. Those guys got tough fast. Lantalvi figured he couldn't block them, so he smoked them. Pete turned around to see what was going on. I was making a fast corner, and the first thing I knew Pete was gone — fallen out. That damn door has busted open before. I've sent Lantalvi back to pick him up. I don't think the revenuers saw him — they were coming along too fast — " And he was thinking: that's what I get for letting the young squirt come along. . . .

McLeary put a cigarette to his lips. He fumbled in a pocket for a match, then remembered. He threw the cigarette to the ground. "The road's full of those guys tonight. A couple of them stopped us."

It was a full twenty minutes before Lantalvi and Pete drove into Landow's. They got out of the car slowly, Lantalvi with a hand at Pete's elbow.

"He was groggy when I picked him up," he explained to Tip. "Was wandering down a field."

Pete insisted with a swagger, "I'm all right, Tip. Just a bump on the head — feel a little dizzy, that's all."

Tip was in high spirits again. "Hell, Pete, you might have left the licorice drops with me — they flew out the car with you."

In Granitetown, Tip handed the load over to McLeary, and used the latter's car. "Take her to the garage." He wanted to see Pete home. Tonight's trip had been successful; he was magnanimous. "You, too, Tiff. I'll take you home." A gray dawn was stealing over Granitetown. Street lights filtered through the early morning mist, refracted into shapeless, dim illumination. He accompanied Pete to his room above the poolroom. Pete's face was drawn, his eyes dazed; but, hell, why shouldn't they be after the scare and bounce he'd taken?

"Sure you don't need a doctor?" Tip urged. "He won't have to know what happened. Tell him you fell down the stairs."

"I'll be O.K.," Pete insisted.

Mister Tiff was thinking: tonight this boy is in no condition to take the lashings of my tongue, but tomorrow I must try to persuade him to stop this smuggling business. It is an exhilarating adventure for one night, but it is dangerous, dangerous. . . .

Tip was in high spirits when he said good night to the older man in front of the Dalli house. "No more falling asleep in my car, see? Hey — " He stared at Mister Tiff who had opened the

back door of the car and was taking out what looked like twigs.
Long green twigs. And when he learned that they were lilac
sprouts for Petra, he threw back his head and laughed loud
and long.

The older man's arms were full. He begged hesitantly, "If you
will lift the rug, please?"

Tip picked up the two bottles, and now his mirth knew no
bounds. He laughed so loudly that his companion worried lest
Pastinetti Place neighbors be aroused. Tip roared, "McLeary
coming through with a load of lilacs and two pints — "

Late that morning Asa Conway was sitting behind his counter
sorting stale candies and making them into "penny bags." The
morning sun poured in on his window display of chocolate bars.
He flapped out a *Granitetown Times* and laid it over the confec-
tions. Veet's meat wagon was rumbling down Pastinetti Place hill;
it must be close to eleven o'clock. Asa's mind was not on the
task at hand. His cheerless face was set in grim lines. He was
pondering the news which his last customer, Dr. Renaud's housekeeper, had given him. Amy Hickox could have no idea that the
information would be of more than casual interest to him, he
argued, or she would not have spoken of it so bluntly. He had
been weighing five pounds of sugar for her when she began, "Have
you heard? Folks are making it hard for that Josie Blaine to
stay in town." Amy hadn't seemed to notice the sugar scoop
halted suddenly in mid-air. She continued, "I suppose it's the
women who don't trust their own husbands — "

Now Asa was twisting the top of a "penny bag." He couldn't
put a finger to his honest reaction to this news. If Josie left town,
would he be sorry? Or would he welcome it? Or both?

Asa's long fingers picked a thread from the green wool of his
sleeve, and he lifted his eyes to Joey Mull who came stamping into
the store with more than his usual energy. Joey's cap hung over
an ear. His ferret eyes gleamed. "Heard the news?"

Asa pushed aside the box of candies. God, news traveled fast in Granitetown! But he asked sourly, "What news?"

"Pete Rocco."

"Well, what about him?"

"He's dead!"

Asa's narrow eyes burst wide open.

Joey opportunely slid a grimy hand into the horehound jar. Asa remembered aloud, "He was in here early last night with Tip Gioffi. Tip bought licorice drops. Pete ate a couple of bananas." He shook his head. "You're crazy, Joey — "

"Bananas or no bananas, he's dead." Joey looked smug. He stared wistfully at a new pyramid of oranges.

Asa snapped, "Dammit, take one! What happened to him?"

"The Dalli boy, Vetch, found him this mornin'. He was goin' cross lots to school — last day of school, I guess — and he wanted to see Pete. Pete helped pull him out of a quarry hole yesterday, you know. Anyway, there was Pete in bed, groanin', and actin' light in the head. Told the boy he'd fallen down the stairs last night and bumped his head. Those're cement steps — I been there. The boy got the doctor. Pete went fast — died about half an hour ago. Concussion, they said."

Asa said, "That girl friend of his, that Marclay girl, she couldn't have known. I saw her standing in front of the poolroom this morning, waiting for the trolley." And he remembered that she had stolen glances over her shoulder at the bedroom window over the poolroom.

What Joey Mull and Granitetown did *not* know was that Vetch, standing that first moment by Pete Rocco's bed, his eyes glued to the strained face and the head twisting in pain, spied a black licorice drop crushed into the curly, matted hair. And he saw, too, the stain of another licorice drop against his neck. And the boy was thinking: Pete doesn't like licorice drops, he always refused them when Tip offered him some. I've heard him. Why should Pete have licorice drops stuck to him? Vetch said, "I bet you

had a fight with Tip — I bet Tip had something to do with this — "
Pete's head ceased its terrible tossing for a moment. "You're
crazy!" he cried wildly. "Do you hear me? I haven't seen Tip —
I fell down the stairs — " Then Pete's eyes burned so fiercely into the
boy's, that Vetch's hand trembled as he loosened the drop from
his friend's hair. He hurried for the doctor.

CHAPTER VIII

Pastinetti Place neighbors were mourning the deaths of Leo Vitleau and Pete Rocco. The Dalli family was unaware of Mister Tiff's nocturnal trip to Canada; and Tip Gioffi, his arrogant face pale and stricken as it had never before been, said to the older man in a voice of biting intensity, "Forget you made that trip, see? Forget any of us did. He's dead now. It's nobody's business how he died — it was an accident. Let them think he fell down the stairs."

And Mister Tiff quietly agreed, remembering with a chill that it was now too late to give Pete the talking to he had planned for today. Instead, he turned haltingly to Tip, but that young man grated out at him through clenched teeth, "For the last time, keep out of my affairs, will you?" And the older man's advice trembled into silence.

Vetch, shaken with his own narrow escape from the quarry tragedy, could not forget the licorice drops he had seen matted in Pete's hair this morning, and he could not help believing that a fight between Tip and Pete had caused Pete's death. It was to Mister Tiff that the boy sobbed his fears.

"No," the man assured him, "Tip and Pete were friends. They had no argument. Oftentimes I have seen licorice drops in Pete's room. He kept them there to offer Tip on his visits."

But Vetch was not fully convinced, and the doubt was to remain with him for the rest of his life.

Aggie Rugg was making Scotch shortbreads, and hoping they would please Miss Ellie. On the stove a beef broth bubbled gently, coddling hundreds of barley kernels. Two tears coursed a V-shaped path from her widely separated eyes down her brown

cheeks to her mouth, and she bent her thin neck, wiping the tears
on her shoulders. It wasn't Pete Rocco she was mourning, she
told herself. Not that swaggering young piece. Nor was she
grieving over the poor Vitleau boy. No, it was simply the way
Miss Ellie was taking it, the way she looked right now as she
sat in a rocking chair by the window. Ellie's red-rimmed eyes lifted
to the crape on the Vitleau's door, and then slanted down over
the rooftops to the windows of Pete's room.

Ellie saw Vetch sitting on the Dalli porch in conversation with
Mister Tiff. It reminded her that Robbie, in yesterday's confusion,
had taken Denny Douglas' velvet jacket home from the picnic.

"Aggie, when you get through, will you take that jacket up to
the Douglas house? It's Denny's." She was glad of this opportunity
to send Aggie away, for an hour, for a half hour — any respite from
those pitying eyes was welcome.

Aggie's face crumpled with distaste. "The Douglas house — ?"

"It's Denny's jacket."

"You know I got no use for them," Aggie whined. "You know
I got it against old Enoch Douglas for buying land from my
grandfather — for almost nothing. Look at them now, rich, rich. . . ."

At last she yielded with a martyred, "All right, Miss Ellie, I'll
go if you say so."

Aggie disliked being on Main Street at four o'clock. A crowd
of people always made her head spin, spin until she wanted to
run and hide herself. Any large group of people could do that
to her. And these homebound stonecutters — Italian, Scotch, Spanish, French, Irish — took so gay, so noisy a four o'clock possession
of the street that she had taken to walking with her eyes lowered
to the pavement. It was a relief today to hear Joey Mull's, "Hi,
Aggie."

He was scratching his back against Asa Conway's awning crank.
He slouched sheepishly into step beside her.

She swung Denny's jacket over a shoulder. "Hi."

"I haven't forgot," he said, "that I owe you a dollar."

"I'm not in a hurry for it." If she were nice to him, he might walk with her past all these men. There was big Tony Bottelli. The skin of his massive neck was creased in diamond shapes like an ice-cream cone. Whitish powder was caked in the grooves. She liked Tony. She started to hum the tune the Pastinetti Place children called after him:

> "There's Tony Bottelli,
> With his big grappa belly — "

Joey said, "Look, Aggie, not too long ago I was goin' to give you a pup, cute little pup — "

"To me?" She was pleased.

"Then I saw it had fleas."

"Oh."

"There's lots of things I'd give you, Aggie, if I was goin' round with you steady. Lots of things I pick up — "

"You ought to work steady first, get a real job."

"Could I come hangin' round again if I got me a job?"

"Maybe." She saw that his small, bright eyes were following the swaying hips of a girl in front of them. She knew she ought to swamp him back to attention. Remembering Ellie's sobbed — "We were going to get married — and now Pete's dead," and hoping to win back his attention, she said quickly, "I know a secret."

"What is it?"

"A big one. Only me and one other in all Granitetown know it."

"I used to let you in on secrets when we were thick last year, remember?"

"You walk to the end of the street with me and maybe I'll tell you sometime — "

"Hell, I know one."

"What?"

"Josie Blaine's gettin' out of town."

"Josie — she's kind of pretty — "

At the foot of Douglas Hill they parted, and she promised, "I'll tell you sometime, Joey."

She liked this smooth sidewalk flanked with velvety green lawns. If Miss Ellie realized how she really hated to go to the Douglas house, she wouldn't have sent her. But Miss Ellie was so upset today. Aggie wondered: would *I* feel so bad if Joey died? She tried to squint up a picture of his monkey face dead, and his sharp ferret eyes forever closed. The picture would not come. Her angular hand languidly brushed back the pile of Denny's velvet jacket. That's how these Douglas Hill lawns looked, close cropped like this velvet, each blade erect.

A gardener was pushing a lawn mower on the green beside her. She liked the droning, whirring sound. Some of the severed grass clung in its sticky life juice to the spiral knives. It smelled sweet and cool even in the sun. And near by must be roses, for their fragrance hung in the warm air. It was funny, she thought, that Pastinetti Place always smelled of good food. These Douglas Hill people had to eat, too, yet passers-by seldom could guess by their noses what was being cooked in the kitchens.

A shadow dulled the hill. A ragged cloud had slipped under the afternoon sun and made a gloomy, tattered design on the Douglas house walls. Grotesque, jagged shadows lay on the yellow brick, and here and there were wispy strands that shone bright gold. There was no crowd to bother Aggie here on Douglas Hill, yet her head suddenly felt as if it were spinning, spinning, and she could not draw her eyes from the yellow-gold color of the Douglas house. Had old Douglas built a house of yellow so that it would look like gold? Look rich? If he hadn't bought that pasture land, perhaps *she'd* been born in just as beautiful a house. Aggie's breath rasped in her throat. She swallowed a sob. It settled in a painful lump in her breast. And it became a violent, aching weight, for the spinning seemed to be draining her head of blood and rushing its added heaviness to her breast.

The Douglas maid opened the kitchen door to her. Aggie's feet stepped over the threshold, but once there they were rooted to the floor. A tumultuous pounding racked her breast. Outwardly she was still; tensely still, head lifted, listening. From the front of the house came the tinkle of glasses and the sound of voices. And above them she heard Minna Douglas' voice, sweet and high pitched.

Aggie wished again that Ellie had not asked her to come. Her head felt strange and light. She droned, "I brought the boy's jacket."

The red-cheeked maid stared uneasily at the mottled, rigid face and at the convulsive swallowing. She was a little frightened. "Denny's? Well, thank you. Say, you look warm — I'll get you a cold drink. And Mrs. Douglas'll want to say thank you —"

"No! Oh, no!"

"Well, a drink anyway —" She went to the icebox. Goodness, that funny creature looked faint, and sort of tortured. . . . "Look," she said brightly, holding up a brown bottle of ale. "This'll fix you." She pitched her voice to what she hoped was an infectious thrill: "It was bootlegged."

Aggie returned the girl's smile mechanically. She repeated placidly, "Bootlegged."

The maid poured the ale. She began conversationally, "That was a shocking accident in the old quarry hole yesterday; wasn't it? That poor little boy — he was a friend of Denny's."

"Quarry hole," Aggie repeated. There was a whirring going on inside her head. It wouldn't let her think. She'd never felt like this before. A steady whirring, like the sound of the lawn mower she had heard.

The whirring clicked off abruptly. "That old Douglas quarry!" The words spat from Aggie's throat.

The maid shrank back from the fire in Aggie's brown eyes.

Alvah Douglas swung open the kitchen door with his foot; his hands were busy balancing a tray of cocktail glasses. "We're wanting more Scotch, Larsa —" he began, and stopped, unprepared for the sobbing, furious presence that was Aggie.

"Good afternoon." His was a pleasant, rugged face. Perplexed, he looked helplessly from Larsa to the visitor. She was the Rugg woman whose grandfather had sold his land to Grandfather Enoch. Minna had once pointed her out to him. It looked as if she and Larsa were having words. . . . "You're Aggie Rugg; aren't you?"

She whirled around, panting at him from the chaos of her mind, "You're Alvah Douglas! Rich Douglas! Yellow house — gold house — gold Douglas." Her long, brittle fingernails broke into the skin of his neck, and left double tracks of raw, bloody flesh.

After the first shocked moment he grabbed her wrists, wrenching her clawing hands free of him, holding her at arm's length. Now she was like a child in his hands; the physical strength of her was lost to her raging emotion. "Here, here," he gasped. "What's the matter?"

Her barbed tongue tore at him wildly. "Douglas! Your folks beat my grandfather out of his land, didn't they, *didn't they?* And now you're rich —" A torrent of words gushed from her twisting lips. Saliva oozed from the corners of her mouth; it dripped to her heaving breast.

Aggie's incoherent cries ceased for a moment. She whimpered, gnashing her hands together, "That poor little Leo, smashed to pieces on that land you Douglases stole from us —" Her agonized breath could sound no more words; they trailed off into a wraith-like moan. She struggled free of Alvah Douglas, and fled the kitchen.

Aggie did not return to Ellie Marclay's house.

Alvah Douglas phoned Ellie, "Something happened to her. She acted, well — as if her mind had snapped."

Pastinetti Place neighbors combed the pasture land sloping behind the Douglas house. At night they searched the flats of Peter's Gate lighting up the picnic grounds with their flashlights and torches. When dawn was fast thinning its shadows for a new day, Officer Jim Riley with Joey Mull, Pietro, and Mister Tiff came upon her near the abandoned quarry. She had dug one small oblong hole. Now she stood ankle deep in a longer and wider one, her hands wielding an old iron shovel. Her drab hair tumbled, uncombed, down her back. Her black shoes and the front of her cotton dress were soaked with mud. Aggie had run through the iris marsh and stumbled upon an old shovel, mired there for years. This blundering into cool mud had soothed her hot flesh. It had quenched at last the burning hatred that had been bellowed to furious flame in the Douglas kitchen. Her mind was happily consumed of hatred and memories. And from this holocaust was born a new Aggie. Innocent, childlike Aggie. She knew only one duty she must perform, and wearily she picked up the shovel and sought an area free of rock. And in her wanderings she discovered the bouquets Petra, Jean, and Peggy had thrust into the wet earth Sunday afternoon and had forgotten in the horror of Leo's accident. Now the bouquets lay at the head of the smaller hole. The tender iris petals were browning to slimy rot. The more rugged Queen Anne's lace was only limp.

Aggie dragged the mud-weighted shovel behind her, and planted it against the ground to rest her back.

"Hi," she said in slow gladness to the newcomers. Her glance traveled the men and rested on Joey. Her face wore a kindly smile.

Mister Tiff wondered if it was the innocence of that smile reaching into her eyes and diffusing them with sweet serenity that made of them the most peaceful eyes into which he had ever looked.

Joey pushed back his greasy cap and scratched at his head. "We been searchin' for you all over —"

She smiled at him again. Under the smile his eyes shifted uneasily to the hole, to the shovel. "What you doin', Aggie?"

The ends of her mouth crooked contentedly. She put her mud-spattered hands at work once more. But immediately her shoulders drooped over the shovel; a plaintive note crept into her voice. "I got one and a half dug — I'm tired, Joey. Awful tired. Don't you want to help me?"

Joey moved awkwardly. "Gosh, Aggie —" His sharp eyes darted — questioning and bewildered — to Riley, and then back to her. "What you diggin', Aggie?"

She pushed back a wisp of hair. "That small one's for Leo Vitleau — I'll pad it soft with cotton on account of his bruises. This one's for Ellie's Pete. But it's got to be bigger. A lot bigger. And I'm tired, awful tired —"

Mister Tiff felt a warm wetness blinding his eyes. He heard Jim Riley's whisper, "Graves. My God, she's digging graves. Poor Aggie, she's gone at last."

Pietro laid a hand to her arm. "You go home now, Aggie, and rest. Tomorrow you can finish —"

"They have to be dug now," she insisted, looking down upon outspread Granitetown where a faint mist was rising. "It's almost day."

She would not lift a foot from the trench until Mister Tiff, after a telepathic message to the other men, coaxed, "Go with Joey and Riley, yes? Me and Pietro, we will stay and do your digging."

She was grateful and docile. "It'll help — I'm tired." She clasped her hands behind her back and followed Officer Riley.

It was a few mornings later that Mister Tiff said to Petra and Vetch, "Tomorrow I go away." But he was leaving Granitetown that night.

In the afternoon Veet Palingetti loaned him the use of the meat van. The man perched himself on the driver's seat, black Pontius Pilate in his lap, Petra and Vetch beside him. He slapped the reins over the dappled beast and drove down Pastinetti Place, bent on brief farewell visits at the homes of his Granitetown friends. Maria Dalli had wet brushed and pressed his suit this morning. Under its freshness his heart wilted in anticipated loneliness. Yet he was pleased that he could summon strength today to fashion a smile for his face, and to hold it there for his friends to see.

On this summer afternoon a blue sky and its blazing sun ceiled

Granitetown. Willow Hollow Road seemed to sag under a motionless heat weight. Branches of river willows drooped close to the sluggish stream; a few thirsting leaves dipped with limp enthusiasm into the scummed surface. Mister Tiff rose from the Tosti porch and took Lucia's finely shaped hands in his. "No more adventures in 'selling,' eh?" he begged in farewell.

And the van traveled Douglas Hill and stopped before the yellow brick house. Aggie's mind, never strong at its best, had really snapped that afternoon in the Douglas kitchen, and now Minna and Alvah Douglas were paying for the woman's keep in one of the state's sanatoria. "You did well for Aggie Rugg," Mister Tiff commended Minna softly. The little man's words, Minna thought, seemed to flow into her with the sweet solemnity and graces of a sacramental. She stood waving after the departing meat wagon, feeling ridiculous at the lump which rose in her throat. She shrugged slim shoulders and returned to the living room where a bridge party was in progress.

He visited his friends Mama Gioffi, Ellie Marclay, the Riley family, and Father Carty. A boyish esteem shone from Father Carty's eyes as the two men stood facing each other on the rectory porch, and the older man found himself basking in their warmth and postponing his farewells.

"The boys tell me they have you to thank for being allowed the use of the baseball field again."

Mister Tiff stroked his nose complacently. "Hah, that was nothing, nothing."

The priest did not explain that he had earlier made the same request of Asa Conway and had been flatly refused. Nor did he add that last week he stopped by to commend Asa on his change of mind, and that the storekeeper muttered, "Don't thank me, thank that Tiff fellow." And as Asa bent behind the counter to get a tin of maple syrup for a customer, he startled the priest by mumbling a sotto voice epithet which sounded very much like "that damn long-nosed snooper." Father Carty wondered, with human curiosity, what lay behind Asa's rancor; moreover, envisioning the myriad personal contacts he must make in his lifetime as priest, he was genuinely interested in learning firsthand this little man's successful method of approach.

The rotund, freckled face above the clerical collar was smiling. "How'd you do it? I may experiment with your technique some day."

Mister Tiff's mouth readily opened, but it closed abruptly and in awkward wordlessness. What could he say? It had been Asa's conscience and fear, pricked opportunely within sight of Josie's house, that had made the storekeeper change his mind. But, surely, he should not impart this knowledge to Father Carty or to anyone else. He wagged a slender finger in front of the priest's face and, hurriedly summoning a tone of scriptural majesty, exclaimed, "Be ye prudent, seek not the whys of secret graces."

A puzzled look was erasing the priest's smile as he groped mentally to place the quotation. "I don't seem to remember —"

Mister Tiff murmured nimbly, "St. Matthew, Chapter 28, Verse 21 —"

"Verse 21!" Almost unbidden the echo leaped from the priest's mouth. Impossible! It so happened that the four last verses of St. Matthew's Gospel — Christ's request that all men be made His disciples, and ending "— and behold, I am with you all days, even to the consummation of the world" — were among his favorite passages in the Gospels. They included Verses 16 through 20 of Chapter 28, and they were the final verses not only of Chapter 28 but of the entire Gospel. Of that he was certain. The priest looked into the pale eyes that were fixed on him with a waiting, breathless quality. "Now, look here, there isn't a Verse 21 —"

"But of course not, of course not," his companion hastily agreed. He fumbled unnecessarily with the kerchief at his neck. Holy Mother, in sparing Josie and Asa he had most imprudently bitten off more than he could chew. And he could sigh with genuine self-reproach, "Hah, the value of prudence!"

The priest waited warily.

"Yes, prudence." Mister Tiff was angry with himself, and with the situation. "You see what happens? You don't wait until I finish speaking — and then you get mad." He ignored the younger man's gesture of protest. "If you had waited to let me finish, maybe I would have added — 'to be sure this verse is not in the Gospel, but I think Verse 21 would be a good place for it, no?'"

Father Carty spoke stiffly. "I doubt if St. Matthew needs a collaborator."

Now it was the older man who was blushing painfully and in all humility, and he was stammering his good-bys, saying that Petra and Vetch were awaiting him in front of the church and that by now they would surely be impatient.

Father Carty leaned his red head to the rectory porch post and watched the limping figure recede down the road. It came to him then that not only had he failed in his request to learn how the man had persuaded Asa Conway to change his mind, but he had been given a doubtful lesson on the value of prudence.

Mister Tiff's last Granitetown visit was to the church. He knelt before his warrior-saint. His eyes lingered on the ruby heart of the altar flame flickering its perpetual adoration, and on the gold-white immaculacy of the tabernacle that housed Him. For a shorter time they sought out the scuffed, wooden floor, and the opaque windows. His mind took a picture of them, so that across the ocean he might remember. He hoped some day Father Down and Father Carty would realize their wish for fine stained-glass windows. Colored windows seemed to spiritualize the raw daylight that streamed through them. The shadows behind St. Michael would bloom with warm, pastel splendor. This rainbow enchantment would not only beautify the house of God but would help aestheticize the mind to the infinite beauty of the divine presence. Mister Tiff firmly believed that spiritual seasonings were as necessary to a frail humanity as salt and pepper and garlic to insipid food.

When the brown-haired Petra slid a hand into his and whispered,

"Vetch says it's almost suppertime and Veet will want his horse and wagon," the smile he had fashioned wavered, and he limped fast from the church.

Of the Dallis only Maria and Pietro were awake to see him off. He passed through the dark, quieted rooms, hovering silently over the sleeping Petra, Vetch, the red-cheeked Gabriella, and the baby Americo, his fingers touching a benediction to the forehead of each. And under a corner of Petra's pillow he tucked the calendar with its richly colored saints.

The two men walked down the crunchy silence of Pastinetti Place. Pietro carried the pigskin bag and a shoe box containing the lunch Maria knew would later tease his appetite. There was tasty gorgonzola, fried chicken, crisp buns. Pietro's simple heart regretted this parting. But he was glad that the *maestro* was smiling, for it must mean that he was happy at the prospect of returning to his homeland. And now he was reminding his parting guest of the *paesani's* messages: "— and Lancelotto says, if you go to Como, to say to his brother that next year, if everything goes well, he will pay him a visit. And for Maria's mother you have the silk shawl, yes? And the steak hammer I made of granite? The picture of the baby Americo —"

The neighborhood poolroom was alight with life, the door open to emit waves of blue tobacco smoke. Across the granite-paved road two lights burned in Asa Conway's store. Pietro murmured, "There must be a Spanish Club meeting tonight or Conway would not be behind his counter at nine o'clock. He hopes for a few late customers, eh?"

Mister Tiff halted. "I might as well bid good-by to that dried-faced one. You wait here, Pietro, I will be but a minute."

Asa was wrapping a pound of coffee and a tin of sardines for a well-dressed, tall man whom Mister Tiff had often seen entering the Granitetown Bank. Asa's sour face had the greedy look of one who listens to profitable news. The customer was saying, "I told them what I told you last week, that there are only two good locations for a sanatorium in Granitetown. Either on that hilly stretch up there —" His hand moved in the direction of Pastinetti Place. "— or on that rise opposite The Hill. I'm for the first location. I —"

There had been talk recently of a proposed tuberculosis sanatorium in Granitetown. Mister Tiff recalled that only yesterday Leo Vitleau's grief-stricken father had said, "We have a chance to sell our pasture and sugar bush to Asa Conway. He's not offering much, but we're planning to leave Granitetown anyway. Going down to my brother's in Georgia, to the Georgia quarries."

Mister Tiff's index finger stroked his beak of a nose. So this was why Asa wanted to buy Vitleau's land — in order to sell it to the city or the county at a good profit. *Dio,* hadn't the deaths of Leo and Pete reminded Asa that the pockets of his last pair of pants would do him no good whether they were empty or full? And he interrupted the well-dressed customer to give the storekeeper a hasty handshake in farewell.

Asa looked over his glasses. "Back to Italy, you say?" He added a mental "good riddance" before pursuing aloud, "Going tonight?"

"I leave now. Now." He burned with impatience to be off.

Asa's eyes fled along the glass counter to the cigar boxes marked *10 cents, 5 cents, 2 for 5;* and he selected two of the *2 for 5's* and handed them to him. "Here," he mumbled. "I never handle those stogies you folks go for."

Outside, Mister Tiff urged the astounded Pietro to go on to the station alone, promising to meet him there in ten minutes, and he hurried his rheumatic legs back to Pastinetti Place, heedless of his friend's alarmed, "The train! Do you think it will wait for you?"

Mister Tiff's narrow chest was heaving rapidly when he was admitted to the Vitleau kitchen. Old Vitleau's shaggy gray head tossed angrily when he heard the reason for Conway's offer to buy. Leo's father merely pressed his thin lips to a thinner line. "Sell it to the city yourself," Mister Tiff puffed. He was tired. And there still remained the fast walk to the station. . . .

Conway's store had gone dark. He turned into a narrow side street. Pietro's short, stocky figure was pacing the station platform. The train was already there, looking like a gigantic, illuminated caterpillar. Tip Gioffi's touring car was drawn up to the platform, and Tip was assisting Josie Blaine and her two children to the train. The bootlegger's head was framed for a few minutes in the train window as he made the Blaines comfortable in their double seat; then he was in the car again, driving away. His appearance with Josie disturbed Mister Tiff, and he wondered if Tip, too, had been attracted to the vivacious Josie. His thoughts did not dwell long on Tip for, from a corner of the station, a green-clad arm that was surely Asa Conway's was handing an envelope to a brakeman and was motioning toward the window that pictured Josie Blaine. A wry smile tugged at Mister Tiff's lips; the brakeman was delivering the envelope to Josie. Her head lowered to inspect its contents, then her face lifted and pressed eagerly to the window, peering into the darkness, trying to penetrate the night. It was only for a moment; then her head, with an indifference that was Josie's, sank to the plush of the train seat.

At the last, Pietro would not remove from him until a lunge of the train sent him staggering down the aisle. His calloused hands locked his friend's. "Take care now in your travels!" he blurted as he jumped from the moving train. Admonition to this teacher was presumptuous, he felt, and sat uncomfortably on his own humble tongue; but because Maria had requested it, he called through trumpeted hands, "And keep a good distance from mealymouthed *ciarlatani*, whether they be men or women. . . ."

Alone, Tiff slumped against the train seat. Hearing again the rumble of the wheels, it seemed but yesterday that he had come to Granitetown. From Ibena, back to Ibena. And Granitetown was but a brief intermezzo. . . . The backs of Main Street buildings passed him. They were black, looming bulks, with only a light here and there to define them. The stream along Shed Row was a long, black pall, unrolling on and on beside the train with the saddening

andante of a dirge. City lights rose dimly above the business blocks
to merge finally into darkness. He was glad he was leaving when
night could dull the memories he had made on sun-bright days.
If he closed his eyes, he was a tiny, helpless spot being sped on,
by some strong power, into a dark space. It was frightening. His
hand reached into his pocket for comforting contact with the
familiar figure of St. Michael. He forced his eyes wide open and
caught sight of Josie slapping a powder puff to her face at the
end of the coach.

Josie's oldest child, Enis, was a pert-faced girl, dark eyes roving
restlessly under a cloud of blue-black hair. She was a little younger,
perhaps, than Petra. She played in the seat facing her mother. Her
sharp teeth were snipping a string into short lengths, and she was
making rings for a sleepy younger brother. He was a round-faced
boy with a running nose. Mister Tiff made his way to Josie, steadying himself along the aisle by grasping the seat backs.

Something of her Willow Hollow Road gaiety and lightness
spurted to her face. "Well, if it isn't you!"

He took the boy on his knees. They talked. She was bound for
her sister's home in the southern part of the state.

"She doesn't know I'm coming. After the first shock wears off,
it'll be O.K. We sort of rub each other the wrong way." She spoke
with spurious confidence, fingering the envelope in her lap. Three
ten-dollar bills showed through the slit, Mister Tiff noted. Asa
Conway's envelope.

The red of contempt for the storekeeper burned Mister Tiff's
cheeks. Thirty dollars. . . . And Tip Gioffi? He pulled at his
mustache in quick confusion, for as if he had asked the question
aloud, she said, "We met that Gioffi fellow tonight by the park. I
hardly know him — but he gave us a ride to the station."

Her voice rang clear with truth.

The little man could believe her.

CHAPTER IX

Maple Junction was Josie's destination. Mister Tiff found he must wait here an hour for train connections. In the station two passengers and a conductor were having doughnuts and mugs of coffee at a corner counter. Josie refused Mister Tiff's offer of food and refused as well his suggestion that he accompany her down the dimly lighted street to her sister's house.

Josie predicted cheerfully, "She's going to let off steam when she sees me. We can do without an audience."

He was having his second cup of coffee when Josie and her children again pushed open the station door. The little boy was clinging to his mother's hand and was whimpering with the monotone of prolonged weariness. She sat on the bench and called out to the counterman, "When's there a train for Millville?"

"There's a bus at six-thirty." He glanced at the wall clock. "Five hours to wait." And as Josie was preparing to settle the children on the bench for the night, he added, "Jeff Ryle's got overnight cabins 'cross the road."

Mister Tiff joined Josie. "But the sister?" he whispered. "What about her?"

She laughed. "The sister says 'no.' I hardly blame her. Three of us — my God, it'll be four soon — is a load for anyone to take on."

He stroked fretfully at his nose. He did not like to picture her curled in sleep on the bench, helpless against the curious eyes of whosoever chanced to come in. "This is no place for you," he said firmly. "Tonight you will stay in a cabin. Tomorrow maybe the sister will change her mind. Anyway, it will give you a chance to rest."

It required no coaxing. The four walked to Jeff Ryle's kitchen porch. Jeff, summoned from sleep, yawned at Mister Tiff from behind the screen door. "Four of you? Guess your family could do with the double cabin — "

Mister Tiff blushed; he was finding it not unpleasant to be considered a partner in the marriage state. He was about to explain that he was not interested in lodging for himself, but the man had already gone in search of the key. He was startled to hear himself say, instead, to Josie, "Me, I think I will stay here tonight, too." Hah, well, one day less in New York would make little difference to him. Tomorrow at this time he could board this same train. And in the meantime it would be but a Christian act to see that this Josie and her children were settled somewhere. He hurried back to the train for his pigskin bag and the lunch box. At the lunch counter he bought two quarts of milk and a dozen doughnuts. He felt warmly protective as, laden with food, he trudged back to the cabin. The children were already abed and asleep. Josie was sitting in a rocker smoking a cigarette and humming a tune. He had intended to pat her back and offer her the advice, "Now, no worrying tonight. Sleep. Tomorrow we can make plans." But Josie, tapping a foot in tempo to her humming, had the look of one who needs no sympathy, needs no advice. He said his good night, went into his own room, and closed the door. Abed he grappled with Josie's problems, weighing the prudence of having a talk tomorrow with Josie's sister or of phoning Asa. . . . Adoption of Josie's worries so unburdened himself of his own heartache that he was able to sleep quickly and soundly.

Here there was no stone-shed reveille to tell him the time, but from force of habit he awoke at seven o'clock. Maple Junction and Granitetown, he mused sleepily, each played its own favorite arpeggio to the day. Granitetown strode noisily into the day's activities with the scream of shed whistles, the drone of trolleys, and the clatter of heavy heels enroute to the stone sheds. Early morning at Maple Junction yawned musically into day with birds chanting their magnificats and with the not unpleasant clank of milk cans being loaded at the station.

Josie's room was quiet. Mister Tiff, basking in his temporary role of family head, snuggled deep in his bed and determined that no sound from him would waken this Josie to the harsh reality of today's worries. He lay there saying a rosary for his Granitetown friends, telling another for the soul of his nephew, and starting a third for the humility of heart and fortitude he would sorely need on the day he appeared again before Mafalda in Italy. . . .

He did not know how long he slept. The pocket watch under his pillow said nine o'clock. The little room was brilliant with sunlight, and stifling. A glistening green fly persistently buzzed and knocked for exit on the window pane. Josie's room was still quiet. He decided with a kindly sigh that Josie was being as solicitous for his sleep as he was for hers. He tiptoed to the lone chair for his pants. They were no longer folded over its back; they lay lengthwise over the seat of the chair, and they could not have slipped to that position. Moreover, the figurine of St. Michael and the moneybag given to him by the *paesani* were slanting precariously from a pocket. Mister Tiff took the shrunken moneybag with trembling fingers, and he counted. Seventy-five dollars were gone! Seventy-five dollars of his passage fare to Italy, of the *paesani's* hard-earned money.

He knew before he opened Josie's door that the room would be empty. And when he went to the station and inquired of the counterman, "The lady and her children, did they manage to catch that Millville bus?" — he was not surprised to hear him answer, "Yup, just made it by the skin of their teeth."

It was at noon, as he was eating Maria's lunch and sipping from a bottle of Pietro's homemade wine, that he became aware of the absence of the two quarts of milk and the doughnuts. He shrugged, and brushed the crumbs from his lap. Poor Josie. When the seventy-five dollars were eaten up, where and how would she get the next? Pietro's clumsy, half-facetious advice to "keep a good distance from *ciarlatani* whether they be men or women" echoed in his ears; it vied with the drumming plea of old Don Benedetto — "Prudence!" Although he was alone in the room Mister Tiff hid his mortified and flaming cheeks in his hands. Hah, what to do? There was not enough money to continue his trip to Italy, and he was ashamed to return to Granitetown and present the remainder of the purse to the *paesani.*

Suddenly he chuckled and drew St. Michael from his pocket. He looked at the saint with quizzical and marveling eyes. "Well," he whispered, "who am I to grumble? We have certainly won the first round, no? To Italy I did not want to return — and now to Italy it is impossible for me to return. . . ."

He straightened his kerchief and made his way to the pine grove behind the cabin where he had seen Jeff Ryle hammering away at new cabins which he was building. The cool pine smell sent his nostrils quivering delightedly.

"Nice country here," he began heartily and with an audible sniffing of the air. "I think maybe I would like to live here."

Jeff, standing on the third rung of a ladder and his lips clamped over a half-dozen nails, nodded his own approval of the countryside.

Mister Tiff queried, "You are building these four cabins all alone? Without help?"

Jeff repeated the nod. Considering the gesture inadequate, he spat the nails in a hand and explained, "We don't get many spare laborers in Maple Junction. Nice enough country, but we're always running short of help. Summer before last a traveling umbrella mender stopped by and decided to stay. He *really* stayed — he up and died on us, and was buried here. Last summer we got another traveler. In the fall he headed for the south. Say, hand me one of those boards; will you?" His eyes followed the limping figure. "Not very steady on your legs; are you?"

Mister Tiff rapped smartly at his modest biceps and mustered a confidence he did not feel, "Hah, I make up for it here."

At six o'clock Mister Tiff's heart was pounding from exertion and there were echoing pulsations in aching legs and arms, but he was jubilant for he had been accepted as Jeff's new handy man. He moved his belongings from the double cabin to the small room off Jeff's woodshed. His careful calculations, set down on paper, looked favorable. The salary was little, but it included board and room. If he worked through September he could save the amount Josie had taken. Moreover, in a corner of his new room he had come across a golf bag filled with the umbrella-mending equipment of the former handy man. This Jeff gladly turned over to him for one of Mister Tiff's pints of bootlegged whiskey.

Might it even come to pass, he asked hopefully of St. Michael that night, that he could not only return the purse to the *paesani* but that he could go back to Granitetown to live independently, from the earnings of the umbrella-mending business?

CHAPTER X

At Shed Row in Granitetown, along the river flats, shed windows and doors were thrown open to the summer. Big Tony Bottelli thumbed the suspenders over his massive chest, his great, Jovian face radiating good humor. "Even the dust cannot resist summer. See how it steals out to meet her."

A swarthy cutter from Frosinone tweaked his ruddy ears and murmured, "Now for the summer anyway — if I listen carefully — I need not dig the stone dust from my ears each time the wife puts a question at me."

Pietro rolled up his sleeves; he put friendly palms to the rough stone in front of him. True, summer coming in at the doors was pleasant. Sun poured into dark corners, dissolved shapeless shadows. The air was somewhat clearer of the powdery gray; his eyes told him so, and his breathing. Yet, in shafts of sunlight one still saw thousands and thousands of particles dancing against each other. Pietro scoffed at the masks some of the cutters wore. He insisted that they were stifling and that they forced an irritating dampness to the skin. Instead, his nose wanted to admit the visiting sun into its every pore. Maria cut two round bits from a sponge. She secured these to the ends of a two-inch string; and Pietro doused them in disinfectant and reluctantly inserted one into each nostril. At the end of the day's work he pulled at the string; the spongy filters came out clogged with mucoid stone dust. It was the one and only time he wore them.

After work hours Ronato kept to the shed, his sensitive hands chiseling beauty to Italo Tosti's memorial. It was a small piece —

this gift of the Gerbatti and McSweeney sheds, this labor of Ronato and Pietro; and Ronato shaped all but life into each passion flower. Yesterday they set the stone over Italo's grave. As Ronato saw grief freshen in Lucia, he himself withered into an apathy of despair. Now when his love for her might blossom into marriage, Lucia was still shaking her dark head and mourning her Italo.

Pietro's brown eyes looked up often from his work and rested on Ronato's long face. *Dio*, love for Lucia flamed so ardently in this pale Ronato that, finding no fuel in her, the fire turned viciously upon himself, burning him to destruction. There was the look of Pompeii in Ronato's melancholy face.

With Mister Tiff gone, the gold and green of summer days lost something of their glory for Petra. She tacked the saints' calendar over her bed. Mornings before she dressed she took it to the kitchen and with the help of her mother read the Italian account of a saint's life. And sometimes the girl's mind possessed so lively a picture of the saint that she felt the need of releasing it, and she must share it in graphic words with Vetch, Denny, Gino, or Peggy.

She deplored their unreceptive ears. The Pastinetti Place boys preferred baseball, afternoons of swimming. Peggy might listen for a time, but she, also, was enraptured of an active summer. Petra, alert to her playmate's restlessness, might then suggest, "Let's act St. Dorothy's life, let's act it just as if we were St. Dorothy." Peggy sometimes played indulgently for a half hour. Then her sober, freckled face rebelled and she murmured, "Oh, let's play hop-scotch." Only Denny, on his infrequent trips to Pastinetti Place, would stretch out with her on the green of Vitleau's pasture. They lay on their backs beneath a maple or a wild cherry, bare legs to the prostrate grass, their eyes on the foliage and the ever shifting designs it made of blue sky. Yet they visioned other scenes. They paid no heed to bees that circled in the scented atmosphere above the tangle of wild vetch beside them, or dipped, droning, into its blue-lavender blossoms. Nor to black Pontius Pilate growling frustration at some hidden, chirping cricket. They paid no heed. They were held in a pattern of some past life. Of Petra's gentle St. Francis and his birds. Of St. Nicholas rescuing the three children from the innkeeper's vat of pickling brine. Of any saint Petra's calendar might that day describe.

But these moments were few and fleeting. Denny's home was the yellow-brick house on Douglas Hill. For three quarters of the summer vacation period he and his mother lived in western mountains that were far from the Green Mountains.

The girl longed for Mister Tiff. When blessedly her mind could be free of him, the little dog was sure to bring before her a picture of the wispy mustache, pale blue eyes, the beaked nose, the mole, the limp. As the puppy lengthened and slimmed from the chubby roundness it had first been, association suffered; and it distorted her memory of Mister Tiff. And after two months she must carefully assemble eyes, beaked nose, and mustache before she could be confident that the picture of him was a true one.

In another measure she missed Leo Vitleau. She had never liked his young-old face nor his too shy, self-effacing manner. But she could not forget that strange understanding, akin to pity, in his eyes when she screamed at Mister Tiff in the pavilion at Peter's Gate. Nor could she forget the green fright on his face and his cry when he dropped into the quarry.

Two day's following Mister Tiff's departure, the Vitleaus had acted upon his advice. They sold their small house and the pasture land to the county for a sanatorium site. Old Vitleau flourished the check in front of Asa Conway's face. "Five-hundred dollars you would have made on that deal if you'd bought from us!" The Vitleaus packed their household possessions in a moving van, and they left Granitetown for one of the granite-working centers of Georgia. The Vitleau house during their ownership had been a humble home, the shingled walls peeling, the front porch sloping under age. But crisp curtains, lights, and the capable hands of old Vitleau had made it cheerfully alive and neat. The house was county property now, waiting to be torn down. It was deserted, uncared for, left standing until that day when the grounds would be swept clean by zealous landscape gardener and architect. Petra often stood on tiptoe and cleaned a circle on the window pane with a handful of grass and she looked into the rooms, pitying the empty house.

By midsummer the mood of the house was translated to the girl. The practical-minded Maria, knowing that she herself missed the *maestro,* said to Pietro, "The child grieves for the man." And with a keenness hinging on jealousy she added, "I doubt if she would grieve more bitterly if you or I were to leave her."

Petra liked to sit in the shade of the front-yard grapevines, on a low, rude bench her father had cut for her from a discarded granite block. She watched the men clear the Vitleau pasture and sugar bush. The Pastinetti Place boys hung at the pasture's end for a closer view of the activities. The girl longed in vain to join them; the Dalli babies stayed her to the front and back yards of her own house. She saw woodcutters ruthlessly trample the blue vetch, the daisies, the buttercups, and she was glad that Leo and Jean were not here to witness the desecration of their play pasture. Axes cut daily into the maples and wild cherry. They didn't sound, she decided, like the sharp, ringing blows Papa's ax made on the dead wood that was piled high in the back yard for kitchen-stove use. She questioned her father, and when he told her the sap in the standing tree dulled the sound, she gave whole hours to fancy. Was the sap of a tree its blood? Did the trees feel those wounds, and were the sounds their smothered cries of pain? And were the quivering of the leaves their tremors of pain? When her eyes wandered from the pasture to the curtainless Vitleau house, that, too, had taken life. She saw it squatting like an unhappy, lonely old woman, staring from empty sockets, brooding silently over the lives she had harbored and lost. At night, if the wind moaned a mutual loneliness, the girl thought she heard the house give vent to its grief, lamenting loudly with staccato bangs of loosened shutters.

Maria was pleased when September came. "It will be good for Petra to put her mind on books again," she told Pietro hopefully. The past few weeks the child had queried continually, "Mama, hasn't Mister Tiff reached Italy yet? Hasn't he been gone long enough to write me a letter? Are there many little girls like me where he lives?" And although Maria, too, wondered why the *maestro* did not write them of his safe arrival, she answered, "Give him time, Petra. He is busy visiting with his old friends."

School did help take Mister Tiff from the child's mind. But now, the mother noted with alarm, Petra was doing so much reading in addition to her studies that her wide gray eyes watered and became wearily red. After school the girl curled up in the rocker beside the kitchen stove, fingers idling with her brown braids, her eyes glued to some brightly illustrated book of fairy tales. Always, after the four o'clock whistle blew and her father's feet sounded on the kitchen porch, she laid the book on its open pages and went out to help him slap the stone dust from his trousers and cap. Pietro would draw off his thick-soled shoes. The girl brought him his Italian paper that had arrived in the morning mail. If it were a wet day, or cold, he would sit there beside Petra, his stockinged toes wriggling comfortably in the oven, his eyes and mind intent on the news.

Maria finally ordered Petra to return her books to the library, and to take out no more until her eyes ceased to redden. The next week there was no improvement; Maria made up her mind. "Tomorrow we shall buy you a fine pair of earrings. Solid gold ones. They will heal your eyes."

"To wear at home, Mama?"

"To wear all the time."

They were at the supper table. Petra broke bits of bread and made soggy islands in her bean soup. "But not at school, Mama, no?"

"To wear in school and out of school. You don't even look pleased —"

"No, no, Mama!" The girl's spoon clattered into the half-empty bowl. She shrank back in her chair, stiffening in horror. "I won't wear them, Mama!"

"Enough, Petra," her father commanded.

Maria, who loved her earrings, neglected a reprimand to ask in honest curiosity, "And why not?"

Petra murmured less vehemently, "I won't wear them —"

Vetch, dark face brooding, thought of plump Sara Stoffi and the long earrings dangling at her round cheeks. Sometimes the boys at school made up funny songs about them, and Sara didn't like it a bit. But he'd better not tell Mama about that; Mama wouldn't like it either.

Pietro said, "To bed, Petra! First apologize to your mother."

Later when the children were abed Maria started once more on the subject. "I think the plain, button-type earring will be best for Petra, no?"

Pietro tugged at his mustache. He could not understand, nor could he forget, the horrified look on his daughter's face. "Well, let us not be hasty, *cara*. We have a fine eye doctor in Granitetown — I will take her to him tomorrow. Maybe an eyewash will help her."

"Eyewash! Didn't my own mother and your own mother teach you that gold in the ears strengthened the eyes?"

"That was in Italy — "

"Eyes are eyes in any country!"

"But here the little ones do not wear rings in their ears." He spoke the words almost absently; but, hearing them, they echoed in his brain and he knew that Petra was reluctant to wear them because they would set her apart from her little friends. "Maria, would you have the little one stared at because she follows the Italian custom of Mama Gioffi and yourself and Lucia?"

Maria's cheeks flamed. "Is she ashamed, then, of her Italian blood?"

"Now, now," he chided. "Of course not. But the day I took my final papers I became American; you, too. If we liked this country well enough to become Americans we must expect our children to go on from there. I'll take her to the doctor, yes?" he coaxed.

"And have her wear glasses? In the old country, did you ever see a child her age burdened with glasses? Not one, except the son of that wealthy family that summered in the count's villa. We called him 'Four Eyes,' remember?"

"Right, *cara* — but remember, too, that your grandmother and my greataunt both went blind in spite of the gold earrings."

"That was old age, and age steals from all our senses."

They could not reach an agreement. And Maria must continue the discussion in their bed, against her will. They did not hear Vetch tiptoe down the hall in his bare feet and put a guilty and hungry ear to their door.

He had to know if they were going to make Petra wear earrings. If they did, he would *have* to tell them Petra would be laughed at. They wouldn't like that. . . . It brought hot splotches to his cheeks to think that Petra might experience the burning shivers he had felt when he was called *Elvecchio,* "the old one."

He listened.

Papa, to be sure, did not favor the earrings. And as he listened Mama's voice lost its supper-table firmness. It softened. He peeked through the keyhole. They sat on the edge of the bed. Mama looking prettier and softer in her white nightgown, and with Papa taking down her black hair and braiding it into two ropes.

For many a week Vetch had been thinking of his mother as two people — a day mother and a night mother. The day mother was firm, unbending, in keeping with her solid, corseted body. The night mother was a gentle person, soft like the snowy nightdress she wore. He had noticed this difference when she came in at night to lower a window, and when she stopped to press a kiss to his forehead. It was a warmer, different kiss from the one she might give him mornings in the kitchen. He knelt in his nightshirt before his mother's door, his haunches resting on his bare heels; and now he heard Mama murmuring, "Ah well, Pietro, all right. No earrings, then. Take her to the doctor —"

Vetch tiptoed hastily into Petra's room. "Wake up!" he whispered urgently. "Wake up, Petra."

But she had not yet fallen into sleep, and she was not surprised to see the white-clad figure. "What's the matter?"

"You don't have to wear earrings."

"Honest? How do you know?"

"You don't, I tell you. I just heard Papa and Mama say so. But don't let on I told you, see?"

The following afternoon she was a little disappointed when the doctor said, "No glasses for you, little lady. For a few weeks do your studying afternoons, not in the evening." There was nothing to show for this trip to the doctor's except a bottle of green fluid that cost Papa a two-dollar bill.

These chilly nights in September and early October Petra was excused from studying with Vetch behind the closed door of the living room. Maria feared the girl would brood and she allowed her to sit in the kitchen watching Pietro and his friends play cards and sip their wine, and listening to their stories about hunting and their plans for hunting this winter. Pietro, like most of the *paesani* hunted rabbits, squirrel, birds, and deer. He liked to tramp the forest beds, whether they held the spongy, springy surface of fern and leaves, or the soft depth of snow. And he liked the tonic freshness of the air at his face and in his nostrils after the hours of dust in the sheds.

Petra remembered that last winter on Saturdays Papa accompanied the boss Gerbatti with his rabbit hound, Circo, to the deep woods where Gerbatti owned a cabin. They interrupted their hunting hours only once during the day; that was when they visited the cabin to warm their feet before the fireplace and to warm their stomachs with hot coffee and grappa. The girl had wondered why these first rabbits he brought home wore fawn-colored coats, and the late ones had soft, white coats. And Pietro told her it was God's and nature's way of protecting the little creatures from keen eyes such as his, for in the fall their brownish fur blended with the bare earth and brown foliage, and in the winter their fur turned white to match the snow. She felt sorry for the furry stillness of the rabbits he brought home, comparing it with the glorious activity of her own body. Yet, she could help her mother tease the wildness from the pink meat by soaking it overnight in diluted wine. And she knew no remorse the next day when her sharp teeth sank into the rabbit stew and *polenta* her mother cooked.

CHAPTER XI

A setting October sun painted the windows of Pastinetti Place a dusky red, and made of the upheaved Vitleau pasture a ruddy wasteland of uprooted shrubs. Petra was returning from Asa Conway's store, five pounds of sugar in one arm, her free hand locked around little Gabriella's. Last year, she remembered, the maples edging the Vitleau pasture land had flared scarlet in their last heightened fire; they had crested the hill and were banked there against the sky for a few days like a bed of glowing embers. She waved across the street to Ellie Marclay who was walking in slow sedateness down the street. Ellie kept to herself since Pete died. And with Aggie Rugg gone, she had given up her work in the adjoining city; she was clerking in a Granitetown department store. Neighbors saw her daily coming home at noon to cook a hurried lunch for Robbie and herself, and again at five o'clock hurrying up the hill with parcels of food for supper.

Petra and Gabriella stopped by the vines bordering the Dalli lawn to pick a cluster of their father's green-purple grapes. If the summer happened to be a short one, the grapes did not fully ripen. But Petra liked their round, hard tartness; and her mouth puckered and watered at the mere thought of them.

A voice spoke behind them. "Hah, my Petra." A mild voice that sent a delicious ripple through her body, and gathered into a lump in her throat, choking back all sound. She stood still, staring at the grapes in her hand, afraid to turn, afraid that her ears had deceived

134

her. Pontius Pilate darted around a corner of the house and set up a joyous yapping.

Now the same mild voice exclaimed, "Surely this sausage-shaped one is not our Pontius Pilate!"

A cry finally broke through Petra's lips. "Mister Tiff!" She whirled and threw herself against him, her red bereted head pushing to his thin waist.

"Hah, easy! Do you want to push me into the vines?" His voice trembled with an emotion that matched the child's. And her clutching, possessive fingers brought a great peace to his heart.

There were first moments when this unexpected joy at seeing Mister Tiff left Petra wordless. Then her agile tongue fashioned questions that had long been churning in her mind, and they tumbled pell-mell from her wide mouth: "Did you think of me on the ship? Why didn't you write? Didn't you like Italy after all? You're going to stay now, Mister Tiff, aren't you? You're going to stay in Granitetown forever —"

Pietro saw them from the *bocce* course behind the Rossi house. He dropped the wooden ball, and his stout legs took high, leaping strides across the lawn.

All but the baby Americo gathered in the kitchen to welcome Mister Tiff. Maria made fresh coffee for him and poured grappa into it. She said fondly, as she would to one of her children, "You were lonesome for us and for America — that is why you hurried back. Tell me, you surely visited with my mother in Ibena? And my sister? How are they?"

The man dipped his face quickly into the steam that rose from the hot drink. Pietro, looking at him, decided that it was a gesture of guilt, and although he, too, was amazed at the return of the *maestro* and was eager to ask questions some sense prompted him to say to his family, "No questions until tomorrow — tonight we will tell the *maestro* all of our own news."

In spite of the little man's protests, Maria hastened to prepare his old cot.

He had not returned to be a burden to his friends, he declared. "Tomorrow I will find a room. Perhaps Lucia Tosti has one to spare, and she can use the extra money."

"You'll be with Gino all the time!" Petra's catapulted words were an accusation.

Pietro insisted, "It is here you belong. Pay, if you wish; but it is here you stay. *Dio*, if you are at Lucia's my little ones will bother her with their presence day and night."

"Then name a weekly sum for my board and room," Mister Tiff declared. His pale eyes twinkled. "A moderate sum, of course. But I *do* have a business these days." From the golf bag he drew two new umbrellas, a sheaf of metal ribs, a kit containing needles and spools of thread.

"An umbrella mender —" Pietro breathed.

The children were staring in fascination at the motley collection, the little man saw. But Pietro and Maria. . . . Mister Tiff's heart sank at the disapproving faces which were silently but eloquently proclaiming this dispensing of service to be no better than the peddling of soft drinks. Inwardly he trembled at causing embarrassment to his friends; and he trembled inwardly because he was in no position to be fussy about a job. He stroked his beak of a nose and smiled. "Hardly a lordly profession, eh? But me, I keep seeing that accursed picture of the fanciful Dante viewing the Proud Souls stooped under their Stones of Humility. And then I say to myself: isn't it wiser — and, indeed, is there any choice? — to carry my Stones in this short life than in the purgatory of uncertain duration?" He chuckled. "Hah, you should have seen the first umbrella I pricked with this mender's needle! Butchery! But I learned. I sharpen knives, too. It hardly fills my pocket with silver, but it provides a living."

"But the walking, and the rheumatic legs?"

"Pah, I discovered the more I torture them in exercise, the stronger they grow. Now, just to spite me, they can endure a good two miles. Besides, it is better to wear out my shoes and earn a little money than to wear out the sheets and earn nothing. One bothers my legs, but the other bothers both back and conscience."

It was well toward midnight when Pietro followed his family up the stairs. Mister Tiff's detaining hand touched his shoulder gently. "One moment in private, eh, Pietro?" The little man dug into his pocket and brought to light the moneybag Pietro had presented to him last spring at the picnic.

He spoke hesitantly, shyly. "All of it is here. You will be kind enough to divide it among the *paesani* who gave it?"

"But they won't accept it, *Maestro*."

"You must make them —"

Pietro's brow knotted in confusion. "They were happy to make this gift. And proud. If you return it, they will be hurt."

"The gift was for passage to Italy, no?"

"To be sure."

Mister Tiff took a deep breath and held it. And lest he be tempted on a second breath to change his mind, he rushed his words into that one exhalation. "Well, I did not cross the ocean!"

"*Dio*, no?"

"Not even to New York did I go —"

"No?"

"Not even out of Vermont." He eked out the words painfully.

Pietro's fingers sought his brown mustache. "Well," he murmured faintly. "Well —"

"I had a little accident the first night — I lost some of the money. But it is all there now," he added quickly.

"Some smooth-tongued fellow, eh?" Pietro guessed. "Did you go to the police?"

"No, no," he stammered. "It was no matter for the police. I lost my money honestly."

"At dice?" Pietro was thinking of how Pontius Pilate had come into the *maestro's* possession. It was not pleasant to think of the *maestro* squandering in chance the money his friends had earned by their sweat. And he was relieved to hear the man deny emphatically, "No, no."

Mister Tiff sighed. Impossible to tell this Pietro that a night of virtuous sleep spent under the same roof with Josie Blaine had thwarted, financially, his trip to Italy. "Look, Pietro, in the first place I found I preferred to stay in Granitetown; in the second place I feared the trip would not agree with me." (Mother of God, to appear in Ibena before Mafalda, and in financial straits, certainly would not agree with him!) "And in the third place someone who needed the money more than I did made use of it. It was in Maple Junction I worked and made my home; and when the purse was full again I decided to come back to Granitetown —" His voice ended on a high, wistful note which pleaded — *must I tell you more?*

Pietro, grasping at the first good excuse which he might present to the curious *paesani*, slapped at his thigh. "The rheumatism! But, of course, the ocean would not agree with you. We shall tell our friends the rheumatism kept you in America, eh?"

Under this unsolicited emancipation Mister Tiff nodded humbly. "Whatever you say."

He had returned in time to join the Dallis in the last fall mushroom hunts. On Sunday he and Pietro mounted the seat of Veet's meat van and with Vetch, Petra, and Robbie drove off to Peter's Gate. There the children might play with Pontius Pilate or amuse themselves picking the common meadow mushroom with whose brownish, scaly caps they were familiar. Pietro and Mister Tiff searched the thickets for choicer delicacies, especially the coral fungi with their pale yellow branches and whitish throats. Maria stirred these into omelets that melted on the tongue. If there chanced to be a warm rain, their noses were on the alert for the spicy smell of tiny garlic mushrooms that sprang up in hordes in the depths of a moist woodland, covering fallen twigs and needles. Dried, the mushrooms would add fragrance to Maria's roasts through a long winter. Petra liked to help her mother peel the skins from the mushroom caps; she liked the fresh, woody smell it left on her fingers.

By mid-October the Dalli back yard was an uneven surface of overturned boxes, and upon them were spread shredded mushrooms. Curling, browning, drying in the sun. Mister Tiff and Pietro brought home so many varieties — corals, puffballs, ear-shaped fungi — that Maria threw up her hands in alarm. She always dropped a well-scrubbed, shining fifty-cent piece into the stewing mushrooms, and she waited in vain for the poison to coat the silver black. It never did.

Once the *maestro* had laughed at her: "If you stew that silver until Gabriel's horn calls us to our reward, it will still be incapable of proving or disproving the goodness of mushrooms."

Maria was indignant. "My mother and grandmother before me used silver. Never once did their stomachs suffer the pangs of poison. It is a rust in mushrooms that is poisonous. Anyone knows that. Now, it is common sense, no, to say that the rust from these mushrooms will, in cooking, stain the silver and so warn us —"

Mister Tiff smiled and sighed. "Hah, if only our great Pliny could rise from his Roman grave to see the thousands who still believe in his teaching! He was a great man, and his thirty-seven volumes of natural history are a project to be proud of, but he was wrong, my Maria, when he wrote that poisonous mushrooms were only those growing near rusted objects and snakes' beds. The great Pliny guessed, but he erred —" He rambled on meditatively, half to himself, as he used to do before Count Mattzo's fireplace. "Indeed, in this instance even the younger Pliny was but half right when he said — 'There is nothing so likely to hand down your name as a poem,' for I wager there are more *paesani* who discuss the elder Pliny's discourse on mushrooms than who discuss the young Pliny's tepid verse. Indeed, when I was in Maple Junction forcing down the fodder Jeff Ryle called food, surely I gave more thought to Maria's spaghetti nestling in its warm nest of red sauce than to Dante's lines. . . ."

But Maria shrugged off such monologues, and clung to the belief of her mother and grandmother: she placed a silver coin in every saucepan of mushrooms.

The mushroom season was over, and now Pietro, Gerbatti, and Rossi together purchased a carload of fine grapes. They took turns using the wine press — their joint possession. The three crushed Rossi's grapes first. Then Gerbatti's. Then they carried the press to Pietro's house. They turned up their noses at Pepino Stoffi, the Neapolitan, and the cutter from Frosinone, who squeezed the grapes just as they came from the train. Bah, they profaned this wine that the *Dio* had immortalized in His miracle at Cana! Let them abuse their stomachs with an inferior wine if they wished! Good wine makers set the grapes free of rot and twigs. They rinsed them well.

On these wine-making days Petra put a plump pillow on the cellar floor and sat cross-legged watching them feed the press. The dark grapeskins broke over the gelatinous green, and the succulent globes were chewed into a purple brew. She rolled a drop of the juice around the walls of her cupped hand, delighting in the scarlet stain it made on the pink flesh, but liking better the rich purple of the drop itself. It was the royal purple of the satin curtain that sometimes draped the tabernacle of the altar in St. Michael's church.

Pietro bottled the first wine for festive occasions; some he barreled for daily use. Then he added water to the grape mash, and made a thinner wine. It would some day become the vinegar Maria sprinkled on green salads.

And the mash was not yet washed of its strength. It must be tried to its last ounce of goodness. Pietro fitted one of Maria's copper wash boilers with tube and coils. He cooked the mash in this boiler until the hot vapors were shocked into liquid state in the cold coils, and it trickled out of the tubes a transparent, potent grappa.

Petra and Vetch enjoyed these fall evenings of grappa making. Outside was the chill night. Inside rose a steamy, racy warmth that nipped their noses. To blind the curious eyes of passers-by, Pietro drew the kitchen shades close to the sills saying that the government did not approve of grappa making. And Petra wondered why the government should care if Papa poured a little grappa into his morning coffee to warm himself these cool mornings, and to make his breakfast taste better. For he said it did. Petra heard her father invite Ronato — "Come up tonight, Ronato. You and Lucia. We will sit at the kitchen table for a game of *briscola*. I am making grappa tonight."

Petra knew that if she breathed the racy grappa steam for a long time, it gave her body a pleasing sensation. Tingling, light, gay. Her mother would make a clucking sound and say, "Look at the child's flushed cheeks. *Dio*, almost *inebriata* she is." And she would allow neither her nor Gabriella to sleep in the little room over the kitchen where the steam rose through the pipe hole in the floor. No, on grappa-making nights the two girls slept in the upper hall where doors were kept tightly closed.

It was on this first night of fall grappa making that Maria committed the crime which she hoped would drive Pietro from the sheds and induce him to other work. She and Pietro were playing cards at the kitchen table with Lucia and the sad-faced Ronato. Mister Tiff sat in a corner mending the giant umbrella Veet carried over the seat of his meat van. Lucia, warmed as were her companions by grappa fumes from the copper still on the stove and from the wine Pietro pressed upon them, spoke glowingly of the new store which a Willow Hollow Road couple had opened in their home. The new store owner had worked for years beside Pietro in the sheds.

Maria exclaimed, "His wife is a fortunate woman!" She lowered her eyes to hide the envy that brooded there. But Pietro had no need to look into her eyes. He knew that she was remembering the countless times she had begged him, "Let us have a store in our home, with a bell on the door that will tinkle when customers come in."

Why, she thought bitterly, why should Pietro be cursed with this ridiculous passion for stone, and why could she not make him see the need for finding other work? Her mind so thrummed with these familiar thoughts that she could not concentrate on the card game nor did she hear but snatches of the conversation, which drifted from one subject to another:

"There should be snow for deer hunting next month —"

"With the sanatorium at the top of the hill the taxes will probably be raised. But it should mean a fine sidewalk." And the *maestro's* chuckle, "Hah, if they are like the Ibena taxes, don't be too sure. Public money, like holy water, is dipped into by everyone."

Someone murmuring, "Eh, Ronato tells us, Pietro, that you are carving a beautiful memorial."

And Pietro's shy supplement, "The best these hands have ever made. Yet, if it were Ronato's work, I would consider it the least of his masterpieces."

Maria snapped to attention. Pietro was saying, "It is a cross, standing just so high." His stubby, calloused fingers indicated a height in the vicinity of his umbilicus. "And it is nearly smothered under vines. The best job I have yet undertaken, and it will be finished next week."

The best job — finished next week.

The words revolved in Maria's mind with the persistence of a catchy merry-go-round tune. Suddenly, their relationship to a former well-remembered threat of Pietro's fired them with potential significance. She well remembered the day when the stone-cutter Gateau had been threatened with dismissal if his hands again slipped carelessly to spoil the stone he was working. Better still she remembered Pietro's fervid, "If by accident my hand should sometime err, just let my boss give me hell. I would throw the job in his face, and quit."

The best job I have done — I would throw the job in his face and quit.

As clearly and as sweetly as an angelus calls laborers from their toil and bids them forget fatigue and defeat, so these words dispelled Maria's fruitless years of begging Pietro to leave the sheds. She must take matters into her own hands: *she must ruin that fine stone of Pietro's, make it appear a careless slip. The boss, Gerbatti, would fume and scold. And against such injustice Pietro would make good his threat.* . . .

Maria's mind was made up. From that moment she directed the evening's activities to the success of her plan. "More wine!" she urged her guests, and made sure to pour a brimming glass for Pietro, too. Ronato, watching Maria's face ripen a joyous red, murmured, "Your cheeks, Maria, are as happily red as that dress you wear."

At midnight, Lucia and Ronato were in mellow readiness to say their good nights, yet Maria detained them with a refilled pitcher of wine. Not until Pietro's words stumbled thickly one over the other and his cheeks bloomed a brick-red, did she close the door behind her visitors. And when Pietro's arm lay in leaden embrace around her waist and his deep breathing bespoke a half-drugged sleep, she rose from their bed, dressed quickly, supplied herself with flashlight and chisel, and stole from the house.

That plunge into chilly night air washed away some of the confidence she had enjoyed in the grappa-vaporized room. A palsied moment of indecision held her slippered feet to the porch. She looked right and left on Pastinetti Place, into the silent drama of darkened windows and deep shadows. In the harsh moonlight the Vitleau sanatorium site was a grotesquerie of exhumed maple roots, standing watch over their open graves. Maria's lips tightened derisively. She stepped resolutely across the granite chip walk and ran in quiet flight down the center of the dirt road.

Down Main Street, on the second block, a cluster of lunch-cart habituees was noisily inviting Officer Riley to a hot dog and coffee.

She breathed more easily after she had crossed the bridge and tracks to the shadows of Shed Row. A darkened car was parked beneath a sprawling river willow. In its interior a quartet of male and female voices woefully harmonized — "Show me the way to go home —" Maria gained the sheds and kept to their back yards. Under moonglow Maria's practical mind waxed fanciful. The weathered structures loomed gaunt specters. Strewn grout pieces lay on the ground like whiting bones. Here and there oblong blocks of stone became overturned tombstones. She looked defiantly at the moon. Her lips curled their scorn at its eerie attempt to weaken her determination: here beneath her feet was the harsh reality of granite chips; each step was a sharp reminder of what stone could do. . . .

The great front doors of Gerbatti's shed were strongly barred against her. She tried to raise one after another of the high, heavy windows and succeeded only in loosing thick showers of gray dust. She crept around the side to the smaller windows of the office. A wire ripped open her thumb. The muscles of her arms strained to aching agony before a window at last gave an inch. She explored the inside sill with her index finger, and discovered a bent spike holding the window secure. She poked at the spike with the chisel until she could turn it in its pocket and pull it.

The quartet's mournful voices drowned the creaking of the window. Maria climbed into the room. Her flashlight threw a circle of light on the floor and revealed dust-filled cracks between the floor boards. She reflected grimly that even Gerbatti, boss though he was, received his share of dust. A door opposite her opened into the dark wet room. It was cluttered with giant saws and polishing machines. Wet room, indeed! *Dio,* here was the earthy chill of some subterranean cave. And cloyed with it was a dank smell of rust and oil that constricted her body into a knot of shivers. What was it Pietro said? Ah, yes — the machinists hate water because it rusts their well-oiled machines; and the carvers detest oil because it stains the granite. Yet, in this machine room, water was truly needed. It had to be fed, she knew, in steady, cold streams to prevent the metal saws from melting as they heatedly cut into stone. Ah, if granite could thus torture metal, what, then, could it do to flesh and blood! But stone was not always the victor. Maria's mouth twisted into a sly, determined smile: stone could not reason, stone could not plot as did her brain. . . .

She pushed open another door to the drier, chalky air of the finishing room. And here she was blind to everything but Pietro's favorite corner where his little masterpiece stood under a stiff covering.

Maria wasted no time. She pulled off the tarpaulin, studied the granite cross dispassionately, and set the chisel point to a corner leaf design where a chip might appear to be a slip of Pietro's hand. With an iron bar she hammered at the chisel. The sound struck into the lofty room with a hollow, sepulchral note. Another blow. A small edge of the cross chipped off and fell to the dirt floor. Another blow. The leaf pattern dwindled to half a leaf. Another blow. Another.

She straightened breathlessly. Now that the deed was accomplished, its magnitude temporarily appalled her. Maria's hands trembled; her heart thrashed wildly against her ribs. And for the first time since she entered the spacious finishing room, she looked about her.

A half-dozen memorials stared back at her, stonily, ghastly in the moonlight. On the boxing platform three little markers plainly lettered — ALMA, GEORGE, and ALICE, held her fascinated eyes with their almost human accusation. She uttered a cry that was half prayer, half scorn. She shook her fist at them, and fled back to the office window, clambering out in such haste that when an outside wire caught at her skirt she tugged it away frantically, undismayed at the tear, only eager to put the river once more between herself and Shed Row.

It was not characteristic of Maria Dalli to stint a healthy sleep appetite with worries. Night, she reasoned, was for sleep. It was during the day that one should worry about getting rid of worries. Wasn't it foolishly inconsistent to nourish the body daily with good food, protect it with clothing, veer it from injuries — and at night to undo this good by punishing the body with wakefulness and by teasing a sensible brain into lunacy? And so it was tonight.

She crept noiselessly into the house. Once again beside the deeply breathing Pietro, she promptly fell into profound sleep. But asleep she was no longer mistress of her mind. Before the seven o'clock whistle could awaken her to reality, it became a shrill police call which gathered together hundreds of blue-coated police. They were marching toward her from the four corners of Granitetown. Hundreds of stern police eyes were riveted to her right hand which clutched a chisel and which was hacking away at the lifeless face of the man for whom Pietro was carving a cross. . . .

The sound of Pietro's voice came to her from a great distance. "Yours is a big head, too, this morning?" he was inquiring sympathetically. She heard the words even as she struggled to wakefulness. He sat in his nightshirt on the edge of the bed, tenderly massaging his forehead.

She murmured, "Big head?" It came to her, then, that he was referring to last evening, the grappa fumes, and the wine. She smiled ruefully. "*Si, si,* we were too generous with the wine last night."

As soon as Pietro and his dinner pail disappeared down Pastinetti Place she fed the children and sent them off to school. Mister Tiff left with them; this was the day for mending umbrellas on Willow Hollow Road. Maria did her housework automatically; mentally she was following Pietro step by step. *Now he enters the shed . . . he chats a moment with Ronato and his friends . . . now the shed whirrs with activity, everyone begins work. . . . Pietro draws the covering off his cross . . . he stares at it with disbelieving eyes . . . now comes Gerbatti. . . . Gerbatti gasps, he fumes and storms . . . the workmen gather around curiously . . . my poor Pietro is shamed before them. . . . "Go to hell!" he shouts to Gerbatti. "I*

quit!" . . . *and he walks out of the shed, never again to return.* . . .
This dreaming was balm to Maria's heart. She bustled about preparing his favorite dinner, for soon he would be home, dinner pail
and all. He would be saddened, perplexed, enraged. She must prepare a good dinner. He would enjoy *salsigi,* and a snappy salad of
endive, tomatoes, and onions.

Vetch and Petra ate their noonday meal and left again for
school. The *maestro,* she decided, must be at Lucia's table today.
But why didn't Pietro come home? Ah, well, he was no doubt
fine-combing Granitetown this minute for another job. *Si,* that was
it. He would find a job, work for a month or two while they
made plans for the little store they would have in their house. . . .

It was shortly after four when he came in, his round face thoughtful and his head bent, and she saw that in his preoccupation he
had neglected to slap the stone dust from his clothes. She knew
he must be grieving at leaving this work he loved, but she felt
little pity. *Dio,* if an infant were attracted to the color red, would
she not remove a red-hot poker from its reach even though the babe
screamed as if its heart were breaking? She waited in vain for
Pietro's, "Well, Maria, I did it. Today I quit the sheds." He muttered
only with his preoccupied air, "The days are getting too brisk for
only a kitchen fire." And in a few minutes she heard him in the
cellar cleaning the furnace.

After supper when the children were abed she thought: surely,
now he will speak. But he shrugged into his coat explaining
briefly, "I promised to help Rossi with his grappa tonight."

She consoled herself: Pietro is Pietro. He will say nothing until
he has found a new job. He does not want me to worry. *Si,* that
is it. . . .

She was alone in the kitchen darning socks when Mister Tiff
entered quietly, the golf bag drooping from a slumped shoulder.
He was hanging back with a strangely hesitant air, ill at ease,
uncertain. Despite the cold evening his high, pink forehead
glistened with perspiration. He handed her a small square of

red-and-white checked cambric. He spoke fast, as if to put an early end to this distasteful mission. "Last night you wore a skirt of this cloth, Maria; the skirt was whole and pretty. Last night in Gerbatti's shed, Pietro's stone was mutilated. This morning this piece of cloth waves accusation from a wire outside Gerbatti's office window. And this morning, I wager, your skirt is minus this little square of cloth — " He shook his head, sighed.

Maria stood speechless. Her fingers clenched the cambric square until her nails, cutting into her palm, smarted her to activity. Her voice was anxious, fierce. "Does Pietro know?"

He shook his head in silence.

"And Gerbatti?"

"No, no. I chanced to be walking the yard on my way to Willow Hollow Road. I saw the cloth — and I remembered." He finished compassionately, "Don't fear, I won't tell."

She gripped his arm in wild hope, and despair. "What happened, *Maestro?* What did Gerbatti say? What did Gerbatti do?"

"Do? Pietro did not tell you?" He was honestly amazed.

"Not one word has he spoken!"

"Nothing happened, Maria."

He felt the trembling of her hands before they fell limp from his arm.

"Gerbatti did not give him hell?" she said tonelessly. It couldn't be true. Her wretched deed in vain. . . . "Pietro did not rebel and — quit?"

The question was a plea. He understood. There might be thousands of wives who blessedly resigned themselves to the hazards of their husbands' work, but it had to be a deeply loving and deeply willful Maria who would try to take matters into her own hands. She was strong of mind and strong of heart; and although strength has its own joys and rewards, it is heir, too, to its own brand of pain. He asked, gruffly tender, "And why should Gerbatti give him hell, Maria? Anyone could see it was no accident. It was the intentional butchering of some malefactor. A beautifully worked stone — in ruin. Gerbatti respects Pietro's love for his work, he had only to see Pietro's stricken face to know he was innocent."

Her shoulders drooped. Her face shrank, beaten, white. Only her black eyes were defiantly burning against this defeat. He shifted awkwardly under their blaze, and he was thinking: if only Lucia could love the poor Ronato as Maria does Pietro. . . .

She whirled away from him. Never had anyone seen a tear glisten in Maria Dalli's eyes, nor would she let the *maestro* see one tonight.

He limped up the stairs after her, his heart fluttering with a great fear. If last night Maria, riding her crest of omnipotence, ruined a costly stone, what greater harm might she do on some tomorrow? And to remind her of what the stone cost Gerbatti would make little impression tonight on her stony mood of defeat.

The door to her bedroom was open. He began timidly, "May I speak to you, Maria?" She did not reply, and he continued, "Forgive me if I repeat what I have already told you — that sometimes for a man there is but one job at which he can be happy. I have seen Pietro at his work. It is as if he has two hearts: one that beats for you and his family, and one that beats for his work. Since the very beginnings of family, the husband's lot has always become the wife's. And justly so. Remember the wise Ruth who even made her mother-in-law's lot her own, when she said — 'Whither thou goest I will go.' And the Roman bride of antiquity formally promised her husband — 'Where thou art, Caius, there am I, Caia.' In the same measure your own promise 'for better or for worse' makes Pietro's lot your lot, and you must accept it if you would keep his love."

She had turned a rigid back on him and was staring, unseeing, through the window.

He gained courage in her silence. "Think how Pietro would feel if he knew his own wife had damaged his stone — "

Her voice carried assurance, and a trace of mockery. "He won't know — unless you tell him — and you won't do that,"

He said quietly, "You are right. I won't do that, Maria. But suppose God had not been so generous with you? Suppose Pietro himself had come upon that all-revealing piece of cloth? Me, I think it would mean the end of everything beautiful and honest between you. Hah, Maria, don't you know that a man is but an oversized boy, and he likes oversized compliments and flattery on the work that is near to his heart? And, instead of flattering him, you beg him to quit his work! *Dio mio,* haven't you known men as fine as your Pietro who have fled for comfort to the arms of other women?"

"Spare yourself the lecture, *Maestro,* Pietro never looks at other women."

Mister Tiff weighed the prudence of implanting a seed of doubt in her mind, but fearful of its catastrophic outcome in the hands of the willful Maria he reluctantly compromised with a — "No? No?"

He did not see the shadow creep into her face. And he turned away, nursing but little hope that he may have touched upon a vulnerable spot in Maria.

Alone, she crouched stiffly on the granite step beside the bed. She was not pondering the *Maestro's* exact words, but rather the poignant associations they stirred, and which now pummeled her, mind and heart. She, Pietro, and the children were happy. Except for her persistent fear for Pietro's health — they were happy. If Pietro ever learned that she had ruined his little masterpiece, how could they continue to love here with the oneness of spirit and body, and the sweet completion that had always been theirs.

The dismal failure of last night's trip to Gerbatti's shed was losing itself now in the vital urgency of preserving the happiness that was hers, Pietro's, and the children's. Her hands clenched over her knees. "God, please do not let Pietro find out."

BOOK II
1941

CHAPTER I

"Mister Tiff!"

The voice was that of Father Carty. His car had just drawn to a stop in front of the Dalli house, and now the priest's sturdy, black-clad figure was stepping with brisk grace across the sidewalk. Mister Tiff's salutation was restricted to an awkward nod of the head for he was in the act of mounting the Dalli porch steps: his right hand was curved to the knob of his cane, his left hand clung to the wooden rail and his teeth were gripping the strap of the umbrella-mending kit which dangled from his sloping left shoulder.

Mister Tiff freed his mouth of strap and asked amiably, "Hah, Father, what can I do for you?"

The round, serious face above the clerical collar flamed in warm discomfiture at the older man's abrupt plunge *in medias res,* but his words had the cadences of a chuckle as he demanded. "Now, how in tarnation did you know I was going to ask a favor of you?"

The older man's pale eyes twinkled. He shrugged slim shoulders. "The *Dio* knows I have not been sinning, that is — not very much. Therefore, you do not want to see me in the — professional way, no? Also, now that you are pastor, you are always too busy to stop for only idle talk."

Mister Tiff's mild blue eyes peered through bone-rimmed glasses to study the priest's face speculatively, and on sudden impulse they sped past him in a widely panoramic sweep, coming to rest at last on the hill above them. A few years ago, on such a May day as this, the old Vitleau pasture would have been a tapestry of chokecherry blossoms against the green tracery of new maple leaves. Today there was no Vitleau pasture. Instead there rose the imposing pile of the county sanatorium. A giant building honeycombed with long windows that were now catching the sunlight and were sparkling and blinking down over green lawns neatly bisected by shrubs and magnificent spruces. Mister Tiff's face was beaming, and it seemed to the priest that the man's great nose was fairly quivering, like a spirited dog scenting a trail. "I know, Father! You have been making your visits at the sanatorium and you find that old Salvatore wants someone to write a letter for him in Italian. . . ."

Father Carty's head, a faded replica of the flaming red-thatched head Mister Tiff had first known, shook. "No — "

" . . . or else Campestri has run out of his cut plug and wants some right away?" Mister Tiff hazarded less confidently.

The priest laughed. "I'm afraid you'll never guess." He observed that his friend's nose had ceased its quivering and had resigned itself to reluctant repose. "Our eighth graders are putting on a Dante-Beatrice scene at graduation. One of the girls recites a short poem in Italian. I wondered if you would be willing to check on the pronunciation."

"Sure, sure." Mister Tiff nodded further affirmation. "I will be glad to, Father."

The priest turned toward his car, but remembering that Mister Tiff's earlier reference to his distaste for idle talk had held a note of reproof, he cleared his throat and inquired pleasantly, "And what do you hear from the old country these days?"

"Nothing. Nothing these many weeks." He hesitated, and then spurted angrily as if the words had long been pounding for release, "It is that Mussolini!"

Father Carty said with all sincerity, "It is a pity that we cannot root out all of a man's evil tendencies and leave only the good. A fellow priest, a good friend of mine who has been studying in Rome, tells me of the fine roads Mussolini has built in Italy and of the improvements in the rural and slum sections."

The other man's white head bent in agreement. With Hitler ruthlessly occupying the weaker countries of Europe, with Mussolini preening hopefully at his feet, the threat of war was a dragnet drawing tightly even around the United States, and the thought hung like a pall on the heart of Mister Tiff who loved both his native land and his adopted country. The old teacher was well aware of the fact that hundreds of others in Granitetown felt as he — Italian granite workers, and a few Germans, who led hard-working lives. No open hostility existed in Granitetown toward these workers of foreign blood, yet how could they but feel shame that their homelands had nurtured the monsters who were selfishly leading the world into another war?

It was with this painful shame of his *paesani* in mind that Mister Tiff dropped to the ground the golf bag bulging with umbrella ribs and suddenly wagged a finger before Father Carty's unsuspecting face. "See what the lack of prudence did to Mussolini! As long as he worked only for the welfare of his people he was all right. If he had gone on — in prudence — to work for the people — all right! But no, he has to blow prudence to the four winds!"

The priest was reminded with a start that somehow, sometime, he had already lived a fragment of this moment. Suddenly he recalled it — it was the doubtful lecture in prudence which Mister Tiff had delivered to him his first year in Granitetown. Time, the priest was reflecting, had generously dug but few inroads in the older man's appearance. He was more frail looking and his shoulders perhaps sloped a bit more than in those early years. The vision of the mild blue eyes was aided, these days, by bone-rimmed glasses. The old man kept his sparse white hair combed back flat to his skull. In the absence of the softening frame of silky, wayward hair, his bony nose with its great mole leaped into prominence and gave him an air of hawk-nosed benignity. The finely textured, almost transparent, skin adhered in tight economy to the bones of his face. The priest was abruptly shaken from this reverie by Mister Tiff's now mournful voice.

"They will not take their lessons from history, these leaders. Always what has destroyed them has been power — or women. But to be sure, each of them, within the realm of prudence, is a delight, no? That blustering pouter pigeon Napoleon, what did lust for power do for him?" he demanded. "And what kept the lovelorn Antony to the Nile? Cleopatra, yes? Pah!" Two spots of angry red were growing into the waxy whiteness of the old man's cheeks. "Me, I have what you call my own private bone to gnaw with this Mussolini. He has destroyed one of my greatest joys — he has spoiled the fine conversation-by-mail which my friend, Count Mattzo, and I have enjoyed for years."

"Thousands of others are not receiving letters from their home-lands these days," the priest reminded gently.

"That is not what I mean," Mister Tiff replied pettishly. "It is the *tone* of the letters that was spoiled, and it was spoiled long before letters stopped coming across the ocean." He blinked through his glasses at the perplexity graven on the priest's face. "Look," he explained, "I have a sister Mafalda who is three or four years younger than I am. Well, a number of months ago I received a short, short letter from her. In it she says only that she is going to marry my old friend, Count Mattzo. Nothing else she says. Nothing." Mister Tiff hesitated. He could not tell this priest that he remembered that disgraceful, gloating note verbatim. *"Well, brother,"* it had said, *"little did you dream when you used to sample the luxuries of Count Mattzo's home that your poor sister Mafalda, in her later years, would possess them to the full. Yes, it seems that your sister has done better than her ocean-crossing brother — next week the count and I are to be married."*

Father Carty cleared his throat.

Mr. Tiff muttered again, "Nothing else did she say."

Father Carty murmured briskly, "Well, now, that shouldn't worry you. The fact that they are not in their twenties does not mean that they shouldn't marry. It will mean companionship for both."

"Pah, it is not their age that bothers me. Let me finish my story," Mister Tiff added testily. "What do I do? I put aside my sister's letter, and I pick up the fat one that has just come from Count Mattzo. I say to myself, 'Here, now, is what I am looking for!' But I am wrong. Very wrong. The first three pages are full of the anticipated tribulations of our Italy under that Fascist upstart. Then comes the fourth page — it groans with the inconveniences the count must suffer, all because he does not co-operate with the Fascisti. You see," explained Mr. Tiff, "the count had said 'no' to the 'privilege' of allowing the profile of Mussolini to be painted on one of the Mattzo-owned ledges near Ibena. For that insult he must pay dearly. What happens? Right away the count finds himself without the services of a housekeeper, without a cook, without a gardener! For the count these equal tragedy; for he is accustomed to the luxuries of life. He hires a new staff. In three days they resign. Another staff comes. These three also resign. It is after the fourth page of these lamentations that the count adds this miserably modest paragraph, *'Perhaps it will surprise you to learn that in my sixty-seventh year I am at last planning marriage. Of late I have become better acquainted with your sister Mafalda, and we have decided to marry. It pleases me, dear friend, that you and I will now be bound by the added closeness of family ties.'* " The older man paused, awaiting the soft sounds of clerical sympathy. Finally convinced that none was forthcoming, he blurted, "Don't you see, Father? Not one word did my sister write of the affection, or even esteem, she felt for this man she was to marry. And the same for the count. Did he marry Mafalda to earn himself a housekeeper and cook? And I ask myself, can this disgusting change in one of the finest men in the world be laid to the door of Fascism? To Mussolini?"

Father Carty's eyes were drawn to the bright red disks in the little man's cheeks. He decided that never before had he seen such a display of anger and hurt in the usually calm features. There was not much of consolation he could offer in the matter, and so he said, "Your correspondence with the count must have meant a great deal to you."

"Of course!" the old man snapped. "We were —" he groped futilely for the desired English word, "We were what we call *simpatici*, and the letters were a joy. But the postnuptial letters! Dehydrated scraps of paper, squeezed dry of character. Each paragraph begins, 'Mafalda says' or 'Mafalda thinks' or 'Mafalda has decided.' And so, then, I cannot stop my heart from stripping my own letters, too; and they become duty letters. I write only the news: that the Dallis added a new bedroom and that now I have a room of my own; that the house has been painted white and boasts a picket fence; that Pietro and Ronato now own a small stone shed; that Vetch is a quarryman and is married to the daughter of a policeman; that Petra is a nurse; that Lucia's son, Gino, has become a doctor; that a fine sanatorium has been built on the hill above us; and that our street is now Pleasant Street instead of Pastinetti Place. All these pieces of news I wrote, and the letters became a pipe line for facts, like the great *AP* — and just as impersonal."

The priest suggested, "When conditions in Europe have improved, when the private lives of men and women are not harassed by invasions and threats of war, perhaps the count's letters will once more become the joy they used to be."

"No, no." It was on the tip of Mister Tiff's tongue to announce that knowing Mafalda he was certain her influence over the count would never weaken, and he blushed a shamed scarlet at the

thought of so belittling his sister to another. Unbidden there came
to him that fascinating first word he had learned in Granitetown,
and now mentally he said "scram" to the ungraciousness he was
harboring against Mafalda. He made much of consulting his watch
which he drew from his pocket. When his face lifted again to
the priest, all signs of anger and pettishness were gone, and the
mild blue eyes even held a hint of roguishness. "I have wasted your
time with this idle talk, yes? Well, Father, I must hurry — it is
time for my transformation." If he had expected his last statement
to evoke a direct question or at least an expression of puzzlement, he
was disappointed. The sober eyes looking into his revealed only
a quick wariness and the black-clothed figure was already turning
away, retreating from further verbal entrapment. Despite this
seeming lack of curiosity, Mister Tiff rubbed a forefinger against
the mole on his nose, and proceeded to grant the unsolicited explanation. "One afternoon a week I am truly transformed. I drop
these comfortable clothes of the umbrella mender, and I put on
the new navy blue serge suit and the stiff white collar, and I go
forth to teach Italian to six of the *paesani's* grandchildren. It proves
the old saying, no? 'Once a teacher, always a teacher.' " Having thus
briefly discussed the weekly sartorial metamorphosis, he took leave
of the priest and limped slowly into the house and up to his room.

He dressed in front of the old bureau he and Vetch had once
shared. On the marble top, on a tricolored crocheted doily Maria
had made, stood the miniature St. Michael. In half an hour he was
neatly clothed in the serge suit. The stiffly starched collar encouraged a pronounced elevation of his chin, a discomfort he willingly
suffered because Petra insisted it gave him an air of distinction.
As a final touch to his toilet he put his hand under the cold-water
faucet and smoothed the wispy ends of his mustache into two thin,
white walrus points. He whistled as he labored down the stairs.

In the kitchen Maria, her hair whiting in slender strands, was
picking over dandelion greens for supper. She sat with her back

to the window, and Mister Tiff knew it was an habitual act of both defiance and weakness: she did not want to look out upon the sanatorium.

Maria's heart still harbored a fear against granite, but she kept it locked within herself. Not once, since that night many years ago when she had destroyed Pietro's little masterpiece, had she voiced her bitterness aloud. No one but she and perhaps Mister Tiff, who sensed the machinations of Maria's willful mind, knew that long ago in frantic prayer that Pietro might not discover her crime, she had promised never more to interfere with Pietro's love for cutting stone. Pietro and Ronato had left the Gerbatti shed to open a manufacturing plant of their own at the time when all Vermont granite sheds and quarries were compelled to install suction hoses and dust-removing equipment. A grateful Maria whispered a prayer each night for those men who had put into effect this law which would lessen the occupational hazards of stonecutters and would also lessen the dread of hundreds of stonecutters' families. To Mister Tiff she had marveled, "It is something of a miracle, *Maestro,* yes? For years I have begged the *Dio* to take Pietro from that dangerous work of the sheds; it never occurred to me to pray that the dangers of the work be lessened! Now here He is, in His own way, satisfying both Pietro and myself. For in freeing the sheds of dust He is certainly putting His stamp of approval on the work Pietro loves, and at the same time He is dwarfing my fears for Pietro's health. . . ."

"How incomprehensible are His judgments and how unsearchable His ways," quoted Mister Tiff humbly. He was thinking back to those first months in Granitetown and how his prayers — that he might not be forced to return to Italy — had been answered strangely indeed when Josie Blaine helped herself to a good slice of the *paesani's* purse. She had not returned the money nor had she again made her appearance in Granitetown.

Maria had spoken in the silence, her words evoking common sense and resignation. "This dust-removing equipment that is being installed — it will benefit the young people who work granite. It will help Vetch in the quarries, and young Robbie Marclay in the sheds; they are young, strong. But for the older devils who have been eating stone dust for a dozen years, this improvement has come too late. . . ."

The Dalli and Ronato shed, modestly small beside the larger Gerbatti plant, vibrated with the roar of Memorial Day production.

Ronato's slender, sinewy hands were putting the finishing touches to a resurrected Christ carved into the semicircular back rest of a massive granite exedra. In the drafting of the design Pietro had spoken longingly of intricate, rococo carvings on either side of the Christ, but Ronato had swallowed his shudders and insisted that the beautiful Christ would appear to better advantage against a bare background. And Pietro had finally submitted to the superior artistry that was Ronato's. In a few days two of these stone benches with their message of soul eternity would flank the entrance to Granitetown's Catholic cemetery. Ronato's melancholy face smiled sparingly at Pietro. He inclined his head toward a lumbering figure engaged in throwing open the shed doors. "See, Pietro. Daily it is Tony who bathes us in fresh air."

Pietro nodded. *Si*, it was big Tony Botelli's broad hands that were jerking open the dusty doors and admitting the sunshine, just as he had been accustomed to do when the three of them had worked together long ago. A few years ago the sheds had been a thick haze of stone dust. A tangible haze. And eyes could not penetrate its substance to the windows in the far wall. Those days, the opening of the great doors was truly an occasion. Fresh air poured into the shed. Dust particles scattered and thinned. And in shafts of intense sunlight the minute specks were seen progressing outward. Relief stirred the breasts of the stonecutters. They gulped this clearer air as if it were simon pure. But today, Pietro reflected, the opening of the doors hardly produced such spectacular results. All because a few years ago Granitetown shed and quarry owners were ordered: "Install dust-removing equipment. Put in suction hoses to protect your workers."

As Tony Botelli was throwing open the shed doors this May afternoon, Pietro was granting the wisdom of Maria's words. A faint tickling was starting in his lungs. A tickling familiar now daily for many weeks. Its beginnings were as exhilarating as the light touch of a feather on the palm of the foot. It excited the senses. But with lightning speed it grew to an irrepressible, gnawing torture. In a moment, in spite of himself, the stubborn lungs would convulse to obtain relief in coughing. Beside him Ronato would hear. Tony would hear. Pietro's trembling hands laid down the pneumatic tool. He ground his teeth in an attempt to choke back the cough. He held his throat muscles taut; the veins swelled hot under the strain; he knew that his face was sweated and crimson. He lumbered past the raptly employed Ronato, blindly pushing aside big Tony Botelli.

Tony muttered, "Did you see him, Ronato? *Dio*, red and puffed up he is, ready to explode! Every day now Pietro races to the toilet. Is it something Maria feeds him, or . . . " He left the unfinished question trembling its suggestion in mid-air. And Ronato, interpreting correctly the eloquence of the unspoken words, shrugged his shoulders and murmured, " — or something that has been preying on his mind of late?"

Within the lavatory walls Pietro gave his lungs free rein. The cough split violently from relaxed throat muscles. A shattering, rending cough. Like the shuddering din of the shed, he thought. When the spasm had worn itself quiet, he sat down exhausted. He was reluctant to join his fellow workers lest they detect the ravages of that cough. Decision came simply: he must see a doctor, soon. Today.

It was not as if this hour was unexpected. Almost everyone of the older stonecutters envisioned it, and with dread, even though he managed to thrust it into the dim realms of a distant future. And perhaps Pietro's fears were unfounded. Perhaps these spasms were but the lingering aftereffects of the cold he had contracted earlier in the spring. *Si,* that must be it. For did he not have a good appetite? Had not his plump figure held to its roundness? True, he tired in the middle of the day's work. But, *Dio,* he was not as young as he used to be. And if sickness were really upon him would not the critical nurse's eyes of the grown Petra have detected it? And the ever watchful Maria? Maria! He groaned. How could he face Maria, who had feared this hour ever since he started work in the sheds? Ah, he would not have to tell her, for the doctor would surely assure him, "Your cold has lingered stubbornly, Mr. Dalli. Take this cough syrup, one tablespoonful every two hours. . . ." *Si,* that was it.

Today, after four o'clock, he was to meet Vetch and Petra, and with them select a watch for Americo who was graduating from high school next month. For this occasion Pietro had taken his Sunday suit to the shed and left it in the office for a quick change at four. He would not have to walk into the doctor's office in his dusty work clothes.

Robbie Marclay, who was both office bookkeeper and cutter for the shed, appraised the neatly clad Pietro with a grin. "Going to a wedding, Mr. Dalli?"

Pietro worked his face into a smile. "Something like."

On Main Street he became painfully conscious of his Sunday suit. He hoped none of his friends would see him entering a doctor's office at two o'clock of a workday. Would they immediately guess? On sudden impulse he hailed the Montpelier-bound bus, but as he stepped into it he remembered that today Gino Tosti was opening an office with old Doctor Renaud in Granitetown. In his mental agitation he had almost forgotten. How proud Lucia must be! He stepped back down to the curb, waving the bus onward. He crossed the street. His eyes caught the play of sunlight on a white placard in a window over the bank. ALBERT RENAUD, M.D., AND GINO TOSTI, M.D., it said. Pietro's heart thumped. He climbed the flight of stairs to Gino's office with reluctant, measured tread.

An immense bowl of red carnations made a splash of radiance in the center of the waiting room. On the edge of the table lay the *maestro's* cane, and the Sunday hat he wore to his Italian classes. It meant that the *maestro* was paying Gino a visit. The old man's voice, of a quavering timber, trickled in from the adjoining room, "It seems only yesterday that you were a barefooted boy insisting, 'I'm going to be a doctor someday.' " Pietro gave a sigh of relief. The *maestro* was simply paying a welcome visit to Gino, and why could he not pretend that he was doing the same.

Pietro walked in upon them. He clasped Gino's hand. "A big day for you, boy! And may you be a success." Despite himself, his own worries were sizing his sincerity into something stiff, ironic. Today Gino was stepping onto the threshold of his career; and here was Pietro, to be told perhaps by this same youth that his career was ending. He truly wished the boy success. He had struggled eight years for this beginning. A scholarship to the state university had helped. And summer vacations the boy had jobs in the quarries to pay the balance of the tuition. *Dio,* yes, Lucia's son deserved success.

The *maestro,* he saw, was exclaiming over the powers of the new X-ray machine installed by Dr. Renaud.

"It sees into you," Gino was saying in Mister Tiff's native tongue, though he suspected that the old man knew almost as much about the machine as he did. "If you break your arm, the ray will photograph the bone. It will picture whether it is a clean break, or shattered. It shows the doctor where the damage has been done and how bad it is. If there is tuberculosis we change the amount of exposure and the X ray will picture the spots on the lungs, and show to what extent they are consuming the tissue."

Mister Tiff stroked his beak of a nose. "Omnivision, eh, Pietro?" He added dryly, "I need no photograph to show me that my old legs have seen their best days. I have but to walk two blocks. . . ."

Pietro scarcely heard him. His suddenly icy fingers trembled over the metal X-ray table. Had many of his long-departed fellow

workers and this Gino's father once stood, as he now was, fear-
fully aquiver to learn the verdict of this metal wizard? No wonder
the stonecutters shied from these cold, heartless machines, even
though they were urged to have periodic and free pictures of
their lungs.

When the *maestro* finally limped toward the waiting room, Pietro
shook his head. "Go along without me, *Maestro*. I must meet some
friends soon — this is a good place to await them, if Gino will
let me."

For long, heavy moments he moved about the rooms, an auto-
maton. He put a numb finger to Gino's shining equipment. He
nodded feigned enthusiasm to Gino's eager explanations. *He was
alone with Gino.* There was opportunity now to tell him his fears.
The words would not come. He was ashamed to suggest to Gino
that his strong body might be breaking. He was startled by the
discovery that Gino had long ago ceased talking and that his
eyes were studying him curiously. Pietro's fingers jerked underneath his collar, easing out the sudden tightness. He must say
something! Anything to end this ponderous silence between them.
It weighted his chest. It would excite him to one of those fits of
coughing.

"Ho!" The inanity popped from his throat. "Ho, Vetch has not
come up yet to see your office?"

"He'll come."

"Nor Petra?"

Pietro sighed. What further emptiness to be said? "Look, boy, I
did not come up here only to look at your office. I — I — "

Gino's sober face broke into a gentle smile. Old Dalli was having
a difficult time; he was no doubt adopting the role of father today,
to congratulate and advise his old friend's son. . . .

"I know," he encouraged. "You want to have a talk — "

"*Si, Si,* boy — " He hesitated, swallowed painfully and whispered,
"The truth is, I want a picture — "

"Picture?" in Gino's bewildered mind there flashed a snapshot of himself in doctor's white, with Pietro standing proudly beside him.

Pietro's hand shot out stiffly to the X-ray machine, the other to his chest. "The lungs. A picture of the lungs."

Again painful silence.

Gino's hand darted toward Pietro and quickly withdrew. Vetch's father, he knew, was one of the stonecutters who had consistently scoffed at the suggestion of periodic X rays, and he would not be here today unless he had reason to believe there was something wrong with his lungs. For a long time Gino had looked forward to his first Granitetown case, wondering who it would be, and what the nature. Here it was: *Pietro Dalli, stonecutter.* Fate was wheeling after Gino with Ixion persistence. His own father's death had seeded in him the determination to become a doctor; and now here was Pietro Dalli, another stonecutter, fated to be the first fruit of that germination. Where was the poise, the easy air of mutual confidence he had planned in his dealings with his patients? He managed to say steadily, lightly, "Sure, we'll take a look, we'll take a picture."

Questions again. Numberless ones. And Pietro jested wryly in Italian. "Questions in a doctor's office belong in the category with taxes and death, yes? They are unavoidable." He suffered Gino to count his pulse. To look at his tongue. Try his temperature. Put him on the scales. Measure his back. Palpate his chest. Listen to his heart. Take a urine specimen. And, finally, to ask him to cough gently and to eject the raised sputum into a small glass container. Even the X ray, it seemed, did not want to give an immediate answer.

Pietro stuffed himself awkwardly into his clothes.

"We'll see the picture in a few days," Gino said. "Then we'll know. We can't judge today, because it isn't right to judge from a wet film. I must send the sputum to the Burlington laboratory. They will study it, they will tell us the truth."

"Look, boy," Pietro pleaded shyly, "let us say nothing to Petra, Vetch, or my wife, eh? Not until we are certain, eh?"

Though, *Dio*, was not the stark certainty staring him sadly from Gino's dark eyes! "I will be careful," he added, anticipating Gino's advice to protect his family. "To Maria I will say I have strained my back at the shed, and that I must sleep alone. To convince her, I shall rub a strong liniment on my back, I shall have a private towel always." He hesitated briefly; it was a plea. "I — I should continue at the shed, yes? Until we know for sure?"

Gino's white-clad shoulders shrugged almost imperceptibly. "That's up to you." Stonecutters were all the same. Men against granite. They hated to admit defeat. He turned abruptly to the window, hiding the young perplexity in his face. He heard himself ask, even though he knew what the answer would be. "Why didn't you find other work when you were younger?" His voice carried accusation. He was thinking of Pietro's family. How each would crumple under this blow.

"I like the work." The older man's words were spoken with biblical simplicity. "I like stone." But because Gino wore the look of one who has received only half an answer, and that an unsatisfactory one, he continued, "Those first years in Granitetown I did not believe all this talk of stonecutters' sickness. You see, boy, in the old country the sheds were open to the air. And the stone was softer — there was less danger. I could not believe it would be different here. Then I began to see one *paesan* become sick. And another. It was the same with the Irish workers and the Scotch — all of them." Despite himself, he chuckled, "There were no favorites. Then I began to believe. Maria, all the time she begged, 'Quit the shed, let us have a store, Pietro.' But — I always put it off. The children, you know. They come one after another, four of them. I told Maria it would be foolish to take work that paid less. And when the children grew up — then, truly, I had no excuse. But then the sheds were ordered to install the dust-removing equipment. Even Maria has not complained these last years."

Gino was transported to his childhood, when Vetch and Denny labored in a miniature quarry. "You and Vetch, you both like stone. I can't see *why* you do. So help me, God, I can't see why!"

"You have to cut it to know. It is hard stone. Beautiful. Lasting. Always when I carve a name on a memorial, I feel, well, important." A half-smile wiped the earlier fear from Pietro's face. It was as if, for a moment, he had forgotten the grim reason for this visit to Gino's office. "I carve the name and I say to myself, 'From up there in heaven the *Dio* creates new life; and when He sees fit to take it away, then we stonecutters on earth take up where He left off. We take up the chisel, we carve the name, we make a memory of that life. Almost, boy, it is being like — like — "

In Gino's mind tiptoed a sentence from an old mythology book: *On Olympus lived the greater gods; and below, the lesser.* He nodded to Pietro, understanding him, and he murmured quietly — "like lesser gods."

"There she goes, boys! Whistle!"

A shrill signal rent the Douglas quarry. Quarriers at the west wall shambled from their labor to the east corner. Opposite them, a mammoth, newly quarried block of granite stirred slowly under derrick power. It lurched, then swung clear of its rock bed, rising slow and sure to the quarry's rim.

Vetch Dalli watched from a low shelf in the east wall. His overalled legs were planted wide apart; his eyes held spellbound to the swinging block. He had seen numberless blocks uprooted from their solid stone beds, yet each time there rose that exhilarated catch in his throat as he watched the stone taken to the upper world, dislodged at last from the resting place it had known for thousands of years.

"Baby!" he exclaimed. "She's the biggest we've taken out!"

The stubby, middle-aged Balideau beside him grunted disinterest. The older man, nicknamed Baldy, removed goggles from his puffy eyes. Leaning back against his drill he put one finger to his left nostril, then on second thought, dug a handkerchief from his pocket, and blew vigorously into it. "What the hell's the difference?" he muttered. "We get paid by the hour, not by the size of the stone."

Vetch's eyes left the block and came to dwell on Baldy. There was a rumor that not once had Baldy visited a bedridden fellow worker so great was his fear of stone dust and sickness.

A mischievous grin lifted the usual droop of Vetch's lids. On quick impulse his lusty voice rang out an almost forgotten parody of childhood, and he sang to the tune of *You're in the Army Now*:

"You're diggin' a tombstone now,
You might as well take your bow,
This old stone hole
Will take its toll,
You're diggin' a tombstone now."

He rammed his fists into his pockets and laughed uproariously at the soundless writhing of Baldy's loose lips. The quarrier's face was pasty with anger; but eclipsing it was a cold, baleful dislike of Vetch. He shot resentful looks at the smirking faces of near-by quarrymen. His gloved hand clutched the foreman. "By damn, have I got to listen to his dirty mouth all day?"

The foreman shrugged. He offered indifferently, "Ah, quit it, Dalli, will you?"

Vetch grinned amiably. He sank cross-legged to the stone shelf watching the huge monolith being hoisted over the quarry brim, then he went back to his job of channeling an oblong block. He whistled the tune through his teeth, aware of Baldy's glaring eyes. The man was surely afraid of stone dust. There he was hugging the suction hose close to his work. He slapped dust from his pants at regular intervals. He blew his nose. He cleared his throat every few minutes. It was unusual in these days of dust-removing equipment to see a quarrier displaying his feelings so openly.

A foreign shadow was breaking into the sun pattern on the quarry wall. Vetch looked overhead. The great metal grout bucket was being lowered. It carried two men — the yard foreman and a stranger. A sight-seer, no doubt. Someone who rated. Every visitor wasn't granted this thrill of being lowered to the deep stone floor in the bucket. Something vaguely familiar in the slight slope of the stranger's shoulders, and in the easy, graceful poise of the blond head held Vetch's eyes. The staccato report of drills deadened the cry, "Vetch! Vetch!" But a moment later Vetch, with a quickened heartbeat, recognized the light-haired man. He set the channel bar against the wall, and vaulted a slab of grout to meet the approaching newcomer. "Denny! Denny Douglas, you son-of-a-gun!"

"Vetch!"

Their gloved hands gripped warmly. Denny's in fine pigskin. Vetch's in grimy, tattered canvas.

"It's five, six years since I've seen you, Denny! It's *that* long since you've been in the pit!"

"How have you been?" The question rushed simultaneously from the mouth of each, and suddenly they laughed together like awkward schoolboys, and left the question unanswered.

"You're here." Denny's hand indicated the vast amphitheater of stone. "It's what you always wanted, remember?"

"I still want it! I got it!" Vetch stopped, a crimson pool eddying in each weather-browned cheek. Did it sound like gloating to Denny? Denny in his fine leather gloves had *not* got what he wanted. The mighty Douglases were closemouthed people; and Denny, strangely, had chosen not to write to his childhood friends these last years, except for a few brief, infrequent notes to Petra. However, the rumored story indicated that Denny's wish to study carving immediately following graduation from high school had been effectively frustrated by his parents. He completed his courses at Norwich University. Once independent of the family, Denny disappeared. Fragments of stories related that he was at last at his beloved carving and sculpturing in one of the mid-western granite states. At any rate, Vetch had one afternoon picked up an art magazine in the quarry office, and during a halfhearted flipping of pages had come upon a photograph of a beautifully carved miniature Pan, with the caption, "Work of Dennis Douglas." Denny had always liked the delicate work of miniatures. A month later, at Christmas, Petra received a card saying that a bad break at the wrist of his right hand had left his fingers weakened, and he was temporarily teaching in a high school. That was a year ago. Vetch's eyes traveled to Denny's right hand. Sheathed though it was in its expensive glove, it wore a slightly effete air.

Against these thoughts, Vetch said brightly, "I'm married, Denny. I've got a copper for a father-in-law."

"Freckle-faced Peggy Riley, I bet. I'm not surprised." He smiled, remembering the young, quiet Peggy of earlier years.

"We're having a baby in the fall. Irish-Italian. Mister Tiff swears there couldn't be a better blood combination."

An eagerness enriched Denny's tone as he inquired for the old man. Petra's notes, as infrequent as his own, had informed him that Mister Tiff was still at the Dalli's. It would have saddened him to return to his home town and to find such a familiar landmark removed. For a moment he was lost in the past, and he did not hear Vetch's question until it was repeated.

"How long will I be here? I don't know. It may be more than a visit. My father's heart, you know. The doctors say he needs a rest. He left yesterday for the south. I'm staying on indefinitely — sort of pinch-hitting for him."

Vetch tore open a pack of cigarettes. Old Douglas hadn't bothered to tell his workmen he was going away. They were just workmen. . . . His lips bit hard around the cigarette, trying to hold down this ridiculous resentment against the moneyed social order above him. He had no right to feel this way, he knew. Old Douglas was a square shooter. Hell, wasn't he always trying to better conditions in the quarry? Yet the resentment persisted. He recalled that much as he had liked Denny in his childhood, he could never feel his equal until Denny stripped off his shoes and let his toes wriggle naked in the grass, like his own. "I'm envious," he decided. And he did not like the thought.

Denny's sensitive face was wincing under the inferno of quarry noises. "Let's get out of here where we can talk."

Vetch hesitated.

"It's almost four — the whistle'll blow in fifteen minutes."

Denny opened his mouth to say, "I'm a boss now, Vetch; take fifteen minutes off." But Vetch, as if anticipating this suggestion, was doggedly retracing his steps to his work. He paused to call, "Petra ought to be up in the yard in a few minutes. We're meeting the old gent after four to pick out a graduation present for my kid brother, Americo. Come along with us, you'll want to see Gino anyway." He was about to add, "He finally got what he dreamed about, too," but he said instead, "He's hanging his shingle in the office window over the bank today."

He could not resist a glance of admiration after Denny's retreating figure. The slim, loose-jointed body towered over Vetch's by a good two inches. He wondered if his own wiry, compact body could carry those expensive tweeds with the careless grace and ease that was Denny's. He wished suddenly, with a humorous twist of his mouth, he had gone up to the yard with Denny to witness his meeting with Petra. The Petra-Gino-Denny triangle had afforded him silent amusement back in high school days. Gino and Denny — always close friends and reluctant to displease the other — had invariably taken turns escorting her to school dances and games. The boys were graduated before Petra and they went off to their respective colleges. And Petra, two years later, studied in a nurses' training school forty miles away. Each was absorbed in his own studies to the exclusion of anything but a sporadic correspondence; and since Denny had never returned to Granitetown, Gino might have been, these later summer vacations, Petra's frequent escort. But Gino, Vetch reflected quizzically, followed his own code: care for Petra though he might, his first obligation was to his schooling which he and his mother earned in sweat. He had no money for dates. And to ask Petra to wait eight years — was not Gino. Vetch pushed back his helmet. He wondered what would happen now that Gino was established locally in his profession, and Denny was in town.

The girl parked the '39 Ford coupe in the quarry yard. Idly she noted the progress of the grout bucket and its cargo as the derrick lifted it neatly over the lip of the quarry. Distance poorly defined the tall stranger. Before the second of recognition there rose in her consciousness an acute awareness of having lived similar moments at some other time — moments when she had watched a blond head, uplifted in silence toward blue skies. The moment fled as swiftly as it had come. And she saw that he was Denny. Her slim, white-uniformed figure wove swiftly among the workmen's cars. Brown, shoulder-length hair lifted in the breeze.

"Denny Douglas!" she called.

"Petra!"

He stared at her. Surely he must have remembered her hair to be this light, silky brown, and her skin this pale gold. Following the supple movements of her body, he sensed that she was both as strong and as delicately wrought as a chalice by Cellini.

"It's about time you paid us a visit," she was saying matter-of-factly.

Her gray-green eyes were enveloping him in a happy serenity, and he found himself nodding agreement, reluctant to admit that if his father hadn't become ill he might have been too stiff necked a fool to return now to Granitetown.

He argued silently with himself that he might have come back long ago if his father and mother had been in sympathy with his wish to make carving his lifework. But how could a son accept the roof of those he loved if he persisted in a line of work that displeased them? After his university days he had lived his own life away from home. The money left to him by Grandfather Douglas had rendered this step easy. After five lonely and sterile months in downtown New York, he eagerly accepted an invitation to share a Village studio-apartment with a struggling Armenian sculptor, and within a week was regretting this move. The immediate neighborhood was the poorest of media for a serious creative worker. It nurtured a garrulous and gregarious group of pseudo artists who aired their projected masterpieces vocally day and night, but who seldom managed to put their art into tangibility. Disillusioned, he packed his bags and drove to one of the midwestern granite-producing states, hoping that here, in an atmosphere that must carry a breath of Granitetown, he could do satisfactory work. Three years later, Denny admitted to himself that he was but a mediocre success. Nothing more. He had always worked with an eye for fine detail, and the results were good. But *good*, he told himself in painful honesty, was not enough. The successful carver and sculptor of miniatures had to be more than *good*. Realization of his limitations and the knowledge that his carving would never obtain the heights of his dreams saddened, rather than embittered, him. In moods of frustration, his mind fashioned a miniature masterpiece but his hands turned out only a good job; he knew that for himself, whether his work was brilliant or just *good*, he would have to satisfy this inborn and perpetual desire to carve. When a bad break at his right wrist kept him from his work, it was not with too heavy a heart that he turned to teaching in the local high school.

His father's letter, suggesting that he "come and keep an eye on the quarry while I go south," arrived on the last day of school, and it was almost with a sense of relief that Denny decided to go back to Granitetown.

He awoke from his fleet dream of the past to hear Petra's "Denny, I've asked you two questions — you've ignored them both, and you've been staring —"

"I was thinking —"

"— right through me, without seeing me. It's not very flattering."

He was so penitent in his embarrassment that she laughingly added, "I've a hunch you were indulging again in the 'guessing games' we used to have with Mister Tiff."

Vetch, living the idyl of his own recent courtship and marriage, would have been disappointed had he witnessed this meeting of Petra and Denny at the mouth of the quarry. For the two, in the warmth of their earlier friendship, simply picked up the threads dropped those few years back when a fundamental harmony had flowed between them. A half hour later, Petra and Denny, with Vetch, trooped into Gino's office.

Vetch was not surprised to see his father sitting there, his lips clamped around a stump of a stogie. To be sure he had promised to meet them downstairs, but wasn't it natural that his father should take a few minutes to look at Gino's new office?

"You beat us to it, Pa!" Vetch said.

CHAPTER II

It was a sun-lashed afternoon of blue sky and lazily moving, ragged clouds.

Pietro was called to the phone in his shed office, and he heard Gino's crisply warm voice ask, "Can you come to the office today, after three?"

Pietro nodded his head at the phone, and words would not come.

The tense knotting together of body and soul that had bound him all week broke now under those few words of Gino. A pulse hammered under his brow. It repercussed in arms, limbs, abdomen, until he was a quivering, throbbing hulk; and he seemed acutely aware, as never before, of the delineations of his plump body. Instinctively, as if to prevent his body from beating into fragments, he steeled himself, and his hand tightened to the phone. Gino's voice had seemed light, not unhappy. Could it be that the X ray pictured good news? Or was this the forced lightness of a kindly doctor loath to impart a bitter truth?

"Si, sure, right after three." His own words sounded strange to him. They were a grating outburst, far removed from Pietro's customary mild tone, and he knew that his voice had jerked to attention the lowered head of Robbie Marclay who was at the desk. Pietro wanted to ask, "Is it good news, Gino boy, or is it bad?" Under Robbie's eyes his tongue flayed soundlessly. At last he mumbled again, "Si, after three." The receiver clattered into place. He stumbled from the room.

In the finishing shed, the screech of whirring machines, the

174

staccato din of drills, the thunderous drone of lumbering, overhead cranes, all noises to which his heart had once sympathetically responded with rhythmic vibrations — now became a distant echo. And he himself was no part of it. He trod the hard-packed floor of earth and did not feel it. Were Ronato's slow eyes studying him from the far end of the room? And was not big Tony Botelli standing arms akimbo, his flabby, unshaven jowls hanging loose in frank curiosity? Even redheaded Robbie Marclay, engaged these five months to Pietro's youngest daughter Gabriella, had followed him from the office, and was bending his fine body over a granite slab — but not before he had sent him a brief, questioning glance. Saints of God, did they know he had been talking to Gino? Did they all know that of which he was not yet sure? But, no! How *could* they know? This was his own excruciated brain warping his vision. Misinterpreting the innocent actions of his fellow workers. He rubbed his hands together, hard and cruelly; and he found a comforting sanity from the warmth that rushed to them.

Ronato, putting the finishing touches to the carved exedra, smiled as Pietro neared him. "Tonight I am having dinner with Lucia Tosti — a special dinner to celebrate Gino becoming a doctor."

Pietro stared at him. It had not been often in fifteen years or more that she had invited him of her own accord and without the usual Ronato-inflicted hints! Ronato's was a beatified smile, yet tinged with the eternal melancholy.

For the moment Pietro's troubles paled beside an overwhelming exasperation. It was ridiculous, yes shameful, of this Ronato to advertise his heart publicly all these years! He was the most skilled carver in Granitetown, and in his years of steady work and bachelorhood he had been able to build a good savings account. He could have husbanded anyone of several Granitetown beauties, and could now be enjoying a home and a family. Yet here he was, an arid, suppressed lover, living a lonely life. And Lucia Tosti. How well she could have used his money in her poor home! Pietro shrugged helplessly.

The afternoon dragged. Of late a lassitude had possessed him at this hour in the afternoon; but today he guided his pneumatic tool into the granite with a great show of zeal, lest he betray his uneasiness to his friends. As he worked, apprehension gave way to vexation. Here he was, one Pietro Dalli, wondering whether or not his lungs suffered a sickness. The doctors at the laboratory in Burlington already knew. Gino Tosti already knew. And he himself whose own flesh was at stake, he did not know. The irony of it! Was sickness like a scandal then, that made its giddy rounds gossiping, galloping into the ears of the whole town yet managing to shy from the ears of those most concerned?

He left the shed at three and walked to Main Street. He was not long at Gino's, though he might easily have been. The two old friends exchanged greetings. They tossed banalities. It seemed to Pietro that they were parrying, parrying, until the older man distraught, demanded, "Tell me, boy, am I sick? Yes, or no?"

"Yes."

Afterward, he closed Gino's door behind him and slowly walked Main Street again. It amused him that he felt no worse physically than when he had opened the doctor's door. In truth, he felt better now that his shoulders were free of the pall of uncertainty. After the first numbing shock of Gino's "yes," he had gradually warmed to resignation.

To his right, a child was chalking an arithmetic problem on the granite-faced front of a department store. Pietro's eyes regarded the stone dispassionately, automatically classified it as second grade, and just as automatically deplored the fact that too few Granitetown business buildings were constructed of native stone. Gino's "yes" had not marred his friendship with stone. It was ridiculous, no, to vent hatred on an inanimate object? If a child, fond of sweets, gorged on the confection and so sickened, did one *hate* the sweets? Was it not the child rather who should be blamed? And if he, Pietro, aware of the fate that awaited stonecutters, had preferred to dust himself at the work he loved, was not *he* to be blamed? He bore stone no animosity. To him the horror did not lie in the future weeks or months, or even years in which he would lie wasting. The older stonecutters were prepared to expect that. The greatest hardship lay knotted in those bitter moments — soon now — when he must tell Maria. Should he shirk it? Should he let Gino tell her? But, no, he and Maria were one; it was his duty. He walked slowly, slowly, in the May sunshine, postponing the ordeal. He smiled at the memory of Gino's suggestion that he would profit by rest and care. Pah, no! When a stonecutter's lungs were really bad, the end was around one of the near-by corners. His mind drummed back to Maria. He must tell her tonight. Tonight. The thought whipped a film of sweat to his back. He loosened the collar of his work shirt.

Joey Mull, the town loafer, slouched in front of the theater. He interrupted the scratching of his back against a billboard to grin at Pietro. The grimy monkey face was blithe; his ferret eyes agleam. "I'm goin' over to see her tomorrow!" he announced.

Pietro's scattered thoughts hobbled together.

"See who?"

"Aggie."

"Aggie?"

"Aggie Rugg — she was Ellie Marclay's housekeeper. Hell, you remember the night she went bats an' took to diggin' graves near the quarry —"

"Ah, yes, the poor Aggie. How is she?"

Joey's mouth slumped, but his sharp little eyes glittered. He still delighted in any reference to the event that had once placed his name on the front page of the *Granitetown Times*. He had been mentioned as one of the rescue party that found Aggie Rugg. He pushed back a soiled cap. "She's batty as they make 'em, but quiet like. She don't remember much. I only see her about once a year. Once Alvah Douglas took me. Another time I got me a ride halfway with Tip Gioffi, and I thumbed the rest of the way. Old man

Douglas' son, Denny — he just come back last week — he's takin'
me tomorrow. Says he'd like to see Aggie, too."

Pietro listened, welcoming this respite from his own mental turmoil, but Tony Botelli and Ronato were emerging from the beer
tavern across the street. They would spy him, bear down upon him,
urge him to a drink. And he must not. He must have time to think
clearly how best to tell Maria, how to lessen her pain. He rammed
limp fists into the pockets of his checked mackinaw and plunged
down the street. The sudden impact of a hard body and a deluge
of licorice drops brought him to a stop.

"What the hell, Dalli!"

It was Tip Gioffi's voice, half angry, half joking. He was tossing
licorice drops to a half-dozen children, watching them scramble
for them. Now the bag lay on the walk, its white sides ripped, the
hill of sweets disappearing under the children's nimble fingers.

"Excuse me, excuse me." Pietro murmured in the direction of
the rakishly tilted felt hat, and pushed on.

Dio, he was almost at his own street corner now. An acquaintance
waved languidly from the window of what had once been the
neighborhood poolroom. It was a combination restaurant and beer
tavern now, one of Granitetown's nine Main Street taverns. Tip
Gioffi had opened it when the defeat of prohibition had ended his
bootlegging career. *The Lucky Truck,* its neon sign said. Tip boasted
that the establishment had cost him the profit on one good load of
bootleg liquor. But Tip's chief business, these days, was in the
distribution of pinball and music machines. He left the management
of *The Lucky Truck* to his friend McLeary. The double doors of
the store were open. The stale, sour smell of beer swept into the
street. Across the road, Asa Conway was cranking up the striped
store awning. He inclined his head toward Pietro in mute salutation.

Pietro's feet rooted themselves to the corner where a neat black-
lettered sign read "Pleasant Street." He must go home. He had
been right when he prophesied to Vetch years ago that the building of the sanatorium on the old Vitleau lot would bring improve-

ments to Pastinetti Place. The rutted road was lost beneath smooth macadam. With this fine cement walk the old granite-chip path was but a bad memory. Even the name of the street was changed. Pastinetti Place twisted American tongues, so the city officials said. It became Pleasant Street. Maria's lips had at first puckered wryly at mention of Pleasant Street. *"Pleasant,"* she mocked. "They name it *Pleasant* to belie that brick morgue at the top of the hill!"

Pietro's legs trembled. He leaned against the unlighted lamppost. In the late afternoon, the many-windowed sanatorium in the Vitleau lot loomed a giant sieve, spilling streams of pallid light. Behind each of those windows lay a pair of sick lungs. Like his own. He tore his eyes from the building. Why had he not listened to Maria and moved from this street long ago? Must Maria's earlier years of warning and pleading be taunted now by that spectral pile of brick standing above their home?

Passers-by were regarding him curiously. He could not stand by this lamppost forever. He kneaded his lips. The time was come. He must go home and tell Maria. His eyes sought out the little white house with its spiral of kitchen smoke slanting from the chimney; but his legs stubbornly carried him past the corner of Pleasant Street and down the main cement road where houses thinned and where cars sped the highway to Montpelier. He trudged the strip of dusty wayside weeds, hands clenched behind his back.

From the riverbank, two little girls were throwing pebbles into the water and watching the circles widen and stretch themselves to imperceptibility. With the sun gone, the water looked cold, unfriendly. Its quiet depth held him fascinated. Suppose he should sit, teeth chattering, in that shallow water for half an hour, only a short half hour — would he contract pneumonia? Pneumonia made short business of finishing off dusty lungs. It would be outwitting fate — if fate it were — and it would be sparing Maria the anguish of a fulfilled dread. And the *Granitetown Times* would say: *Pietro Dalli, of the Dalli and Ronato Monumental Company, died of pneumonia after a brief illness,* instead of — *Pietro Dalli died this morning. He had been confined to his home and the local sanatorium for several months.* . . . He shook his head. Ah, good *Dio*, he was not afraid of death. Not that. He was afraid only to tell Maria and to hear her heart wrench out, "Pietro, Pietro, if only you had listened to me!"

His eyes still held to the river. Cold water . . . pneumonia . . . quick death. If he became ill with pneumonia, no one would know it had been self-induced. Neither Maria, nor his children, nor the *maestro* — none of those he loved would know him for a self-murderer, a suicide. *None of those he loved?* It came to him then with all the pain of acute embarrassment that he was being disloyal to his own soul and to God. Yes, what of the omniscient God whom he had taught his children to love? What of God who created eternal life and to whom he had felt a close, intimate relationship through all those years when his chisel had been creating granite memorials of mortal life?

The two little girls stared curiously at his plump rigidly hunched figure. They exchanged whispers and suddenly ran away, throwing quick glances at him over their shoulders. His hands unclenched; his fingers moved to his face feeling out the expression there. Had he frightened those children? Was the evil look of a murderer graven on his face? He stood still, head bowed and trembling, and time seemed to stop about him. But in that moment of victorious defeat Pietro became quietly sure of himself, with the ageless certainty of a man whose mind and soul recognize the fundamentals of life and eternity. Come what may, he knew he must respect to its poor end this life God had given him. He turned his back upon the river, and began trudging again toward Granitetown.

A blue sedan screeched to a stop beside him. Gerbatti, his former boss, spoke around a long stogie. "Come on, *paesan'*, I'll drive you home. What the hell you doing on the road at suppertime?"

There was nothing to do but crawl in beside him. Pietro's thumb indicated the bend in the road where the family of one of Gerbatti's employees lived. "Maria sent me on an errand to the Delsanti house."

Gerbatti's mouth, preparing for speech, loosened around the cigar. He changed his mind, tightened his lips, and puffed furiously. He, himself, had just left the Delsanti house. He had never before known Pietro to lie. And why the devil was his passenger acting so nervous?

Gerbatti let Pietro out in front of the Dalli house. Light flooded the bedroom where Americo was doing his studying. The shade in the next window was not drawn and the rectangular pane disclosed the red-cheeked Gabriella raptly beautifying her face. He could not stop an indulgent smile. The willful Gabriella would rush them all through supper in order that she might tackle the supper dishes early and so have a longer evening with Robbie Marclay. Robbie! A dull pain plunged into Pietro's heart. Robbie was a stonecutter. Would Robbie one day be standing in front of his own home, like Pietro, dreading, hating to go in and tell his wife that his time had come? And that wife would be Gabriella! Lovely, red-cheeked Gabbi. Pietro wondered if he had sinned in turning a deaf ear to Maria's pleas; and if his sin was in later years to be visited on his child? It was not uncommon to overhear Gabriella advising Robbie to leave the sheds. Another Maria, she was. Would Robbie listen to her? And Vetch, in the quarries? Would he, too, be confronted one day with this agony of mind? Did a wheel of fate roll relentlessly through generation after generation of stonecutters' families? Pietro's mind spun these thoughts, churned them, until it seemed that chaos would burst the bony confines of his head.

And at this point he would reason sanely that, with the suction hoses and dust-removing equipment, the greater share of the hazards of stonecutting was removed. Vetch and Robbie were comparatively safe. The bright kitchen window drew his heavy steps across the brief lawn. His palm stroked the wood of his house. It was his own house. Yet he stood there, his back flat to the wall, his neck craned, his eyes straining through the pane, furtively, like some trespasser. He peered through the glass. His eyes embraced the scene hungrily. Vetch and Peggy were visiting tonight, he saw; and now Maria hustled about in a flowered house dress. Their faces looked happy. *Dio,* that it should be his duty to utter the few words that would wipe that joy from their faces. . . .

The kitchen looked warm, cheery. He could remember to the day when they had bought the glistening electric refrigerator, the spotless white sink, and the white stove over which Maria was now bending. It was a snug little home which he was proud to own, and it had been his work as stonecutter that had made it possible.

A familiar step, punctuated by the tap of a cane, sent him scuttling guiltily from the wall of the house. The *maestro* was slowly climbing the front steps, his frail shoulders stooped under the golf bag. Black, fat, aged Pontius Pilate waddled behind on short legs as stiffly rheumatic as the man's. The dog's coat threw off an unpleasant pungency these days and no amount of soap and water could dispel that odor of old age. Maria had spoken, lately, of doing away with the dog, but Petra and the *maestro* would not hear of it.

"You had a good day?" Pietro greeted the older man, though he well knew that the *maestro's* legs restricted his earnings to approximately a dollar a day. It was Mister Tiff's mild complaint that many housewives no longer bothered to have their umbrellas repaired. They bought new ones in the chain stores for a dollar. And as for sharpening knives and scissors — he must grind at better than six pairs to earn a dollar.

Mister Tiff slanted a thin shoulder and let the golf bag slide to the porch floor. "Only so-so," he replied in answer to Pietro's question. He sank to the porch rail, stroking the curve of his nose, waiting for Pietro to strip off his mackinaw and shake out the stone dust before entering Maria's kitchen.

Pietro fumbled with the mackinaw, shook it. He shook it again and again. The *maestro* was waiting for him, he must go in now.

He must tell Maria. But how? In what words? He would have to think through the supper hour, and tell Maria in privacy later on.

Maria's kitchen was savory with the smell of mint crushed and ready to go into a pitcher of lemonade, and there was a faint suggestion of garlic from the roast browning in the oven.

"Come on, Mama, I'm hungry!" Vetch was drumming the table in mock impatience.

Maria thrust out her lower lip and blew upward a wisp of gray hair that straggled before her eyes. "Only twice a week you and Peggy visit here," she complained in Italian, "and then you are always in a hurry."

Peggy stared. Accustomed though she was from childhood with visiting at the Dalli house it was always disturbing to hear her name in a flow of language she did not understand.

Vetch grinned. "She wasn't calling you down, Peg. She was saying we don't visit here often enough."

Maria sighed and promised herself once more to remember to speak English in Peggy's presence. Peggy was a splendid girl. Plain faced and lacking the distinctive beauty of either Petra or Gabriella, but possessing a sweet wholesomeness. She was a good wife to Vetch, steadying to Vetch's restlessness, and she was practical. Yet, like a hundred other Granitetown mothers, Maria wished Peggy could have been of Italian blood, and that the grandchild, the unborn babe in Peggy, would some day be able to chat with her in Italian. But her position was not unique. All over Granitetown, she told herself, there were Spanish, Italian, Scotch, and French grandmothers who would not know the joy of talking to their grandchildren in their native tongue.

Peggy, uncomfortable under her mother-in-law's subconscious scrutiny, said, "It looks easy to make that sauce. I'll have spaghetti tomorrow night and if Vetch doesn't rave about your spaghetti, I'll know I made it right." She went to the stove, watching the red, bubbling, tomato mixture. "See if I've got it right, Mama Dalli. First, you heat a little olive oil and melt a good-size piece of butter in the frying pan. Second, you fry a pork chop, and with it a diced onion and a diced clove of garlic. Strain this or not, just as you wish, then add a bay leaf or mint, a few curls of parsley, a cup of sliced tomatoes, a little water, and let it stew gently for a couple hours. Stir in a tin of tomato paste, salt and pepper it, and let this simmer for another half hour. Right, Mama Dalli?"

The older woman was brisk. "*Si*, that's the best way to make *salsa*." She heard Pietro's step on the porch. After more than twenty years of being a wife to him, his step could still strike up a swift gladness in her heart. She raised a welcoming face.

Pietro murmured to the room at large, "Hello, hello, everybody," and darted into the next room.

Maria's eyes followed him, and a faint frown creased her brow. For years it had been an unbroken custom of Pietro's to remove his heavy work shoes as soon as he entered the kitchen door, and to stand in his stocking feet at the sink sloshing cold water over his dusty face and arms. She watched his silent retreat to the dining room. It came to her that all week he had seemed something of a stranger. Yes, ever since the afternoon he came home complaining of a strained back, and had decided to sleep his nights on the narrow cot in the hall. The back, she reflected wryly, apparently rendered him no discomfort during the day, for he went daily to the shed and managed to do his work as usual. It was only at night. A red hotness leaped to her cheeks: were Pietro's the actions of an unfaithful husband? Mother of God! A knife slipped from her hand and clattered to the floor. Her Pietro unfaithful? But no! Age must at last be cursing her with an imagination. Making a suspicious old woman of her. True, Pietro was concealing something. But nothing important. He had loaned a friend money perhaps, and was reluctant to tell her . . . or he had lost money at cards . . . or he was contemplating the purchase of another new suit for the *maestro*. . . .

Vetch and Peggy ate Maria's spaghetti and roast and left before the family sat down at the table. The supper hour passed quickly. Americo ate in silence, his dark eyes fastened to a science book opened beside his plate. Since learning of his scholarship to the state university, he walked, ate, and slept with his books. Maria saw her husband's eyes dwell often upon the boy. She was happy that this last of her children had come another Pietro. The boy's round face was sober, composed; his brown eyes, warm and gentle, and the short, solid body seemed ever at peace.

Gabriella hummed as she deftly removed the spaghetti plates.

Over his book, Americo grumbled mildly, "Say, I haven't finished —"

"If you'd eat at the table and study elsewhere —"

"Aw, why don't you marry the guy before you starve us all! We've been racing through supper for months, ever since you got the diamond."

She slid his plate in place again. Her round cheeks flamed. "Do your own dishes then!"

Pietro, his mind riveted to the moment that was drawing inexorably nearer and nearer, was only dimly aware of their discord. But he was always responsive to Maria's voice, and now he heard her interrupt their wrangling with, "Your Robbie, is he going to take that job with the State Highway?"

And he saw Gabriella hesitate, the dishes piled in front of her. "He — well, no, Mama," Gabriella answered lamely. Robbie spent his hours contentedly in Papa's shed where he served as both bookkeeper and stonecutter. Why, he had argued with her, should he take another job that didn't pay as much? "Papa pays him too much!" Her laugh was forced.

Pietro cleared his throat and let fall the little pellet of bread he had been rolling nervously between forefinger and thumb. This was not the first time Gabriella had hinted dissatisfaction with Robbie's work. "Maybe it would be well for him to take the state job." *Dio*, were those words sprung from his own heart, and fashioned from his own lips? He saw the eyes of the family turn upon him in amazement; even Americo temporarily forgot his book. He felt a Judas to the stone he loved, yet he said, "Robbie's heart is not really in the stone business, so why should he stick to my shed?" His heart ached dully as he spoke the words. How comforting it would be to rest assured that Robbie would stay in the shed to manage the Dalli interests after he had gone. There was no one of his own children to follow in his footsteps. Vetch's heart beat to the tune of quarry work, and Americo spoke of becoming a high school athletic coach and instructor.

Unexpectedly, Americo spoke, "Gosh, Pa, why don't you fire Robbie? That'll solve Gabbi's problem. He'll take the state job. Then when Gabbi meets him after four he'll be all dressed up instead of in shed clothes." He laughed with youthful candor. "That's what bothers you about the shed job, isn't it, Gabbi?"

Mister Tiff's calm, maintained diligently throughout the meal for digestion's sake, suffered a rude jolt. He had taken it for granted that Gabbi's objection to shed work stemmed from health hazards just as did Maria's, years ago. But one glance at Gabbi's crimsoning, guilty face convinced him that the boy Americo had guessed correctly and that Gabbi wanted to see her handsome Robbie in a white-collar job for reasons of pride.

"There doesn't have to be any firing," the girl flung at her brother coldly, "I'll see that he takes the state job!"

Before she fled from the room, Mister Tiff caught a glimpse of flashing black eyes, and of willfully clamped lips. His frail body slumped in his chair, and he sat there frozen with horrifying suspicion, for Gabbi's face was that of the long-ago Maria when she had "taken things into her own hands" in order to drive Pietro from the sheds. For a moment he considered forsaking his glass of wine and following the girl to the kitchen. He could hear her moving about in the kitchen, making the homely little sounds that are a prelude to dishwashing. His body relaxed, and Mister Tiff told himself that old age was making him suspicious. What harm could Gabbi do? Robbie's work was plain, very plain stonecutting. Robbie had no granite masterpiece which Gabbi could destroy.

Pietro, beside him, was saying, "Well, it looks like Robbie will take the state job, eh, Maria?"

Maria's thoughts were bewildered ones. Those were not Pietro's words when, a few years ago, she had pleaded with Vetch not to go into the quarries. Could it be that a strained back had warped his heart, too, and rendered him more solicitous for a future son-in-law than for his own son? She said to Gabriella who had returned for more dishes, "Your Robbie is as stubborn as my two." All her persuasive powers had moved neither her husband nor her son from their stone. She did not speak unkindly. How could she, when here was her grown brood of children, well and strong, and beside her a robust Pietro, a living lie to her years of fear?

The kitchen door opened. Petra came in, pulling an orange kerchief from her head. She did not miss the quick flight of Gabriella's eyes to the wall clock. "No, it isn't seven yet, Gabbi. I'm home early — my patient died."

Mister Tiff made the sign of the cross. "May she rest in peace."

Petra poured a glass of cold milk. "Don't make room for me, Mama, I'm not hungry. I'm going out later. I'll have a bite then."

Maria smiled. She said to no one in particular, "Denny is a fine fellow."

Petra murmured into the tilted glass, "It's Gino I'm seeing tonight."

Maria bristled. "Denny last night — Gino tonight. I don't like it!" But Petra's feet were already climbing to her bedroom.

Gabbi spoke in her sister's defense. "She likes them both. Besides, going to see Gino means they'll sit in the office half the night talking medicine!"

Americo, with a resigned shrug of his shoulders, closed his book and left the table.

"I don't like it!" Maria repeated. She helped Gabriella clear the table. Petra's nurse's cap sat primly on the icebox. She could never understand why this imaginative daughter had chosen the sober business of nursing which would seem to have no room for her swiftly changing moods. But it was good for her. It kept her subdued. Maria suspected that the grown Petra still walked with her head in the clouds, though she could rest assured that at the same time the girl's feet trod the earth sensibly, carefully.

Pietro and Mister Tiff dallied over their wine. Tonight Pietro's throat could not enjoy the dark liquid smoothness, nor could his body warm around it. Ah, to be drunk, drunk! To forget these nightmare hours since he had left Gino's office, to forget that he must tell Maria. He gulped his wine. "I think I'll take a little walk, Maria." As he spoke, an ambulance chose to whine past the house. The sound of shifting gears broke the early evening quiet. A new patient was being carried to the hilltop sanatorium. Of a sudden, this cheery room became Pietro's only sanctuary. He would not go out. He would not go out and allow the lighted sanatorium windows to draw his eyes like a magnet. He would sit here by the stove, pretend at reading his newspaper, but his mind would be planning how best to tell Maria. . . .

It did not happen as he planned. Big moments seldom do, he thought.

The quarrier neighbors, Lancelotto Demenecini and his wife, dropped in for an evening of chatting. They spoke endlessly of a nephew Jo-Jo and of his success as a granite salesman.

The moment they left, Pietro, harassed in flesh and mind, labored upstairs to the hallway cot. When Maria came up he would follow her into their room, and there where they had been closest he would tell her. So deep were his thoughts that he did not hear her until she was suddenly beside him.

"All that boasting and lip showing from the Demenecinis," she laughed. "We have done as well as they. Better, I think, we have raised four children. And with you still in the sheds —"

All the day's restraint in Pietro broke. The carefully chosen phrases scattered. He blurted, "I left the sheds today!"

She was staring at him as if he had suddenly taken leave of his senses. "Today?" she echoed.

He nodded mutely.

"But it's your shed — why should you leave?"

Unable to speak, his right hand tapped significantly at his chest.

She could not but understand. His face was white, humbled, drained of all but compassion for her own feelings. A ponderous pain, sprung from the fierce throbbing at her temples, bore down into her flesh, into her face, her throat, into each member of her body. It weighed her down until she felt she was mercifully being drawn senseless to the floor. Then the same throes surged rebelliously upward, fiery now and consuming, leaving her giddily empty, purged of all but a nameless ache. There came to her, in one of those swift flashes that can pierce intense agony, the memory of those moments when she had for the first time been a wife to Pietro. Strange that such widely separated and vastly different emotions should travel the same course in one's body. Her husband had indeed impelled that surging of an exquisite pain. And it had indeed purged her at last, leaving her giddily empty of all but a sweet ecstasy. Was there then but a breath between the ecstasy of joy and agony?

And was it only tonight she was counting her blessings, half boasting that in spite of her years of fear her Pietro was still well and working? She wanted to laugh wildly, bitterly. But here was Pietro before her, remembering her pleas, standing here sheepishly, expecting her to cry, "I told you so! Why did you not listen to me years ago?"

She said calmly, "You have seen a doctor?"

And so, slowly, he told her all.

"I could go on working — still," he added humbly, "but we thought it best not to. . . ."

Maria's eyes found the liniment bottle lying on the cot. "Your backache was only an excuse, yes, Pietro?"

He nodded, his cheeks red.

She turned down the covers on the cot. She pulled the stopper from the bottle and poured the brown liquid over the sheets. Her strong arm crooked itself through his. "See, the cot is not fit to sleep on. Come on, Pietro, to our own bed." And she added with a hope she did not feel, "A month or two in the spruces beside some pond, and you will be well again."

He slept late the next morning. Maria waited until her children and Mister Tiff were gathered at the breakfast table and then she told them. She finished, her voice biting at them hard, "Remember, act no differently toward your father! Be as cheerful as you always were. I will not have him see your pity, your grief. I will not tolerate a single long face under this roof!"

When the door closed behind them, she sank into Pietro's rocker by the kitchen stove and burst into tears.

Pietro brooded through five days before he found it in his heart to visit the shed and collect the familiar tools he had first used in the Gerbatti shed and then in his own shed. Petra understood his reluctance to face his fellow workers. One afternoon after the four o'clock whistle, with the shed empty of men, she drove her father to Shed Row. It was a brief visit. With his tools in his arms, Pietro stood for a moment, drinking in the vast room, his thigh to his unfinished stone, remembering the years. Perhaps he would be back some day, he dared hope. But no. If, miraculously, he and health should some day be one, he must not pain Maria again by resuming this work. *Si*, this was the last time he would stand in this shed with his cherished tools in his hands. He shifted the tools, and passed a palm gently over the rough surface of the stone. And because a lump rose persistently in his throat, he turned on his heel and fled.

CHAPTER III

The lethargy of an unseasonable warmth clung to this early day in June. At Chisel Point Pond, fifteen miles north of Granitetown, a listless breeze stirred sporadically, flagging even at its birth so that the water lay unwrinkled, a sparkling smoothness under the sun.

The pond was bowled between rugged, dark old spruces and an outcropping of spurious granite. The water lay in the shape of a chisel point, as if thrown there by some gigantic stonecutter's hand. Its sagittal lineations followed, on one side, a façade of summer camps owned chiefly by stonecutters. A few were spacious cottages. Most of them were but humbly comfortable camps. A lesser number were crude shelters designed for a week end of fishing or hunting. A pioneer stonecutter, his name long since forgotten, had built the first camp as a release from the dusty air of the sheds. In a short time many of his fellow workers followed his example.

On this side of the pond, beachless and deeply cragged, only an occasional cottage rose in the spruce clearings. Ronato's camp was a simple, one-story square structure, painted white. His artist's hands had trained vines to cover the white walls. Only the front door, the granite steps, the garlanded windows, and the great granite chimney evidenced the labor of man. From a distance the house gave the appearance of a mammoth but squat green plant, sprung from the soil. And Ronato's eye must have a beautiful setting for this verdant haven. He studded the gentle rise behind

191

the camp with clumps of wild flowers and ferns, and ran among them little paths paved with granite blocks. Facing the highway, on a dais of natural rock, stood a life-size granite statue. It was a guardian angel in flowing robes. Her hands clasped, her face seraphic and reassuring, she nevertheless extended the protection of only one complete wing. Ronato had carved the angel in Gerbatti's shed many years ago. A wealthy Virginian had ordered it for a memorial piece. A wing tip had been accidentally broken as it was being boxed for shipment. An angel with a clipped wing was useless to Gerbatti, and Ronato had shuddered at the thought of his beautiful work being scrapped. If an armless Venus survived the ages, why not his dewinged angel? He paid Gerbatti the value of the rough stone, and gave the statue a position of honor at Chisel Point Pond. A path, bordered with white-painted stones, wound behind the statue and extended some one hundred feet over rocky terrain to a brief oasis of three spruce trees and trampled grass. Here, beneath the spruces and directly overlooking the water, Ronato had built a rustic picnic table and benches.

From here could be seen the windows of Ronato's corner bedroom. The two windows were raised to their highest, but today no breeze stirred the ruffled, white curtains. Behind them Pietro was taking his afternoon nap. At first Pietro's graying brown head had shaken at Ronato's suggestion that he spend the summer at his camp, but when Maria, Petra, and Mister Tiff added their pleas he had finally and listlessly yielded, and one afternoon he and Petra drove to Chisel Point Pond, their car laden with clothing for the two of them, with bedding and provisions.

On Sundays, Maria cooked the family dinner on Pleasant Street and carried it to the camp, where they all dined together. Americo often "hitched" rides to the pond during the week. The week after Pietro left home, Maria noticed that Mister Tiff was spending fewer hours at his work of umbrella mending and was devoting long hours to sitting on the porch, a book in his lap. To her frank questioning, he replied, "That rain last week, it seems to have encouraged my rheumatism." She believed him, and she believed also that separation from Pietro and Petra, the two he held most dear in Granitetown, was making him restless and unhappy. And when she hinted that a few days at camp might be beneficial to his leg, he responded with alacrity, climbing the stairs as nimbly as legs allowed to pack pajamas, shirt, and underwear in his ancient pigskin bag. Perhaps it was the sight of the old bag, stored in the attic these many years and its Mattzo coat of arms still faintly visible, that brought to him in vivid illumination the past he had left in Ibena. It reminded him poignantly of Mafalda's crude reference to her marriage and of the luxury she might now be enjoying, the latter depending, he bethought himself with a grim smile, upon Mussolini's wishes. Memories crowded upon him as he limped painfully down the attic stairs, and when a sharp twinge in his leg compelled him to drop the shabby bag and cling to the railing, Mafalda's taunting "I-told-you-so" rang in his ears. He was powerless to dispel a fancied picture of himself in Ibena, and Count Mattzo saying solicitously, "Ho, a touch of rheumatism, my friend? Let us see what a sun bath in my *giardino* will do for you." And a servant would whisk off his clothes, wrap him in one of the count's silken lounging robes, and before long he would be reclining on a cushioned couch in a corner of the lovely garden, the sun pouring balm into his aching leg, the near-by flowers making perfume for all his senses, Mattzo's engaging voice beginning an engrossing discussion, a servant plying them with wine and sweet cakes. . . . The enticing picture vanished as soon as Mister Tiff entered his room and his eyes fell on the St. Michael figurine. He blushed in acute dismay. Was he envious of Mafalda's fortune? "My age is telling upon me," he scolded himself. "What difference does it make whether I end my days in a city poor farm or the count's garden? At any rate, I don't expect to starve." As if to bolster his philosophy he remembered that more than 1500 years ago Augustine had written, *Thou wilt carry us . . . when little, and even to hoar hairs wilt Thou carry us.* The slight bulge under the doily on which St. Michael stood gave him added comfort. Under the doily lay a bank book, and the three little figures printed at the end of the last column assured him that his funeral, whenever it might be, would not be that of a pauper. But even this comforting thought pricked a discomfort to his pride, for he remembered, with quick humility, that Christ's was a pauper's funeral even to the burial clothes and tomb.

Now on this warm June afternoon Mister Tiff sat in Ronato's oasis, his back to the rough bark of a spruce. He wore an old shirt, his neckerchief and a pair of Americo's athletic shorts. His spindly legs were extended straight before him to catch the warm rays of the sun. He was reading aloud from an English translation of *The Confessions of St. Augustine*. Occasionally the youth interrupted to correct the pronunciation of a difficult word, although Americo's first attention concerned his game of solitaire. Mister Tiff was well aware of the fact that he spoke English better than Maria and Pietro. He was also aware of the reason for this good fortune. His own education had far exceeded Maria's or Pietro's; a new tongue was mastered with less hardship when one already had a basic knowledge of other languages. Also, Mister Tiff had had more leisure hours to put to the reading of English books; and in his early Granitetown days he had struggled daily through the *Granitetown Times* while Maria and Pietro sought the more pleasurable reading of the Italian newspaper to which they still subscribed.

Mister Tiff's thin voice droned on — *So then after the matter of the Academics (as they are supposed) doubting of everything, and wavering between all —*

"*Wavering,*" Americo corrected, punctuating the interruption with the slap of a card against the table. "A like the *a* in *May.*"

Mister Tiff accepted the correction with a nod of his head and continued reading. After a few minutes he missed the almost rhythmic slap of cards and heard instead the restlessness of the boy as he fidgeted on the bench. He looked up to see Americo's eyes staring after a rowboat that was making its way to the beach opposite them. A thin figure in a red bathing suit bent over the oars.

Mister Tiff cleared his throat, and automatically he rubbed the side of his nose. "Somebody I know?"

"It's a — well, it's a girl."

"That I can see," the man remarked dryly.

"It's Aster. I met her at the wayside stand. I bet she's going for a swim — "

And I bet you follow suit, the man thought silently. He closed his *Confessions,* and the act was dismissal for the boy. He rose and stretched unhurriedly; but his steps to the camp were fast and eager.

Alone, Mister Tiff removed his glasses and hunched himself more comfortably against the tree. With gentle fingers he brushed away a noisy, iridescent fly that had taken a fancy to his bony knee and was walking the knobby surface with stiff, erratic movements. In front of the man the water stretched smooth and quiet, and over it soared an arc of cloudless blue sky. Mister Tiff sighed a deep, satisfying sigh. To think that only yesterday he had half yearned for the luxuries of Mafalda! His only great sorrow these days lay in Pietro's illness, and in the persistent, nagging thought that he himself might have urged Pietro to leave the sheds years ago. Even as this thought gnawed at him he knew instinctively that if Pietro were given another opportunity to live his life, he would live it again with his granite tools in his hands.

Earlier in the afternoon Gino's car had stopped beside the front door, and Gino had made his almost daily visit to Pietro. Now Mister Tiff blinked lazily as he watched the young doctor and Petra walk to the smooth boulder behind the camp. The girl had changed to a sun suit. She stretched out under the sun, with Gino sitting beside her. They were deep in conversation. Mister Tiff remembered that when they were children Gino's had been a protective, brotherly affection for the girl, while from Denny there had radiated a spirit that seemed to merge with that of Petra. . . . The old man's eyes closed drowsily.

On the sun-warmed boulder Petra was saying quietly to the man beside her, "It's doing him no good, Gino." Daily, her father's temperature had soared, and he had forsaken his daily strolls.

"Give him a chance. A new environment always sets one back a bit. Like — well — like transplanted flowers or vegetables. They're bound to suffer while they're making a new root hold, while they're getting acclimated, then — "

"Bluffing and hedging from you, Gino?" Her gray-green eyes smiled wanly. "I've seen a lot of them. I know better. So do you." Last week Gino had driven her father into Granitetown for another X ray. "How did the X rays read? Why didn't you bring them with you today?"

He abandoned pretense. "They weren't encouraging."

She was wearing a short, backless play dress of bright India print. Her brown, silky hair sprayed her shoulders, and short, damp tendrils curled at her temples. She tensed at his words, her fingers pressed hard to the rock.

Gino saw the pink, oval tip of a fingernail bend, then crack against the rock. Mechanically she plied it back and forth until it broke off. The sun made it a small glistening crescent against the dark stone. He knew the ridiculous urge to pick it up and to hold it shining in the palm of his hand.

Her voice was low. "It — it'll be over soon then. Four or five months?" The thought left her cold, shaken. But, dear God, it was better for him to go soon. She remembered Jose Peridez who lingered seven years with tuberculous-silicosis. It was a capricious bug, devouring some fast, some slowly.

"It's impossible to say," Gino answered honestly.

They lay for some minutes in silence. She frowned pensively, speaking more to herself than to him. She went on, knowing that she was talking futilely, childishly, "Why couldn't it have been marble he liked? You haven't seen the Rutland marble carvers die off like our stonecutters — "

"Marble doesn't contain the silica that granite does — "

She interrupted, her mind chasing at a vague tangent, "Didn't some school of medicine believe that wherever a sickness is common to a region, that same region produces a medicine to combat the sickness?"

The sober lines of his face dissolved into brief humor. "You mean that there might be some herb growing around here that'll perform the cure? No, it's got to be better than that. Or, who knows? It's the silica dust that does the harm. The sheds' suction hose system isn't perfect yet — some day it may be. Preventive measures are the important thing in this business of health." His brown hands clasped eagerly. The dark eyes suddenly faltered in their gaze, avoiding hers shyly like a child who has lifted a veil to expose a part of his heart's ambition and is uncertain whether to expect praise or ridicule. "There's one group of doctors — silicosis experts, and they know their stuff — their idea is that if a man gets his lungs coated with a good film of aluminum dust *before* he begins cutting stone, it'll help prevent silica dust from reaching into that media where it thrives best."

She stared at him, her hand making a visor for her eyes against the sun. "Wouldn't the aluminum dust do just as much harm?"

"It's an inert dust — "

"But the film of aluminum particles will bring about a condition of dusty lungs. Any kind of dust will eventually impede the function of lungs. They can't get a healthy contact with air, with oxygen. They'll weaken anyway, won't they?"

"At least it might postpone silicosis," he said gravely. "You see, Petra, some dust doesn't affect lung tissue as granite's silica does. A union of silica and lung tissue effects a decided chemical reaction — silicosis. And strangely, the t.b. bug has an affinity for silica-infected lungs. It flourishes. We did an experiment at school. We injected the t.b. bug in a healthy guinea pig; then we gave the same amount to a pig with silica-infected lungs. We gave both the same treatment, the same food. What happened? The bug didn't do so well for itself in the silica-free lungs. The pig got well. But things happened fast in the other pig. The bug thrived. That pig died."

Her heavy heart warmed to his zeal. She knew he had reason to be more than casually interested in this cross the older Granite-town stonecutters must carry. She liked Gino's zeal, his sincerity; yet an uncontrollable restlessness seized her. She heard him speaking, a dull drone, " . . . same thing happens in our lungs as did in those pigs. . . ."

Petra looked across the quiet waters. *Pigs . . . pigs . . .* The warm air suddenly became an oppressive weight. She was tired, weary. *Pigs . . . pigs . . .* Her harassed mind, unleashed of discipline, silently took up the nursery rhyme — "This little pig went to market, this little pig stayed home —" She shook off the nursery chant, scorning herself for not listening to Gino, who was doing his best for her father. But *she* was doing her best, too, a part of her argued. And for these few minutes shouldn't Gino help her forget her troubles? Over there across the pond stood ancient spruces, their lowest branches richly weighted almost to the ground with fragrant needles. A warm sun burnished them. A generous sun gilded the pond. Why weren't they out there in a boat, skimming that liquid gold, laughing, chatting of pleasant matters? Why must her mind agonize continually with her father? Tears of self-pity stung her eyes. A thin shred of common sense aroused her to shame. Dear God, she was truly grateful that her services as a nurse kept her beside her father. . . . Gino was still talking, talking. She lay tense, forcing herself to listen.

" . . . and there are other doctors who have dished out other food for thought. Autopsies on tuberculous-silicosis victims have revealed silica particles in the kidneys. If they're in the kidneys, they must have been carried there in the bloodstream. These fellows say, why not rid the body of as much dust as possible? Why not remove this blood, give them transfusions with a healthy, dust-free blood? If it's tried on a patient in the early symptom stages, it may do some good. There are hopes — all in the experimental stage." He sighed.

Without warning, she sprang to a sitting position, her hands flat and tight to the warm stone. It was a swift, restless movement indicative of the tension that bound her, and he saw that the slender body was painfully taut. Her face blazed in one of its unexpected chameleon moods. "Guinea pigs! Experiments! No one's going to experiment with my father — "

Gino was silent. Knowing her, he waited quietly until the short-lived fury burned itself out.

When she dropped again to the stone, she was self-reproaching and embarrassed. There was something of infinite patience and kindness in Gino's face.

Her bare arm flashed in the sunlight and her fingers sought his hand. "I didn't mean that — "

He had known these moods of hers since she was a child, had seen her lost in rapture when she was no part of this world, had seen her hands clawing madly at Peggy Riley's hair, had seen her drop to the ground in ecstatic abandon to press her lips to a straggling violet. Of course, she never truly expected him to experiment with her father. "You're tired," he said. "And maybe I'm overzealous." His laugh was wry. "Come on, you're going up and get some real rest."

Still she hung back, vaguely aware of something unfulfilled in this afternoon's plans. Vetch? Vetch? "Why didn't Vetch come with you this afternoon? He'd planned to."

A brief hesitation. "I had some calls to make. I missed him."

She searched his face. "Gino, Gino, you'll never make a successful liar — you're too much like my father. Vetch is drinking; isn't he? Oh, it isn't any secret, my mother and Gabbi hinted at it last week."

"Vetch'll be all right — "

"It's Peggy I'm thinking of, and the baby that's coming. It's no time for Peggy to be worrying about her husband. Papa's illness is a sorrow to all of us. Vetch should take it like a man, and not let Peggy feel its repercussions!"

Because Vetch had been in Gino's mind these few days he could answer quickly, "Don't be harsh with him, Petra. Ever since we were kids prowling around some abandoned quarry, he's always had something of your father's feeling for stone. I know. And now, with your father sick, it's as if stone had, well, stabbed him in the back. He'll get over it. Come on, now, get back to camp and take a nap." He drew her to her feet. "I'll be over tomorrow."

There was no need of his visiting her father daily. "It's a long trip, Gino, and it interferes with your other patients — "

He replied cheerfully, "I've only eight patients."

"Being away so much, you're probably missing out on new ones — "

"It's not only your father I come to see." He halted beside her, his hand enfolding hers. He was the boyishly hesitant Gino she had always known. "Don't you know that, Petra?" And now her startled eyes were propelling the words he was not yet ready to speak. "I suppose I've no right to say anything now, but some day when I've built up a practice, when I've paid what I still owe the university — " He broke off helplessly, for the call of a car had caught her attention, and it must be a familiar, welcome sound for she was turning her brown head toward the dirt road leading from the highway to the camp. It was as if she had not heard his words at all.

Denny Douglas stepped from his dark blue roadster and strode through the scant jungle of ferns, a long, plump watermelon under his arm. He bowed in blithe courtesy before the granite angel and cut across the path toward them.

Petra waved, her head high, expectant.

Gino pressed close to her in slow urgency.

"Is it Denny, Petra? Is it Denny you love?"

She turned puzzled eyes on him.

"Are you in love with Denny?" he insisted.

He had to admit that her reply rang with honesty. "No, oh no! No one, Gino —"

Yet he could not help feeling that the joyous lilt in her voice was better tuned to a, "Yes, oh yes!" He scowled. She surely was being honest! Or didn't she know her own feelings? And, too, he might be wrong in interpreting her feelings. For that matter, what did one person really know of another except those things that he or she chose to disclose.

He said, "I'll stop by and see your father a minute. No, don't come along — I'll be over again tomorrow afternoon."

Petra watched them pass each other, dark Gino and blond Denny. It was good to have them both in Granitetown once more, and to keep open house for them in her heart! The two exchanged a few words, then Gino was gone, his measured tread crackling through the scant brush.

Denny was gay. "Asa Conway's got the edge on all the Granitetown grocers today! His store window's full of the season's first watermelons." His jackknife cut into the melon; it split open. "Conway's store has never been so popular! I had to elbow my way through the crowd —"

His unexpected nonsense was balm to Petra. "Let's take half of it with us — we'll row across Chisel Point, and tramp that spruce knoll over there —"

He saw that her eyes were shadowed. She needed relaxation, not exercise. This cottage of Ronato's made too much work for her. "I could do with the boat ride," he admitted, "but let's omit the tramping. It's too hot."

It was lazy fun sitting in the old boat, hands dangling in the water, feeling power even in her static finger tips as, motionless, they cut the smooth surface. Fun to wriggle bare toes in the warm rain water that had not been drained from the boat floor. Fun in seeing

Denny's muscles ripple as he worked the oars. Best of all was the comfortable, mutual silence in which each traveled his own thoughts. It did not last long.

"Petra, why don't you and your father try our lodge in the Adirondacks for a while?" It was not a new thought born of this afternoon's meeting with her. He had discussed it with his mother and although she had displayed no eagerness, she had nevertheless yielded.

Petra had never visited the Douglas Lodge. Two years ago one of the leading architectural magazines carried colored photographs of that luxurious mountain home. There were close-ups of the huge stone fireplace, the beds, chairs. At the time the pictures tended to thrust Denny far above and beyond her horizon, yet here he was, his slender face carelessly stained with the pink flesh of watermelon, and his bare toes touching hers.

He was saying, "My father's in the South, you know. And my mother insists upon summering with me in Granitetown. The lodge isn't doing us any good, it might as well be used." He was mentally comparing the modern heating and the well-equipped kitchen with the more humble facilities of Ronato's cottage. "Besides, Gino admits that mountain air is drier, more bracing."

She shook her head. "You're sweet, Denny." Her father and mother would never accept this luxury, even as a token of friendship. She could make Denny understand that without being hurt. "Papa won't go, Denny. He boasts that he hasn't left Vermont since he came here twenty-five years ago. He won't leave — now."

And then, hardly aware of the conversational bystream, she found herself struggling once more deep, deep in the ever engulfing talk of stonecutters, quarriers, silicosis. Gino was concerned with making sick stonecutters well again, and with keeping the dust from healthy stonecutters. This latter enthusiasm, she learned, was transmitting itself to the new Denny who spent the day's working hours in the office of his father's quarry.

The boat had been drifting. Now it was still, caught in a marsh where weeds pierced the surface of the water, and scum lay in green, wavering patterns. A frog or two croaked in cross complaint against intrusion of its domain.

"To be shamefully honest, Petra, I haven't given the stonecutters and quarriers much serious thought until recently, even though I grew up in the business and even though the Dallis and the Tostis were my best friends." He was apologetic. "You know the saying about not being able to see the trees when you're deep in the woods. . . . Being away has helped. I seem to see the picture with new eyes. The shed and quarry owners have done a lot to help the workers these past years. They'll probably do more. And if there's ever better dust-removing machinery to be had, they'll re-equip their plants. They're human — "

There was a hint of her mother's voice in Petra's words, "The workers would still be waiting for the installation of suction hoses if it hadn't been made compulsory!"

A bright glow suffused his cheeks. "The smaller owners couldn't afford it," he said.

Once more there was silence. A less comfortable silence. And suddenly he was off again, this time on the subject of stonecutters' compensation. She sat rigid, her hands clenching her knees. Dear God, she begged, don't let me explode as I did with Gino! Her smarting skin and taut nerves warned her that she could endure no more. She said, saying out each syllable in forced calm, "Let's go back. It's time for my father's eggnog, and I have to send Americo to the village store for groceries."

He obediently picked up the oars. Back at camp he visited for a few minutes with Pietro, and then paused in the combination living room-kitchen to admire Ronato's paintings. On either side of the fieldstone fireplace were large murals in oil. One depicted the countryside of Ronato's Italian homeland, broad sweeps of rolling pasture land, a humble home of plaster and stone and an ascent of rounded hills growing against a distant background of snow-tipped mountains. The other mural, Petra explained above the whirl of the egg beater, was Ronato's conception of the birth of Christ had He been born in this day and age in Vermont. "Ronato has imagination," she added.

Denny whistled. "Imagination! What an understatement!" he offered, for Ronato had truly introduced Vermont flavor into the picture.

The nativity was seen through the wide door of an abandoned sugar house. A corner of a great syrup vat was visible. The haloed Infant, covered with a gay plaid blanket, lay in a metal syrup pan. Mary sat on an overturned sap bucket, smiling at her Child. A blue kerchief covered most of her dark hair, and she wore a plaid-lined parka and woolen skirt. Beside her, in the warm clothing of a Vermont lumberjack, stood Joseph. To the left of the sugarhouse were visible the back wheels of an automobile almost hub-deep in snow. In the distance a red silo towered over the barns of a farmhouse, and far beyond rose a great hill, its grout-topped height faintly discernible. A collie was running across the field of snow, and from a small wood of spruce and pine peeped a wide-eyed slender fawn.

But it was a charcoal drawing of Lucia Tosti's face, boldly alive in light and shade, that held Denny longest. There was the slightly rounded face, the dark eyes quietly brooding, happy yet unhappy, and uncannily holding a little of the mystery of La Giaconda. Denny, brought up to date these past weeks on the status of most of his Granitetown friends, felt that the lovelorn Ronato had truly caught Lucia's changeless love for her dead husband. An inner confidence shone through the woman's face and seemed to say, "I have loved one man. I do not want anyone else." Denny pitied the man who was so much the artist that he could sacrifice his own feelings to reproduce faithfully Lucia's spirit, and could keep it there on the wall to haunt him.

But as much as he admired the sketch and the murals, he had to admit that the most sublime of Ronato's artistry lay in the sculpturing of granite. Da Vinci had found inspiration from every thing — living and inanimate; Gauguin had drawn powerful artistry from colorful Tahiti; but Ronato's inspiration was in granite itself, and he could shape the stone into all but life.

Denny lingered to smoke one cigarette, then another. Petra guessed that he hoped to be invited to their simple supper. But she couldn't ask him today. Another hour of the grueling conversation she had had this afternoon with Denny and Gino and she would become an hysterical, nerve-frayed woman.

After he left, she sat on the doorstep, pointed chin in her hand, listening to the disjointed rhythm of Americo's ax as he chopped the kindling she must use tonight. The day's oppressive warmth was being washed away in a clean-sweeping breeze. The spruce boughs purred like a gentle surf. The sweet scent of pastures and woods was carried across the water.

Americo carried an armful of wood to the kitchen. It spilled, clattering into the bin. Then he was beside her, wiping his hands on his blue denims. He kept his eyes awkwardly to the tips of his shoes. "Mind if I ask someone to supper tonight?"

"Heavens, who?"

"It's a — well, she's the girl whose mother runs the wayside stand beyond the dance pavilion."

Petra smiled at his awkwardness. She thought: it's his first date — he's never taken a girl to high school parties, not once in four years — he simply hadn't been interested in a girl; his interest had been books and athletics.

"That'll be fun. But don't expect a banquet."

His deep breath was one of relief. "What do you want at the store? I can stop in and ask her on my way back." His hands moved clumsily through his hair. "Gosh, Petra, I've been bragging about your cooking. At her mother's place they serve only sandwiches and hot dogs — the usual wayside stuff. You — we aren't going to have anything out of a can tonight, are we?"

She had planned just that. She was infinitely weary. It would have been easy to open a can of asparagus and serve it creamed on toast. She made a quick mental survey of their food supply. "How about a mushroom omelet and a green salad. And soup, of course." Papa insisted daily upon a thick soup. "A quart of milk and a quart of ice cream, that's all you'll have to get at the store tonight." She watched him walk off toward the highway with an almost jaunty stride.

Tonight her father's temperature was still high. He raised no objections to taking his meal abed. He lay there in an apathy unusual to him. Her throat choked back an aching lump. She had seen so many like him, daring at first to hope, then as fever reigned, as flesh wasted, as coughs racked more mercilessly — this hopelessness.

Americo's guest, she decided later, was no beauty. Aster Mitcham was small; her thin body indrawn with an almost self-excusing air, like some retreating, defeathered bird. Perhaps, as Americo suggested, the girl didn't get the right food. Her unrounded body, under the red piqué dress, was that of a child of twelve; yet Aster was old enough to have been graduated from a Florida high school last year.

"Aster's a pretty name," Petra began encouragingly.

"It's the nearest to my father's name that my mother could think of," the girl said and Petra was startled at the unexpected rich timbre of her voice. "Perley Mitcham was my stepfather. My real father died before I was born."

"Aster wants to go to the university this fall, too," Americo put in eagerly. "She's been saving money for over a year."

"I need a hundred and fifty more," Aster admitted in raw frankness.

Petra scarcely heard them. She was back at her childhood game of guessing, picturing Aster's mother when she had been heavy with this child. No doubt the girl's mother had wanted this child a gorgeous bloom, as colorfully beautiful as autumn asters. And, in all hope and confidence, she had christened the scrawny babe *Aster*. A giggle curled in Petra's throat. The name Aster was not entirely incongruous. Asters were fall flowers, many of them frost-nipped before maturity. And certainly this Aster wore that pinched, frozen air. But the girl was not without charm. Aster's creamy skin was flawless, smooth. Her eyes were clear violet depths, and her hair, worn in straight bangs and falling to her shoulders, was a finespun cloud of lustrous black. That pale, oval face might some day be truly lovely. Petra started, shaken from her thoughts. "What — ?" she asked.

"We're going over to the pavilion tonight," Americo repeated self-consciously. "Jerry Dole's orchestra from Granitetown's playing. You come, too, huh?"

"Yes, you come, too," Aster chimed breathlessly.

Later Petra's father insisted, "You go, too, eh? The *maestro* will be here, and I have my papers to read."

She went. She had long ago learned that her father fretted himself into relapses if he thought she was sacrificing relaxation on his account.

The dance pavilion, of weathered pine, spread over a broad flat rock, and reached out thirty feet over the shallow end of the pond. It was a summer pavilion, enclosed by a low rail, and open, except for the ceiling, to the evening air. Petra did not accompany them inside but preferred to sit on the narrow veranda, sipping a coke and idly surveying the new arrivals. Most of the couples were from the neighboring countryside and near-by villages. Conspicuous tonight in the motley assortment of cars was a cream-colored roadster that belonged to Mama Gioffi's son. The Gioffis these days boasted two Packards, thanks to Tip's success with pinball machines and juke boxes. She scarcely knew Tip beyond a casual nod. He was older than her crowd and Vetch's. She often caught glimpses of that hard, arrogant face as he sped the roads in his powerful car.

At intermission Aster excused herself to go across the road and help her mother at the wayside stand during the brief rush. Tip

Gioffi was amusing himself with a youthful, song-inclined drunk. They stood in a bright pool of light shed by the parking-lot lamp. The boy lolled against the fender of Tip's car, his unsteady voice filling the night air with popular tunes.

The lone voice was a magnet for a curious, fast-assembling crowd, and Tip, enjoying the limelight, tossed the boy a bill. "How about a hymn this time?"

A girl, whose round face was a pale moon under a halo of plump, yellow curls, scolded, "Don't you do it, Johnnie! Let's go home."

Tip pressed another bill into the boy's hand.

The young voice began: *"Mine eyes have seen the glory of the coming of the Lord. . . ."* Tip's eyes darted about the crowd, lapping up their gay approbation. His glance grazed Petra's unamused face, and returned to dwell on her in pettish contemplation. Another bill passed from Tip to the boy. There was another hymn. Another popular song. Tip's eyes darted often in Petra's direction, and when the orchestra's first swing bars drew the couples inside the pavilion, Tip smoothed his black hair, straightened the flower in the lapel of his pencil-stripe suit, then was on the veranda bending confidently over her chair. "How about this one?"

She didn't like his brazen assurance nor the "city racketeer" air he chose to wear. "Thanks, I'm not dancing." She pretended interest in the stretch of meadow where fireflies were turning their lights on and off.

His smugness retreated behind an angry flush. "Kind of high-hat, aren't you, Miss Dalli?"

Americo rammed his hands nervously into his pockets, "Listen, I guess she can say 'no' if she wants to."

"Shut up, kid." Tip turned and shouldered his way to the floor.

But he was not yet through with her. Between dances he appeared often in the shadows of the veranda, the glow of a cigarette revealing his features. And he approached her again, some of the cockiness ridden from his manner. "You've been sitting here an hour and a half, how about a jaunt around the pond before you stiffen up?"

Mosquitoes had been feasting on her bare legs. They itched and smarted. She was weary of the whole day and evening, and the hint of challenge in his face promised diversion. "All right, you can drive me home. Wait, I'll have to tell Americo first."

He grinned. "*I'll* tell him, and like it!"

The cream-colored roadster swung north. "It's the other road," she directed. "We're staying at Ronato's cottage."

"Balmy night air's what we need. We'll take the long way back."

She didn't care. They skirted the pond, rolling smoothly over macadam road. A breeze lifted her hair, cooled her skin. He spoke briefly of her father. "The old man's sick, huh? That's tough."

Her hands clenched. He switched off the subject as if it had been a statement expected of him, and now forgotten. "There's Scotch in that pocket," he suggested.

"No, thanks."

His arm slipped around her shoulder. She shrugged it off.

"Trying to be different?" he taunted good-naturedly. His arm reached over her shoulder again.

She told herself that it was her own fault for coming and that she might have expected this overture. Silently she again shrugged off his arm. She felt his quick, baffled glance.

"O.K., O.K., don't get excited!" he mumbled.

Time passed swiftly. They circled the pond, drove to Greenville, back to the pond once more. It was Tip who did most of the talking. Boasting of his bootlegging days, recounting the neck-to-neck races with revenue men. Her father was absent from her mind until Ronato's camp came into view and her heart began to thud with the sickening beat of a grim reality.

He didn't open the car door as Gino or Denny would. She opened it herself. He sat there behind the wheel, his arrogant face smiling. "Good night, kid, I'll be around again."

The kitchen light sent a path of brightness through the window. Americo was on the kitchen cot, a blanket over his drawn-up knees, his head nodding over a book. He could not hide his relief at seeing her.

She hesitated at the door of her room. "Was Papa all right?"

"Sure. He was asleep when I got in and Mister Tiff was snoring in the chair. They'd had a bottle of wine."

Some time later, her father's persistent, rumbling cough woke her. Automatically she groped for her bathrobe and just as suddenly her arm fell back to the bed. He would reproach himself for having disturbed her. She drew the blanket over her head, trying to deaden the sound of that coughing. The luminous hands of her night clock pointed to four. In the cough-ridden darkness the clock was skeletonized a spectral green. She twisted and turned under the blanket, knowing that if the coughing continued she *must* go to him. Americo's cot creaked. The coughing ceased. She heard her brother pad across the kitchen floor, and heard his concerned, "Papa — " and the rest of his words was lost in a mumble.

Her father gasped testily, "Go on back to bed, boy! *Dio*, do I run to your side every time nature demands a sneeze from you, or a blow of the nose!"

Petra smiled in the dark. Yes, she was glad she had not gone to her father.

CHAPTER IV

In Granitetown, Maria was making *ravioli*. She had always enjoyed fashioning these tasty morsels of meat and pastry: a song blossomed in her throat, and her capable hands kneaded the dough in gay tempo. But today the rhythm of her hands was a plodding adagio. Tomorrow would be the Fourth of July; also it would be the twenty-fifth anniversary of Maria's and Pietro's marriage. Pietro was failing fast. She anticipated little joy in the anniversary dinner at the pond. After the family dinner, he would come to sleep his anniversary night in his own bed in Granitetown, and the following day he would take Gino's advice and go to the sanatorium atop Pleasant Street, within stone's throw of his home. It had not been difficult to reach this decision. Pietro welcomed this opportunity to be near his family. And Maria's old bitterness was dissipated by the knowledge that he would receive expert treatment at the sanatorium and — she would be able to visit him daily.

Mister Tiff stood washing his hands at the sink. He had been mixing the meat filling for the *ravioli*. He had come to Granitetown yesterday to assist Maria with the dinner preparations. Close to his feet, plump Pontius Pilate lay in quivering sleep, his twitching legs and restless nose revealing that he was actively living his dream. A car stopped in front of the house, and a swift tattoo of steps beat on the porch. Mister Tiff drew aside the curtain. "It's Petra come for the supplies."

Black Pontius Pilate opened his eyes and drummed the floor with his tail. The old dog rose with rheumatic slowness and waddled to the door. Uncontrolled excitement trickled from him, left a long, wet trail across the floor. Mister Tiff, thankful that Maria's keen eyes were fastened to the pastry in front of her, limped quickly to the cellar cupboard for the mop. He had to admit that the old dog's time had come at last. Maria's saddened household could well do without the added care of an age-ridden dog.

Petra stooped and scratched dutifully behind the dog's ear. "Is everything ready to take to camp, Mama? We're going back right away."

Maria's black eyebrows grew into horrified question marks. "*We?* You mean Americo came with you, and you left your father alone?"

"No. Americo's with Papa."

"You said *we —*"

"Tip Gioffi drove me in."

Maria stiffened as she wiped floury hands. She had paid little attention to Americo these past weeks when he spoke of having seen Tip Gioffi at Chisel Point Pond. But now those casual references leaped into grim significance. Her voice was brittle. "I don't like it. He's too old for you! He's not your kind." *Dio,* didn't Mama Gioffi herself often admit, and tearfully, that Tip amused himself too freely with this girl and that?

Petra was packing fresh *ravioli* in a cracker carton. "It's nothing like that, Mama. He's just a friend."

Mister Tiff peered questioningly at the red stains in the girl's cheeks, and despite Tip's well-known reputation, he could believe her. Yet he sighed uneasily. Maria's few words today brought to a head the feeling he had been harboring that a portentious cloud was gathering itself around Pietro's children. Vetch was beginning to frequent the beer taverns, Petra was spending too much time in the company of a man with whom she had but little in common, and Gabbi's vivaciousness was losing itself in quiet moments of brooding. Gabbi, since her father's illness, spoke no more of the state job for Robbie. It was as if she considered it fitting that he replace her father in the shed.

Maria pushed back a wisp of hair with the back of her hand. She hinted to Petra briefly, darkly, "Friendship with him may forfeit other dearer friends."

The old man asked suddenly, "All right to ride back with you to camp this afternoon, Petra? Me and the little Pontius Pilate have business to attend to."

A pressing quality in his voice drew her eyes to his hand as he gestured, behind Maria's back, toward the newly mopped tracks on the floor. Petra nodded although she was not sure of his meaning until she heard him climb the attic stairs for her father's gun.

Maria took a deep breath. "Your father looks forward to this dinner tomorrow?"

"Of course, Mama."

"It will be his last anniversary dinner with us —"

Petra paused. She said frankly, "I think so, Mama. Gino thinks so, too."

"He will be able to sit at the table with us?" Maria's tone was dull.

"I think so —"

Tip's horn blasted impatiently.

Maria whispered fiercely, "We'll make this dinner festive, you understand?" Her hands clamped hard to her daughter's arm. "No long faces."

They packed the groceries in Tip's rumble seat, stacking them around the excited dog. On Main Street, Petra's eyes picked out a slim, muscular figure striding jauntily into a beer tavern. It was Vetch. And in the middle of the afternoon when he should be working in the quarry! She said impulsively, "Take the next side street, will you, Tip? I want to stop a minute at my sister-in-law's —"

In the blue-and-white kitchen, her astounded ears drank Peggy's calm, "It's not the first day of work he's missed, it's the third. Don't be alarmed, Petra."

"But it's you —" Petra stared at her friend.

The summer sun had lavishly painted freckles on Peggy's white face. It was the same serenely plain face Petra had known in her childhood. Utterly futile to say against that placid expression, "It's *you* who should be alarmed. It's *you* who is having his baby soon."

Peggy sank into an armchair covered in gay Scotch plaid. She said matter-of-factly, "Vetch'll snap out of it in his own good time. Speak to him if you want to, Petra, but don't ask me to, because I won't!"

Behind the calm features Peggy was silently telling herself that she was smart enough to know what had attracted Vetch to her. And she was not going to spoil it now. Vetch was quite handsome. He had always been popular — he could have had a dozen better-looking girls. He liked her because she paid no apparent attention to his sullen, restless moods, because she didn't question him, and because she cleverly did not intrude into that aura of independence which he loved.

She added simply to her friend, "I — I understand how he feels, Petra. Your father's sick — it's made Vetch wonder about granite. It's disillusioned him. He wants this baby as much as I do. He knows his responsibility. And if he doesn't — well, I'd rather lose him that way than send him away from me by criticizing him."

Petra could find no answer. She uncrossed her legs, and smiled. "See you tomorrow at dinner, Peggy."

Once out of Granitetown's streets, Tip's car picked up reckless speed. His alcoholic breath drifted to Petra. He must have drunk, she decided, while she was visiting with her mother.

Beside her Mister Tiff, blue kerchief flapping at his neck, was reminded of the wild ride he had long ago taken to Canada. In an attempt to engage Tip in conversation and so slacken his speed, and at the one time to remind Petra of Tip's too colorful past, he leaned forward and sideways toward Tip. "This is like the time we went to Canada, eh, Tip?"

And the old man chuckled, for Petra turned her head to say tolerantly, "When did you ever go to Canada, Mister Tiff?"

He ignored her, and screeched across her to Tip's head, "Like the time we came down with a load of liquor, eh, Tip? Bootleggers, we were —"

A laugh roared from Tip's mouth. "You sure surprised us that night!"

The puzzle in Petra's eyes delighted the old man. He caressed his beak of a nose, and yelled, "Let me see — it was the night Pete Rocco was with us, no? The night he fell out of the car and was killed?"

The car swayed under Tip's hands, and slowed. The muscles of his neck were taut. Why in hell did that old fool have to open his mouth now after so many years! Not that it would make any trouble, but —

Petra asked slowly. "Pete Rocco bootlegged with you — and was in an accident?"

Pete Rocco made a dim picture in her memory. She knew of him chiefly through her father and mother. They sometimes spoke of that orphaned Pete who might have married Robbie Marclay's Aunt Ellie had he not fallen down the stairs and received a fatal concussion. And they spoke of Vetch's devotion to Pete, and how he had mourned his death. She stared with new eyes at the rugged, arrogant face beside her, and she wondered if Vetch knew something about the accident — and if that could account for her brother's intense dislike for Tip? The sharp, bold profile seemed to belong to a stranger. These last weeks as Tip boasted of his bootlegging adventures, had he never felt a pang of sorrow for the dead Pete? She said, "I've always heard that Pete Rocco fell down the stairs —"

"As good a story as any, isn't it?" he laughed. Then harshly, "Hell, it wasn't my fault he spilled from the car!"

The conversation ended there. But a quiet thoughtfulness was graven on Petra's face, and Mister Tiff was satisfied. The old man's pale eyes twinkled. The landscape was moving past them less hurriedly now. He sank contentedly to the leather cushions.

They found when they reached Chisel Point Pond that Pietro, with the help of Americo, had shaved his mustache. True, in the sheds it had served as something of a dust catcher, but abed it proved only a nuisance. Sans mustache, Mister Tiff decided, Pietro's face looked thinner and spoke more eloquently of his illness. The cheeks flamed a feverish red; and the firm, vital roundness of his body was shrunk to a flabby flesh that clung with listless tenacity to his frame. Mister Tiff thought wearily that the wise Hippocrates had indeed been justified in naming this sickness a "wasting."

Tonight Pietro had his supper abed, saving energy for tomorrow's dinner. And Americo, ever reluctant to embarrass his sick father with the presence of a guest at the supper table, again grasped the opportunity of inviting Aster to the camp for her evening meal.

A red July sun was hovering at the horizon when Mister Tiff limped away from Ronato's cottage, rifle slanted against a frail shoulder, Pontius Pilate waddling behind him. After a half hour of walking he saw, beyond an unkempt sweep of dusty, tough grass, a sprawling wayside stand. Hah, this must be the place where the beauty-stinted but brain-endowed Aster Mitcham helped her mother. The grimy wood of the little business establishment had long been weathered of its one coat of paint. But a wooden dachshund, boasting a fresh paint job, topped the roof, its tail bearing the sign — *Hot Franks, 5c Each.* The old man's fingers scurried into his vest pocket: a pencil stub, wooden rosary beads in a worn leather envelope, and, *si*, four dimes and a few pennies. He pushed open the door.

A half-dozen scarred booths dotted the floor. An open door at the back revealed a small, cluttered kitchen. Beyond the kitchen, Mister Tiff had remembered Aster saying, was the bedroom she shared with her mother. Tip Gioffi was unlocking the money box of one of his pinball machines. The drawer tipped. Nickels rained brightly into his leather satchel. He glanced at the newcomer, "Not a bad haul, huh, Tiff? How about a cup of coffee with me?"

Mister Tiff said, "No, but thank you." He watched the money pour into the bag. Hah, what an easy way to earn money! This Tip simply cruised the countryside in a fine car, stopping here and there to burden himself with jingling coins. Beside a limply curtained window, a juke box ground out the popular *Maria Elena*. A stout, dark-haired woman, red arms bulging from short, snug sleeves, was wiping a table and humming.

Mister Tiff coughed for attention. "How much for just frankfurts, not steamed, and without the little breads?"

The woman continued wiping in great arcs. "I'm not runnin' a meat store —"

"I know, I know. It is just that I want a little meat for my dog."

"I'll sell you some, three for ten."

"Hah, six then, please!" The old man laid two dimes on the table she was wiping. Her head snapped upright in sudden curiosity.

His pale eyes stared into a rouged, familiar face. Life had worn wayward paths into the forehead and cheeks that sixteen years ago were of velvet smoothness. And her figure sprawled a bit. But here were the same lively eyes and pert mouth. He could not be mistaken. "*Dio mio,* Josie Blaine!"

"Well, if it isn't Mister Tiff!" The woman pumped his thin arm in vigorous recognition. "You must be the old gent Aster's new boy friend talks about." She giggled. "Funny he didn't mention your name. I'd have known." Then memory surged over her in a hot wave. Her cheeks shone red under the purplish rouge, and her bright eyes shifted. "Listen," she said, "about that money, I always meant to pay you back, but there were the kids, and you know how it is —"

He shrugged, rubbing his beak of a nose. "Pah, that little bit!" Little bit! Mother of God, it had been the hard-earned wages of his *paesani* — his fare to Italy! "Forget it, eh, Josie? So this is your place?" It came to him that years ago he had given Pontius Pilate his first bath in front of Josie Blaine's house, and now here he was garnering the little dog's last supper from Josie.

Josie spoke her relief. "Well, say, that's nice of you." If he could forget, *she* certainly could. "I rented this stand for the summer. It's just a dump. This fall, I'm headin' for Florida again. There's a stand down there I been runnin' for ten years, every winter. I leased it out this summer. Say, I'm Mrs. Mitcham now, not Blaine. He's dead now, too — I mean my second husband."

The oldest girl was married, Josie told him, and the boy was going in the army. "There's only me and Aster now. Maybe it'll be Josie-on-her-own in Florida this fall. Aster's got crazy ideas about goin' to college. Well, I won't stop her, but I can't help her either."

It all came spinning to him across the years: the train trip; Josie's little girl and boy with their running noses; and Josie herself heavy with new life. . . .

"Aster is a sensible girl," Mister Tiff offered. "And bright."

"Mm-m, I suppose so." It was a compliment for which Josie could muster but little enthusiasm.

He saw that Tip was at the far end of the room intent on counting his money. He asked casually as if the question had not been poised on the tip of his tongue these ten minutes: "Have you seen Asa Conway?"

"Kind of nosey, aren't you?" she said flatly. Then she laughed, but it was not a happy laugh. "Get this — I don't have to run after men —"

"Of course not!" breathed Mister Tiff. "That, I did not mean!"

"Not even Asa, not even if I have good reason to. See?"

Mister Tiff quivered and caressed his beak of a nose. He was remembering the pinched look of Aster's face and comparing it with the face of Asa Conway. And surely Josie had just now confirmed what he had been thinking. "So," he murmured thoughtfully.

Later he followed the footpath behind Josie's stand to where it split into three thin, earthy fingers that poked their ways into scrubby woodland. He chose the path at the right. When he was out of sight of Josie's stand he opened the paper bag and shook out the linked frankfurts. Seven, Josie had given him, instead of six. "Eat then, Pontius Pilate, eat," he said to the dog. The animal's teeth tore into the skins. Mister Tiff braced himself against a tree, rifle poised. It was hard to part with one of the first friends he had made in Granitetown. "We were both beggars of sort, weren't we?" he whispered.

The heavens, he saw, were a picture-book sky of bare, cool blue but feathered warmly in the west with rosy fragments of clouds, as if a flock of giant robins had shaken their breast feathers there. Shadows would soon be lengthening across the countryside. His eyes came back to the dog; they blinked away a moisture. "The end of your day, too, Pontius Pilate." He aimed and fired.

Afterward his thin hands wrapped the warm body in a potato sack, and he sat beside it until darkness thickened between the trees. When he reached the camp, the grounds were quiet. From across the pond came the gay voices of *paesani* and the faint click-click which meant they were at their game of *bocce*. Fewer and fewer *paesani* went to the trouble these days of building *bocce* courses. Pietro's bedroom was lighted. In the kitchen, Petra would be preparing for tomorrow's dinner. He moved stealthily to the shovel he had earlier concealed in a hydrangea clump. He dug a grave beneath Ronato's granite angel, shoveling painfully, noiselessly. From the spruce oasis a bird started its evening chant. "Your requiem," Mister Tiff murmured to the shrouded form beside him. "And, think of it, you have for your tombstone the work of Granitetown's most skilled carver! True, Ronato might not like the idea of your sleeping here, but he does not have to know."

The anniversary dinner was eaten.

Pietro's night in his own bed in Granitetown was slept.

He scorned the family's suggestion that he ride from his home to the sanatorium atop the hill. Twenty-five years ago he had walked proudly into the humble doorway of 23 Pastinetti Place; today he would close the door behind him and, as proudly, walk away from 23 Pleasant Street. And all the twenty-five years between the opening and closing of that door were his. All his moments with Maria. The births of his children. Those gay fall evenings of grappa making. The earlier winter evenings when he warmed his wool-dressed feet in the oven, and read his Italian newspaper. The low-swinging kitchen light, and Maria's face in its radiant pool as she darned the children's stockings. The children studying. Himself oiling his gun. Skinning a rabbit. His children grown, healthy, strong. Making their own way in the world. Twenty-five years. All his. And it had all been made possible by the beautiful, time-enduring stone he had worked. It was a short lifetime; but a golden achievement. An achievement he could relive mentally now, and proudly, at his will. And so today he could walk out of that door proudly, too.

Maria grimly stifled her emotions; under her Sunday dress she was one tight ache. For the first time in her life she savagely touched a disk of rouge to her pale cheeks. She pinched her grief-locked lips until pain forced them to lie softly parted in numbness. She crooked her arm in Pietro's, and walked up the hill with him, she on one side, Petra on the other.

Mister Tiff sat on the porch and watched their slow progress. Ah, why could it not be his old body plodding to his Calvary instead of the more youthful Pietro's! Instead, why did not the *Dio* recall him, just as he himself had yesterday put the little black dog to eternal rest? A picture of the *Dio*, armed with a .22 flashed before him. He buried a wry chuckle, and limped down Pleasant Street to Asa Conway's store.

Joey Mull was in need of cigarettes again for he slouched over a broom, lazily sweeping the sidewalk in front of the store.

Inside, Asa's gnarled fingers fondled the coins in his cash register. "All alone, eh?" Mister Tiff inquired brightly.

The cash register closed with a slam. Asa grunted a surly affirmative. All Granitetown knew that since his housekeeper-sister died, his daughter Hester was away half of the time visiting her married sister, leaving him alone. Asa's pasty face raised warily. "Why the hell do you care, Tiff? You worrying about my health?" Throughout his years of association with the little man he had found himself growing more and more suspicious at each meeting.

"Well, you get older every day, no? You should take it easy now," the man said mildly.

Asa's laugh was harsh. He directed his words to the ceiling. "My God, now he wants me to retire!" He leaned across the showcase. "Where do you get all these ideas, Tiff? From crystal gazing? Well, you'd better look for another picture in your crystal ball because I've no intention of retiring!"

"Oh, but wait!" Mister Tiff protested. "Of course you do not want to retire. And me, I would truly miss seeing you in this store. I say only that you should take it easy —"

"Like you, I suppose?" Asa sniffed the words. Mister Tiff blushed. He was not proud of the fact that his work in Granitetown lacked a robust nature. "You should have help in the store —"

"I can take care of my store!"

"I know a young girl, a fine girl, she wants work."

Asa struggled for calmness. He picked a thread from his sleeve. He still had a weakness for green. Dark green predominated in the weave of his suit. "Tiff, we're getting too old for arguments. Once and for all, will you keep that snooping nose of yours out of my business!"

Mister Tiff stared at him, and his heart lurched in a sudden rush of affection and pity. Invectives he had expected, but an almost-pleading Asa was something new. A warm, kindly feeling rose in the old man and reached out to the storekeeper.

Asa was muttering moodily, "I got enough troubles without you adding fresh ones."

"We all have our troubles," reminded Mister Tiff very gently. He was remembering his old and unfaded sorrow at having to leave the seminary. "Think of the Delmonto family: the father dead, the mother sickly, and both children cripples. Actually, you are lucky, my Asa. Your children are grown and independent. You have comfortable bachelor rooms, you have your health and a store that makes money." He might have added compassionately, "Also, you are very, very lonely." Instead Mister Tiff chirped brightly, "That Socrates was right indeed when he said that if all our misfortunes were laid in one common heap from where everyone must take an equal portion, most of us would be content to take our own troubles and depart."

Asa's comment was a brief snort.

"This girl I was telling you about — she's a smart girl, Asa."

"My own brains were good enough to run this store for thirty years. I don't need anybody else's!"

"Hah, but this girl wants to cultivate her brains. She wants to go to college this fall. She needs money; she wants to work."

"Dammit, Tiff, for the last time, get the hell out of here! You trying to run my business for me?"

Mister Tiff sighed. Despite the disapproving face of old Don Benedetto which appeared to him mistily, he decided to toss prudence to the winds. He plunged desperately. "Me, I think she looks like you, Asa. A young girl, she is. She was born not long after they talked Josie Blaine out of town. About sixteen years or so ago, remember? This girl and her mother, they work in a wayside stand at Chisel Point Pond —"

Asa's face purpled. The veins in his neck swelled. Tiff's words did not exactly loose a bolt from the blue. Joey Mull had smirkingly stated, the other day, that he'd seen a woman at the pond who resembled Josie Blaine. Asa had tossed it off as one of Joey's poor jokes. Nevertheless, he had spent a few sleepless nights, and he could not decide whether the news pleased or displeased him. "Damn you and your hawk nose!" he spat at the man. "I said get out of here!"

"Sure, sure, if you want me to." The old man retreated a step from the counter, and from Asa's clenched fists, but he continued regretfully, "It would be bad, bad to have people wagging their tongues again about Josie and — and maybe you. And that will happen for sure if the girl and her mother come to Granitetown for this other steady job I know of. But if the girl works here and then goes to college, the mother can go back to Florida —"

"You damn blackmailing foreigner! You held the whip over my head when my daughters were kids, but I'm alone now — your talk won't bother me."

Mister Tiff trembled under Asa's terrible wrath. The old teacher stared in fearful fascination at the storekeeper's twitching mouth. He said weakly, honestly, "Me talk? Oh, no! I am thinking only what a fine chance this is for you to wipe a few black spots from your soul, and also to give yourself a little rest in your old age. This girl could work down here in the store, she could cook upstairs, she —"

Asa's writhing hands groped under the counter. Mister Tiff, with a surprised gasp, ducked from the path of a well-aimed five-pound sack of sugar. It burst against the wall, the crystals showering into a little white hill on the floor. The old man pulled open the door; he peered around it determinedly, his quavering words tumbling fast. "Let your mind chew on it, eh, Asa? This girl, I will send her to you tomorrow. She knows nothing about you except that you have a job for her, maybe. And pay her well — she's got to have money for school —"

Asa hurled an orange after him. Another. Another. Before the door slammed shut one of the oranges rolled out to the sidewalk. Mister Tiff stooped, picked it up and put it in his pocket with trembling fingers. Nor did the trembling cease until he left the business section and caught sight of St. Michael's church where he was going to make his daily visit.

Father Carty, slowly pacing his porch and reading his Office, was distracted by a joyful whistling of the triumphal march from *Aida*. He watched the whistling and limping Mister Tiff until the frail figure was lost behind the heavy doors of the church; and he knew that for the next half hour the old man's mild eyes would be fastened alternately on the tabernacle, the ancient statue of St. Michael, and the stained-glass window depicting St. Michael. The thought of that window always sent a warm red creeping into Father Carty's cheeks. He had an uneasy feeling that he had been literally swamped — naturally or supernaturally — into installing it. Ten years ago, when he became pastor and had found himself in a position to redecorate the church, he had planned that the new windows should portray scenes from the lives of Jesus and Mary. He had hoped, privately, that there might be enough money to depict his own patron saint, the poor St. Francis, on at least the smallest of the windows.

Father Carty had no proof that Mister Tiff had captained the successful crusade for a St. Michael's window, but he was reasonably sure. Only once had the old man complained that the wooden statue was showing signs of rot — and he had added, "It is fitting, yes, that the patron saint of our church be enthroned forever in the glorious rainbows of stained glass?" Mister Tiff had never mentioned it again. But soon hundreds were speaking to the priest enthusiastically of a window he had never planned. Neighborhood children asked excitedly if the St. Michael window would "look just like the statue." And was it true that the "new school, when built, would be called St. Michael's School"? The priest felt a ridiculous guilt for not being able to muster an enthusiasm equal to this wave of childish fervor, and he increased his prayers for divine guidance. Then one morning, in the mail, he received a check for one-hundred and fifty dollars from a well-known non-Catholic resident of Granitetown. With it was a simple note explaining that it was for the "new stained-glass window of St. Michael." At least ten smaller donations were received by mail, each one accompanied by a note directing that the money be used for "the St. Michael window." Father Carty accepted them, feeling something of a traitor to his beloved Francis, but it simply would not be a Christian act if he, by negative action, squelched this parish interest in the truly great archangel. Besides, didn't the church belong to the people themselves? And so St. Michael it was who finally adorned the window. A triumphant, beautifully winged Michael.

CHAPTER V

Mister Tiff told himself that had he not gone to the band concert in the park that evening and stayed until the end, he would have gone to bed early, without seeing Gabbi. And he would not have heard from Gabbi's lips the startling sequel to that presentiment he had felt in the spring when she had stated grimly, "Robbie will quit the sheds! I'll see to it that he takes the state job!" He invariably shuddered when he thought that if she had not emptied her heart to him, she might have stumbled into greater difficulties.

Granitetown's weekly band concerts drew Mister Tiff irresistibly. He liked music. Better, perhaps, he liked the park itself filled with the tantalizing odors of fresh popcorn and hot dogs, and the melee of men, women, children, and youthful lovers, all in holiday spirit.

He spent the greater part of tonight's concert hour mingling with the crowd, chatting with acquaintances and watching children and dogs tumbling over the green. The benches were filled, and he feared the ground might prove damp for his legs. He had decided to return home, when his alert eyes spied a couple dislodging themselves from a narrow bench beside the giant granite statue which symbolized youth. He sank gratefully to the seat. This last musical selection of the evening was proving to be a collection of modern and classic arias. Mister Tiff's smoldering imagination was so easily fanned into flame that, from the opening bars to the last quivering note, he lived a score of fancied scenes: he heard Eve warbling a solo to Adam, providing man with his first alfresco musicale . . . he saw Assisi's Francis listening to the orchestration of birds . . .

he caught a glimpse of ancient tribes answering the insistent rumble of war drums . . . Gable smiling at an inevitable blonde . . . nineteenth-century couples gliding before him in graceful waltz step, and managing with lightning swiftness to become black, nude figures with bare feet beating out a rhythmic, African patter. As the last concert note died, quivering in the night air, he hastily recalled himself to the present with quick shakes of his head, and he started for home.

Again he would have missed seeing Gabbi had he gone straight to bed. Instead, he paused for a moment's rest before attempting to climb the stairs to his room. He was sinking into the hammock in the shadows of the Dalli porch when Gabbi and Robbie arrived. The car door slammed. Then silence until they reached the porch. He was about to call out to them but Robbie's voice suddenly came, strained, stiff, youthfully bitter.

"You aren't going to ask me to come in, are you, Gabbi? That would be asking too much! This way it's a perfect zero of an evening for both of us — and that seems to be what you want — "

"I do want to get to bed early — "

"Nine-thirty!" Irony and pain tinged the words. "It's been like this for the past two weeks. Why have you bothered to see me at all, Gabbi? My God, if you're trying to kill off everything we had between us, you're doing a good job — "

Mister Tiff squirmed, and wished desperately that he had gone to bed. Strange, he told himself, that he would not have objected to accidental eavesdropping had the lovers been strangers or even casual friends. . . . He wondered if he should announce his presence with a cough. Gabbi was speaking now, her voice so faint that the words did not carry to his corner of the porch.

And Robbie sounded like a stranger. "O.K. Have it your way, Gabbi. Good night." He started down the steps, halted, and said over his shoulder, "Just remember that if this develops into one of those soured-up romances, it'll be your fault."

Mister Tiff could not see Robbie's face, but he knew it must be drained of the quality of good humor which one noticed first of all in him and which seemed to flow from him toward everyone he met. In coloring, he was like his Aunt Ellie — fair skin, reddish hair. There the resemblance ended. Ellie's face was pretty, but weak. Robbie's strong features matched his muscular body. Mister Tiff's mind went twisting over the years to the picnic at Peter's Gate and to the vision of a young Ellie radiant with love for Pete Rocco. A radiance that was destined to last for only a few minutes of her life, for Pete Rocco died the very next day. Mister Tiff was drawn to the present by the slamming of the car door. The car throbbed into life and drove away. Still Gabbi did not enter the house. Despite her earlier insistence that she wanted to retire early, she walked now to the top porch step and sat down. The old man wondered anxiously why Gabbi had said so little tonight and why she had quietly accepted the blame for their quarrel. To lack a spirited reply was not in line with Gabbi's nature. Unless — she was guilty. Mister Tiff trembled with an unknown fear. Guilty of what? He suddenly voiced a long, noisy yawn and hoped it sounded as if he had just awakened from sleep.

Gabbi uttered a startled cry and stared into the shadows.

"It's only me!" He laughed merrily, and babbled over his confusion, "I know I should say, 'It is I' but it sounds wrong. Hah, tell me, is it right that a sentence should *sound* wrong when it *is* right!" He limped over to her and sat beside her, at the same time managing to produce another yawn. "I heard the car start. It was Robbie?"

She was thinking only of rushing the question, "Did you — I mean, were you asleep?"

He felt her dark eyes on him, suspicious, questioning. He said, "I went to the band concert tonight. When I came back I was tired. The minute I felt the hammock under me — " His Latin shrug was eloquent. "Well, you know how it is — "

The answer must have satisfied her for she said no more. And he had to begin again, "Wasn't that Robbie's car I heard?"

She nodded. And in the very brief time it took her to nod she was living again the whole miserable evening she had spent with Robbie. . . .

The evening had started like many another. Unless they went to a movie or visited at the home of friends, they usually took a drive and stopped for a bite to eat before returning home. Tonight they drove to Montpelier and up the winding road to the top of Capitol Hill where an observatory of natural stone rose pinnacled against the sky. It was a warm evening, refreshed now with the tonic scent of spruce and pine. The little capital city, snug in its nest of hills, twinkled with a medley of lights; and the sky of velvet darkness was so spattered with stars that it seemed that sky must reflect Montpelier, or Montpelier reflect the sky. The lulled countryside called for moments of calm and contentment. But Robbie, hunched tensely over the wheel of his car, plunged into the theme that had been ravaging him for the past few weeks.

"When are you going to marry me, Gabbi?" They were sitting in their respective corners like strangers. Or like contestants waiting for the fight to begin, he reflected bitterly. And it had been so ever since that night a month ago — or was it longer? — at Peter's Gate. He and Gabbi, a strange, demonstrative Gabbi, had loved as they had never loved before. And now he did not trust himself to the nearness of her. It occurred to him that perhaps her blood, too, pounded with the nearness of him and that now her emotional and physical distance was an armor to protect herself against the repetition of that night. But if that were so, he reasoned, why did she not see the necessity of marriage, in fairness to himself and to her?

"Your father's illness shouldn't hold us up. I visited him this afternoon. He's just as eager to see us married as we — as *I* am," he corrected ruefully.

"I've a headache tonight," she said simply. "I don't even want to think of making a decision — "

"Decision! My God, Gabbi, you decided to marry me when you accepted my diamond, didn't you?"

Whatever answer she made was lost in the furious throbbing of the motor as he angrily jerked the car into motion and shot down the hill. But as they drove past the State House with its golden dome ablaze with lights and topped by a gracious Ceres, his fury had given way.

"Are you sure you aren't still holding that business of the state job against me? I swear, Gabbi, I'll take the damn job if that's what you want! But you haven't said any more about it — I thought — "

"No," she said quickly, honestly, "I'm glad you're staying on in my father's place. It seems — right that you should." For the first time tonight the old eagerness and vitality flowed into her voice. "I think Papa's glad, too. You've spoken to him — don't *you* think he's glad?"

Yes, Robbie agreed that the sick man was pleased. The conversation drifted, then, to small talk of the shed and the workmen. When they reached the Granitetown park the concert was still holding its crowd of men, women, and children to the confines of the little square. Gabbi expected Robbie to join the parked cars beside the hotel so they could listen to the music. But he drove straight ahead. Just beyond the sign which read *To the Quarries* he made an abrupt left turn and put the car in second for the steep climb ahead.

"Robbie!" Her voice was sharp with uneasiness. "Let's go home! My head — "

"I won't keep you very long!" He spoke grimly. "We're going to Peter's Gate whether you like it or not — "

"Take me home!"

"We haven't been up here since that night. You've seen to that, Gabbi! Maybe you're afraid it will happen again. Well, it won't! God knows — "

"I've never blamed you for that night," she reminded quietly. A wave of tension settled on her as he stopped the car on the spot where they had been on that other night. Above them spread the branches of a sturdy sugar maple and ahead of them lay the flat of Peter's Gate where summer picnics were held.

"Relax." His laugh was harsh. He took her hand in his and felt the blood pound along the fingers. "There are three questions I want to ask you — then we'll go home. First, that night, that last night we were here, you really loved me then, didn't you, Gabbi."

"Yes."

"And now, Gabbi, right this minute, do you love me any less?" He could not keep the dread from his voice.

"No."

Relief stirred in him like a long sigh and he said, "Then here's the third one: *When* are we going to be married?"

But he had to be content with her reply that she would tell him "in a day or two" and it seemed to him, as they once more reached Granitetown, that although she had answered his first two questions as he had hoped she would, there still rose between them a baffling, unpenetrable wall. . . .

He did not take her home. In his wearied mind lingered a hope that they might still, tonight, defeat the obstacle between them. They stopped for a sandwich and a nightcap at *The Turinese,* one of the many Granitetown restaurants that specialized in Italian foods. It was a popular spot. Robbie's hopes for intimate conversation with Gabbi sank dismally as they threaded their way among crowded tables. They passed a table occupied by Dr. Renaud and three of his friends. The old doctor's fork was breaking into a very tender portion of steaming chicken *a la cacciatore.* A side dish, heaped with *ravioli,* stood beside the main dish. Flanking the doctor's table, to the right, sat four Granitetown workmen chatting noisily over their wine, the smoke from cigars and cigarettes curling overhead to the already smoke-misted lights. Gabbi knew that here in *The Turinese* laborers, state officials, businessmen might mingle and eat side by side. Only last week she and Robbie had come in for a late dinner and had seen the governor and one of the United States senators at a small table beside a party of Gerbatti's workmen, and occasionally a friendly word was exchanged between them. A warm surge of pride for the democratic camaraderie of her home town swept through the girl; and hard on the heels of this emotion pressed a more personal feeling, a love and respect for Robbie who could take pride in the work of his choice even though it did not mean sitting at a handsome desk all day.

Gabbi lingered over a coffee and brandy while Robbie consumed two thick *salami* sandwiches. As Robbie had suspected here was no opportunity to reopen the subject that possessed him, mind and body.

And soon they stood on the Dalli porch, Robbie, sounding like a stranger, saying, "Good night — it'll be your fault." Then the slam of the car door, and Mister Tiff mushrooming from the darkness of the porch and sitting beside her. . . .

Mister Tiff was asking, "Wasn't that Robbie's car I heard?"

Gabbi nodded.

A car, making a turn at the Pleasant Street corner, grew long fingers of light along the street; they fumbled briefly over the old man and the girl and then the Dalli steps were left once again in darkness. In that moment Mister Tiff saw her tightly clenched hands, and the dry, tearless eyes in a wan face. He longed to lay his old hand on the short, black hair. He knew it would feel crisp and unruly with curls, so different from the smooth silkiness of Petra's brown hair. But a questioning, comforting hand had never been the key to unlock Gabbi's heart, he remembered, not even in childhood.

He snatched her hand in a playful swoop and said heartily, "Your marrying Robbie is the first smart thing a Dalli has done for a long time! Look at Petra, wasting her hours — "

"I should have been married long ago!"

The words leaped from an overburdened heart. As if that heart could no longer contain them, he reflected. And Mister Tiff knew that regardless of his method of approach she would have spoken them.

"You mean that Robbie's love is beginning to cool? Pah!" He punctuated his disbelief in such nonsense by slapping her hand smartly to his own knee. "That, I will never believe!" Mother of God, hadn't he himself heard the lovesick Robbie tonight? "Robbie is as changeless in his love as — as poor Ronato," he ended triumphantly.

She pulled her hand away with a fierce tug. "You don't have to tell me how Robbie feels!" Haughty, youthful assurance was speaking.

"But — "

"You might as well know it now." Suddenly she was breathing fast. Hysteria struggled against relief as she unburdened herself. "Everyone in town will know it soon enough. I'm going to have a baby! Do you hear? I'm going to have a baby!"

He could only stare at her dumbly in the darkness, his thin face flushed hot, as if the humiliation were his alone; and his back was atremble with icy chills.

"Go on, say it!" she cried bitterly. "Say that things like that don't happen to the Dallis of Pleasant Street! Say that things like that don't happen to girls who have a family like Papa and Mama! But it's happened, I'm going to have — "

"Quiet!" For Mister Tiff it was a roar. It was not time yet to be gentle with Gabbi. Not yet. The old man's breath poured noisily through long nostrils. A shaky finger futilely sought consolation at the wart on his nose, at the droop of silky mustache. He knew Gabbi from those early days when he shared Maria's household duties by changing the little one's diapers. He had seen her grow up strong, willful to be sure, but strong in morals and in the religious principles into which she was born. There was more to this, he told himself miserably, more. He was conscious of swift movement beside him. He clutched the edge of the soft yellow skirt as she made to rush into the house, and drew her back down beside him. He struck out in verbal relentlessness at what he sincerely hoped was Gabbi's weak spot. "Pah, what kind of a half man is this Robbie of yours! Why hasn't he insisted upon marriage? Why — "

"Leave Robbie out of this! He doesn't even know about it — " She tried to draw away again, felt his old hands holding there. "All right," she said desperately, "all right. I'll stay here, and you'll hear it all, then you can hate me, loathe me, despise me."

"I could never hate you, Gabbi." He spoke from his heart now, gently, kindly, for her own words were at last washed of fierceness and they trembled out to him, tear streaked and infinitely weary. "I could never hate you," he repeated.

"It's — it's awful," she whispered. "I've heard of girls who — do what I did — to win a husband. I've always despised them. Well, I did it intentionally, too! I planned it deliberately. . . . Not to get Robbie to marry me, but to make him quit the sheds." She felt the quick pounding of racing blood in the old hands that held hers, and the start of his body. "It — it was when he had a chance for the state job, and he refused to leave Papa's shed. And I thought I could — could tell him there was going to be a baby and that I wouldn't marry him unless he took the other job. I was sure he'd want to marry me right off, and that he'd leave Papa's shed — "

"But, dear Gabbi," he interrupted mildly, "you have little to fear for Robbie's health. In the old days, yes, but not now — " His heart was battering at his chest. Gabbi was another Maria! Here was the cycle. . . . In blind love for Pietro, Maria had entered a night-darkened shed, like a thief, to destroy a granite memorial. In blind love for Robbie, Gabbi had willfully broken the law of God.

"It wasn't his health I was thinking of," she sounded old, weary. "I — I didn't even have a good excuse for doing what I did. That's why I hate myself, that's why I — " She broke off, and when she spoke again her voice was heavy with shame. "I just didn't want him working in a shed; I was ashamed to be seen with him in his working clothes after four. Americo guessed how I felt. He knew I wanted to see Robbie dressed up. It was shabby and cheap to feel like that, and it was shabbier and cheaper to do — what I did. And then the day after, Papa told us he was sick. If Papa had only told us the day before. . . ." She was like a child, thinking it aloud and sorrowfully.

"Just as soon as I knew Papa was sick, I suddenly became very proud of all his years of cutting stone. And, just as suddenly, I was proud of Robbie for sticking to the job he liked even though it didn't mean a white collar and wonderful office. And I was happy that Robbie'd be — well, continuing Papa's work in the shed. So I said no more to Robbie about the state job. I know he was surprised — and thankful. But all the time I was hating myself more and more. And then, when I knew about the — baby, I felt that I couldn't tell Robbie without telling all — I mean, that I had planned it cold-bloodedly and deliberately. He would hate me, and I couldn't bear that — "

Gabbi's black head fell to Mister Tiff's knee, and he felt her shaking with silent sobs. There had only been a few times, since she reached school age, that he had seen Gabbi in tears. He caressed the short, crisp curls. Yes, she was another Maria. Let her cry the bitterness and sin from her heart.

Finally he asked, "None of the family knows?"

"Only you." She hesitated. "And Father Carty — in confession."

Again she was aware of her companion's quick start. She mistook it for a movement of surprise, and could not guess that his blood was leaping joyfully through his old veins, and that his heavy heart was lightened by this sign of her contrition. A tear was loosed from his blinking eyes; he wiped furtively at his cheek.

He detected a youthful reproach in the words muttered beneath her lowered head: "I *told* you I was sorry the very next day, didn't I?"

He raised her head and said briskly, "Hah, don't you think I have served as your 'wailing wall' long enough tonight?" The epithet had been attached to Mister Tiff years ago by a ten-year-old Petra. He had showed them a picture of dark-veiled women wailing beside the wall of Jerusalem, and Petra, accustomed to bring her troubles and tears to Mister Tiff's shoulders, immediately dubbed him her "wailing wall." "Now then, the thing to do is simple. You and Robbie must marry, soon, soon —"

"He'll hate me," she said in cold quiet. "He'll hate me when I tell him it was deliberate —"

Mister Tiff started to speak, but his thin lips flapped soundlessly, for it seemed to him that old Don Benedetto's face was struggling to pierce its way through the darkness, a strangely unfathomable expression on the vague features. He closed his eyes against the apparition and he prayed silently, *Please, please go away this one time. This is the daughter of my good friend Pietro. I want to see her happy. Surely it is the best part of prudence to start three souls on the road to happiness. Please go away.* He kept his eyes tightly closed, and he said on a fast, quivering breath, "Your child, Gabbi, has two parents. Since you love Robbie very much you do not for a minute think of asking him *why*. Nor will it occur to him to ask *you* the why of it. Tell him only that there is to be a child — I know he will want to marry you in a hurry. As for your family, tell them only that you have decided to marry now while your father is still with you —"

The girl raised her head. "When you put it that way —" she began hopefully.

"It is the only way." He spoke firmly, prepared to challenge even the persistent Don Benedetto. But no challenge was needed for, surprisingly, Don Benedetto's misty features drifted gently into a tolerant, understanding smile and then disappeared into the darkness.

Mister Tiff rose painfully, his legs stiff from their cramped position on the steps. "Up now, my girl. Get in there and phone

Robbie right away, quick. Tell him to come over now, and then the two of you make your plans."

He waited outside until he was reasonably sure that she had completed the telephone conversation. As he passed the living-room door on his way to bed he saw her curled in an armchair, the phone silent in her lap, and he knew she was waiting for Robbie. The ravages of shame and tears stained her cheeks, but through them shone a radiant peace. She was aglow like an altar candle, he thought through sudden tears — a candle that had been warped and twisted, but whose wick within still bravely sent a clean flame to God. Something in her joy stirred to wakefulness the great, single sorrow sleeping in his heart. And he guessed wryly that tonight, sleepless, he would ponder over the peace he had known in the old days at the seminary, and he would reproach his flesh for the weakness that had kept him from the priesthood.

Gabbi had already left for the office next morning when Mister Tiff came downstairs. And it was Maria who told him what he wanted to hear. She was too deeply enmeshed in thoughts of her beloved Pietro, he saw with relief, to feel more than quiet interest in her younger daughter's approaching marriage. "Gabriella," she said, "tells me she and Robbie want to be married soon. In two weeks or so. A quiet wedding. Ronato had planned a trip to Oregon where a new agency is to sell their memorials. Now, it seems, Robbie is going instead, and they want to make it their honeymoon trip. Ah, well, Pietro will be pleased, no, *Maestro?*"

As the earth traveled its course around the sun, some cranny of the Douglas quarry was usually left in cool shadow through even the hottest of working days. But today at two, a fierce over-head sun, free of cloud filters, blazed into each corner of the vast stone bowl. It bored into bare and browned backs perched along the quarry walls, and shuddering over pneumatic tools.

Denny mopped his glistening forehead with a handkerchief. He was in the pit chatting briefly with Vetch before climbing back to the comforting cool of his father's office. He was well aware of the fact that of late Vetch frequently failed to report for work, and he was acutely aware of the concern it was causing to Petra and to Peggy. Denny began to make daily trips into the quarry to chat for a moment with his friend not only because he enjoyed these conversations with Vetch but because he hoped that Vetch might recapture the old enthusiasm he had felt for his work. "We have a new Maryland order for some of our best granite," he was announcing confidentially to Vetch. "It's to be used for columns on a federal building." Denny was justifiably pleased. The order was from new customers and made through his own contacts.

Vetch scooped up a dipper of water from the pail. Interest spurted for a moment to his restless eyes. "Ought to come out of there," he suggested, indicating a sheer, flawless expanse of dark gray wall opposite them.

Denny nodded. "Mm-m, so engineer Olsen says."

Vetch had taken off his sun-drenched shirt and was rubbing it to his sweating back and chest. He rolled the garment into a ball and tossed it in the corner beside his dinner pail. "God, it's hot!"

Beyond them, water welled up through a crevice in the quarry bed. It spread, a shallow, greenish pool. A hose always lay in this water, sucking noisily and pumping it up the quarry walls and spilling it, finally, down a slope of thick spruces. Baldy and a rugged old Scot stood a few feet above them drilling a block that rose near the mouth of the hose. Baldy's thick hands jumped with the rhythm of the drill. The nozzle of his dust hose lay at his feet, close to the hole where it inhaled the spurting dust. His puffy lids squinted venomously toward Vetch. "That Dalli's takin' it easy again, takin' time off to mouth with the boss! He started this block with us — what's he want to do, wait till we've finished it for him?"

The Scot pushed up his helmet. He was tired of this fellow worker's open dislike for Vetch. "An' more power to him! You'd like to be in the lad's shoes yourself these hot minutes, wouldn't you?"

Baldy's mouth puckered. He whistled the opening bars of *You're in the Army Now*, but he was thinking of the parody with which Vetch used to taunt him. And Vetch was reminded of it, too, he saw, for the younger man had glanced up at him, his body taut.

The Scot mumbled, "Shut up! You know his old man's down flat abed. 'Tisn't a pleasant tune for the lad to be hearing."

"If he used to sing it, I can!"

The Scot eyed him in disgust.

Baldy interrupted his whistling. "Look at him, suckin' around the boss for a ten minutes' lay off! His pay check won't be any thinner'n ours, I bet! Not by a damnsight! Young Douglas's sweet with his sister — "

A piercing whistle blasted the air, warning the quarriers to stay clear of an ascending block. Baldy switched off his drill, forgetful that his heated voice was ringing loud. " — her holdin' her head high, and all the time she's messin' around that Gioffi fellow. Hell, she's no better'n his other women, she's — "

A fist smashed into his jaw. His chunky body spun around. He staggered on buckling knees against the wall. Vetch's eyes blazed into his. "Take it back, Baldy." He spoke in deadly quiet.

Baldy's eyes darted desperately toward the approaching foreman. He was trapped flat to the wall. Vetch's open palm smacked his cheek into stinging pain. Baldy's thick hands clawed at Vetch's throat.

The foreman was running to them. "Break it, you two!" During all the years he had been in the Douglas quarry there had never been an open fight.

Denny leaped the pool of water. He reached the stone shelf just as the two men, locked together, swung off the edge to the floor three feet below. The impact broke their grip. Instantly they sprang to their feet again, Vetch's knuckles rapping fast, sharp blows to Baldy's chin. A knot of men gathered on the narrow shelf. They crowded to the edge, pressing, in their excitement, to Baldy's drill which leaned against a small, jagged piece of grout.

"Watch out, up there!" Denny warned.

Baldy's hand fastened to Vetch's belt; with his free hand he jabbed wildly at his stomach. Wind belched from Vetch's throat. He tripped over the hose. His head lolled giddily against the shelf. The workers surged closer to the edge of the block. The grout piece was slipping. Denny yelled futilely, "Vetch!" He lowered his head and charged at him, shoving him to safety just as the stone slipped over the shelf. Denny's hand, outthrust to Vetch, knew a knifelike pain. Then he was snapped to the ground, his hand pinned beneath the jagged stone.

Vetch started dizzily toward him. The old Scot held him back. "He's all right, lad. Let me stop up that bloody hole in your arm." A short, deep gash in his forearm was spurting a scarlet stream. The Scot didn't wait for the first-aid kit. He ripped off his undershirt and bound the wound.

With the stone lifted from his hand, Denny stood up, swaying, staring at the gory mass that was his fingers. He tried them weakly, a fathomless expression on his pallid face.

In a few minutes, Denny, Vetch, and the foreman were being lifted from the quarry. Vetch's mind leaped backward to another accident, in a deserted quarry, when he and Leo Vitleau hung from a cable and this Denny had run breathlessly to bring them aid. And Denny had helped him again today — His throat ached with gratitude, with reproach. He touched Denny's arm awkwardly. "Thanks, Denny."

A faint smile hovered at his friend's mouth. "It isn't much of a hand anyway, you know." At the quarry's brim he waved aside the advice that they get attention in the first-aid room beyond the office. "Might as well go straight to the hospital. Vetch here can stand a few stitches in that arm of his." The strange expression still haunted Denny's face.

They climbed into the foreman's car. It crunched down The Hill's winding granite-chip road to Granitetown.

In front of the Granitetown hospital, a ruddy-faced gardener looked up curiously from the hedge he was trimming. Joey Mull slouched beside him, his jaws snapping at a wad of gum. His ferret eyes widened in fascination as Denny was helped from the car. Vetch followed, bedraggled in a tattered and bloodstained shirt.

"Cripes, lookit!" Joey whispered. "There's been an accident in the quarry —"

It was a matter of an hour and a half before Vetch was ready to call a cab and go home. The gash in his arm was sutured in six neat stitches. Dr. Renaud's work. They had not been able to get in touch with Gino. Dr. Renaud was still in the room across the hall, working over Denny's hand. Oh God, Vetch was thinking, Dr. Renaud might this minute be working over his own battered, gory head if Denny hadn't interfered! His stomach pumped under a sick nausea. He was unaware of the white-clad figure beside him until he heard Dr. Renaud's, "Three of his fingers are pretty bad."

Vetch grinned feebly. "Don't give him any more stitches than you gave me, Doc. He'll brag about it."

The doctor's eyebrow twitched. He was about to speak, but Vetch was already at the door. "Here's my cab — see you later, Doc!" Dr. Renaud shook his head slowly. He retraced his steps to Denny's room.

Vetch found his apartment locked. Peggy must be shopping or visiting his mother on Pleasant Street. He cut cross-lots to his mother's house. Americo was alone in the kitchen. The boy stared at Vetch as if he were an apparition; he stammered with relief, "Gee, it's true then! You're not hurt bad at all. That's what the hospital said when Petra called. But first — when Joey told us — we were scared —"

"Joey? Joey told you — what?" he demanded. He saw that his brother's cheeks were drained of color, his soft eyes strained.

Joey must have given him a big scare. He remembered vaguely of having seen Joey outside the hospital.

Americo hesitated. "You — you didn't see Peggy at the hospital?" He wished Gabbi were here to tell Vetch the disturbing news. But Gabbi and Robbie were married two days ago and were now honeymooning in Oregon.

Vetch groaned in irritation. "So that's where Peggy is! She went up to see me. What'd they have to tell her for? Well, she's probably home by now — "

His brother's hand held him from the door. "Look, Vetch, she — Peggy didn't go to the hospital to see you. She — she's sick herself. I mean — " The sharp question in Vetch's eyes pricked him to greater coherency. "That stupid Joey Mull, he must have been hanging around the hospital this afternoon. He — he must have seen you. Peggy was out here on the porch saying good-by to Mama — they'd been up the san to see Papa — and Joey came rushing up the street yelling, 'There's been a quarry accident! I just saw Vetch and Denny Douglas go to the hospital!' Peggy fainted. She — she fell down the steps. Gee, Vetch, don't look like that! Gino said she'd be all right! She had pains — Gino said maybe the fall would — well, maybe the baby'd be born sooner, so he took her to the hospital. It was just a little while ago. Maybe they're just getting there now."

"You call me a cab!" Vetch ordered his brother.

At the hospital, he panted at the startled office nurse, "Where's Mrs. Dalli's room? Where is she?"

His heart thumped at sight of Peggy on one of those high, narrow beds. Like his father's. He brushed past his mother and Officer Riley to the drawn face on the pillow. Her freckles seemed enormous against the pallor of her face; her eyes, dark with pain. "Peggy! God, Peggy — "

"I'm all right, Vetch." She struggled to make her voice ring strong, convincing. "Gino wanted to make sure — "

The complete certainty in her reassured him. He stroked her forehead. "That Joey Mull, that damn fool Joey Mull."

She did not return home the next day as she had expected. The pains came in the morning. Short pains, and stabbing. Vetch forgot the quarry; he would not leave the hospital.

Gino said, "Stop worrying. There's nothing seriously wrong with her. You're having your family a little earlier than you expected, that's all."

Vetch haunted the hospital lobby. Toward evening, a woman's white, beringed hand touched him on the shoulder. "Mrs. Douglas!" He was surprised. "Hello, Mrs. Douglas."

"I've just heard about your wife. I hope she'll be all right. They tell me the quarry didn't notify your family about the accident because you weren't seriously injured. In this case it would have been better if they had —" Mrs. Douglas' whiting hair, drawn upward in a cluster of small curls, added to the softly patrician look Vetch had admired as a boy.

"How's Denny's hand?"

"They've just given him a hypo. He'll sleep in a few minutes. Petra, your sister, will be with him tonight —"

He stared at her, "Denny's still here — at the hospital?"

He was shocked to learn that Denny was still at the hospital, that he needed a nurse. His own troubles today had driven Denny far from his mind.

He said, "I thought he'd gone home. I thought —"

Mrs. Douglas' eyes were dry, but her words trembled softly over to him, "Then you haven't yet heard that Denny's had three fingers amputated —"

He stood as if turned to stone. It was Denny's right hand that was hurt! The hand that carved! And it was Vetch's fault — if he hadn't gone wildly at Baldy, Denny's hand would still be whole. To think that such a small piece of granite could wreak this havoc. Small, yes, but a cubic foot of rough Granitetown stone weighed approximately two-hundred pounds. . . . He passed shaking fingers through his dark hair. Did Mrs. Douglas know that Denny had crushed his hand while trying to protect him from injury?

Mrs. Douglas, as if in tune with his harassed mind, said, "You're not to blame yourself, Vetch. You would have done the same for him — I know that. It's one of those accidents that happen, why — we don't know." She added in the same tone, as if it were no change in subject, "Your Mister Tiff called on me this afternoon. Such a comforting person. . . ."

Vetch's tight lips twitched with a sudden rush of warmth for the older man. He wondered how much of Mrs. Douglas' generous attitude — and genuine — could be laid to the door of Mister Tiff's endeavors.

Minna Douglas' eyes looked, unseeing, through the hospital window. She could not tell this young man that in her heavy heart she believed the accident was in punishment for a sin of her own. From the day a young Denny had shown interest and talent in sculpturing she had ruthlessly thwarted his every attempt to cultivate this God-given gift. She touched Vetch's shoulder in a silent gesture of good-by.

It was Gino who later came across Vetch, hunched and stunned, on the lobby bench. He whacked him heartily on the back. "Peggy's fine! It's all over, Vetch — you have a healthy, squawking six-pound son —"

CHAPTER VI

Pietro was learning in his bed at the sanatorium that the friends who had multiplied his joys in days of robust health, were now subtracting from his personal sorrow, by their visits. Coming back to Granitetown was as if he had signaled his friends for their company. They came regularly. His family, Mister Tiff, Father Carty, his fellow workmen, and all his neighborhood friends. Although night must fall here at the sanatorium, just as at Ronato's cottage, it did not seem to shroud him alone, but rather blanketed the whole of Granitetown snugly, himself and his family and friends together.

When, occasionally, the melancholy and reticent Ronato spoke enthusiastically of a current piece of carving, Pietro let him speak and could be happy with him, for he knew that honest speech was the picture of one's mind and heart and that Ronato must love his work. During the long hours of day and night he did not for a moment regret the years spent in carving memorials that were sent to the four corners of the country, to stand eloquent testimonies to lives that might otherwise be forgotten. They were testimony to his own life, too. To a bodily and spiritual courage — although Maria chose to call it foolhardiness — in pursuing the work he loved, despite its grave hazards in those earlier years. And a testimony to his freedom of will, and to his liberty, for other work would have shackled him, mind and heart, into slavery. Pietro preferred a lean liberty to a plump slavery. Actually, he reflected, his life had been far from lean even in the early years: he had gloried in his work, in his family. And he knew that an abundance of life was what a man could enjoy rather than what he possessed. Daily, unless rains veiled the countryside, his eyes sped from his little eyrie atop Pleasant Street, traveled over the Granitetown rooftops, and dwelt beyond them on The Hill where pyramids of grout rose outlined against the sky. And on "good" days when he was able to sit by his window he could look down upon the large stone sheds located just outside of Shed Row. He heard the morning whistles calling the men to work, and the afternoon whistles proclaiming that they were through for the day. And it was comforting to know that for hundreds of years after he was gone Granitetown men would be able to live comfortably, raise their families by working the beautiful stone that came endlessly from The Hill.

The marriage of Gabbi and Robbie pleased him. A father, he told himself, should feel great satisfaction in seeing his daughter settled in marriage with the man of her choice, and that man dependable and industrious. Robbie would never become Granitetown's wealthiest man but he would always provide his wife with a good living. On the Sunday Gabbi returned from her wedding trip, Pietro took her firm white hand in his. "Twice last summer I heard you say you hoped Robbie would take another job. Do you still want him to, Gabbi?"

She was prepared. She spoke lightly, shaking her dark head in the childish way he knew so well, and he could not guess that her eyes were purposely avoiding his. "It's the funniest thing," she admitted, "I certainly *did* want him to take that state job. Now I want very much to have him stay in your shed. He does, too — so that settles it!" She began brightly to tell him of her and Robbie's plans. They had finally found a small apartment next door to the apartment of Robbie's Aunt Ellie. The owner had agreed to paper and paint the three rooms. "They'll be ready for us in about three weeks," she added.

"I am glad, Gabbi, I am glad." He might have spoken to her then of his hope that some day Robbie would buy the Dalli shares in the partnership firm of Ronato and Dalli and thus keep within the family the business he had started. But Petra appeared at the door followed by Pietro's nurse. His older daughter's uniform was almost hidden under a white polo coat. Denny had left the hospital a few days ago. Petra was caring for him days at the Douglas home, but each afternoon she drove across Granitetown for a short visit with her father.

Petra's wide gray eyes kindled in warm excitement. "How," she demanded, "would you like to take a peek at your first and newly baptized grandson this afternoon, Mr. Dalli?"

Her father's soft eyes responded quickly to the warmth in hers before they flew questioningly to his own nurse.

"No infant visitors allowed here," the nurse said briskly, "but there's no reason why you can't go to the sunporch and look out at him."

They helped him to the wheel chair and he clung to Petra's every word as she described the baptism of Vetch's son, Peter Michael. "Wait till you see the long dress Mama made for him — it's a cascade of lacy ruffles. Peggy says it's lovelier than any of those she's seen advertised in the New York papers. And she ought to know, she's had her eyes glued to advertisements of baby clothes for weeks before Peter Michael was born . . . and do you think Peter Michael cried when Father Carty poured the water over his head? Oh, no — just a look of surprise on his little face, but not a whimper . . . you should have seen Mister Tiff, Papa — proud as a peacock that the baby's middle name is Michael! After the christening he insisted that Vetch hold him for a minute in front of that old wooden St. Michael statue, and Mister Tiff fondled his nose and beamed and winked up at the saint just as if the two of them had shared secrets all their lives, and he said, 'Here's another Michael, take good care of him.'"

When the little group reached the sun porch they saw Vetch standing on the close-clipped lawn, close to the windows of the sun porch, his son in his arms. And Mister Tiff hovered there, solicitously alert as a hawk guarding its young. For ten minutes

Pietro sat in his wheel chair and his hungry eyes feasted on the tiny face which was almost lost in the white froth of baptismal garments. And he told himself that God was good to allow him the consolation of looking upon this tiny part of himself that would not die with his own flesh but would continue living in this new Peter Dalli. He noticed that Vetch was using his injured arm with stiff awkwardness. But Pietro was not worried, for each member of the family had already assured him that the injury was not of a serious nature and that Vetch would return to his quarry work in another week.

And now the baby's brief visit was at an end for Vetch was already turning away, but Pietro saw the ever understanding *maestro* fumble with the baby's blanket and lift the lacy dress to reveal tiny, well-shaped legs. The old man raised the baby's arms, too, and boasted, "Dalli arms they are, Pietro, strong and active! They'll do a lot of good work in this world."

And Pietro was grateful to the old man.

Afterward, the subjects of birth and death were to stay with Pietro, entertaining him persistently for days. Everyone was born — a natural function. Everyone died — natural, too. Life and death; the beginning and the end. One as natural as the other. Yet death, he reasoned, was not as extreme as birth. For birth was the beginning of all, the commencement of both mortal and eternal life; and death was but the end of mortal flesh, while life continued immortally in the soul. And with this in mind, it was a relief to loose at last his tiring hold on the life of his flesh. It was a relief to relax his muscles, and never again to flex them against spells of racking coughs.

Gino climbed the broad, curving staircase to Denny's rooms. The door to what Denny called his den, but what was actually a spacious combination living room and studio, was open. He could see his patient, in brown lounging robe over tan slacks and soft white sport shirt, sitting before a large wooden packing case. The box was spilling over with fine wood shavings, and a flurry of them had settled like fresh snowflakes on the deep wine of the rug and on the screw driver and hammer which lay there. Denny's left hand was poking into the box. He lifted out a small tissue-wrapped object, carefully shook it free of shavings and then unwrapped it. Gino knew it was one of the many miniatures Denny had carved during those years in the West. Soon after his return to Granitetown Denny had one of the pale green walls of the den broken into niches for his carvings. Now the wall space on either side of the fireplace was a honeycomb of bare shelves awaiting the figurines. Yesterday Petra spoke to Gino of Denny's intentions to unpack the miniatures. Gino considered it unwise for Denny to face these poignant reminders of a career that was now definitely closed to him. Before the quarry accident there had been hope that the weakened hand and fingers might some day gain strength enough to resume their work, but now those fingers were — gone. But Petra, her smooth brow wrinkled in concern for Denny and speaking to Gino not as a nurse to a doctor but as a lifetime friend of both Gino and Denny, suggested that it might be better if he wasted no time in facing "these reminders." "I know, Gino, that he's suffered a shock, a mentally depressing shock, but if he's willing, even if it's a forced willingness, to face what's left of his career, why not let him? It will be easier now than later. I've seen some of the articles he's written for art magazines. I'm not qualified to say whether they're good or not, but they must have some merit if they've been published. He might even discover that *writing* about art can be to him a second best to creating his miniatures. It's strange, isn't it, Gino, how some of us will see a goal when we're children, plan it, and cling to it through our teens and into manhood or womanhood until we achieve it." (She was completely woman now, he thought, and not Petra, the nurse. The gray eyes were softly rapt, held in dreams to something infinitely precious. And he wished with all his heart that his own being and nearness could evoke that steadfast radiance.) "Robbie," she was saying, "Robbie had dreams of becoming a great criminal lawyer, but somewhere along the way he lost sight of that goal, and now he's perfectly satisfied in Papa's shed. And as for myself, I never thought sincerely of nursing until I was a high school senior. But Denny and Vetch and you —" (The rapt light faded from her eyes. They turned to look into his now and he was disappointed that in their personal message for him he could interpret only warm admiration and affection.) "— you three held to your young dreams. Vetch wanted to be a quarryman, Denny wanted to carve, you wanted to become a doctor. Suppose you were suddenly forced to give up general practice, Gino; wouldn't you turn, if possible, to work associated with medicine even if it were — well, being salesman for a medical company? I — I keep thinking that if Denny can at least make a hobby of some work associated with his art that he will be a whole Denny again, regardless of the loss of his fingers. It seems such a little thing — to unpack those miniatures now and put them there as reminders on his shelves, but it may be just the thing to either jolt him or ease him into his natural being, even though there's bound to be pain —"

And Gino had agreed.

But he had not expected that Denny would attempt to pry open a good-sized packing box with only one good arm.

The deep pile of the Douglas' rugs muffled his footsteps as effectively as the deep wood moss of Granitetown's forests. From the doorway he growled, "Hey, who gave you permission to do carpenter work?" Denny gave a start, and the miniature fell into the soft wood shavings of the box. A hell of a doctor I am, Gino reproached himself silently, startling a patient out of his wits.

Denny picked up the figurine, a tiny schoolboy of reddish stone with books strapped to his shoulder, and inspected it carefully. There was relief in his voice when he said, "Listen, fellow, if that had dropped to the floor and been broken, you'd be nursing a couple of black eyes of your own!"

"Yeah?"

"Yeah."

Gino opened his bag and took out bandage scissors. "Let's take a look at that hand." He expected, as he changed the dressing, that Denny would speak of the carvings packed there in the case beside them. But Denny, it seemed, was not yet ready to discuss his work, not even with his friend and doctor. His sole oblique reference lay in his brief, "Incidentally, it might soothe that medico's soul of yours to know that I didn't open the case. Johnson did."

Johnson, the Douglas' gardener-chauffeur-handy man, was married to the maid, Larsa. Both of them had been with the Douglas family for as long as Gino could remember.

With the new bandage in place Denny went to the window seat where he had left his cigarettes. This double window looked down the slope of Douglas Hill to Granitetown while the west windows of this corner room offered a view of the lacerated bulk of The Hill. Gino returned gauze and scissors to his bag. As he raised his head his glance fell on the open doorway to Denny's bedroom and beyond to the bathroom. He told himself ruefully that fate was conspiring to throw Petra and Denny together while he himself was thrust away from Petra, alone, making his calls on the sick.

He snapped together the bag with a loud click. "Where's Petra?"

"At the baptism. Vetch's baby. And then she was going to see her father." His blue eyes sought his wrist watch. "She should be back soon. Stick around and we'll have a drink — to the baby."

He shook his head. "I'm a workingman," he said, and mentally kicked himself for the red that was spreading over Denny's cheeks. "I've some more calls to make," he amended. He took a step toward the door, hesitated.

"Denny."

His friend lifted inquiring eyes from the cigarette he was lighting.

"About Petra." Gino could not hide his hesitancy to speak the words that would keep Petra and Denny together for a few more weeks. "Her father's getting weaker every day. She mentioned that she would like to stay with him."

Denny rose from the window seat. Tall, lean, gracious, more the host than the patient. "I suppose I can get along, if her father — "

"Let me finish, will you?" the other complained. "Her father says he'd rather not have her, not now when he's nearing the end. A case of her distress adding to his. And I guess he's right. Besides, he already has excellent nursing care. I may not be able to reach her by phone, so if you'll tell her for me that she should stay on here — "

Denny stared at him curiously, aware of a restraint or perhaps reluctance in the other's words. A silence, foreign to the two friends since it carried with it discomfort, grew between them. Voices grew up to them from the terrace below, and Denny grasped the opportunity to bring the uncomfortable silence to an end. He drew aside the flowered drapes from the open window. "It's Petra. Nice car," he offered. "It's a newer edition of mine."

Gino was suddenly beside him looking down at the stony, arrogant profile barely visible in the car. "Tip Gioffi."

"Oh."

Denny was remembering the last time he had heard that name. In the quarry just before the accident. If Vetch hadn't overheard Baldy's reference to Gioffi and Petra, he might now have his fingers. And Vetch might not now be torturing himself with daily visits to Denny, torturing himself because Denny had maimed a hand to save him. And Gino, his eyes on the departing car, passed despairing fingers through his dark hair. He was in love with Petra, Gioffi appeared to want Petra whether he was in love with her or not. How could one know? Love was such an abused, maltreated word. And as for Petra's feelings, and Denny's — In his harassed mind he saw the four of them chasing ineffectively around and around, like a merry-go-round. Imagination did not easily sway Gino, and now angrily he closed his mind to the picture.

Denny was saying half to himself, "You don't suppose she's serious about him — "

Gino had had enough. "Dammit, if you want to know why don't you ask her!"

Once again this afternoon Denny stared at his friend, but it was at the broad back disappearing down the well of the stairs. Gino's attitude was clear enough now. Gino was in love with Petra, and he, Gino's friend, could not feel happy about it. He strode restlessly to the packing box before the fireplace.

"Hi!" Petra greeted unprofessionally, and vanished into the closet to hang her coat.

Above the rattle of clothes hangers he heard her running account of the baptism and her visit with her father. "Gino's mother was at the house afterward and Tip Gioffi drove by as she was inspecting the baby on the front porch. He stopped to take a look, too, with Vetch scowling for all he was worth. Vetch has little love for Tip, I guess. Tip heard Americo asking to borrow my car — by the way, he's leaving for the university week after next — and so Tip offered to drive me here."

She was ignorant of the cause of the quarry accident, Denny and Vetch had kept that much from her. Her words continued to come in light conversational snatches from the clothes closet. His heart thumped high and hard against his ribs, and he wondered if this was purely a physical weakness or if it was relief at having her explain her presence with Tip as a coincidence. Even when he was convinced that it was the latter, it left him hollow and cheerless. All his life she had been dear to him. But it had to be now, when he suffered a useless hand and when he discovered how desirable she was to Gino and to Gioffi, that she was suddenly grown more desirable to him.

She chatted on as she came into the room, slim and straight in her white uniform. "Gabbi and Robbie are back. They said they'd be up to see you tomorrow night."

She spied the packing case and then the stone figurine on the chair. An exclamation of delight escaped her lips. Her finger tips touched the chubby legs and arms. "He's sturdy — yet dainty, like a Hummel figurine." And she decided aloud, "It's good."

"It's good," he granted dryly. "Talent, nothing more."

"I'm hardly a genius as a nurse," she countered, "but I think the world stands more in need of everyday talent than the hard-to-find genius." She tried hard to keep her eyes from his bandaged hand, from which even that talent had been crushed. She set the figurine in a niche beside the fireplace, stepped back with brown head cocked to one side to study it. "Why not unpack all of them, Denny, then we can better judge how to arrange them?" She insisted that he sit in a plump, overstuffed chair, while she sat on the floor removing the figurines from the box. Larsa brought them iced tea, cast a grim look at the storm of wood shavings on the rug, and departed silently determined that since Johnson had let himself be talked into bringing that box into Denny's room he could jolly well help her clean the mess.

A half hour passed. The box was nearly empty. Petra knelt on the floor, her right hand groping in the box. "The last one," she announced, retrieving the tissue-wrapped object. She caught her breath sharply. In her hands was a group of tiny figures stemming from a single base. The outstanding figure was a faithful replica of the wooden archangel in St. Michael's church, and beside it stood a thin, frail man, unmistakably Mister Tiff even to the neckerchief, cane, and beaked nose. Three smaller figures huddled under the archangel's great wings. A slender boy, his head familiarly upraised and questing, could be only Denny himself. The second child had the sturdiness and strength of a young Vetch. A little girl completed the group, a pig-tailed figure with the edge of a panty leg showing beneath the short dress.

"It's us, Denny!" she cried. And the past came tumbling back, the patter of their childish footsteps along the aisle in St. Michael's church and the tap of Mister Tiff's cane, and Mister Tiff whispering, "St. Michael . . . be our protection. . . ." The Dallis and the Archangel, she reflected with a smile, had been irrevocably united through the efforts of Mister Tiff. Even today, an older Mister Tiff offered the newest Dalli to the protection of those wide wings. And Denny, with his hands, had preserved that union in stone. Suddenly her very existence seemed to take on new meaning. The little figures in her hand and the feelings they stirred were like a swift shift of a kaleidoscope changing the pattern of her life, and she knew clearly that her own happiness lay in making Denny happy.

She had been kneeling on the floor as she groped in the box. Now, intent on her thoughts, she still knelt there, the little figures raised before her.

Denny looked at her silently. At the pale, triangular face; wide, gray eyes under level eyebrows; and wide generous lips. Her brown hair had fallen forward and it hung shoulder length soft and full like the hair of Cranach's *Saxonian Prince.*

Vitality, health, and a rapt tenderness surged through the paleness of her face. Almost unaware of his thoughts he decided that such qualities could be made more successfully alive in oils than in sculpturing. He had always sketched his miniatures, and more often than not modeled them in clay, before carving them. He felt a compelling urge to attempt to portray the face before him. Again his heart thrashed in his breast, but it was the thrashing of a caged bird who sees a chance for freedom. He told himself it was not too much to hope that with thumb and index finger he might be able to sketch, to wield a brush. He might not be a genius, but he might be able to transpose some of his talent to canvas.

He asked casually, "How long before this bandage comes off?"

He had to repeat the question, and she had to hurry herself to the present before she answered, "Only a few weeks, I think." A tense quiet in his face made her add, "Why?"

He laughed. "After all, why shouldn't I be interested in learning when I can go around unswathed." He must not tell her. He must tell no one. If further disappointment lay ahead it must be for him alone. He must wait and see of what the remaining fingers were capable.

Pietro never saw Peter Michael again. A week after the baby's christening Petra arrived at the sanatorium for her usual afternoon visit and found her father napping. She sat beside him for a while, watching the tired lids quiver over the sunken eyes. Then she slipped out to one of the comfortable wicker chairs in the sun porch. Her own eyes soon closed drowsily, and she was gliding into the tranquil days of childhood when she and Peggy tramped Vitleau's orchard for the summer's first violets. A hand shook her. She woke to the urgent words of one of the nurses. "Miss Dalli, your father —"

Petra flew past her down the hall. Gino was attempting, with ice packs, to prevent the ever-widening of those bright patches of red on her father's pillow. She knew he was dying. It was added torture to see his soft eyes humbly pleading forgiveness of her: as if he were saddened at causing her this grief, yet himself were quite willing to go.

They came quickly from their corners of Granitetown: Father Carty, Maria, Gabbi, Americo, Mister Tiff. Pietro wished wearily that the white-tunicked Gino would keep his busy hands from him and let him die in peace. The boy's efforts were delaying, only for a few minutes, the great and final moment of release. This business of dying would be a drifting, not unpleasant sensation, were it not for the grief-ravaged faces around him that tore at his heart.

Of all the eyes about him only Maria's were dry, bright; her face, an inscrutable mask. He was proud of her. As strong, as unflinching as granite she was, he reflected, in his last earthly flicker of humor. The same qualities in these two he loved. . . .

The faces around him blurred. He was soaring giddily above them, out of and above himself. He could scarcely see his family and friends; yet in a strange lucidity he was viewing the complete panorama of Dalli life in Italy and in Granitetown. He was with

his childhood friend, Italo Tosti, in the hills of northern Italy . . .
he stood at Italo's grave in Granitetown . . . and here he was testily
suffering Gino's tireless hands . . . he was embarking with Maria
on the blue Mediterranean . . . he was beside her in their bed at
Pastinetti Place . . . he was here at the Granitetown sanatorium
watching her face grow dimmer and dimmer . . . he plowed
brown fields under an azure Italian sky . . . he hunted mushrooms
at Peter's Gate . . . he was in Gerbatti's shed caressing beauty into
stone . . . he and Italo were boys, pilfering eggs from the hennery
of the village priest Don Ricardo. . . .

Redheaded Father Carty, breathless from this hurried sick call,
stood gravely over Pietro. Pietro saw him as another Don Ricardo;
and he murmured the deathbed plea of the old world *paesani*,
"Gesu, Giuseppe e Maria!"

But his last breath did not come. He was in Gerbatti's shed
once more, his hand guiding the steel into the pattern of a slender
cross. He sweated over his work, eager to finish it before the end
of the day's work. . . .

A four o'clock whistle began screeching to Granitetown that
stonecutters were through for the day. In Shed Row, another
whistle, and another, took up the cry. Pietro heard them. A smile
settled on his gray face. His head dropped forward in a nod, and
then he was dead.

CHAPTER VII

" — fifty-six, fifty-seven, fifty-eight!" Joey Mull's dirty nails scratched ecstatically in his unkempt hair. "Cripes, fifty-eight cars! Kind of funny though," he mused, "him goin' before the leaves turned. Asa always says most of 'em go in the fall or spring."

"Is — would you call that a *large* funeral?" Aster Mitcham asked. She was thinking of Americo Dalli's heart, tight with grief over his father's death. Perhaps pride in an unusually large and fine funeral would displace some of that grief. She was ashamed that she could not sincerely mourn Pietro Dalli. She was concerned only with his son's state of mind.

Joey's ferret eyes gleamed. "Leave it to them Eyetalians! Biggest funeral in 'bout four months." Assured that the girl's attention was riveted to the tail end of the funeral procession winding down Main Street, he edged to Asa Conway's counter, his fist stealthily entering the wide mouth of a peanut jar. A peanut or two rapped to the counter.

She swung around, surveying him levelly under a cloud of dark hair. "You better put those back, Joey Mull. He'll blame me. I'm not going to be blamed for stealing. Put them back — or pay for them."

"Cripes, how's he goin' to know?" Joey plopped them into his mouth. "He's right there in that funeral parade; isn't he? How's he goin' to know?"

Aster fished a note pad from her apron pocket. It was one of Asa's store aprons; it traveled twice around her slim waist. "I have to jot down every sale. Besides, his eyes always take inventory

258

before he leaves the store and when he gets back. Even if he goes out for only five minutes. He'll know there's some missing —"

"Nuts!" He smirked. "Peanuts!" He rattled the rest of them in the scoop of his hand, and shoveled them into his mouth. "I washed his car for him this mornin', didn't I? What'd I get? A lousy fifty cents, that's what. I oughta take a quarter's worth in trade from the old tightwad. I'm a mind to tell him so, too."

"You'll have a chance to." Her old fountain pen scraped across the pad. Her violet eyes were intent on her writing. "I'll put down — 'five cents worth of peanuts. Not paid for. Joey Mull.'"

"Hell, you're as stingy as Asa!"

"This is a business establishment, Joey," she said practically, "and you *can't* give things away and expect to make yourself a profit."

Joey licked the salty palm of his hand. "When your face screws up over figures, you even *look* like the old sourpuss."

Mr. Conway *was* stingy, she admitted to herself, or was it thriftiness? But he was kind to her. Wasn't he making possible for her this year at college? It seemed like a dream that she should actually be planning to go to college. A rosier dream than ever, for Americo would be there, too. Why shouldn't she repay Mr. Conway with honesty? She'd been working here ever since early July. Ever since that day Mister Tiff said to her, "Go to the Conway fruit-grocery store at 129 Main Street. I hear he wants a girl to work for him." She'd been nervous those first few minutes with Asa Conway. He had peppered her with surly, irrelevant questions. He himself had fairly trembled with a sort of nervousness. She was sure it was not dislike for her because he offered her twenty dollars a week plus board and room. Much more than she had hoped for.

He didn't seem to mind if Americo hung around the store. He seldom spoke to her, except when it concerned the business; and he kept his eyes averted. Yet, sometimes, as she worked, she felt his eyes following her. If she turned, he shifted his gaze with lightning speed, his sallow cheeks flushing with something like fury. Strangely, it didn't frighten her, she felt sorry for him. He needed company. His globe-trotting daughters appeared to show little interest in him. Aster slid the note pad into her pocket and wondered if Mr. Conway would miss her when she left for the university in a few days.

Suddenly she wanted very much to see his long, sour face round into a smile. "Joey!" She rocked thoughtfully on the balls of her feet, her hands clasped behind her back. "Joey, how long does a funeral last?"

"I had a girl once what used to hold her hands like that — behind her back. Aggie was her name. Aggie Rugg. She's gone now."

"Did she die, Joey?"

"Sort of."

"Joey Mull, be sensible! Either you die, or you don't!"

Joey touched a finger to his head. "She sort of went off up here. I got a *Granitetown Times* clippin' that tells you all about it. My name's in it, too."

"Oh, that's too bad — I mean, about *her*."

She hesitated for the respectful pause she felt was due such tragedy and then repeated, "Joey, how long will the funeral last?"

"All depends."

"On what?"

He wasn't sure, but he told her, "Well, some get sermons and some don't."

"Oh —"

"But 'bout an hour, I'd say."

"Look, Joey, let's surprise Mr. Conway. You sweep the sidewalk and wash it with the hose. Oh, I'll pay you — I'll pay you from my own money. And —" What could she do to please Asa Conway most? She had to admit that he looked happiest when fingering the day's receipts. "— I'll polish the cash register."

CHAPTER VIII

Two days after his father's funeral Americo left for the university. Maria, in black cotton house dress with neck and short sleeves piped in white, stood on the porch in a pool of warm September sunshine. She watched his short, stocky figure, so much like that of a young Pietro, piling tennis racket, baseball bat, and other sport accessories onto the back seat of Vetch's car which was to carry him to Burlington. He returned to the porch for the small bags resting on the steamer trunk beside her. His soft, limpid, brown eyes wore the glaze of painful uncertainty. For him the experience of his father's death was a new and penetrating knowledge, kneading itself into emotions and feelings that had never before been stirred in his young life.

He said uncertainly, striving to gain certainty and comfort from the assurance and firmness which he had always associated with his mother, "I still think I should stay home with you another week. Gabbi'll be gone and Petra and Mister Tiff will be at work —"

She shook her head, smiling. "It's all settled, Americo. You're ready to go now. It's best that you start with your classmates on the very first day. Besides, didn't you promise Aster a ride to the university? If I know Aster she will want to be there on time."

She could see the uncertainty make way for his little disappointment. "Oh-h, old Conway decided to drive her up himself."

Of them all, Maria told herself for the thousandth time, Americo was the only one who was truly another Pietro in body and emotions, and she would have preferred infinitely to keep him beside her. She had loved Pietro more than anything and anyone in the whole world, better than these her children who were woven of her own flesh, blood, and bone. Lucia, after those three days when Pietro lay in his coffin in the living room, had recalled her own Italo's death and she had marveled quietly to the dry-eyed Maria, "You are brave. Braver than I." But Maria had mentally shaken her graying head. Nor did she explain that it was not really a braveness, but simply her way of life. In her earlier years she had even committed a criminal act to safeguard the health of the man she loved. When she learned, with pain, that neither threats, pleas, nor wits could change Pietro's deep-rooted regard for his work, she had become reconciled to it. Grimly and bitterly, perhaps, but reconciled. And now that Pietro was gone, she must become reconciled to that, too. Bitterly perhaps — because she could not forget that years ago she had envisioned the stony hands that would choke off Pietro's breath — but reconciled. She agreed with the *maestro's* reminders, put to her subtly in so many different words each day, that if she grieved for Pietro it would be far more painful for her and her children than if she accepted the *Dio's* word that death meant but a short separation and that some day she would join him in the unknown world he had reached before her. In moments of such thought she almost forgot that it was Christ and not Pietro, who had said: "*Let not your heart be troubled . . . and if I go and prepare a place for you . . . I will take you to Myself; that where I am, there you also may be.*"

A school child skipped down the street waving a maple twig, its leaves early crimsoned and poignantly prophetic of approaching autumn. Maria, an alert eye on the luggage Americo was stowing in the car, was reminded of the heavy socks she had included in the boy's wardrobe. *Si*, fall would soon be here, and winter. With warm sunlight pouring over her she trembled helplessly in a sudden chill. Unless she acted quickly Pietro's grave would remain unmarked during Granitetown's long winter months. Half of Pietro's satisfaction in his work, she knew, had lain in the joy of perpetuating in stone the memory of some once-living person. It seemed to her of the utmost urgency that he should not lie for a lonely winter in the Dalli cemetery lot, bereft of the stone he had loved.

When Americo's waving hand disappeared around the corner of Pleasant Street, she went to the telephone with the ready resolve that had always been hers. She gave the number of Pietro's and Ronato's shed, and her restless eyes fell to the little pad on which Petra had noted the phone numbers frequently used by the Dallis. Halfway down the column, between Denny's number and the grocer's, was an underscored *sanatorium — 28*. Automatically she picked up a pencil. The blunt lead swept a broad black line through the notation.

"Ronato," she said into the phone. "This is Maria, Maria Dalli." She lapsed into Italian, "I want to put up a stone for Pietro before winter. Will you design it?"

And now, scarcely ten days after Pietro's death, she gathered her family together in her home for the purpose of selecting a memorial for him. They finished the simple noonday meal just as Ronato's steps were heard on the porch. Maria untied the white apron from her supple waist and bustled her brood into the living room.

The long-faced Ronato wasted no time. Slender, strong fingers drew two sheets of paper from a manila envelope. One of these he handed to Maria.

"It is not an accurate print," he explained. "It is simply a sketch I made. A new design, especially for Pietro — there is no other exactly like it."

Maria looked at the penciled sketch, Gabbi, Vetch, Petra, and Mister Tiff pressing at her sides for a view of it. They knew, after the first glance, that Ronato had spoken the truth when he said that they would not find its duplicate. The upper and solid rectangular block was not unique. Its beauty lay in the classic simplicity of line, a beauty that would be enhanced, they knew, in the flawlessly smooth sheen the granite would wear after it was polished. But centered just above the base was a narrow twelve-inch panel depicting two sinewy arms, the hands of which held a chisel to the rough lines of a small, unfinished memorial. The panel, carved by Ronato, would be a masterpiece of beauty. To Mister Tiff it called up a picture of the delicate artistry of the Robert Burns Memorial beyond the park; to Petra it brought memories of Denny's little miniatures. And in the silence Maria sensed their approval. During the years when her children were growing to maturity Maria had realized more sharply than ever before that although she and her children were one in blood and close together in heart, yet each was an individual alone in himself, a tabernacle of thoughts which could be kept secret or disclosed as one saw fit. But in this brief moment she could feel the silent swelling of their approval, and she spoke for all of them as one. "It is beautiful, Ronato. It is truly meant for Pietro."

A swift smile lessened the melancholy of the sculptor's face. Yes, it was beautiful, he prided himself silently; of that the artist in him was sure. And it was meant for Pietro. Or at least he had thought it was until yesterday when, glancing idly through one of Pietro's old folders, he had come across this second drawing which he now held in his hand. The edge of the sheet had protruded from the folder, dog-eared, yellow, and furred with granite dust. He had recognized the drawing of the rococo cross. It was what Pietro had called his little "masterpiece." Was it fifteen, sixteen, or seventeen years ago that Pietro worked on it? The cross had been near completion when one night someone had stolen into the Gerbatti shed and ruined it. Pietro was angry over the destruction of his work and deeply pained that, as he put it, "anyone should hate me so much that he would destroy the best of my work." The incident had remained a mystery to Pietro and his fellow workmen. Ironically, Pietro had no opportunity to start another such cross, for the customer who had ordered it immediately chose another stone from Gerbatti's stock of completed memorials. But Pietro must have loved the cross, Ronato knew, or he would not have kept the design all these years. Perhaps he had hoped that some day there would be another customer who would turn proudly possessive eyes on the intricate carvings of the cross. But no customer had ordered it; and Ronato now believed with all his heart that Pietro would prefer for his own memorial this cross of his own design and worked by the hands of his friend and partner.

Ronato was not a man of many words. He said to Maria as he handed her the second sheet, "This is Pietro's cross which someone destroyed many years ago. To be sure *I* meant the other design for Pietro, but I think *he* would like this one."

Mister Tiff was proud of Maria, standing straight and untrembling under the shock of Ronato's words. For surely, he thought, as his fingers sought comfort from the long ridge of his nose, she must be remembering; she is no longer in this cozy room of plump over-stuffed chairs and divan; she is remembering that fall night in the cold darkness of Gerbatti's shed when her hands rained blows upon Pietro's cross.

Maria's eyes lifted from the sheet and met his. For a fleet second there might have been no one and nothing in this living room, nothing but the locking of her black eyes with his mild blue ones. And he saw memories growing in Maria's eyes, memories that would never be told in words, not because words were inadequate but because she had purposely buried those memories so deep within her that words could not reach them.

Maria felt her children crowding to her, their eyes on the cross. They were all acquainted with the story of the mysterious destruction of their father's "masterpiece." Gabbi, with a bride's impatience to get back to the new apartment she was scrubbing for occupancy the following week, said, "It's too fancy, Mama, I like Ronato's better."

The young brutality and rawness of Gabbi's words were lost on Maria. It was as if she were hearing no words but Ronato's earlier, "*I* meant the design for Pietro, but I think *he* would like this one."

Maria's eyes held to Pietro's cross. "It *is* Pietro," she said.

She was experiencing a strange sensation, as if her husband were here with her and knowing, at last, that she, his wife, had been guilty of the crime. She felt sodden with shame. And she knew she must give him in death what he had cherished in life. He must have his little "masterpiece." In later years when she looked back to this scene in her living room she realized that this decision, more than time itself, healed her of the bitterness she had felt for granite, and helped her to see that stone, beautiful and lasting, was worthy of being claimed as a lifework for Pietro and for any man. And in later years, too, she would realize that the *maestro* had then and there caught the almost miraculous significance of that moment, for once again his eyes had locked with hers, and in his she saw understanding and a quiet satisfaction.

Petra peered over her mother's shoulder. A strand of light brown hair spread like taffy against the black of Maria's dress. Once, many years ago, while walking with her father she had exclaimed joyfully over the formal garden of a Douglas Street home, pointing out the oval and circular plots of grass with only a few flowers in their centers. But he had shaken his head. "Too few flowers, Petra. See, they look lonely. Besides, it is a shame to waste all that good earth when it is capable of producing many more flowers." Perhaps, Petra reflected, her father had felt the same way about granite, and that was why he had worked the entire surface of this cross in an intricacy of design. "Yes," she said, "Papa would like it." Then, her wide gray eyes were drawn back to the panel in the first sketch and she could not but envision the carved hands and chisel as they might stand in rugged relief against a shining surface of polished stone. The panel reminded her of the miniatures filling the niched wall of Denny's room. On her father's last day at the sanatorium another nurse had offered to relieve her of Denny's care for a week. She had accepted. Now Denny was well enough to get along without nurses. He still kept to his rooms except for his meals which he had with his parents downstairs. He had sent over the three Douglas cars for use on the day of the funeral, and each day there had been his phone call. She missed the unexplainable peace and the quiet conversations of those days in his room. They had seemed an unbroken extension of childhood; and time, from her graduation to the day of Denny's return to Granitetown, was as if it never had been. She straightened, remembering Denny's last phone call yesterday. He had asked lightly, failing to disguise an undercurrent of eagerness, when she was coming to see her "former patient on Douglas Hill." "As soon as I can," she had promised. And tonight Lucia Tosti was coming to spend the evening with her mother. It would give her a chance to see Denny again.

Ronato extended an arm to the level of his shoulder. "The cross should stand so high."

Maria nodded. It had not been necessary, after all, to get her family's verbal opinion on the choice of the memorial. As soon as the second design was recognized as Pietro's modest "masterpiece," the choice had been a foregone conclusion, except to Gabbi.

Vetch was silent. The longer he looked at the design the more convinced he became that he was experiencing an about-face of all those thoughts that had been tormenting him since his father's illness. And he could have cried for sheer relief. The stone his father had designed in life would stand over him in death. Vetch was sure — why, he could not explain — that his father, wherever he might be, was rejoicing over this fact. And surely if his father could still hold a kindly feeling toward stone why should not he, Vetch, rid himself of the torturing feeling that in returning to his quarry work he would be disloyal to his father?

He was aware of the drone of voices about him. Ronato assuring his mother that the cross would be standing over the grave before the first snowfall, and Gabbi wheedling Petra to "come along and help me get the new apartment cleaned." He passed a hand across his forehead. His throat and eyeballs ached with the burning dryness that comes from lack of sleep. He promised himself that he would not stop at the beer tavern today, that he would go home to Peggy.

He slipped out behind his family to the kitchen and turned on the cold-water faucet, waiting for the water to come cold and free of bubbles. He gulped the water. His stomach received it with icy, exhilarated tremblings that were part of this new lightness of heart and mind. It was part of the joy of knowing that he could again open up great blocks of granite. He could lay his hand against virgin stone and thrill to the knowledge that his was the first contact since, as a molten mass, it had been conceived in The Hill thousands of years ago.

The thump of Mister Tiff's cane sounded on the kitchen linoleum. The bulging golf bag hung from the old man's shoulder. He was saying thoughtfully, "I can't make up my mind what to do. Shall I work this afternoon, or shall I accept Veet Palingetti's invitation to ride out to Chisel Point Pond in his meat truck?"

"The pond road should be good today," Vetch encouraged. "There won't be many more nice days left in September." He moved away from the sink to make way for Petra who had entered the kitchen with Gabbi in time to hear their conversation. Petra was rummaging in the utility cabinet beside the sink for scouring powder and brushes. "I'm helping Gabbi at the apartment this afternoon, Mister Tiff. We'll drive you down to meet Veet, if you want."

She closed the drawer. A little cry escaped her lips. "Darn, I caught my finger." She rubbed the finger briskly. "Just a little pinch — and it hurts. Denny's fingers must have pained him a lot before they were amputated —"

Mister Tiff saw the quick stiffening of Vetch's compact body. He knew only that Denny had injured himself in coming to the rescue of Vetch, but he suspected that there might be more to the accident. Vetch's brooding told him that. Beneath the almost sullen indifference of Vetch lay a deep sensitivity. Mister Tiff had become acquainted with it that first night in Granitetown when the boy had warned him that the high heels on his foreign-made shoes would make him the laughingstock of the town. It was revealed again when the boy quietly mourned Pete Rocco and Leo Vitleau. And now the boy was blaming himself for the loss of Denny's fingers. Perhaps it was justifiable, but it was helping neither Denny nor Vetch. The old man's frail voice said to no one in particular, "It seems to me that you are making melodrama of Denny's misfortune —"

Petra forgot her finger. Face and voice reproached him. "He carved with that hand."

The old man looked at his own white hands where veins rode high and blue among the wrinkles. And I, he thought sadly, I wanted more than anything else to use these hands to elevate the Host at Mass. He said humbly, "Perhaps the *Dio* took his fingers for a very good reason. Losing his fingers doesn't mean the end of his life. Denny has health, a beautiful home, education, an opportunity to do a fine job with his father's quarry. Denny will make out well, that you need not worry about. Right now he is busy, reading all the histories of quarrying he can get hold of. Some I brought to him myself from the library —"

Vetch interrupted harshly, "Denny never wanted to quarry." There was a pinched look around his mouth.

Mister Tiff shrugged. "And I never dreamed I would mend umbrellas, but I am quite happy at it." His white head nodded slowly, and he said what he truly believed, "Denny will be happy. You'll see. Stone is his heritage just as it is yours. He cannot help but respect the business which his grandfather founded and which has meant a good living for hundreds of Granitetown families. Can one help but hold a genuine liking for what his heart respects? His heritage is perhaps as old as yours. Who knows? Your father has told you that your great-grandfather hewed stone in Italy. When your forefathers were working at stone in Italy perhaps Denny's forebears were doing the same in Scotland."

The tight line of Vetch's mouth relaxed. "Cripes, the arguments we had when we were kids! I used to tell him I bet my ancestors worked in the old da Vinci quarry hundreds of years ago. He'd

come back at me with the bet that his ancestors helped carve the
Sphinx, and that was hundreds of years before da Vinci's time! I'd
say, 'The Sphinx isn't in Scotland, so how could your ancestors have
had anything to do with it?' And he'd suggest that maybe some of
the Sphinx carvers could have migrated to Scotland. And I'd say,
'Listen, Italy's nearer to the Sphinx than Scotland, isn't it? If they
did any migrating I bet they went to Italy where there was plenty
of stone. Granite, and marble, too.' 'But lot of it is lava stone,' he'd
argue —"

Gabbi cut in impatiently, "This isn't cleaning my apartment." She
rolled her pile of clean rags into a neat bundle. "Do come along,
Petra!"

Petra's wide eyes held seriously to Mister Tiff's. She had reason to
believe him. He had never failed her with truth ever since the day
he had come to them as a temporary guest but had remained to
become one of the family. She wanted to believe that she and
Vetch were dramatizing Denny's misfortune, she wanted to believe
that Denny could be happy managing his father's quarry. "You —
you seem so sure he's going to like being in the granite business."

It was a statement, but the man saw the question in her eyes and
in the entire bearing of her eager body. "Hah, how can one think
he is not truly interested when all this week he digs into those
books and when he pelts me for a whole half hour — *si*, I was up to
see him for a half hour last night — when he pelts me with stories
of early quarrying in the Old World and here? About Denny, no
one should worry. He is the kind that makes himself invulnerable
against the world. One of these days some smart girl will grab him,
like that —" His fingers made a faint snapping sound. "— and his
happiness will be com — complete." He stumbled over the last words
not realizing, until he was actually voicing them, that he had made
almost the same remark to Denny last night.

He and Denny had spoken of the closeness of spirit between
Petra and her father, and Denny had said, "She's going to miss him
a lot." Mister Tiff, managing a carelessly prophetic tone, had coun-

tered with, "One of these days some smart fellow will find her, he'll make her happy." He warmed with a hopeful inner smile at the flush that rose from Denny's neck and spread over his cheeks. But the warmth chilled in his veins for Denny, after a glance at the pink, healing stub of a hand, said, "You mean Gino, don't you? Is it that way with Petra, too?" The question and resignation in Denny's voice had sent his old heart thumping wildly. "No, no!" he had cried at first, had then modified it to, "Well, I don't think so," and in a conquering burst of truth ended miserably, "Truly, Denny, I don't know." He had scolded himself mercilessly for his well-intended interference, calling himself a senile meddler. He could quite understand why Don Benedetto had stressed the need of prudence. Perhaps Denny and Petra belonged together. Perhaps Gino and Petra belonged together. Perhaps Petra, like himself, needed no partner in this world. It was frightening to think that a few words of his might bring sorrow to Petra who was dearer to him than any other of her family.

And today, despite yesterday's resolution, he had thoughtlessly made the same goading remark, this time to her. And the words were striking at her as they had at Denny. A deep red rushed to her pale cheeks.

He was spared further agony over his own shortcomings by Gabbi who was urging Petra to the kitchen door, "*Are* we going to get at that cleaning, or aren't we?"

For the time being Denny was forgotten. On the porch Petra paused. "You mentioned going out to the pond, Mister Tiff. Isn't this your 'transformation' day?"

"There's a late afternoon movie for school children today. A colored picture of animal life in Africa." His pale eyes smiled. "Me, I would have gone, too, but it would be poor business to suggest by my presence there, that the animal pictures are more important than the language of their forefathers."

Petra drew the forgotten golf bag from his sloping shoulder. "If you're going to the pond there's no need of being burdened with this." She laid the bag on the hammock and tucked her arm under his. It was a gesture of affection and he responded with a slight pressure of his thin arm. Her slender, warm body brushed his side as they walked to the car. Petra had once told him that his was an ageless heart. But he was an old man, he knew; his was a paternal love for her and, paternally, he was vexed that Denny could not or would not respond to the tantalizing nearness of her.

Gabbi sat in the driver's seat of Robbie's car, Petra beside her, Vetch and Mister Tiff in back. The sisters began a discussion of furniture for Gabbi's apartment. It was a scant ten minutes before the car drew to a stop in back of Veet's meat truck on Main Street.

Mister Tiff climbed out. Vetch followed. "You're coming to the pond?" the older man inquired.

Vetch shook his head. "No."

They were standing in front of a men's clothing store. Vetch said, "I'll have to buy a couple of work shirts if I go back to the quarry Monday." He hesitated. "I don't suppose you know it, Mister Tiff, but I'd almost made up my mind not to go back. To the quarry, I mean. Then, a few minutes ago when I saw the stone my father designed and carved, well —" He left the sentence dangling in mid-air, and made for the clothing store.

Mister Tiff stared after the young man until he was lost from view in the store. "I don't suppose you know it," Vetch had said. Mister Tiff smiled. Had Vetch actually thought that no one could see the turmoil of his mind the past few weeks, and that no one had guessed why he stayed away from the quarry?

"*Maestro!*" Veet's rich bass sounded from the near-by meat truck.

He took fast, limping steps. Veet's broad, hairy hand reached down and pulled him up to the perch beside him. The motor throbbed. Veet backed the car from the parking space.

"Just one more trip to the pond this year," Veet began conversationally. "Most of the camps are already closed."

"Mm-hmm."

"I am thinking next year to put a meat stand there, and stay there."

"Mm-hmm."

"But I would have to eat sandwiches at a wayside stand, or do my own cooking —"

There was no reply. Veet glanced at the seraphic smile on the old face. The *maestro* was paying no heed to his words but was making silent conversation with himself. Veet began humming *La Spagnuola.*

Mister Tiff fixed unseeing eyes on the countryside. Truly, this was one of the most comforting days of his life. Vetch was going back to the work he had dreamed of even as a child, and without which he had seemed lost these past weeks.

During Pietro's illness, when doubts were forming in Vetch's mind and when he was beginning to neglect his work, Mister Tiff had found himself questioning his own belief that good produced only good. He reasoned: Pietro lived a simple life, a good life, faithful to God, to his family, to the work he loved; yet his illness, which came as a result of his lifework, had unwittingly willed to Vetch a bitterness toward that selfsame life. And toward stone itself. To sow goodness in life but to leave a son to gather a harvest of bitterness did not seem to him to be in the nature of God's ways, devious though they might be. Maria's bitterness had been born in the early years of Pietro's work. To be sure she had not given voice to it these many years but it must have lain there in her heart, quieted. Today when Mister Tiff saw Maria select Pietro's own "masterpiece" for a memorial and when his eyes locked briefly with hers, he became confident that she was at last washed of this bitterness. And his heart exulted. Vetch, on the other hand, had painfully thrashed out the problem in his own heart these past weeks even when seeking temporary comfort in the Main Street beer taverns; and he, too, had reached his decision today.

Mister Tiff became very quiet. The world was suddenly one great hush and he heard neither passing cars nor the rush of the road underneath him. He heard only his thoughts.

The little man basked under a great peace. He should never have doubted his own convictions. Pietro's kindly sowing had not resulted in an evil harvest. Pietro's memorial was a symbol of Pietro's lifework. Of himself. As such it had today given its benediction of peace to Maria and to Vetch.

Veet's hearty voice sent his thoughts scampering. He saw with surprise that they were already beside Josie's wayside stand. The door and windows were closed, but juke box music seeped out to them thinly.

"Just a ten-minute stop I got to make up the road, then I'll be back for you," Veet said. "Most of my customers are on the other side of the pond."

Mister Tiff was humble. He apologized. "Me, I wasn't very good company for you today, eh, Veet?"

Veet grinned. He dug into the pocket of his white butcher jacket for a stogie. "That's O.K., *Maestro*. I know. Sometimes I feel like that. Sometimes all the talking I want to do is with myself —" He tapped his forehead with the cigar. "— up here." He helped the older man from the truck, and over the throbbing of the engine reminded, "In ten minutes I'll be back."

A small truck and a blue coupe were parked beside Josie's stand. But the neighborhood wore the usual after-Labor-Day air of desertion. Most of the little colony had returned to Granitetown. But the pond area would not be completely deserted. Fall and winter days, stonecutters drove out to their cottages for week ends of hunting and fishing. Today a single rowboat broke the monotone of blue water. Occasional roadside maples, with early ripened leaves, flushed scarlet between the green cool of pines and spruces. Beyond a bend in the road he caught a glimpse of Ronato's dewinged angel. Even though it stood on a highly elevated position only the top of its head was visible over the treetops.

Josie was not alone. A teen-age couple sat in the booth near the juke box. The girl's hand was beating time on the table and she was paying little attention to the boy's seemingly earnest flow of words. A blue-jowled stranger, lanky under loose slacks and pull-over sweater, sipped coffee and smoked at a small table near the counter as he chatted with Josie.

Josie raised a plump arm in greeting. Her heels clicked as she went behind the counter to get more coffee for the stranger. She wore high-heeled pumps today and she had discarded the usual cotton work dress for a blue dress of silky material. Two unrelated brooches and a bar pin cluttered the straining front of her dress. Josie's dressed-up appearance suggested to Mister Tiff that she might be planning to close her stand this very day.

"Cup of coffee?" Josie asked him. She moved to the end of the counter, leaned across it, and added *sotto voce,* "On the house, Tiff."

Over the steaming cup he smiled into the heavily powdered face. And he was thinking that he had her to thank, as well as St. Michael, for being here in Granitetown and not in Mussolini-ridden Ibena.

"I came to say good-by, Josie, and to wish you good luck in Florida."

"Good luck — I can use plenty of that. But Florida, well, haven't quite made up my mind. I mean —"

She did not explain what she meant but Mister Tiff was certain that her eyes, for a flickering second, held a strange, eager light. He wondered uneasily if she and the blue-jowled stranger had been making plans.

Josie's fingers flipped away a few pieces of doughnut from a post card lying on the shelf beside her. "Heard from Aster," she announced. "Read it," Josie offered.

He took the card. Doughnut grease stained the colorful depiction of sunset over Lake Champlain. On the other side Aster had written: "Hi, Mom, I have two classes with Americo D. We're planning to do some of our studying together if we can. My courses aren't easy but I like studying. In fact I like everything here. Love, Aster."

The old man's index finger caressed his beak of a nose. "So," he murmured softly.

"Study, study, study." Josie gave a good-natured snort. "It don't take much to give some people a lift!"

"Perhaps it isn't the studies alone," he suggested. "Perhaps Americo helps give her this — what you call it — lift. He's a fine boy, like his father."

"He's nice enough," she conceded, "— quiet though. When I was her age I liked my company to have a little pep."

Their conversation was brief. It seemed as if only five minutes had passed before Veet's horn blared away in front of the stand. Mister Tiff shook hands formally with Josie, hastily repeated his hopes for her well-being, and departed.

The day was growing progressively comforting, he reflected happily, as he once again took his place beside Veet. The money Asa had paid Aster was contributing toward her education and, if the post card told the truth, toward her happiness. He decided to ask Veet to drop him at Asa's store. Asa should be told about Aster's brief post-card message and about the good his money was doing. Money lying untouched did no good, but once it started circulating. . . . A chuckle bubbled in Mister Tiff's throat. From the depths of memory he had stirred up an almost forgotten picture.

"Did you know, Veet, that my father was a homely philosopher and that I heard my first lectures on the good and evil of money while standing beside a pile of manure? When I was a little boy in the Old Country my father used to take me out, each spring, to the edge of his great gardens and chestnut groves. He would point out a towering pile of manure standing hot and steaming under the sun. And he would say, 'Look at that pile, Michele. It is the winter's accumulation from our barns and stables. It is doing no good standing there, is it? In fact, it is covering ten square yards of earth which could be made to grow a profitable little vegetable garden.' He would ask, 'You agree with me, Michele?' I would answer, 'Si, Papa, I know it is doing no good.' He would continue:

'The manure itself is too strong for most seeds, but when it is spread over the earth the soil is enriched and its goodness makes better trees and vegetables.' And he would always add, 'It is no sin to be wealthy, Michele, but it is a sin to be a miser. Remember that money is like manure, it does no good until it is spread.'"

Veet laughed. "Your father was right, *Maestro.*"

The stone-shed whistles were blowing by the time they reached Asa's store in Granitetown. The sun was still bright but a September chill hovered in the air. Mister Tiff drew the kerchief higher around his shriveled neck. Aster's post card message had filled him with kindliness and warmth for Asa, and he admitted to himself that it was the first time during all his years in Granitetown that he was looking forward with genuine pleasure to a little visit with the storekeeper. Two customers came out of the store as he entered.

Asa's half-bald head was deep inside a showcase and his arm, stretched full length, was arranging chocolate bars in a far corner. He heard footsteps and looked up into the newcomer's beaming countenance. He asked without moving his head from the showcase, "You want to buy something, Tiff?"

"No, but —"

"I thought so."

"— but I have good news for you." Mister Tiff smiled. He wanted very much to reach out and take Asa's hand in his own and tell him what a fine thing he had done in making it possible for Aster to go to school. But under the wariness in Asa's eyes he could say only, "Aster writes that she is studying hard and that she likes college. I know she is grateful to you, Asa."

Asa drew his head from the showcase.

Mister Tiff's pale eyes widened. For a second he felt that a stranger stood there in Asa's clothes. Surprisingly Asa's features were twisted into a smile. It was a smile which his face had long outgrown and which no longer fit but, nevertheless, a smile.

"Had word from her myself," he announced.

For the second time today a post card depicting a sunset over

Lake Champlain was put into Mister Tiff's hands. This card was free of doughnut grease. Asa had placed it for safekeeping in the sanctum of his cash register. Mister Tiff read: "Dear Mr. Conway, I rather miss being in the store with you but that doesn't mean I don't love it here. I do! I'll write you a real letter when I know more about my courses. If you happen to come to Burlington sometime I'll show you the campus and buildings. Aster."

A knot of tenderness rose painfully in the old man's throat. He said in all innocence, "It's a shame, Asa, that she cannot make this her home for week ends, no? She will be alone and —"

The rest of the words suffered a silent death for Asa was beside him, and Asa's hands were wiry bands around his arms. The cane clattered to the floor. Mister Tiff's startled eyes sought Asa's face. A deadly tenseness was graven there.

"You snoop!" The tense, low whisper matched Asa's face. "I beat you to it this time! You hear me, Tiff? I beat you to it!" He punctuated each phrase with a shake that left the little man dizzy. "You didn't even give me the idea — I had it all figured out and decided long before that limping, meddling carcass of yours got out of bed this morning —"

"Please —" The plea quivered from Mister Tiff's lips.

"Aster's going to live here, see? Right here — and it wasn't your idea, it was mine. *Mine!* And I'm marrying her mother next week! I'm marrying Josie — go ahead and peddle that around Granitetown —"

The spoken promise sapped Asa of speech and strength.

Mister Tiff squirmed loose, picked up his cane. He protested automatically, "Asa, I don't gossip."

Asa recovered quickly from his outburst. "Why don't you get out and stay out, Tiff," he muttered wearily. He marched behind the showcase and his hands began puttering again among the chocolate bars.

Despite the fear that was urging Mister Tiff away from the store he wanted to explain to the storekeeper that he had been unjustly accused; and in the same breath he could not help thinking wistfully of how flattered he would have felt had he truly made these commendable suggestions to Asa. He was ashamed of his thoughts. God — and Don Benedetto, he added wryly — were no doubt pleased that Asa had acted without assistance on his part.

Out in the sunshine he turned in the direction of the church. He guessed that today's visit might be a long one, there was so much for which he was grateful.

CHAPTER IX

At the moment when Mister Tiff was slipping away from Asa's Main Street store, Gabbi's hopes for completing the cleaning of her new apartment were being shattered by the unexpected appearance of Gino. Petra and Gabbi had scrubbed the kitchen linoleum and were starting on the front bedroom. Gino, driving past the house on a neighborhood call, saw Petra framed in a window washing the glass with great, circular motions of her arm.

Gabbi welcomed Gino with a grin. Her face and arms were smudged with dirt, and the usually crisp curls lay in moist sculpture to her warm forehead. She indicated a pile of cleaning cloths in the center of the room. "Personalized cleaning cloths, no less — and a swell variety to choose from, Gino. There's a couple of Robbie's work shirts, a shredded pink silk shirt which Mister Tiff insists used to belong to a count in Italy, and one of Mama's serviceable cotton slips. Help yourself to a couple and pitch in."

Her cheer was short lived. Gino sat on an overturned pail. The conversation drifted to Denny. Gino said, "I removed the bandage yesterday. I think he can go without from now on."

Petra asked quietly, "How is it?"

"Oh — healing."

"Two fingers left — ugh, it must look horrible!" Gabbi twirled a cloth and inspected the window near Gino. It was speckled with tiny dots of white paint. "Look at that!" she wailed. "Painters ought to be fined or something for leaving windows like that. It'll take an hour's scraping to get the darned stuff off. Petra, you didn't bring a knife, did you?"

But her sister was untying her apron with unmistakable I'm-through-with-work deliberation.

There was a strange quality of intentness in Petra's eyes. She did not want to wait until tonight to see Denny. "Gino, have you time to drive me over to Denny's now?" And despite the dismay on her younger sister's face, she washed her hands, drew a comb through the pale brown hair, and powdered her face. She tossed her coat over her shoulders. "I'll come back after supper and work like a beaver."

"We've just started — "

"Truly, Gabbi, I'll come back later, and I won't leave till the whole place is spic and span. Robbie will be here tonight, and the three of us can finish in no time."

"It's all your fault," Gabbi accused Gino.

He admitted wryly that no doubt it was. This morning Dr. Renaud suggested that they take on an office nurse. He left the matter in Gino's hands. The younger doctor's thoughts had flown hopefully to Petra, and when he saw her at Gabbi's window the hope had flared with new brightness. But the mention of Denny's name had released her, as if she were an arrow poised on a taut bow, and like an arrow she was going swiftly, surely, to her destination. He knew what her answer would be, but because he could not help himself he explained to Gabbi, "My reason for dropping in on you was to see if Petra would like an office job with Dr. Renaud and myself, but — "

Petra stood slim and impatient by the door. "It's sweet of you, Gino. Thanks. But an office wouldn't suit me — I'd rather do private duty." It was plain that her words were merely words and her thoughts were elsewhere.

They left for his car, turning once to wave to Gabbi who was scraping industriously at the window with what looked like a nail file.

At Denny's house Larsa opened the door to them. Two tables of bridge were in play in the chintz-draped living room off the hall.

Mrs. Douglas made excuses to her guests and hurried to the hall in time to lay a soft, detaining hand on Petra's shoulder. Gino went up the stairs.

"It's good to see you again, my dear," Minna Douglas murmured. She had not seen Petra since the day before her father's funeral when Denny had asked her to call on the Dallis. She appeared at a loss for further words and she turned away eager to return to her bridge guests.

At the top of the winding stairway, Petra heard Gino's low whistle and his words, "What the Granitetown executive will wear on his desk this fall! Or *is* that a desk under those books, boy?" And Denny's, "Bet you never knew that early quarrying was accomplished by dropping heated iron balls on granite and — "

There was a lilting lightness in his voice that sent her heart into a joyous racing. Mister Tiff was right. Denny *was* interested in his work. . . . He was sitting at a book-and-pamphlet littered desk beside the west window which gave a view of The Hill. His fair hair was tousled. The index finger of his left hand was marking a place in a heavy volume.

Denny saw her in the doorway, then. He rose, and as he stared at the palely golden features, his flow of words stopped.

Gino did not miss the quick, happy union of their eyes. He suspected that from the opposite ends of a crowded ball park those two pairs of eyes would find and hold each other to the complete exclusion of everyone else. And he suspected that subconsciously he had known right along that the field had been Denny's alone. Ever since he was of high school age he had sensed Ronato's devotion to his mother. He had resented it with the extreme and not unusual sensitivity of youth which argued that only the members of his family should share in devotion to her, and that anything else was a departure from the normal and was therefore shameful. It never occurred to him to pity the man. Never, until this moment. He said awkwardly to Denny, "You'll get your professional call tomorrow. I came only to deliver your visitor. Be seeing you — " He left them and started down the stairs, hoping at each step to hear Petra or even Denny call him back, and knowing they would not.

Denny broke the hush. "I thought you were coming tonight, Petra. I'm glad you made it this afternoon. I've been counting the hours."

"Liar!" She was smiling her generous smile at him, facing him across the desk. "You were deep in these books, having a time for yourself — "

"Killing time," he insisted. "Yet they *are* interesting at that. For instance, d'you know that early quarrying — "

"I heard you — they dropped heated balls on granite."

"*Iron* balls."

"Iron then."

They laughed together. Her eyes went to the desk and came to rest on a sketching pad. Laughter left her. She took the pad with unsteady fingers and went to the window where late sunlight slanted through the pane. Her coat slipped unheeded to the floor. He picked it up and laid it over the back of his chair.

She was looking at a crayon sketch of herself, head and shoulders and arms; the hands were holding Denny's wide-winged St. Michael figurine. There was her hair falling shoulder length and straight underneath a nurse's cap; and there was the plain Peter Pan collar of her white uniform. She remembered the afternoon she unpacked the figurine in this room; it had recalled to her the days when as children they stood beside the wooden statue in St. Michael's church. In the sketch Denny had captured the half-dreaming expression which must have been on her face. Her throat tightened with an aching joy as the full significance of the sketch grew upon her. Denny must have sketched it either yesterday or today, for Gino had taken the bandage from his hand only yesterday. She guessed that the drawing, like his miniatures, would be classed as "good." Nothing better than that. But that was not the important thing. What was truly important was that his hands could still give satisfactory expression to whatever of the artist there was in him; the proof was here before her, in black and white. She could reproach herself now for making tragedy of Denny's accident.

Denny did not ask her if she liked it. He said, "What do you think of my trying it in oil? I — I sort of experimented with a brush this morning — it can be done."

"Yes, it can be done," she agreed softly.

He moved closer to her.

"Petra, you're crying — "

"Not really. I mean, it's because I'm glad."

"Petra — "

His arm went around her, and her head was cradled against his shoulder. For a second she glimpsed the mutilated hand, pink skinned and ugly at the knuckles, hanging idly at his side.

"Petra, I love you."

"I know." And she knew that she loved him. The marvel of it was that it had always been Denny and the discovery had not come until today. The revelation held no element of surprise to her; it was simply recognition of a feeling with which she had long been familiar. But recognition carried with it a jarring, discordant note that had not sounded itself during simple friendship but had waited until now when love was pointing out the sweetness of a closer relationship. She was a Catholic, Denny wasn't.

"Wait, Denny — "

His hand swiftly sealed her lips. "Let me speak, Petra. There are things I should have told you before I said I loved you. I know what you want to say. It's been with me night and day for a week. You don't have to tell me it's anything but helpful for a husband and wife to have different religions. But — I have to be sure." Her slender body trembled against him. His arm held her more tightly. "The little theology I studied was the Sunday school type, and very little at that. But I grew up with you and Vetch and Mister Tiff. There are some things about your Church that have appealed to me — ever since those days. Maybe it's the philosophic system that seems to remain changeless through the ages and has made it an institution of antiquity, something to hold on to in a world where everything changes — "

She nodded against his shoulder. She could understand how the antiquity of Catholicism would appeal to him. Half of the charm which the carving and quarrying of stone had held for Denny and Vetch in childhood, and now in manhood, was due to the antiquity of these crafts and to the endurance of stone.

"There's something else," Denny began, and then fell silent. How could he tell her that there was a sort of nostalgia, a groping for a past that might now appear most desirable to him chiefly because of its irrevocability. It was all mixed up with Mister Tiff, his Michael, and those moments when they trooped with him into the church, hot and grimy. He said, "I'll learn more about your Church, Petra. I'll go to Father Carty. If it's what I think it is — "

Her wide gray eyes were troubled. "Your mother won't be pleased, Denny."

He didn't tell her that he had already discussed it with his mother, and that she had said in some bewilderment. "I'm sure, dear, I can't understand why you should want to put yourself in the unpleasant position of considering as sinful something that the rest of us do not look upon as a sin. Like not going to Mass on Sundays — it's an enormous sin, they say — and eating meat on Friday. And if you want to be a good Catholic and are determined not to commit these sins, why think of the discomforts you are asking for. It's all very complicated." She sighed, perplexity wrinkling her forehead. "But if it agrees with Mister Tiff it might agree with you." She appeared mildly surprised at having introduced Mister Tiff's name into the conversation for she said, "But then, it's Petra you're interested in, isn't it? Not Mister Tiff." And she had left him to dress for dinner.

Denny smiled at Petra. "Mother won't mind." With his father it would be different.

"It's going to be all right," he promised huskily. He would have to make it be all right.

She could believe him. It seemed to her that all his life Denny had been in quest of such a moment as this, a slender fraction of time which was holding out to him a composite pattern of a way of life and of their future together.

His lips touched her forehead, her eyes, and clung to her wide mouth.

From downstairs came the gentle tinkle of glassware and china, and the murmur of women's voices swelling over teacups.

Outside the slanting rays of sunlight lingered on The Hill. Its lacerated bulk was quiet and faintly tinged with the lingering gold.

Mister Tiff's head bobbed acknowledgment to the greetings of homebound stonecutters and children. When he reached St. Michael's church he did not know that there were blue marks on his arms left there by Asa's wiry hands; he was equally unaware of the pain that pulsed beneath these markings. Asa's grim face and his own tremblings of a few minutes ago were lost for all time beneath the delight of knowing that Aster was going to have a home with both of her parents. A home that was not perfect, and parents who were far from perfect. But at least — a home and parents. His was a feeling of exaltation, a sensation of well-being that came from the knowledge that today five of his friends, each in his own way, had gained in well-being: Maria, Vetch, Asa, Josie, and Aster.

The church was not empty of people. Five grade school girls knelt in the rear pew. A plump, oldish woman was making the Stations of the Cross. She read from a prayer book, and her flabby lips made sibilant sounds. The little girls looked at one another and stifled their giggles. A man in work clothes followed Mister Tiff into the church. In front of the main altar a nun was instructing two little boys in their duties as altar boys. She was a young woman. Her cheeks bloomed pink above a white, starched guimpe. With each movement of her body the long rosary beads rattled cheerily. Mister Tiff knelt first at the center of the communion rail; he kept his thin body straight. His lips fashioned formal prayers, and his heart and eyes directed them to the Presence in the tabernacle. Then he picked up his cane and moved to the wide-winged old statue of St. Michael. Here he knelt, too, but he eased his body by leaning back on his heels, for this was but a statue and not the Presence, and the statue like himself was comfortably old and worn. With the Michael whom the statue commemorated he was apt to slip from prayer into reverie, into long interludes of homely experiences which his patron saint had shared with him.

He prayed dutifully for the welfare of Mafalda and Count Mattzo. It seemed incredible that only a few months ago his thoughts of them may have been tinged with envy. He felt infinitely richer than they. Instead of servants who obeyed Mafalda's dry commands for the sake of a salary, he had his Granitetown friends. To be sure, Josie had once used his friendship for financial gain, but it had turned out to his advantage. He prayed that the count and Mafalda would survive whatever misery Mussolini seemed intent upon bringing to Italy. He did not add the hope that some day he might meet with them again. He fingered the blue kerchief at his throat, and with the act came the disturbing picture of Mafalda's disapproving eyes. During Ibena days he had insisted to her that the kerchief made him feel more at home with the peasants and those of the villagers who wore them. Here in Granitetown he repeatedly told himself that he continued to wear it through habit, but he knew that it was because he took pleasure in defying Mafalda, even with an ocean between them. He blushed guiltily, dug into his jacket pocket and felt out the thinness of a dime. He touched a match to a red vigil light and offered it "for the general welfare of my sister."

He reached into his pocket again intending that another candle should burn in thanksgiving for the little individual victories won today by Maria, Vetch, Josie, and Asa.

There were only three pennies and a nickel left in his pocket, and he remembered with a warm blush that he had mended but one umbrella today. This morning. And he had spent the rest of the day chatting with friends. Well, his Granitetown friends would have to share in the benefits of Mafalda's vigil light although Mafalda, if she knew it, would turn a sour face upon the suggestion of being coupled with Josie. But that was to be expected. Mafalda's mind, unfortunately, was weak, and like a weak wine was expected to sour at the slightest provocation.

His eyes moved from the peeling statue to the stained-glass window at his right. Late afternoon sunlight slanted through the Michael depicted there. The archangel's body was a shimmering glory of scarlet, blues, greens, and flesh tints.

He had no way of knowing that in the yellow-brick house on Douglas Avenue Petra and Denny were at this moment making plans for a future together; yet, strangely, he was free of the concern he had felt for her earlier today. The old man's sigh was blissful. He reflected that if he were a character in a book the author might seize upon this moment to bring his aging life to an end. But blood, not ink, flowed from his heart. And he wanted to stay longer in Granitetown, for whatever pains and joys awaited him.

His eyes returned to the wooden statue. The tip of one of the wooden wings appeared to be deeply cracked. Forgetful of the other visitors in the church he rose and touched it. The scant inch of wood dropped into the palm of his hand. He stared at it silently. Yes, a new statue was surely needed, a statue that would last longer than this one. Granite was lasting. Strange that no one had thought of providing the church with granite statues. He blinked up through his glasses, mentally replacing the painted wooden statue with a wide-winged archangel in the subdued gray of granite. He rubbed thoughtfully at his nose, and looked briefly at the plaster figure of Mary to the right of the sanctuary, and at the brown-mantled St. Joseph to the left. If all three were of granite what a distinctive tribute it would be from Granitetown itself, from all her people regardless of religious belief. . . .

It would be costly. St. Michael's church could not afford it. And he could hardly picture Granitetown quarry owners vying with each other to contribute granite for this perhaps unique honor. Still, he reflected, as he limped out of the church, in his lifetime he had seen seeming impossibilities grow into possibilities and become realities.

A black-cassocked form was coming up the steps.

Mister Tiff exclaimed, "Hah, just the one I want to see!"

Father Carty's round face smiled. "Yes?" He waited. His eyes rested quietly on the thin face with its skin drawn fine and translucent over high cheekbones and great nose. He thought he detected, far back in the old man's mild eyes, the beginnings of a determined light, and something else to which he could not give a name. It was disquieting to the priest since it reminded him of the look Mister Tiff had worn during the mystifying crusade for the St. Michael stained-glass window.

"Yes?" he repeated.

The older man sensed an uneasiness in the politely spoken word. He changed his mind. The idea for a granite Michael had just been conceived. It must not die at birth. To assure its survival it must be strengthened and made to stand on its own legs before being handed over to as busy a foster parent as Father Carty.

Mister Tiff smiled apologetically. "What I have to say will take a few minutes. Quite a few minutes. It will keep you from your prayers. Some other time will be better, Father, yes? Good afternoon — "

The priest looked after the frail figure as it walked the sun-dappled walk beneath coloring maples. The man's left shoulder sloped noticeably although, today, no umbrella-mending kit was suspended from it.

Afterword

The novel you hold in your hands has been brought back into print by the New England Press for several compelling reasons: it is a well-conceived and well-told story, a story about an important chapter in Vermont's past, and, yes, a story written by a woman who was a native Vermonter. *Like Lesser Gods* is a novel about the plight of the Italian granite quarriers and stone carvers of Granitetown, Mari Tomasi's fictional rendering of Barre, Vermont. The novel celebrates not only Barre's Italian community but Miss Tomasi's personal heritage as well. Nor is the novel restricted to Barre's Italian influence: "in Granitetown, the Italian, Spanish, Scotch, Irish, French—all lived in harmony," as Pietro and others had written Mr. Tiff. Equally important, here is a woman writer of the 1930s and 1940s, a thoughtful and compassionate, largely self-taught writer, a knowledgeable and careful researcher—and, for all that, a writer almost totally ignored today. By making this, her second novel, readily available, it is hoped that Mari Tomasi and her work can be recalled from the shadows and be reintroduced to a whole new generation of readers.

Mari Tomasi was born January 30, 1907, in Montpelier, Vermont, and went to school there before attending Trinity College in Burlington. Both her parents came from northern Italy. Her father settled in Vermont after a tour of South and Central America convinced him he would be happiest in the Green Mountains, an area that closely resembled his native lake region of northern Italy. Information about her early years is scarce, but as a youngster she was apparently operated on in Burlington for a hip problem. Mari wanted to study medicine; her sister was a nurse and her brother and four of her cousins practiced medicine in Vermont. But when her father died, she abandoned that goal and decided instead to become a teacher.

Writing, however, seems to have been her major interest, and before she took her degree, she left Trinity College to become a free-lance newspaper and magazine writer. Later, in 1940, she published her first novel, *Deep Grow the Roots*. The next year she won a Breadloaf Writer's Conference

Fellowship. She also worked at this time on the Vermont Writer's Project and served as the city editor of the *Montpelier Evening Argus*. The most interesting work to come out of the Vermont Writer's Project was "Men Against Granite," a collection of interviews and stories, some written by Roaldus Richmond (in manuscript). "Men Against Granite" is concerned with the history of Barre, Vermont, the Italian immigrants who lived there, and the granite industry, subjects that serve, in part, as the basis for *Like Lesser Gods*, first published in 1949.

Mari Tomasi apparently continued to write after the publication of *Like Lesser Gods*, but little, if any, of this work was of a fictional nature. For many years she was a very active member of the Vermont Poetry Society. She died, after a brief illness, in Burlington on November 10, 1965.

Favorable comments by three prominent women novelists of the day—Dorothy Canfield Fisher, Mary Ellen Chase, and Faith Baldwin—appeared on the dust wrapper of *Deep Grow the Roots*, but the reviewers were too kind, damning the work with faint praise. They implicitly passed it off as a slight production by praising its lyric qualities while ignoring the fact that the novel ends in tragedy. Structurally, the work is overly long for the simple tale it tells. Also, it ends not only in too contrived a manner but also too quickly in comparison with the earlier, more laconic pace of the exposition.

In the novel, Luigi, a young man of Ibena, in the Piedmont region, nurtures his chestnut grove with the expectation that it will provide him a handsome-enough income to marry the beautiful Nina. Just as all appears to be headed for a happy ending, Mussolini, whose ominous footsteps are heard throughout the novel, makes his presence felt in the remote hill town, and Luigi is drafted into the army to fight in Ethiopia. Luigi attempts to avoid the army by smashing his foot with a large stone, but ironically the wound turns gangrenous and kills him. For reader appeal, the novel relies almost entirely on the love affair between Luigi and Nina, an affair that has a delicately balanced tension between its outward actions and a sexuality and coyness that run beneath the surface. More important, the novel is a subtle attempt on Miss Tomasi's part to present even native Italians as innocent victims of Mussolini and, in so doing, further distance and dissociate Italian-Americans from Mussolini's actions and Italy's involvement in the war.

Whatever strengths *Deep Grow the Roots* has, they lie outside the areas of story and plot. The sense of place that Miss Tomasi creates is almost symbolic, but it is neither overdrawn nor overly abstract. Ibena is an Arcadia and is as idyllic as pastoral Vermont; the characters that people the setting are durable and interesting, even if at times they appear stereotypic. The village priest, Don Paolo, and the witchlike Tonietta are well contrasted but coexist as each strives to be the spiritual leader of the community. One of the more interesting characters in the book is Luigi's little friend Gobbo, who inherits Luigi's land. Late in the novel Luigi kidnaps Gobbo and ties him to a tree, a folk remedy he had seen villagers employ to cure a sick goat. This stratagem is intended to ward off his misfortune—the diabolic Mussolini, the destroyer of his pastoral happiness. As he flees the scene after tying Gobbo to the tree, Luigi stubs his toe; he later speculates that it was no mere accident but an event directly occasioned by his kidnapping Gobbo. The stubbing of his toe leads him to the thought that if he were to damage his foot permanently, he would avoid being drafted. As he lies in a near coma for several days after inflicting the wound on himself, he dreams that he is in the arms of the Virgin—only to awaken and find himself in Gobbo's arms. Gobbo forgives him the kidnapping, and Luigi feels that superstition and divine intervention have joined to relieve him of his problem.

The curious mixture of superstition and religion represented in the characterizations of Tonietta and Don Paolo must be the same that Miss Tomasi recognized in Italian-Americans in Vermont and in Italians she encountered in the hill country during her only visit to Italy. This flavor of authenticity, without ever becoming superficially ethnic, gives Miss Tomasi's first book the strength that it has.

Like Lesser Gods, Mari Tomasi's second novel, is a realistic story set in Granitetown. The novel is divided into two books: the first takes place in 1924, the second in 1941. In the novel, Miss Tomasi chronicles the growth of the family of Pietro Dalli, a quarrier who came from Ibena, the setting of *Deep Grow the Roots*.

The novel begins with the arrival of an important unifying character, Maestro Michele Pio Vittorio Giuseppe Tiffone, who soon becomes familiar to all the townspeople as Mister Tiff. Pietro Dalli's teacher in Ibena, Tiff moves in with the Dalli family and represents throughout the novel an un-Americanized, old-world morality. The major conflict in the lives of almost all the people of Granitetown is, of course, narrowly focused in the conflict between Dalli and his wife, Maria. She wishes, indeed begs, her husband to quit the carving sheds before he dies of tuberculo-silicosis, the dreaded sickness caused by the silica in the dust of the granite he works. He refuses, working the stone being tantamount in his view to religious devotion. Later in the novel, when Pietro goes to young Dr. Gino Tosti to get the results of his X-ray examination, we hear an exchange that must have been spoken many times in the history of the granite industry in Barre. When asked by Tosti why he never quit the sheds, Pietro says that he doubted at first that he would get sick and that later he needed the money for his growing family. Tosti still doesn't understand why Pietro didn't look for other work, and Pietro again attempts to give an answer. Then Tosti has an epiphany that makes clear the meaning of the title of the novel:

> "You have to cut it to know. It is hard stone. Beautiful. Lasting. Always when I carve a name on a memorial, I feel, well, important." A half-smile wiped the earlier fear from Pietro's face. It was as if, for a moment, he had forgotten the grim reason for this visit to Gino's office. "I carve the name and I say to myself, From up there in heaven the *Dio* create new life; and when He sees fit to take it away, then we stone-cutters on earth take up where He left off. We take up the chisel, we carve the name, we make a memory of that life. Almost, boy, it is being like—like—"
>   In Gino's mind tiptoed a sentence from an old mythology book: *On Olympus lived the greater gods; and below, the lesser.* He nodded to Pietro, understanding him, and he murmured quietly—"like lesser gods." (p. 166)

In the most poignant scene in the book, the scene that is also the heart of Miss Tomasi's short story "Stone," Maria awakens from her sleep, rises from her bed, abandoning as it were her husband and her marriage, and steals to Gerbatti's shed where Pietro has been passionately carving an ornate granite cross, the design and execution of which he hopes will be his crowning achievement. Maria angrily enters the shed, vandalizes the cross, and, as she leaves the shed, sneers at the work being done on the tombstones of those she neither knows nor cares about. In so doing she actualizes her fears and vents her anger on a symbol so rich that it resists complete explication. The cross is a symbol of her love for her husband, her marriage, and her religion. Working the stone is killing her husband, but the cross represents all of Pietro's artistry and inspiration as well. The cross that Pietro has designed is entangled in vines smothering other vines in a baroquelike ornateness symbolizing the complexity of the life/death, love/work struggle that lies at the heart of the novel. Maria slips back to the house and into bed and never tells Pietro that it was she who, in desperation, tried to discourage him from his work.

The strategy fails. Pietro continues to work in the sheds, but he never finishes the cross. However, Maria's fear of an early death for Pietro is also unfounded. As expected, he contracts tuberculo-silicosis and endures considerable pain, but he lives to see his family grow. After a stay at Chisel Point Pond, he is admitted to the sanitorium, situated on a Granitetown hilltop (where it still stands today). One day he dreams that the four o'clock whistle blows, signaling that work for that day is completed, and then he dies contentedly. His beloved cross is reintroduced as plans are made to have it completed and erected as Pietro's own cemetery marker. Thus, Pietro and Maria are finally reconciled by the stone and symbol that had been the cause of the major tension in their otherwise happy marriage.

With the publication of *Like Lesser Gods*, Mari Tomasi's novelistic talents showed remarkable improvement. Her sense of story, now more panoramic and detailed, and her recognition of the need for a plot and a unifying theme lead one to believe that if she had produced any subsequent work and had continued to show the same refinement of her talents, we would be reading yet more of her work today. But perhaps this is too facile. In *Like Lesser Gods* she uses a beautifully rich, unifying symbol for the story that she tells, but it is one that, if exploited thoroughly, she perhaps could not use again. The question remains then whether or not, in any subsequent novel, she could have found as easy a vehicle for the expression of the human condition as she had found in the granite of Barre. How fortunate we are, however, to have this solid attempt to render in fiction the passion and anguish of the Vermont quarriers' special plight.

Miss Tomasi was extremely knowledgeable about the quarrying of granite, and it was as if her whole life had prepared her for working out the symbolism attached to granite. She had grown up in her father's grocery store in Montpelier listening to the quarriers' tales of the old country: tales of excavating a softer granite in northern Italy and the even softer marble from the Carrara quarries, where marble had been cut from the mountains as far back as Roman times. She later worked on the history of the granite industry for the Vermont Writer's Project and still later, in an even more scholarly way, she gathered information for "The Italian Story in Vermont," an article she published first in *The Stone Cutters Journal*, a trade publication, and then in *Vermont History*. Her notes, correspondence, and bibliography for "The Italian Story in Vermont" show how comprehensive and meticulous she was in gathering information that went beyond her own reminiscences. For her second novel Miss Tomasi used her youthful reminiscences and her later research in a fictional account of the granite story.

Mari Tomasi was deeply aware of the treachery of the granite that brought Italians to Vermont. She knew the torture of the tuberculo-silicosis—or "stonecutters' TB," as it was called—that lay in wait behind the incredibly durable and stately granite. The hardness of the stone allowed it to be polished to a mirrorlike finish. Unlike marble, however, its hardness necessitated methods of tooling that created a fine granite dust, which like microscopic razor blades lacerated the lungs of the workers who inhaled it. The hacking, wrenching coughs of the older workers, coupled with their devotion to the stone and their jobs, must have entered Miss Tomasi's consciousness early in her life and later compelled her to attempt, in *Like Lesser Gods*, to actualize the irony of the quarriers' calling. And the ironies are indeed heavy here. The more the workers dedicated themselves to the stone, the more they created their own figurative and literal tombstones. But it was this aspect of their lives, as Miss Tomasi embodied it in her title, that gave the workers their almost godlike power to achieve immortality. The granite they excavated and the tombstones they carved were also the very markers of their own passing. In a startling and profound way, Mari Tomasi realized that the granite workers continually celebrated and memorialized their own deaths in the stones they quarried and carved for others they would never know.

As a symbol, the granite is even more interesting. It is not merely blasted, hoisted out of the earth, sawed, carved, polished, and shipped to far-off places. Certainly, the granite is reminiscent of the ice in Thoreau's Walden Pond, which in winter was cut from the top of the pond and sent all over the world. Like the ice, the granite celebrates a region but also, by its distribution, achieves a level of both actual and symbolic universality. Yet the granite is more than this. It can be artistically tooled into sculptures that are unique in the combination of boldness and mysticism they reflect. The granite workers were not, however, artists in the truest sense of the word. Their interest was not, for example, in brilliance of conception, imaginative flights, or in experiments of form. Rather, it was in identifying with the stone, in being in harmony with the substance, of having a true understanding of it and the techniques used to work it. They were dedicated craftsmen and artisans in a far more literal sense than we normally use these designations today.

Herman Melville's whale hunters surrounded themselves with functional and artistic by-products of the bones of whales to serve as symbols of their love of whale hunting and of the dangers that necessarily went along with that calling. Similarly, the quarry workers used granite for windowsills and doorsills, for roads, and sometimes in personal ways. Pietro and Maria, in yet another interesting symbol, use a large block of the stone as a step to their bed. The step, the granite, is what makes their marriage, allows for it, but it is also the substance that generates the tension in it. The stonecutters are also described, in images reminiscent of Fitzgerald's wasteland in *The Great Gatsby*, as being completely covered with the stone dust, thus looking like the stone they worked. Like the New England transcendentalists, who considered water the universal element because their very bodies were constituted largely of water, the stonecutters identified with and were obsessed by stone, since it, too, became a part of their bodies not merely externally but internally, but with vastly different and sadly ironic consequences.

There is much to admire in Miss Tomasi's *Like Lesser Gods*. In addition to the vivid characterizations, the ethnic contrasts, the rich symbolism of the granite, and the strong story, there are passages reminiscent of the works of her contemporaries—Sinclair Lewis and F. Scott Fitzgerald in particular. She is especially good at portraying small-town life and the emerging importance of the automobile as an American institution. But the central theme is, of course, the granite and its cultural importance, and no one has handled this theme better than Mari Tomasi.

Alfred Rosa
Shelburne, Vermont
September 12, 1988

A Note on the 1999 Edition

During the ten years since the New England Press first reprinted Mari Tomasi's *Like Lesser Gods* in 1988, interest in Italian-American literature has flourished. A new generation of readers has experienced the literary imaginations of an immigrant people and come to appreciate their often difficult assimilation into American life by reading the works of such writers as Tony Ardizzone, Helen Barolini, Don DeLillo, Tina DeRosa, Pietro di Donato, John Fante, Jerre Mangione, Giose Rimanelli, Gilbert Sorrentino, Gay Talese, and Mario Puzo. And critics such as Helen Barolini, William Boelhower, Mary Jo Bona, Fred Gardaphe, Paul Giordano, Anthony Tamburri, and others have examined the significance and offered their interpretations of that large body of work. Books by two of these critics deserve special mention in this context: Helen Barolini's *The Dream Book: An Anthology of Writings by Italian-American Women* (1985) and Fred L. Gardaphe's *Dagoes Read: Tradition and the Italian/American Writer* (1996) and *Italian Signs, American Streets: The Evolution of Italian American Narrative* (1996). Clearly, these critics have not only shown us the worth of Italian-American writers but they have modified our views of the landscape of American literature as well. Thus, there is also a new respect for Mari Tomasi's achievements and her place within our literary tradition. Not only have scholars found genuine worth in *Like Lesser Gods* but instructors at all levels have adopted the novel wishing to share it with their students in American literature courses in general as well as in more specialized courses in immigrant and ethnic literature. There is every reason to believe that with this new printing many more readers will find their way to *Like Lesser Gods* and the history, insight, and pleasures it provides.

September 1998
Shelburne, Vermont